HARDEMAN LODGE

A NOVEL

W. W. McNEAL

FORT WORTH, TEXAS

Library of Congress Control Number: 2020939947

TCU Box 298300
Fort Worth, Texas 76129
817.257.7822
www.prs.tcu.edu
To order books: 1.800.826.8911

Cover and Text Design by Preston Thomas

FOR

CATHY

CONTENTS

ONE

SWIRLS OF DUST ROSE UP BEFORE HIM AS BILLY MCCULLOCH turned his mare down the road beside the Plum Creek post office and over the bridge across Plum Creek on a hot July day in 1874. It had been a long trip from Mississippi. A new railroad was under construction, and although rails were yet to be laid, the roadbed had been built up all the way from the old town of Atlanta, east of Plum Creek, to the place where a new town was to be built, a few miles to the west. He had heard reports about this new town and was excited to see how much had been done toward its development. He rode beside the roadbed, and as he came up a rise, he began to pass piles of cut trees. They had been cleared from the area in front of him, which promised to be a street in part of the new town. A few structures were being built on both sides of the roadbed. After a while, he could see that a crowd had gathered up ahead, standing around a small platform erected on the side of the street.

The streets, though unpaved, were broad. Wagons and horses stirred up clouds of dust. A handmade sign indicated he was traveling on South Railroad Avenue. Billy rode up to the rear of the crowd at noon, just as a tall man wearing a black hat in the July heat was introducing a woman who stood beside him. She was dressed in unusual attire, wearing an English riding habit and a brown derby hat, as if it were a chilly day in November.

"This new town will be christened by our distinguished guest, Lady Leah Cahar," the man said as the woman stepped forward. He guided her down the steps at the front of the platform, where another man reached for her other hand, holding it until the woman had reached the bare dirt of the street. He then handed her a small sledgehammer and bent down below Billy's line of sight. Billy walked around the edge of the crowd until he could see the man bending down, holding a silver spike in his left hand. The woman drove the spike firmly into the ground. The man stood again and turned around, revealing that where his right arm should have been, his coat sleeve was pinned up just below his shoulder. It was Everett Hardeman. He was sharply dressed in a summer suit. He looked the same as he had before Billy had left for Mississippi.

The woman stood with the hammer in her hand and held it up, then said, in a Scottish brogue, "This is the center of this town I name Luling."

The audience applauded and began to disperse. Billy dismounted and led his mare around to the side of the platform where Everett Hardeman stood talking to the man in the black hat. He turned as Billy walked up and brightened when he saw him.

"Well, the scholar has returned," he said. "Welcome home, Mr. McCulloch. Meet George Polk."

The man smiled and extended his hand.

"My pleasure," he said.

"Billy has just earned his degree from the University of Mississippi," Ev said. "I believe he is now a bachelor of arts. Is that true, Billy?"

"Yes, sir."

"Mr. Polk is the chief engineer for the railroad and my boss. And this is Lady Cahar. Lady Leah, this is Master William McCulloch."

She extended her hand palm down. He hesitated, then shook it lightly.

"You have a fine-looking mare there," she said, gesturing toward Julie, his father's horse that had become his. "But she has some mean scars on her neck. How did that happen?"

"A mountain lion got her. It was few years ago."

"That's too bad," she said, rubbing her hand along the side of the mare's neck.

"Did you ride her all the way to Mississippi and back?" Ev asked.

"Oh, no," Billy replied. "Gruder brought her to Joe Fairchild's place in Harwood and left her there for me. I took the train and picked her up there."

He had made the trip from Oxford in only five days, by stage to Natchez, then by steamboat to New Orleans and Galveston and by train from Galveston to the end of the line at Harwood, nine miles to the east.

"Gruder's still alive?" Ev asked. "He must be a hundred by now."

"Nobody knows how old he is," Billy said. The black man, a former slave of his father's, had never been told his birthdate. He chose June 19, *Juneteenth*, so, as he said, he could celebrate his birthday with "lots of folks." He was an old man on the day that word of emancipation reached Texas and decided he would say that June 19, 1865, was his sixty-fifth birthday. "He claims he is only seventy-four," Billy said. "But he doesn't really know."

"I hope your trip was comfortable," George Polk said. "We only have limited passenger service and our personnel are new."

"It was a good ride."

"Splendid," Polk said. "It's time for lunch. We have the privilege of escorting Lady Leah to the luncheon. Please join us, Mr. McCulloch."

He agreed and followed the three of them down the street to a large circus tent that was set up next to the construction site for the new hotel. Boards laid across sawhorses served as tables. Billy followed the others to the serving line along a long table in the middle of the tent. The railroad had indeed furnished a feast. Platters of barbecued venison, beef, chicken, and quail lay along the table, followed by bowls of cooked vegetables, a giant bowl of macaroni, and loaves of bread. A large beer keg sat on a stand at the far end of the table, next to a vat of lemonade. Although many of the men wore their Sunday best, the workmen, farmers, and cowboys in the crowd were dressed in their work clothes. There were few women. After his metal plate had been filled by the servers and he had grabbed a glass of beer, Billy turned and noticed Lily Poe sitting at a table with Ashley Maitland and Lily's daughter, Barbara Ann. He had not seen them since he left for Mississippi three years before. Barbara Ann seemed to have changed from a girl to a woman. She sat smiling at him as he followed Ev Hardeman and the others to a table across the way. He set his plate down and excused himself, then walked to the table where Lily, Ash, and Barbara Ann were sitting. Ash stood up as he approached.

"You're back," he said, extending his hand.

"I am," Billy replied.

Lily extended her hand and he took it in his, holding it lightly for a few seconds.

"Your father would be proud," she said. "And you are so grown up. Isn't he Barbara Ann?"

Barbara Ann nodded, smiling.

"Billy, would you like to join us?" Ash asked.

"I would like to," he said, staring at Barbara Ann, "but I'm sitting with Ev and Mr. Polk."

"And that lovely Scottish lady," Lily said. "Welcome home."

"Thank you." There was a history with Lily Poe that he had not forgotten. He was not sure how to take her friendliness.

"I'll see you at my office come Monday morning, sharply at eight," Ash said. "We've got work to do."

Billy returned to the table where Lady Leah, obviously the guest of honor, sat as the only woman in a group of men. She was holding forth.

"I see this new town as a great city, the hub of the entire area," she said. "It will be the end of the line for a year or so, until the bridge is built, and that will give it a good start. It is perfectly situated to be the stopping-off place for Austin and points north, even after the line makes it to San Antonio."

"We'll need to improve the roads between here and Austin," a man with gray sideburns said. "And build a bunch of bridges."

"It'll all come together," said another. "It's gonna happen."

Their faces were bright. They ate rapidly while their guest of honor picked at her plate.

"I hear you are to be a lawyer," she said to Billy.

"Yes, ma'am. I hope to be."

"He'll be studying with Ashley Maitland," Everett Hardeman said.

"Good for you," she said

"Ash is a fine man. A good friend of Billy's father," Ev said.

"So you'll be reading law?" George Polk asked.

"Yes, sir. Ash helped me get into college and he is going to let me learn with him. He said he would show me which shelf to start on."

"I assume that would be the bottom one," Polk said.

"I hear you have quite a reputation already," Lady Cahar said.

"Not really," Billy said.

He had wondered when it would come up He had shot and killed a man several years before. A bad man. At first, he liked the attention he received because of it, but it soon grew old. He was glad that no one at college had known about it. He had accompanied Jack Hays and two of his uncles in pursuit of an outlaw that had kidnapped Hays's niece after murdering her family. Gruder was with them. Although Hays and his uncles rescued the girl, the renegade escaped. Later, in San Antonio, the outlaw confronted Billy, his uncle Wonsley Baker, the girl, and two other women on the St. Mary's Street Bridge. Billy shot the man with the Remington pistol his father had given him for his birthday. He became a local hero at the age of sixteen.

He excused himself from the conversation at the table after he had finished eating. It had been three years since he had been home, and he was anxious to see his mother and the farm. He found his way to the old road that led west to the McCulloch place, along the river banks. Almost four miles down the road he came to the shack Gruder had erected on the high ground above the river. It was bordered by a cotton field with a good stand of cotton that would be ready to pick in another two months, when the sharecroppers would be in the fields over the whole area. The corn in the uplands had already been harvested. Gruder's shack was built from crudely sawed lumber that Gruder had retrieved from the discard pile at the sawmill three miles downstream. The front porch roof was held up by three post oak trunks that had been put in place unfinished, their bark cracked and peeling with age. Gruder came around the corner of the shack as Billy rode up. The black man's hair had turned a light shade of gray, and he seemed to be more stooped over as he walked, but his steady gaze and easy smile were the same. Billy stayed in the saddle as Gruder walked up to him.

"You made it back," he said, looking at Billy from boot to hat.

"Yep. I did."

"I guess you're anxious to see your mother."

"How is she?"

"She's gettin' along good," Gruder said. "Real good. We've had some good crops and prices are holding up. I guess you know that from the mail."

"Yes, Mother wrote me. Thanks for getting Julie to me."

"She's holding up, too," he said, patting the mare on the side of her neck.

"I'll come by later on, if you'll be here," Billy said.

"I won't be going nowhere."

Billy did not want to ask him if he was still doing some work.

"I'll come by a little later," he said.

"I want to hear about Mississippi," Gruder said. "Last time I saw it, they had slaves all over."

"They're still there. It's like here. They're sharecroppers now. Those that have work."

Gruder looked at him through narrowed lids. Billy sat looking back at him, and a long moment of silence passed. He was imagining what the black man had seen in his time and how things had changed and would change even more in the future. Billy was about to embark on a new life, a life of learning and working with his mind rather than his hands. His father had once told him that the most important thing was to learn how to think. He now had an understanding of what he had meant. But he also knew that the knowledge gained from books was not any more important than what he had learned from experience and that the future would teach him more. And the man who looked up at him now had taught him more than anyone else about how to live in the world.

"I guess I'll be getting on home," Billy said. "See you later."

He turned his horse toward the road. After he had ridden a ways, he turned and looked back. Gruder was still looking at him as he rode away. A mile up the road, his mother was waiting for him in a rocking chair on the front porch, as if she had word he would be home that afternoon, although no one had told her. She stood as he rode up and waited for him to come to the edge of the porch before stepping toward him with her arms out for an embrace.

TWO

WONSLEY BAKER TIED HIS HORSE'S REINS ON THE GATE post of Mrs. Elliot's fence on Soledad Street in the late morning. He had visited regularly for the past four years, but this spring morning was different. He wore new cotton pants that had been altered to fit in length and a new shirt and brush jacket that had been purchased for this occasion. He also wore a new Stetson instead of his usual leather cap. He had on a pair of handmade boots that he had ordered from Lucchese weeks before and had just picked up that morning. The stiffness of the clothing, particularly the boots, made him uncomfortable. He was used to wearing moccasins and Indian boots made of soft deer hide. And he was itching in a lot of inconvenient places.

The new duds had not come cheap, and he was bound and determined to suffer through the discomfort they caused him. He had not seen Martha Roberts in over a month; he knew that this coming Sunday would be her last Easter at the Ursuline Academy, and the time had come for him to begin to talk to her about their future together. She had recently turned eighteen. He was nine years older. He had picked out a place on the Baker spread in Guadalupe County where he would build a house for them. It was on a high spot near a bend in the river, with a stand of oaks to shade the cabin and a good spot downhill for a garden patch. His father, Eli Baker, had even promised to deed him one hundred acres around the house location, so that he could consider it his and be on his own with a place to raise his family, just as his older brother John had done on his place farther downstream. Wonsley had been doing his own farming and ranching on part of the family land, and with sharecroppers of his own, had made enough in the last few years to be able to save sufficiently to afford a wife.

He had sent Mrs. Elliot a wire saying that he would be pleased to visit in San Antonio on the Saturday before Easter, so he knew he would be expected. He untied the bouquet of flowers from the saddle horn, stepped up to the front door, and used the cast-iron knocker on the wall. The inside door was promptly opened by Rosa, Ellen Elliot's maid.

"Good morning, Mr. Wonsley," she said as she pushed open the screen door. "Please come in."

"Buenos días, Rosa." He stepped inside.

"I'll let Miss Martha know you're here," Rosa said. "Please have a seat in the parlor."

He sat on a chair in the parlor, next to the fireplace. A clock on the mantel ticked out the seconds. Martha would always take a few minutes to come into the room when he visited. He looked at the clock and the memories came back to him again, as they always seemed to when he was waiting for her in Mrs. Elliot's front parlor. Carrying her through the thunderstorm five years before, as she kicked and squirmed in his grasp. Her blank face as they rode away from the San Saba valley to San Antonio and eventually to Katherine Johnston's house, where she was turned away because she had been with a half-breed renegade—and it did not matter to Mr. Johnston that she was his wife's niece, nor that she certainly had no say in the matter of her rape. Wonsley and the others waited at the Menger Hotel as her uncle, Jack Hays, took Martha to Mrs. Elliot's, to leave her in her charge. And the night Martha's teacher, Sister Rosella, had been shot in the head on the St. Mary's Street Bridge, her blood spilling over Martha and Mrs. Elliot as they crouched down on the planks of the bridge. And the devastated look on Martha's face at Sister Rosella's funeral.

In the five years since, he had seen her at least once a month, first with Mrs. Elliot present, then alone in the parlor, then on rides in a rented buggy around San Antonio. He was always elated when he was with her and was confident she would be his wife someday. He was not sure what he would say to her today, but he was hoping that they could talk about their future together, for the first time. He had never had the courage to bring it up, but it was Easter weekend in 1875, and it was high time that they had a talk.

She entered the room from the back hallway as she always did. She wore a light blue dress with a high collar, and her wavy red hair was done up, with ringlets hanging down around the collar. He suddenly remembered to remove his hat as she walked toward him, her hand extended.

"Welcome, Mr. Baker," she said.

"Thanks, Miss Roberts," he replied, taking her hand lightly in his.

She withdrew her hand gently and took a seat in a chair on the other side of the fireplace, lightly spreading the skirt of her dress out as she sat.

"Happy Easter weekend," she said. "I hope you have been well."

"Yes, thank you."

"And your family?"

"They're well too," he said.

She looked at the bouquet he was grasping tightly in the same hand in which he held his Stetson.

"What beautiful flowers! Are they for me?"

"Oh, yes," he said, standing up and awkwardly shifting his hat to his other hand, then extending the bouquet to her. She took it, then brought it to her nose.

"Oh, they smell lovely. I'll get Rosa to put them in a vase. Rosa!"

Rosa came in almost immediately from the front hallway. She had obviously been close by, within earshot. Martha smiled at her.

"Rosa, would you please take these lovely flowers back to the kitchen and put them in a vase with water for me? Then you can bring them back here. Would you care for some tea, Mr. Baker? I think I should like some tea."

"If you do, that's fine with me," he said.

"Rosa, also put a kettle on and prepare a teapot for us. Mrs. Elliot will be joining us shortly."

His face revealed his disappointment as Rosa left the room with the flowers.

"Then after tea, perhaps we can go for a walk," Martha said, still smiling. "It seems like a lovely morning for a walk."

He brightened.

"That would be nice," he said.

They talked about local events in San Antonio and about the new town of Luling, which Martha had yet to visit. Mrs. Elliot came in with Rosa and the tea tray, and they chatted some more over tea about the cattle business, cotton prices, and the weather. It was obvious to him that they were trying to discuss topics with which he had some familiarity. In the past, whenever Martha had mentioned matters she had learned in school, such as history or current events, he had difficulty in keeping his ignorance of the subject matter a secret. After a while, it was obvious that he was only nodding and agreeing with whatever she and Mrs. Elliot said and not really engaging in conversation.

After tea, Mrs. Elliot excused herself, and he and Martha went on their walk. They walked up Soledad Street to Main Plaza, then turned west on Commerce toward the market. On a previous occasion, when he was taking her for a buggy ride, he had made the mistake of riding across the St. Mary's Street bridge, which brought back bad memories. She was visibly upset, tearing up and becoming stiff and quiet. She had indicated she had an upset stomach and asked him to take her home. He had not made the same mistake again.

It was a cool morning with a nice breeze and a good day for a walk. She was talking about her female friends at school and how she enjoyed her studies, then stopped and turned to him.

"Wonsley, I have been accepted to the teacher's normal college and plan to enter there this fall."

She said it quickly, as if it was hard for her to say it. He stood and stared at her. It was as if all of his plans for the future had been crushed.

"I really value our friendship, and I wanted you to be one of the first to know. I think I can become a school teacher if I continue to study hard. I have made good marks, and in this day and time a woman can do whatever she wants to in life. I think I would make a good teacher."

She said it without conviction. He was silent, still staring at her for a long time, then he looked away, across the street at some market stands where people were buying fruit and vegetables. She reached and touched his arm.

"I hope you'll wish me well," she said.

He looked back at her.

"Sure, I do," he said haltingly. "I wish you thc best."

She tugged on his arm, encouraging him to continue their walk. He looked down at her hand on his arm and back at her face, then moved along with her. She told him about her dreams of learning more about the world and how much she had enjoyed school. She never mentioned Sister Rosella, but she had often referred to the good teachers she had at the academy and how much she respected them. At one time in the past, he had feared that she might become a nun, but other things she had said convinced him otherwise. After they had walked a block, he stopped and turned to her.

"I have something to tell you too," he said. "I have decided to become a Texas Ranger."

"What? Oh, no," she said. "But that is so dangerous. I was hoping you would be near and I could see you often."

He looked down.

"My father and brother John, and Wes McCulloch, Billy's dad, were Rangers, and I've always wanted to follow them," he said.

Wonsley had never taken to book learning and had stopped going to school when he was nine. He could barely read and write. He knew about forests and fields. He could track a mountain lion over hard ground and herd cattle in a thunderstorm, but he was unaware of what was happening in New York or London, and the only history he was interested in was the history of his family and his region, which he had learned from fireside conversations with his elders. He knew about the Tonkawa and the Comanche, but nothing about the ancient Greeks or Romans. Walking along Commerce Street with this girl, who was the love of his life, he had finally come to believe that they would never be together as husband and wife, in spite of their mutual attraction. He was silent during the rest of their walk and she talked intermittently about trivial matters, but the mood that had existed was gone, and after he took her home, he rode to the sheriff's office on Main Plaza to ask where he could join up with the Texas Rangers.

THREE

MRS. MOORE WAS RESTLESS AS SHE LAY IN HER BED. She had not heard from her daughter, Ada, for days, and she sensed that something was wrong. Then she heard a faint tapping coming from her front room. She pulled on a wrapper and slowly stepped into the front room. Moonlight spilled through the windows. She stopped by the front door and listened. After a few seconds, she heard the tapping again. Then she heard a high-pitched voice saying, "Mama." When she opened the door, her daughter stood there in the moonlight, in her nightgown. Her hair was tousled and her left eye was swollen shut. She staggered into her mother's arms.

"What has happened to you, Ada?" her mother breathed, pulling her into the room and sitting her down in a rocker. Ada dropped into the chair as if using her last reserve of strength. Mrs. Moore lit the lamp on the sewing table, turned and bent down to her daughter, who was leaning back in the rocker, her eyes closed.

"I can't do it anymore, Mama," she said weakly. "I can't do it anymore."

Her mother took her hand and looked her over. Ada's face was purple around her swollen left eye, and there were fresh scratches on her chin and neck. Her right shoulder, bare under a tear in her nightgown, was deeply bruised, and her naked feet were swollen and bloody.

"Did he do this to you?"

Ada did not say anything, but her reaction was an answer. She was clearly frightened by the thought of her husband. Mrs. Moore had seen evidence of abuse before, but Ada had always denied that Gilbert Adams had assaulted her, blaming her bruises on her clumsiness, even though her mother knew that she had always been quite agile and not the least bit clumsy.

"Tell me about it, child," Mrs. Moore said.

Ada started to sob. Her shoulders shook and tears ran down her cheeks, making tracks in the dust on her face. She and her husband lived four miles from Mrs. Moore's house, and from the look of her feet, she had run all the way.

"I can't do it anymore," she said again, through her sobs.

After what seemed like an eternity, Ada stopped sobbing and sat still, silently staring ahead, looking at nothing, as if her mind had gone blank. Mrs. Moore took a pan with water and washed the blood from her feet and bandaged them with cotton cloth. She managed to get her to stand and slowly moved her to the bedroom and her bed. Ada lay down and closed her eyes. Mrs. Moore looked at the clock on the wall. It was three o'clock in the morning, and she remembered that it was Easter Sunday. She sat in the chair by the bed listening to her daughter's moans until daylight, when Ada appeared to have finally fallen asleep. She stood up and went to the chair in the corner, where she had laid out her best Sunday dress for church, picked it up, and hung it back in the wardrobe by the washstand. It would be the first Easter Sunday service she had missed since she received word of her husband's death in the war.

Mrs. Moore dressed in a weekday dress and combed her hair. Her servant, Mattie, would be there soon, and she had to be ready to send her for help. When Mattie arrived in an hour, later than usual, Mrs. Moore had a note ready for her.

"Here, Mattie. Miss Ada has had some trouble, and I need you to take this into town to Mr. Maitland."

She handed her the note and watched her walk down the lane toward the road to town. She then went to the closet where Tom Moore's rifle and shotgun were stored, pulled out his twelve gauge, loaded it with buckshot, and went out to the front porch. She pulled a rocking chair to a spot near the front door and sat down with the shotgun across her lap, waiting.

Ada slept fitfully until midmorning, when she suddenly sat up in bed and looked around as if she had forgotten where she was. Mrs. Moore was seated in the ladder-back chair next to the bed.

"You're here at home with me, Daughter," she said. "Mr. Maitland and the constable are here. You needn't worry. Everything is going to be all right."

The swelling around the eye looked worse in the daylight. After looking around the room and then into her mother's face, Ada spoke in a voice that seemed broken.

"I've got to get home," she said.

"You are home, Ada," Mrs. Moore replied. "You can't go back there. You can't go back to that man. He'll kill you."

Ada turned and gingerly put her feet on the floor. When she tried to put weight on them, she drew back, surprised at the pain she felt, and looked down at the cotton bandages.

"I ran," she said. "I ran all the way."

"Yes, you did, girl. And you can't go back there."

She started crying again. This time the sobs turned into a paroxysm of tears and shaking. Mrs. Moore sat on the side of the bed and took her in her arms, holding her as she cried.

"He'll come after me," she said. "I can't stay here. He may hurt you, too."

"Constable Stagner and his deputy are here, Daughter. The constable says he will leave the deputy here until they pick up your husband, but you will have to talk to them first."

"No. I shouldn't have come here. He'll get you, too."

Then Ada noticed Ashley Maitland standing outside the bedroom doorway.

"What are you doing here?" she asked.

Ash stepped inside the bedroom and walked over to her.

"I'm here as a friend, Ada. I'm here to help."

"Don't tell Ev about this," she said, tears still running down her cheeks. "Mama, he'll tell Ev and Adams will kill him."

"You need to bring charges, Ada," Ash said. "Then he'll be locked up."

"He won't stay locked up," she said. "He'll get out. He's crazy."

"You need to let the law take care of this, Ada. Constable Stagner is going to wire the sheriff and Adams will be arrested before he can do anything. You need to tell the constable what happened so he can be arrested." Ash said it gently but firmly, looking down at her.

"I can't do that," she said. "I can't do that."

"We'll leave the deputy here, Mrs. Moore," he said. "I'll come back with the sheriff."

After they were gone, leaving the deputy in the chair on the front porch with his rifle across his lap, Mrs. Moore coaxed Ada into the metal tub filled with warm water in the bathroom. Ada had scrapes on her legs from the brush she had run through and bruises on her back and buttocks. Bathing and drying her and getting her into one of her own cotton nightgowns, Mrs. Moore led Ada back to the bed, propped her up, and got some stew down her. In a short time, Ada was asleep again.

FOUR

ASHLEY MAITLAND WAS LATE FOR EASTER SUNDAY DINNER at Lily Poe's. The episode with Ada Adams had taken up much of his day, and it was after two in the afternoon when he finally let himself in the front yard gate and walked to the porch. The inner front door was open, and Lily could see him through the screen. She called out to him as he reached the porch steps.

"Well, Mr. Maitland. It's about time."

He opened the screen door and stepped into the parlor, where Lily, Barbara Ann and Everett Hardeman were sitting at the dinner table, finishing up a turkey dinner.

"Sorry, Lil," Ash said. "I had an emergency."

"Oh? What was it?"

He stood there for a while looking at Ev Hardeman, then said, directly to him, "I'm afraid it was Ada."

Ev stood immediately.

"What did that bastard do now?" he asked. "Did he finally kill her?"

"No, but she's pretty bruised and battered."

Ev stepped to the hat rack and retrieved his hat.

"Is she at her mother's?" he asked.

Lily came quickly to his side and grabbed his arm.

"Wait, Ev. You shouldn't be getting into this," she said.

He looked down at her hand.

"Let me go, Lily," he said. "You know I can't let him do that to her."

Ashley moved between him and the doorway.

"Let the law handle it, Ev," he said. "The sheriff is on his way to the Moore house."

"The law? The law won't do anything. He'll just get away with it. He needs killin'."

"I'll pretend you didn't say that, Ev. He'll be punished. I promise."

"Get out of my way, Ash." He said it with menacing determination.

They stood staring at each other, until Ash finally stepped aside. Ev pulled out of Lily's grasp. "Thanks for the dinner, Lily," he said, then pushed the screen door open and stepped outside. He was quickly on his horse and rode off at a gallop.

"Oh, Ash. Go after him. That crazy man will kill him."

At his age, Ash was not as active as Ev Hardeman. It took him some time to mount and head after him, and Ev had a better mount. He knew that Ev would cover the several miles to the Moore place at a pace he could not match. When Ash pulled onto the lane that led to the house, Ev had already dismounted and was standing on the front porch in front of the deputy constable, a young man whose eyes were wide with surprise. He held his rifle up and Ev grabbed it and jerked it out of his hands.

"Get out of my way," he said. "I need to see Ada."

The young man, obviously frightened, stepped aside. Ev burst into the front room. Mrs. Moore was sitting in her rocking chair by the sewing table, calmly rocking back and forth as if she had been expecting him.

"Where is she?" he asked, still holding the Winchester.

"She's all right, Everett," Mrs. Moore said. "She's resting. She needs some rest. Won't you sit down?"

"I need to see her," he said.

"You can peek in on her, but don't wake her up. She needs her rest."

She stood and quietly walked to the bedroom door, holding her finger to her lips as he followed, then cracked the door and held it partially open as he looked in. Ada was asleep, lying on her back with the covers up to her chin. Her dark hair covered the swollen left eye. She was breathing easily and did not appear to be in any distress. He stood looking for a long moment, until Mrs. Moore slowly closed the door.

"What did he do to her?" he asked.

"She'll be all right, Everett. I think she was scared more than anything."

"I'll kill the son of a bitch," he said.

He stepped to the front doorway, pushed his way through the screen door, and handed the rifle back to the young man on the porch. Ash was waiting at the steps.

"Hold up a minute, Ev. Let me talk to you."

"It can't wait, Ash. I've got to go."

"It can wait. You'll be better off if you sit down and cool off first."

"You know I can't do that, Ash!" Ev said as he bounded off the porch. He was in his saddle and riding down the lane before Ash could reach his mount. With a head start, Ev would cover the four miles in a short time, and Ash's horse again had trouble keeping up the pace. He fell further behind after Ev turned onto the road off the Moore's lane. Ash lost sight of him after a mile. After he turned his horse into the lane leading to the Adams place, he could see Ev stopped ahead of him a hundred yards or so. Gilbert Adams was sitting on the seat of his wagon, which was hitched to two mules, stopped in the lane fifty feet ahead of Ev. The two Adams sons were also in the wagon, the older in the seat to the left of his father and the younger one standing in the bed.

Before Ash could bring his horse to a stop, Adams, looking at Ev, reached down with one hand to the bed of the wagon. Ev Hardeman dropped his reins, pulled his Colt revolver in a smooth, practiced motion, and fired. The bullet struck Adams in the chest. He slumped forward over the front edge of the wagon frame. The Adams mules shied, but stood their ground. The boy in the seat jumped out and ran to the rear. The younger one stood frozen, looking in Ev's direction.

The smoke from Ev's pistol rose into the still air. Everything was unusually quiet as Ash dismounted and walked forward. There were no bird sounds. No wind in the trees to rustle the leaves. The shot still rang in Ash's ears. Ev was still pointing his pistol at the wagon as Ash walked up to his side. Ev was staring at the boy, who was standing frozen behind his father's slumped-over body, his eyes fixed on the pistol in Ev Hardeman's hand. Ash stopped beside Ev's mount. After a long pause, Ev slowly lowered his pistol.

Ash moved to Gilbert Adams, who lay in a strained position, apparently being held in the wagon seat by the metal frame at its side. Ash hesitated to touch him. It appeared that he was not breathing. The boy in the back of the wagon was crying now. Ash leaned over the wagon to look into the bed. A single-barreled shotgun lay there in front of the seat. He walked back to where Ev still sat in his saddle, his pistol still held at his side.

"He looks to be dead," Ash said.

"Good," Ev replied.

"I'm going to have to contact the sheriff," Ash said. "You best be going on home now."

Ev stared down at Ash for a long time, then nodded, looked at the pistol in his hand as if seeing it for the first time that day, then slowly holstered it. There was a squeak from the wagon springs, and as Ash turned that way, he could see that the younger Adams son had jumped to the ground and was running back in the direction of the house. Then Ev turned his horse and rode in the opposite direction.

It was almost dark when Ash returned with Sheriff Ellison, his chief deputy, and the deputy constable who had been stationed at the Moore place. The sheriff had been attending an Easter Sunday picnic in Lockhart, and a deputy had to be sent to find him. When they turned into the lane leading to the Adams house they discovered the wagon had been moved. It had been pulled up in front of the house, the mules hitched to the gate post. They dismounted and the sheriff and his chief deputy examined the wagon and the ground surrounding it. Barely dried blood was on the bed of the wagon in front of the seat and on the wheel by the near side. A trail of blood led through the yard gate up to the front porch. They followed it to the front door, which was ajar behind the screen. The sheriff led them inside, where the trail led to the rear bedroom. Adams was laid out on the bed, lying on his back, a pool of blood coagulating under his left arm on the rough army blanket that served as a bed covering.

They found the two Adams sons in the back by the well house, hiding. They had to be coaxed to come around from the rear of the small structure. They said they thought that someone was going to come and kill them to eliminate them as witnesses. The older son, George, was twenty-one and the younger, Harry, was eighteen. They had been to town rarely and had never been to school. Their father did not believe in schooling, saying that they needed to help him with farming and cutting cordwood and that schooling was a waste of time. Neither could read or write. When Adams found out that Ada was secretly teaching Harry to read, he became angry and whipped her and the boy with a saddle quirt.

A search of the house quickly revealed the shotgun in a rack over the front door. The boys said it had been there all along. According to them, the one-arm man had shot their father without warning as they were going to fetch their stepmother, who had run off. They said their father was unarmed and unable to defend himself. They claimed that the lawyer man had come up later, after the shooting, and was not there when it happened. George did most of the talking. When Harry was questioned, he looked at George before answering.

It was several hours later when the justice of the peace came and declared Adams dead by gunshot wound. His body was taken by the undertaker to the new funeral parlor in Luling. The sons said they had no relatives and insisted on staying at the Adams place. The sheriff took the shotgun with him when he and the last of the deputies left.

FIVE

BILLY MCCULLOCH HAD DECIDED TO ATTEND A MINSTREL show with his uncle, Wonsley Baker. His mother had always refused to let him attend one, and he had always been curious about them. Now that he was an adult, he felt he was entitled to see for himself what the minstrel shows were all about, even though he told his mother he was going to an Easter Sunday get-together. Wonsley had invited him and suggested the white lie. As they were riding to the rodeo grounds where the show was to go on, Wonsley told him that he had decided to join the Rangers.

"I thought you were going to become a gentleman farmer," Billy said.

"I changed my mind," Wonsley said sharply.

"Where are you going to sign up?"

"Corpus," Wonsley replied. "Captain McNelly is down there getting a company together to go clean up the Nueces Strip. Brother John knew him during the war and said he was the man to serve under. He's givin' me a letter of introduction."

As they turned off the main road onto the pasture that served as the rodeo grounds, they could see that a large circus tent had been erected on the far edge of the field. It was dusk and lanterns had been hung on posts leading up to the tent. After dismounting and tying off at one of the hitching posts, they walked to the entrance of the tent, between the rows of lanterns. The tent was open on three sides. Lanterns were hung around the perimeter. Folding wooden chairs were lined up for the audience, with a center aisle. A wooden stage was bordered by more lanterns with reflective panels. They lit up the stage quite well. A seven-piece orchestra was seated in folding chairs at stage left, tuning their instruments. Billy and Wonsley entered and took seats near the back. By Billy's watch, it appeared that the show would be starting on time.

A row of folding chairs was placed in a semicircle on the stage. As if there had been some secret signal, the conductor held up his baton and turned to the audience and then back to the orchestra, whose members had stopped tuning and held their instruments at the ready, then began to play with a downstroke of the baton. The piece was a march and a line of gaudily dressed performers in blackface marched in from around the edge of the tent at stage right, in single file, led by a tall man in tux and tails. They strutted, kicking their heels high as they marched around the stage. One slim blackface played a tambourine, banging it against his leg as he marched, swaying from side to side. Another with a huge belly played bone castanets. One man played a banjo.

Two of the marchers were men dressed in women's clothing, one with a gray wig and large waistline, the other a slim hussy with lighter skin, who wiggled her hips as she marched. One of the male characters sported a wiry gray wig and appeared to limp as he marched, playing the part of a decrepit old darky. Another was dressed in shiny, baggy pants and an oversized top hat with red and green stripes. He kicked higher than the rest, performing what Billy was later to learn was called a cakewalk. After one circle on the stage, they burst into song. The song was "Camptown Races," well known to the audience, some of whom began to sing along.

There were no black faces in the audience and only a few women. The subject matter was considered "racy" by many women, who could not be talked into attending. The only true blacks were behind the stage end of the tent, hired for fifty cents a day to crew the show by doing the manual labor involved in setting up. They were allowed to stay for the show as long as they stayed out of sight. Lucius Jackson attended with his wife, Sally, who was hired as one of the kitchen helpers. Accompanying Sally the previous day, Lucius had pitched in with the setting up of the tent and stage and was rewarded by being put on the payroll. He and Sally sat near the back tent wall so they could hear every word.

After the last strains of "Camptown Races" and the applause died down, the man in tux and tails stood front and center and addressed the group on stage.

"Gentlemen, be seated," he said. He was the only person on stage not in blackface. He turned to the audience.

"Ladies and gentlemen, allow me to introduce myself."

This brought cheers, hoots, and hollers from the cast members. The bones rattled and the tambourine clanged.

"I am Mr. Interlocutor, your master of ceremonies. Welcome to the greatest show in Texas."

Amid more hoots and cheers from the cast and intermittent applause from the audience, he introduced the *dramatis personae.* The tambourine player was Brudder Tambo and the bones player Brudder Bones. They were seated at opposite ends of the semicircle. The man in the fancy pants and colorful top hat was Zip Coon and a thin man in rags seated next to him was the slave, Jim Crow. The old woman was Mammy and the light-skinned hussy was Prima Donna. A brown-faced man seated next to Prima Donna was introduced as Jasper Jack, the "trickster." The old man was Old Uncle. Several children were also in blackface. All of the blackfaces wore fuzzy wigs, exaggerations of African American hair.

Billy had heard about minstrel shows, but was not prepared for the brand of humor. Almost all of the jokes made fun of former slaves. Some were reserved for Yankees. Puns were commonly used. The audience was eating it up, laughing uncontrollably. The jokes and tales were interspersed with songs: "Nelly Bly," "Carry Me Back to Old Virginny," "Old Dan Tucker."

Old Uncle longed for his secure home on the plantation before the war and mourned the death in battle of his former master. The dandy, Zip Coon, mocked free blacks and slaves alike. He asked Jim Crow how to get to China. After rubbing his chin and looking up for a long time, Jim answered, "Why, you jes goes up in a balloon and waits for the world to rotate below you." The audience roared. Each joke was punctuated by the rattling of bones, the banging of the tambourine, and the plunking of a few notes on the banjo.

The final part of the show was a short play, modeled on *Uncle Tom's Cabin,* but rewritten to show the Southern view of slavery as a benign institution that gave the inferior black people refuge from the consequences of their ignorance. Contrary to the plot of the novel, the overseer was a good man trying to help the recalcitrant young slaves do their duty and avoid the consequences of being "uppity."

The show closed with the singing of "Dixie." The audience stood and joined in enthusiastically. Billy and Wonsley stood with the rest of them but did not sing.

Many of the black crew behind the stage also laughed at the jokes. Some joined in and sang along softly with the songs. Most listened silently.

After the show, as Billy and Wonsley made their way back toward town, Billy suggested that Wonsley join him for a drink at Ashley Maitland's office. Wonsley quickly agreed. They reached the office on North Railroad Avenue in a short time. The office was located upstairs, above a hardware store. Ashley sat in his leather chair in his office, a glass of whiskey in his hand. A bottle of bourbon was open on the desk. He turned as Billy and Wonsley entered. His face was flushed.

"Well, welcome, gentlemen," he said in a slurred voice. "Have a drink." He gestured unsteadily toward the bottle. "You know where the glasses are, William."

"That's what we came for," Billy said. He retrieved two glasses from a shelf and poured out two drinks.

"Have a seat," Ash said. "Sit a spell."

They sat beside the desk.

"This has been an eventful day," Ash said.

"What happened?" Wonsley asked.

"Oh, not much. Just that Ev Hardeman shot and killed Gilbert Adams."

Billy stood abruptly.

"What?"

He and Wonsley had yet to drink from their glasses.

"Shot him through the heart," Ash said. "One shot. From about fifty feet."

"My God," Wonsley said.

"Yep. Didn't know he was that good with that left hand."

"What happened?" Billy asked. Ash gave him a familiar look, one that indicated he was asking a stupid question or repeating himself. "I mean, how did it come about?"

"Adams beat up his wife," Ash said. "Ev said he would kill him and he did."

Billy and Wonsley looked at each other. Wonsley downed his shot of bourbon.

"Shot him on the lane to the Adams place," Ash said. "His two boys were in the wagon with him." He reached for the bottle and poured into his glass, his hands shaking. "You better bone up for the bar exam, William," he said. "You may be needed."

"What do you mean?" Billy asked. "Won't you be representing him?"

"I'm a witness," Ash said. "I saw the whole thing. I cannot appear in court on his behalf. The prosecutor will name me as a witness and seek disqualification." He gave Billy a red-eyed stare. "But I can act as your clerk."

Billy stared back at him.

"How can I do that? I've never tried a case."

"Yes, you have. You have sat in with me on three jury cases already and by the time the case goes to trial, you will probably be second chair on a couple more. You've made two jury arguments already." Ash smiled. "I haven't told you yet, but I think you are cut out to be a lawyer, just like your daddy thought you would be."

"Do you think I am ready for a bar examination?"

"You will be in a couple of weeks. The tradition is to bring a bottle of bourbon with you, for the judge. It had better be good bourbon, though. Judge Daughtry will not be satisfied with anything but good Kentucky. And it's about time for your name to be on the shingle out in front. I do think you should be known as 'Will' from now own. The shingle can say 'William' or 'William Wesley,' if you prefer."

They sat and drank for another hour and discussed the details of the shooting and the events leading up to it, until Ash was wavering as he stood from his chair. Billy and Wonsley helped him stand and urinate in the chamber pot beside the couch, then laid him down on it and pulled his boots off. He was snoring loudly as they left the office.

SIX

WONSLEY STARTED FOR CORPUS CHRISTI ON THE WEDNESDAY after Easter Sunday. After a two-day ride, he broke his camp early in the morning and rode along the coast road, which eventually led him across the bridge over the Nueces near its mouth and onto the streets of Corpus. A fair-sized settlement with a couple of big stores and a number of small ones, it was surprising that at midmorning the streets seemed to be all but deserted. There were no women or children and few men. The window shutters on store buildings and houses were closed, as if prepared for a storm, although the sky was clear. He soon learned that Corpus was a town that had been frightened by regular raids by bandits who had come up from across the Rio Grande in large groups. On the main street, he came upon a group of men standing in front of a large store building. They were roughly dressed. Each wore a pistol on his belt as well as a Bowie knife. The older men were bearded. He was sure they were Rangers.

The men were loading a wagon with supplies, and two of them were handing out Sharps rifles from the store. Wonsley had only seen one of the rifles before, in the company of an old buffalo hunter he had encountered with his father many years before. The Sharps was a fifty-caliber single shot with a very long range. Each Ranger who was handed one turned it over in his hands, examining it. Wonsley dismounted and asked a young Ranger, who was apparently waiting for his gun, where he might find Captain McNelly.

"Why, he's right over there," the young man replied, pointing toward two men standing on the porch of the store. One of the men was large and rotund, with a heavy beard, wearing a leather apron. The other was a small, swarthy man, dressed in rough clothing, with a black cigar clenched between his teeth. He was gesturing toward the men carrying out supplies as if directing them. Wonsley walked over to the edge of the porch.

"Captain McNelly?" he asked, looking at both of them. The small man answered, "Yes," looking down at him from the porch.

"I'm Wonsley Baker from Guadalupe County. I've got a letter from my brother, John Baker. I'd like to join up with you if you could use another man."

McNelly stared into his eyes.

"You have a letter, you say?"

"Yes, sir." Wonsley pulled the letter from his shirt pocket, unfolded it and handed it to him. The captain read it, then refolded it and handed it back to him.

"You mounted?"

"Yes, sir. That's my sorrel over there."

"I see you have a pistol and knife. Know how to use them?"

"Oh, yes, sir. And I'm a fair tracker."

"You ever handle a Sharps rifle?" the captain asked.

"No, sir. But I'm sure I can. I can shoot."

The captain turned to the portly man.

"Sol, you think he can handle one?"

The man looked him over.

"He looks hardy enough," he said.

McNelly said, "Your pay will be thirty-three dollars a month, paid in state scrip, and found. The state will furnish a Sharps and ammunition. You want it?"

"Yes, sir."

He turned to another large man standing nearby.

"Sergeant, sign him up."

He followed the sergeant to the wagon, where he signed his name in a small book. He was given a Sharps and boxes of ammo for the rifle and for his Colt pistol. The sergeant then introduced him to a younger man whose name was George Durham. He was told Durham would show him the ropes. After the sergeant walked away, Durham turned to Wonsley.

"That sergeant's got a sense of humor," he said.

"How's that?"

"I just joined up myself a couple of days ago," Durham said. "Where you from?"

"Guadalupe County," Wonsley replied.

"That in Texas?"

"Sure is. You must be from somewheres else."

"Georgia," Durham said. "Just got here to Texas a few weeks ago. My daddy served under Captain McNelly with his Texas guerrillas in Louisiana. He said he'd take a chance on me."

"My brother John knew the captain during the war, but he didn't say where. He don't talk much about the war."

"I get it," Durham said. "Sherman burned and stole us out back in Georgia. Wasn't much left to farm. We don't talk about it much either."

When the wagon was loaded, they mounted up and followed the captain, the sergeant, and the other men on a trail up the right bank of the Nueces to a rough camp about a mile out of town. After being situated in camp, they were ordered to fall in.

"What's that mean?" Wonsley asked Durham.

"Follow me," he replied. "You'll see."

He followed Durham to a point in front of a row of tents, where the men were forming into a single line. The sergeant, whose name Wonsley later discovered was John Armstrong, passed in front of the line and made a nose count. Captain McNelly appeared out front, and Armstrong reported, "There's forty-two, Captain."

"Does that tally?" McNelly asked.

"Yes, sir," the sergeant replied.

McNelly then commanded, "Count off by eights." The men shouted out numbers, eight at a time. Then the captain said, "All number eights step forward two paces." When they had done this, he continued. "You will be acting corporals until further orders. You'll be held responsible for the men in your dab. You'll post a guard of four men in three-hour tours, beginning at the head of the line. It'll be all right to light up some fires. When you bed down, bed down at the ready at ten-pace intervals, behind your mounts."

Wonsley was not familiar with such orders, but it appeared that most of the men were, and those that were not followed the lead of the others. He drew the second watch. In the morning, they were told to saddle up without breakfast. Wonsley later learned that it was not unusual to ride without breakfast.

Bandits had been plundering the entire area south of the Nueces for a long time. They crossed the Rio Grande downstream from Laredo in groups of fifty to one hundred men and had struck up through Duval County as far as Beeville and toward Goliad and Refugio, rustling cattle and robbing stores and homesteads. Ranchers all over the area had raised vigilante posses to chase the bandits, but were seldom able to catch up with them before they crossed back over the river. One of the more recent raids had been on Tom Noakes's store at Nuecestown, about thirteen miles from Corpus Christi. Noakes had taken his five children into a tunnel he had built to the Nueces River, but his wife, Martha, had tried to save her feather bed from the burning store and had been whipped with a saddle quirt and "mistreated" by some of the bandits. The bandits had made off with eighteen Dick Heye saddles from San Antonio, which were considered the best-made saddles in the state. McNelly had learned about the saddles in detail so that he could identify them, and had the storekeeper in Corpus, Sol Lichtenstein, describe them to his men, telling Sol not to sell any that he might receive in the future until there were further orders from him.

He then told Sergeant Armstrong, "Order the men to empty those saddles on sight. No palavering with the riders. Empty them. Leave the men where you drop them and bring the saddles to camp."

It was very clear from the beginning of Wonsley's time with McNelly's Rangers that Lee McNelly, though small in stature, was a tough leader. He carried a large book in his saddle bag that contained a list of men who were wanted by the law, with a description of each. As the company made its way through the Nueces country, name after name was crossed off the list. McNelly also informed the local sheriff that he and his men would not need any assistance and that all posses of vigilantes were to be disbanded. He made it clear that any man trying to act on his own against the bandits, or as part of a posse of vigilantes, was subject to being shot on sight. Every Ranger in the company referred to him as "the captain." Every utterance indicated respect for him. The word was that he was a hard man who drove himself as hard as his men and that he was not to be crossed.

SEVEN

HARDEMAN LODGE WAS ESTABLISHED AS A MASONIC LODGE on Plum Creek in the 1850s. The decision to move to the new town had been made several months before, and by 1875 construction of a new two-story hall was underway on a lot a block north of Railroad Avenue. The lodge was named for a relative of Everett Hardeman. Billy McCulloch, now determined to be known as Will, was not a Mason, but his father had been, and he felt the need to help with the construction. Like his father, his cousins, Henry McCulloch and his son Ben, were Masons, and they were involved. Will was passing by the construction site early on a Monday and saw Ben working as part of the crew. He waved as he rode by, and Ben walked over to the edge of the street. Will said that he could not help out today, because he was on his way to Lockhart, the county seat, to take his bar examination before Judge Daughtry.

"So you're actually gonna make a lawyer, huh?" Ben asked, looking up at him with a wry smile.

"If I can convince the judge I know how to talk like one," he replied. "Ash Maitland says it's all about learning how to talk like a lawyer and if you can do that, you can make it."

"You was always a good talker," Ben said. "Not much of a fighter, but a good talker. Not to say you can't shoot. You can sure as hell shoot."

Will looked over the construction site. The beams and floor joists for the first floor had already been set on the piers after only a couple of days' work, and the men were working on laying out the framing for the walls. Almost all of the workers were Masons, who were there with their families. They had volunteered for the building project. The men were spending the early morning hours working on the building, starting at dawn and working until noon, then breaking for lunch, which was served by their wives and daughters at tables laid under the large oak tree at the rear of the site. Each day after lunch, they returned to their farms and businesses.

Will's father had not shared much about Freemasonry with him, but he had told him that Masons believed in truth and justice and that one should be tolerant of the diversity among humankind. He had been taught that all differences of religious belief should be respected and that honor was of the utmost importance to living a fruitful life; that it was the duty of every honorable man to help out others who were in difficulty and to exercise independent judgment about the problems of the world. It was important to be honest and truthful to others.

Shortly after he had returned from Mississippi, Ben had asked him if he would allow him to sponsor him for membership in Hardeman Lodge. He had said he would think about it. His father had never expressed interest in his joining the lodge, but that may have been because he considered him to be too young at the time. He was not quite sixteen when his father died. When Ben asked, he said he would think about it. He was curious about Masonry, but he did not like the idea that it was a secret club, with secret rituals. And in the last few years, he had become more skeptical about the mysteries of religion.

"I can be here tomorrow morning," Will said.

"See you then, Cousin," Ben replied.

Will continued on the road to Lockhart, which lay fourteen miles to the north. He had appeared in Judge Daughtry's court a number of times in the past months, but he had not been there alone. Ash Maitland had always been lead counsel. In fact, it was only after a couple of months that Ash had asked the judge if Will could speak for their clients. He had previously only taken notes, sitting next to Ash at the counsel table. In response to the request, Judge Daughtry narrowed his eyes at him from the bench, looking down on him by expression as well as position. After a long pause, he said, "We will allow the young McCulloch to appear in the presence of Lawyer Maitland and speak to the court and jury." The hint of a smile crossed the judge's face. Since then, Will had actually put on some direct testimony and had given two jury arguments, though he had not yet cross-examined a witness. As he rode into Lockhart, he was still not sure of the judge's opinion of him. Judge Daughtry had always addressed him in an exaggerated, formal manner, talking down to him.

In front of the courthouse, he dismounted and pulled his documents and a bottle of bourbon out of this saddlebag. He had brought his birth certificate and his college diploma as well as the whiskey, which his mother had placed in a brown burlap bag to hide it from the public. He walked up the stairs to the judge's office. The door was ajar. He looked inside. Judge Daughtry was sitting behind his desk, his head down, apparently asleep. Will knocked on the open door. The judge jerked up in his chair and looked his way, a groggy look on his face.

"Ah, it's Mister McCulloch," he said gruffly. "Come in, sir, and have a seat." As Will stepped toward the chairs on his side of the desk, the judge eyed the burlap bag. "What's that you're carrying, young man?"

"It's for you, Judge," he replied.

He handed the bag to him. The judge took it, held it up before him for a moment, then pulled the bottle of bourbon out and looked at it with a sparkle in his eye.

"This is mighty fine whiskey by the look of the bottle. Evan Williams, eh? Haven't had any of this in a while. Grab a couple of those glasses from the shelf over there and we'll have a snort."

Will grabbed two of the thick bar glasses and placed them on the desk before the judge, who uncorked the bottle and poured liberal portions. He took one of the glasses and gestured to Will to get the other one, then held his glass up.

"Here's to the legal profession," he said. "May it forever stand as a bastion of reason and justice." There was a hint of sarcasm in the way he said it.

The judge downed his glass and looked to Will, who was obviously expected to do the same. He tilted his glass and felt the whiskey burn its way down his throat. He was not used to strong drink.

"I am sure Lawyer Maitland advised you to bring the whiskey," the judge said. "You should know that it doesn't mean you will automatically pass."

"No, sir," Will replied. "He said it was a tradition."

"Indeed it is, and a fine one at that."

The judge placed his glass back on the desk.

"I am sure Lawyer Maitland has been directing your studies and obviously thought you were ready to be accepted to the bar. Tell me what you have been reading."

"Ash said I should make a list," he replied, pulling a sheaf of paper from his vest pocket.

"Ah, let's see," the judge said, reaching for the paper. "*Paschal's Digest*, 1870, good," he read. "Wharton's *Law of Homicide*, very good. Blackstone, of course. Story's commentaries on American law. Pomeroy on equity jurisprudence. Pomeroy on constitutional law.. Chitty on contracts and pleadings. Sayles's *Practice*. And several more. Very good. It looks like Lawyer Maitland has a respectable library. And you have read all of these?"

"Yes, sir."

"Very well. If Ash has recommended you, that is almost good enough without further inquiry. But I shall put some questions to you."

"Yes, sir."

"I have a suspicion that you will soon be on a criminal case in my court," the judge said. "You must not consider any subject we discuss here as indicative of my future rulings from the bench."

"Yes, sir. I understand." He wondered what Ash had told the judge about Everett Hardeman's situation. The grand jury was in session and scheduled to make their report soon.

"Very well. What are the two classes of manslaughter?"

"Voluntary and involuntary, Judge."

"And what is the difference?"

"Involuntary is when the accused is performing an unlawful act and unintentionally kills someone."

"But there is a qualification to that, isn't there?"

"Yes, sir. The unlawful act has to be less than a felony."

"Correct. What about voluntary manslaughter?"

"Where the killing is intentional, but under the heat of passion."

"Or . . . "

"Or in a sudden quarrel."

"Yes. But when is a killing in self-defense and therefore justifiable?"

"When in lawful self-defense."

"And the qualifications?"

Will stopped to think. He knew where the judge was going with these questions and felt the need to be very cautious.

"Well?" the judge finally asked.

"When there is reasonable ground to believe that the person killed was going to do some great personal injury."

"And the qualification to that?" The judge's lips were pursed.

"Imminent danger."

"Exactly." The judge paused, looking him in the eye. "But when there is reasonable apprehension of imminent danger from the other person, don't the grounds have to be real and not imagined?"

Will paused to think. He looked away from the judge's stare for a moment, then spoke slowly.

"If the apprehension is reasonable and honest, then the grounds need not be reasonable," he said.

"But what if the grounds don't exist and that fact is undisputed?"

"Then I suppose self-defense would not apply."

"Might there be manslaughter?"

He hesitated again. "There might," he finally said.

"But on what condition?" the judge asked.

"Sudden passion," Will replied

The judge's stare continued without speech, for what seemed like an eternity. Will shifted in his chair, but held his gaze. Finally, the judge cleared his throat.

"Pour us another shot, young man," he said, smiling. "I'm going to give you a few pieces of advice."

Will poured two more shots, being careful to approximate the amounts the judge had previously poured. They held up their glasses again and downed the whiskey.

"Value your profession. Don't take it lightly. Always charge a reasonable fee, unless it's a *pro bono* case."

"Yes, sir."

"Don't believe everything a client tells you. Even good men stretch the truth sometimes, especially when the chips are down."

"Yes, sir."

"And follow Ash Maitland's advice," he said, in a more serious tone. "He is a good man and has had a lot of experience. Rely on his judgment."

The judge paused again, looking at the ceiling for a moment. "Do you have any questions?" he finally asked, looking at Will again, no longer smiling.

"No, sir."

"Very well," the judge said, then reached for a sheet of paper and took up a pen, dipped it in his inkwell, and began writing. After he finished, he blotted it with a large curved blotter, then handed it to Will.

"This will serve as a certificate of your admission to the bar until you receive a license from the clerk of the Supreme Court," he said. "Congratulations." He stood and extended his hand.

"Thank you, Your Honor."

"*Judge* is sufficient here in my office," the judge said. "You can save the *Your Honors* for the courtroom."

Will clutched the folder with his new certificate and other papers in one hand as he descended the stairs and walked out of the courthouse to the street. He felt a lightness in his step that had not been there before. It had all happened so fast that he found it hard to grasp the reality that he was suddenly a lawyer.

EIGHT

LILY POE ARRIVED AT MRS. MOORE'S HOUSE IN MIDMORNING. Lucius Jackson, her employee, drove the carriage. She had sent Lucius around the previous afternoon with a note asking if she might visit and received a written reply saying Mrs. Moore would be pleased to see her the following morning. It had been weeks since the shooting.

Mrs. Moore met her on the front porch. She was not smiling.

"Good morning, Mrs. Poe," she said.

"Good morning, Mrs. Moore."

"Please come in, Mrs. Poe. I'll put a kettle on the stove."

They entered the front room. Ada was seated in the rocker by the fireplace. She wore a black dress. Her hair was up in a bun. She had changed since the last time Lily had seen her. It was more than the dress and her hair. There was an air of fragility about her that she had not noticed before. Lily walked over to her.

"Hello, Ada."

Ada was staring straight ahead, then slowly turned toward Lily. She had a vacant smile on her face.

"Hello," she said.

"I hope you're feeling better," Lily said.

Ada stopped smiling.

"I'm feeling much better," she said. "Did Everett send you?"

"Not exactly," Lily replied. "I wanted to see how you're doing."

"Is he coming to see me?"

"Not right away. I don't think Ash wants him to see you just yet."

"Why not? I need to see him. Where is he, anyway?"

Lily glanced at Mrs. Moore.

"You know why, don't you, Ada?" Mrs. Moore said.

"Because they think we're lovers," Ada said.

"No one has said that," Lily said. "Ash thinks it's better for the two of you not to see each other. You're a witness."

"I wasn't there," Ada replied. "I wasn't there and I don't know anything but what I was told about it."

Mrs. Moore and Lily exchanged a look.

"I think Ash believes you are a witness, although not of the fight itself," Lily said. "You know what happened before. How your husband treated you."

"Do I have to talk about that? I don't want to talk about that."

"You know, Billy McCulloch is going to defend Ev if they indict him. Ash can only help. He was a witness."

"Billy? He's just a boy."

"Ash needs to talk to you. He asked me to ask if you could come to his office."

"Why didn't he come out here?" Ada asked.

"He felt it would be best for him to see you in his office."

Ada looked to her mother, then back at Lily.

"Why am I a witness?" she asked. "I wasn't there."

"He could best explain that himself. Can you come into town tomorrow?"

"She hasn't been anywhere," Mrs. Moore said. "She's been here at the house."

"I'll come pick you up with my carriage tomorrow, if you'll come in," Lily said. "You may want to ride in with us, Mrs. Moore."

"I don't know anything," Ada said.

"What time?" Mrs. Moore asked.

"How about nine o'clock?"

"Ada, will you be willing to go in and see Mr. Maitland?" Mrs. Moore asked.

"I guess so," Ada replied. "But I don't know why he wants to talk to me."

"We'll be ready at nine," Mrs. Moore said.

"Thank you," Lily said. "I'll see you then."'

She turned toward the door.

"Won't you have some tea?" Mrs. Moore asked.

"Not today, thank you, Mrs. Moore. I really must be going. I'll see you tomorrow."

Lily led them up the stairs to Ashley Maitland's office at nine thirty the next morning. Will was there waiting for them in the reception room. He had not seen Ada since he had returned from Mississippi. Her appearance startled him. She was thin and pale. Her strong spirit seemed to be missing.

"You'll remember Mr. McCulloch," Lily said to them. "He is now an attorney at law."

Mrs. Moore stepped forward, extending her hand.

"I am so proud of you, Billy," she said.

Ada looked up at him briefly, then quickly looked down. After a brief silence, Lily again spoke.

"Ada, you remember your cousin, Billy McCulloch, don't you?"

"Yes," she said, again looking up at him for only a moment.

"Mr. Maitland is ready to see you, ladies," Will said. "I think he wants to see you first, Ada."

She looked to her mother.

"You'll come with me, won't you?"

"I think he wants to talk to you in private," he said.

"Why?" she asked. "Why can't my mother be there with me?"

"I'll ask him," Will said. "If you'll wait a minute."

After a moment's absence, he returned.

"You may come in too, Mrs. Moore."

They entered the office, Mrs. Moore holding onto Ada's hand. Ash met them inside the doorway.

"Good morning, ladies," Ash said. "I'm so glad you came in to talk. Please have a seat."

When they were seated beside his desk, he gestured to Will to have a seat beside him.

"I know this has been a difficult time for you, Ada," he began, "but I think you know that we represent Everett Hardeman and I need to talk to you about what has happened and some of the surrounding circumstances."

"Surrounding circumstances?" Ada asked.

"Yes. I need to know some background."

She looked at her mother, then back at Ash.

"What do you want to know?"

"Your husband. What did he do that made you go to your mother's that night?"

She was holding her hands tightly together in her lap. She looked down again as she spoke.

"I was scared of him," she said, her voice barely above a whisper.

"Why were you scared of him?"

She looked at him. Her eyes reddened.

"He beat me."

She started to sob. Ash hesitated before speaking again.

"Did he do this often?"

"Yes," she said.

Ash and Will exchanged glances.

"Had you cried out before?" he asked.

"No. He was my husband. I was supposed to obey him."

"Was there something different about this time?"

She looked at her mother. Mrs. Moore was tearing up.

"I don't want to talk about that," she said. "What difference does that make?"

"I need to know all of the facts of the case," Ash said. "What he had been doing may be relevant."

"I don't see why."

Ash and Will looked at each other again. Ash reached for his pipe, picked it up and examined it, thinking.

"Your husband had a shotgun. It was in the wagon that day. Were you familiar with where he kept it?"

She looked surprised.

"Over the doorway," she said, glancing again at Mrs. Moore. "Why?"

"Was he in the habit of taking it with him when he left the house?"

"When he was hunting. Or when he was going to town. He always took the wagon to town. He was always buying things to bring back home."

"So it was a customary thing for him to take the shotgun with him when he used the wagon?"

"Yes. He didn't use the wagon much, though. He usually rode horseback."

"Did the boys have horses?"

"There are a number of horses on the place. I don't know how many."

"The boys were with him in the wagon that day. Why would they be with him?"

"He would take them with him to town to help load or unload, or if he was going to cut cordwood and haul it. They'd go with him then."

"Why would he beat you?" he asked quickly.

She stood up.

"Because I wouldn't do just as he said," she said, her voice breaking. "If I didn't please him, he would give me a whipping, just like I was a child. I've had enough of this. I don't want to talk about this anymore."

Her hands were shaking. Mrs. Moore stood and tried to reach for her, but she shied away.

"He's dead and I'm glad of it," Ada said. "There. Is that what you wanted to know?"

Ash fondled his pipe and leaned back in his chair.

"I wasn't going to ask you that question, Mrs. Adams," he said. "I wasn't going to ask you that."

"Let's go, Mother," she said, turning to Mrs. Moore. "I've had enough of this."

She turned toward the door. Ash stood up.

"Ada," he said. "Don't leave."

She turned toward him.

"I know you represent Everett," she said. "I want to help you, but I'm tired of this."

"Then perhaps we should wait until another time," Ash replied.

"Perhaps we should," she said, then turned and left.

When Will returned after showing them out, he found Ash standing by the window watching the women mounting the carriage below. Ash was smoking, looking out the window with a calm expression.

"I don't think I am the one to interview her further," he said, turning to Will. "You would do a better job. Besides, I just realized that I may have to claim the privilege when I am on the stand."

"I agree. I have known Ada all my life. I'll go talk to her."

NINE

MRS. MOORE HAD RETRIEVED THE LETTER FROM THE NEW post office in Luling. It was her first trip to the post office in several weeks. She was reluctant to see what may have been waiting for her, and her fears were confirmed when she found the letter addressed to Ada, with no return address. It was fine stationery, folded and sealed neatly, and it gave off the air of an important message. When she returned to the Moore place, she found Ada sitting in a rocker on the front porch, waiting for her, as if she had known Mrs. Moore had picked up the mail, although she had only said she was going into town for supplies. She hesitated before stepping down from the buckboard. Ada was watching her closely as she came into the yard with the bag of supplies and her purse. When she stepped onto the porch, she reached into her purse, retrieved the letter, and handed it to Ada.

Ada took it and held it up before her, her hands shaking slightly. She looked up from the letter at her mother and back again, then gently broke the seal along the edge with her fingernail, untied the ribbon around it, and unfolded it. It was several pages.

"I knew he would get in touch," she said, her eyes brimming with tears.

"Oh, Ada. He shouldn't have. He has to be careful."

Ada began to read. Mrs. Moore sat in the other rocker and watched her. She read quietly, without looking up, until she had finished the last page, then she read it a second time. After she finished, she looked at her mother.

"He said to burn it after I read it."

"Where is he?"

"He's in Austin," Ada replied. "Or at least he was then. It's dated two weeks ago. He said Ashley Maitland advised him not to contact me, but he couldn't help himself. He wants to see me."

"He had better follow Ash's advice," Mrs. Moore said.

"Billy is his lawyer now. Ash is just his assistant."

"You know better than that, Ada."

Ada stood and tucked the letter into her bodice.

"I'm going to fix some tea," she said. "We could use some tea."

She stood with her back straight and looked down into her mother's eyes.

"Everything is going to be all right," she said. "I will see him and it will be all right."

TEN

ASHLEY MAITLAND AND WILL MCCULLOCH WERE WAITING for their client to arrive. It was already half past ten in the morning. He was thirty minutes late. They were sitting at their respective places at opposite sides of the double desk, with the doors to the reception room open.

"I'm getting a lot of pressure to stand as a delegate to the Constitutional Convention," Ash said. "The election is in August. The convention will follow in September."

"We don't have a trial date yet," Will said. "Maybe you could do it."

"I don't see how," Ash said. "If the indictment comes down next week, the judge will likely set it for the fall term. I can't be off in Austin then."

"Isn't there going to be an automatic continuance if you are counsel of record?"

"That's not clear," Ash said. "Judge Daughtry might grant one, but it is subject to interpretation. A delegate to the convention is not a legislator in a regular session. He could force us to trial. Besides that, you are going to have to be lead counsel."

"I thought the exemption applied to co-counsel," Will said.

"It has been so interpreted. Maybe the judge will let us know in advance what his ruling will be."

They heard footsteps in the stairwell. Will met Everett Hardeman at the top of the stairs. They shook hands, and Ev followed Will into the office, where Ash stood and greeted him.

"Have a seat, Ev," he said. "You are a bit late."

"I had to ford Clear Fork on the way from Lockhart," Ev said. "The creek is still up from these nice June rains we've been having, so I had to detour a little bit."

Ash noticed that his pants were wet above his boot tops. He offered him a cigar from the walnut box on the desk, but Ev declined.

"We want to cover a few things with you," Ash said.

"All right."

"I'm going to give it to you straight. We've heard rumors about you and Ada," Ash said. "We've tried to talk to Ada, but she won't really talk to us. I've got to ask about that."

Ev shifted in his chair.

"Everybody knows about Ada and me from long ago," he said. "It's no secret. And I still love her."

He waited for Ash to respond. Ash looked over at Will but did not speak.

"What do you want to know?" Ev asked.

"Have you been seeing her since she was married?"

"I've seen her a couple of times in public," he replied. "What about it?"

"Have you seen her otherwise?"

"No. I haven't."

Ev was looking down at his boot tops as he spoke. Ash looked inquiringly at Will. Will cleared his throat before speaking.

"We've talked to the Moore neighbors," he said. "Some of them say they've seen you turn into the lane to their house."

Ev looked at Will.

"I had to see if she was all right," he said. "It was after the shooting."

Will looked down at the desktop before speaking again.

"You know, Ev, we've got to know what to expect when this comes to trial. If we are surprised, it will not be a good thing. You see that, don't you?"

"Sure. I understand."

"Is there anything else we need to know?" Ash asked.

Ev hesitated. Ash and Will exchanged a glance.

"That's all," he finally said.

"I know you're concerned about her, but it doesn't look good for you to be seeing her, Ev," Ash said. "Don't you see that?"

"Sure. I understand."

His gloved hand was shaking.

"All right," Ash said. "We think the case will be called to trial in October. Looks like I might be a delegate to the Constitutional Convention. That could get it postponed until the next term, maybe until next spring."

"I don't want that," Ev said. "I want to get this over with."

"It will probably be better for you if it's postponed," Will said. "Gives the gossip time to die down."

"Gossip? Why should gossip have anything to do with it?"

"Maybe it shouldn't, but it almost always does," Ash said. "We won't know who's in the jury pool until the week before trial. If you stay away from Ada until then, maybe there won't be any talk still going on."

"I don't want to stay away from her," Ev said, standing up.

"You must," Ash said. "If you want to survive this."

"You were there. You saw he had a shotgun."

"Yes, and I probably made a mistake agreeing to represent you and be your lawyer at the same time I am a witness," he replied. "I decided they would know we were friends anyway, and it was worth the risk, but my credibility will be an issue. That's why Will will be lead counsel. I may not even be in the courtroom except to testify."

"You can still decide to change counsel," Will said. "It's not too late."

"I don't know anybody else. Which means I don't trust anybody else. You'll do."

Ev smiled when he said it.

ELEVEN

THE GRAND JURY WAS SEATED IN THE JURY BOX. The chairman had just handed a sheaf of papers to the bailiff, who handed them to Judge Daughtry. The judge began to announce each indictment or failure to indict presented, in the order they were given him. Everett Hardeman's name was not called until he held the last document before him. He hesitated, looking down from the bench at Ash and Will, seated at the counsel table. When he spoke, it was in a deeper voice than before.

"Everett Hardeman, a true bill. Murder in the first degree." He hesitated again, placing the other sheets of paper on top of the last one on the bench before him, then announced in a lighter tone, "These cases will be set for the October term of court, beginning the first Monday in October, with motions to be heard the Thursday before. Hearings on bail will be this afternoon at one thirty."

Ash and several other lawyers stood. Ash spoke first.

"May it please the court. Your Honor, I anticipate that I may be a delegate to the Constitutional Convention, which is set to begin in September and may well last into the October term of court."

"There has not been an election yet," the judge said. "How do you know you will be elected, Counsel?"

"I don't, Your Honor. But I wanted to apprise the court of that possibility now, to aid the court in its scheduling."

"We will take that matter up when the time arises," the judge said.

A tall, thin man stood up at the opposite end of the counsel table from Ash.

"Your Honor," he said. "On the Hardeman case, I understand Mr. Maitland may be a witness. If so, as prosecutor, I will object to him being in the courtroom as counsel for the defendant."

"Mr. Clark, I appreciate your sharing your position with the court, but that is a bit premature. But perhaps I should ask Mr. Maitland if he is going to appear as counsel for Mr. Hardeman." The judge looked down at Ash.

"I intend to, Your Honor, and in fact, I ask that my appearance on behalf of Mr. Hardeman be entered into the record now," Ash said.

"That disqualifies him as a witness, Your Honor," Clark said.

"Hold on, Frank," the judge said. "Maybe it is best if we have a hearing on all these matters this afternoon, after bail has been set. I'll consider motions regarding counsel and witness issues then, but I may take any ruling under advisement until the proper time. Is that acceptable to counsel?"

Both lawyers assented. After court was adjourned, Clark approached Ash.

"You can't have your cake and eat it too, Ash," he said.

"I don't expect to," Ash replied. "I know that the judge will not allow me to participate as counsel over your objection, but I can still assist outside the courtroom."

Clark appeared to be puzzled.

"Then who is to be lead counsel?" he asked.

"Mr. McCulloch, here," Ash replied, turning to Will, who stood beside him.

Clark looked from Ash to Will, then smiled.

"I see," he said. "Well, I am looking forward to it, Mr. McCulloch."

"Thank you," Will responded.

After they left the courtroom, Ash walked briskly toward Friedman's Saloon. Will had trouble keeping up. When they were inside, Ash stepped up to the bar. The bartender, without a word having been spoken, poured a shot of bourbon and placed it before him. He downed the shot and flipped a coin onto the bar, then turned to Will.

"Don't be intimidated by Clark," he said. "He is sloppy and mostly bluster. You'll do just fine."

"All right," Will replied. "But why did you bring the convention up now? You haven't been elected yet. I didn't even know you had decided to run."

"It's better overall if I am a delegate. And I want the judge to be thinking about it. I don't expect him to rule today. You heard what he said. He usually takes matters like this under advisement, and I didn't want to spring it on him in the fall, when he might make up his mind too fast."

Later that afternoon, the judge set bail at five thousand dollars and gave Ash a week to surrender his client and post bond for his release. As Ash predicted, the judge took the matter of his appearance as counsel and witness under advisement, without comment. As they were leaving the courtroom the second time that day, Will turned to Ash.

"What if you don't get elected?" he asked.

Ash smiled.

"Then you better be ready for trial in October," he said.

TWELVE

LILY POE OFFERED EVERETT HARDEMAN A CIGAR. They were seated at the dinner table at Lily's house. Barbara Ann had excused herself and retired to her room after clearing the dinner plates from the table.

"How about some coffee?" she asked.

"That would be nice."

"Come into the kitchen with me while I fix it."

In the kitchen she filled a kettle with water and placed it on the wood stove, then turned to him.

"I've had something I've wanted to talk to you about for some time," she said.

"That's what I thought."

She put her hand on his shoulder.

"I know you've been seeing Ada," she said.

He held the cigar up.

"Nice Havana," he said, smiling.

"You know you shouldn't be seeing her."

His smile went away.

"No one knows about it."

"Hah! I know about it. Do you think I'm the only one? It's the talk of the county."

"So what? We have a right to be together."

"Are you out of your mind? You're charged with killing her husband.

Don't you think being with her is a bit dangerous for you? I've always loved you and I know you are obsessed with Ada, but you've got to stop seeing her."

"Lily, we are going to be married. I'm going to marry her as soon as this is over."

"You won't be alive to marry anyone if you're not careful," she said, her eyes brimming with tears. She turned away from him. He put the cigar on the edge of the stove and took her by the arm.

"Look, you can't know how I feel. I know you care about me and I value your friendship. But I know what I'm doing. Ada is part of me. I can't let her go."

She turned around.

"You have to wait. She won't be going anywhere. You just have to wait."

"I can't leave her by herself. I have to see her."

"Were you seeing her before Adams's death?"

He backed away from her, frowning.

"You were, weren't you? I can see it in your face."

He turned and walked out of the kitchen, retrieved his hat from the hall tree, and walked out the front door. She stood in the kitchen, looking after him through the kitchen doorway. The kettle began to sing, but she just stood there, listening to the lingering sound of the front door closing behind him.

THIRTEEN

ASHLEY MAITLAND WAS ELECTED AS A DELEGATE TO THE Constitutional Convention in August. Judge Daughtry had ruled that he was to report to him after the election. The returns had been counted, and Ash reported to the judge, as ordered. The judge was on the bench during a court recess. He stared down at Ash.

"Are you going to be participating in the trial as defense counsel?" he asked.

"Yes, Your Honor," Ash replied.

"When is the convention to be over?"

"That has not been determined, Your Honor, but I expect it may go into early November."

Frank Clark stood next to Ash.

"Your Honor. My motion to disqualify counsel . . . "

"Hold on, Mr. Clark. I'll get to that," the judge said sternly. He studied his leatherbound calendar, which lay open before him. "I'm going to set the Hardeman case for trial the second week in January," he said. "Can counsel be ready then?"

"Yes, Your Honor," Ash replied.

"I have no problem with that date, Your Honor," Clark said.

"Very well," said the judge. "On the prosecution's motion, I rule that Mr. Maitland will be allowed to be seated at the counsel table to assist lead counsel in the case, but if he is to be a witness, he will not be allowed to interrogate witnesses or address the jury. Do you intend to be a witness, counselor?"

"I do, Your Honor," Ash replied.

"Your Honor. If Mr. Maitland is to be a witness, I intend to place him under the rule."

"He will be excused from the rule for this case, Mr. Clark."

"But, Your Honor. That will give the defense an unfair advantage. The lawyer will be able to hear other testimony that may affect his own."

"I have given this considerable thought, counsel. I believe this witness will not let his testimony be so affected, but I will entertain a motion during trial as to his presence during any particular testimony. You will approach the bench to make any such motion, which shall be made outside the presence and hearing of the jury."

Clark looked down, then up at the judge again.

"Yes, Your Honor," he said.

"Any other matters regarding this case, gentlemen?"

Both indicated that there were none.

FOURTEEN

DELEGATES FOR THE CONSTITUTIONAL CONVENTION OF 1875 came from all parts of the state, three having been elected from each state senatorial district. Seventy-five members were Democrats. Fifteen, including six black men, were Republicans. None of them had taken part in the Constitutional Convention of 1868-1869, which had resulted in the radical Constitution of 1869, enacted when virtually all of the former Confederate soldiers and state office holders were disqualified from voting on it. It had concentrated power in the governor's office, which had led to the appointment by the Republican governor of a state police force that was detested by most Texans.

The political wounds from radical Republican rule were still tender. The election of delegates to a Constitutional Convention was held in August.

Ashley Maitland was one of twenty-nine lawyers among the delegates. There were forty-one farmers. About forty delegates were members of the Grange, a strong farmers' organization. The convention was almost entirely composed of old Texans: John Henry Brown, Sterling C. Robertson, Rip Ford, and John H. Reagan were part of a bevy of generals who had worn the gray. Of the ninety members, more than twenty had held high rank in the Confederate States of America. In an effort to reverse the perceived Republican excesses of previous years, restrictions were placed on state salaries, expenditures, taxes, and the state debt. State banks were abolished, some activities of corporations and railroads were limited, and term limits were placed on many government offices.

The majority of the convention believed so firmly in economizing they refused to hire a stenographer and would not allow the proceedings of the convention to be published. The document they produced provided for short terms of office, low salaries, and limited powers for officials. It removed the power of the governor to declare martial law. It indicated a general mistrust of state government. The convention first met on September 6, 1875, and adjourned on November 24. The new constitution was passed by the voters in an election held on February 15, 1876. It remains, with numerous amendments, as the governing document for the state of Texas.

Ashley Maitland had been a member of the standing committee on railroads. Even though he had lobbied for legislation in the past on behalf of the Galveston, Harrisburg and San Antonio line, that was not perceived as a conflict of interest. He returned to his law office from Austin on the day the convention adjourned, the day before Thanksgiving. It was dusk when he rode up to the hitching post in front of the building. He could see lantern light coming from the upper window and found Will waiting for him at the double desk.

"Welcome back," Will said. "Did you do right by the people of Texas?"

"We'll see," Ash replied. "How about a drink?"

Will pulled the whiskey bottle and two crystal glasses down from the top bookshelf and poured shots for them. They raised their glasses.

"To Texas," they said in unison, and downed the shots.

"So has our client been behaving himself?" Ash asked.

"I hope so," Will replied. "I haven't heard of him being arrested, but I have heard he has been spending a good deal of time at Friedman's."

"I don't like that," Ash said. "I can picture the conversation that happens there."

They had another drink and discussed getting ready for trial. After talking about the state's witnesses and their own, Will brought up another subject.

"What if there were two shotguns?" he asked.

"I've thought of that," Ash replied. "But where did the other one go?"

"Exactly. I think we need to search the Adams place."

"But the two sons are there."

"I don't think they are now. I heard they were staying with their aunt in Prairie Lea. I think we need to inspect the premises."

Ash packed his pipe, thinking.

"We would need some law enforcement with us, but it would have to be friendly."

His face lightened up. He looked back at Will.

"Stagner," Will said.

"Yes. Constable Quill Stagner. He can be trusted. I'll call on him first thing tomorrow."

"You know tomorrow is Thanksgiving."

"So it is. I'd better get over there early, before the drinking starts."

FIFTEEN

JURY SELECTION FOR *STATE OF TEXAS V. EVERETT HARDEMAN* began on the second Monday in January. Sixty prospective jurors, veniremen, had been called in by the sheriff, who had selected them from a list. Only the first forty would fit in the courtroom, so the judge directed the sheriff to furlough the others, who were to remain subject to recall should they be needed. At nine o'clock, not all of the forty men had been seated. The lawyers and court reporter were gathered close to the bench, where Judge Daughtry asked if they had any motions before the beginning of *voir dire.* "The defense does, Your Honor," Ashley Maitland responded.

"Then let's retire to chambers to hear it," the judge said.

They crossed through the side railing gate and the door at the back of the courtroom, through the jury room and into the judge's office. The court reporter sat on a stool at the edge of the judge's desk.

"Be seated, gentlemen," the judge said as he took a seat behind the desk. Frank Clark and Ashley sat in the two available chairs. Will McCulloch stood next to a young lawyer he did not know, who stood behind Clark. He was gangly, with a trimmed beard and a large nose.

"Judge, I want to introduce my associate counsel in this case, Mr. John Singleton of Austin," said Clark.

The young man stepped forward, and the judge shook hands with him.

"Welcome, counsel," he said. "Are you in private practice?"

"I have the honor of being an assistant district attorney for Travis County," he responded.

Ashley exchanged glances with Will. It was obvious that Clark wanted to counter the youth factor Will brought to the case, but there may have been more to it.

The judge turned to Ash.

"You have a motion, counsel?"

"More of a need for clarification, Your Honor," Ash said. "I wish to address the panel in *voir dire* and interrogate the veniremen. I want to make sure that does not violate your previous order."

"My order was intended to prohibit your direct involvement in interrogation of witnesses or addressing the jury," the judge said. "That would include questioning veniremen and making any kind of statement to the jury. I think it's hard for jurors to separate argument from testimony, and that would be true in jury selection as well as during trial. Does that clarify, Mr. Maitland?"

"It does, Your Honor," Ash replied.

"Very well. Is there anything else to take up in chambers?"

No one spoke up. They returned to the courtroom. The first prospective juror was called to the witness stand and sworn in. He wore a shirt without a collar and held a worn brown hat, which he switched from his right hand when told to touch the Bible held before him for his oath taking. He had a visible tan line where his hat had touched his forehead. Frank Clark began the interrogation by asking his name, residence address, and profession. Singleton was seated beside him, taking notes. Clark then asked if he had heard about the case.

"Everybody's heard about it," he replied.

"Have you formed an opinion about what happened out there?"

"Naw. I wasn't there."

"What did you hear about it?"

"Aw, just that that Hardeman boy shot ol' Adams. That's all I heard."

"Do you know the defendant?"

"I know Ev. Known him all his life."

"Would you consider him a friend?"

"His daddy was a friend of mine. I knew him good. A good man."

"He's charged with murder in the first degree. Do you think you could be fair as a juror in this case?"

"Oh, sure," the man said. "I don't know nothin' about what happened out there. Just what I heard."

"Could you find the defendant guilty if the evidence called for it?"

"Sure could."

Clark stood up.

"This juror is acceptable to the state, Your Honor," he said.

The judge looked at Will, who was listening to Ash whisper in his ear. Will then stood.

"We have no questions, Your Honor. This man is acceptable to the defense."

The state was entitled to ten peremptory challenges, in which the prosecution could strike a prospective juror as a matter of right, without assigning any reason for his disqualification. Ash knew that Clark was familiar with most of the men who had been called by the sheriff for jury duty. He also knew that the district attorney's office kept a card catalog on every man who had served on a Caldwell County jury in the last twenty years, and it was likely that Clark knew that the man just questioned had a background in law enforcement and thus did not strike him. For Ash, it was not worth using one of the defense's twenty peremptory challenges on a man who had been a friend of Ev Hardeman's father, even though he was a former deputy sheriff of Gonzales County. Ev had given him a nod of approval from his end of the counsel table, and that was good enough for Ash.

The next panelist was sworn in. He was a ruddy-faced man in his early twenties. Clark asked the same question about his knowledge of the case.

"I don't know what case you're talking about," the man said.

"What do you do for a living?" Clark asked.

"I do a little farming with my daddy."

"What is your daddy's name?"

"Martin."

"Is that his first or last name?"

"That's his given name," the young man said. "His last name is the same as mine."

"The defendant is charged with murder in the first degree," Clark said. "Could you find him guilty if the evidence showed he was guilty?"

The man squinted and hesitated.

"Did you understand the question?"

"I think I did," the man said. "I guess I could if the evidence showed it."

"This man is acceptable," Clark said.

Will cleared his throat while looking at his penciled notes.

"Do you believe a man has the right to defend himself?" he asked.

"Sure do."

"If you believe the defendant shot in self-defense, would you be able to return a verdict of not guilty?"

"Sure could."

"This man is acceptable to the defense," Will said.

The third panelist was a thin man wearing suspenders. Clark asked him his profession.

"What's that?" the man asked.

"Did you hear the question?" Clark asked.

"What question?"

"What is your profession?"

"I don't guess I have one," the man said.

"What do you do for a living?"

"Oh. I raise a few crops and run a few head of cattle," he said, frowning.

"Have you heard about this case?"

"I heard somebody shot Mr. Adams," he said. "I don't know who."

"Did you know the decedent?"

"The what?"

"Adams. The decedent."

"Oh, him. Yeah, I knew him."

"How well did you know him?"

"Pretty good, I guess. He was my daddy's cousin."

In answer to Will's questions, he would not admit to any bias and Will used one of his peremptory challenges on him, leaving nineteen to be used on others. Ash advised against ever letting a relative of the decedent on the jury.

The next panelist was a former Indiana resident who worked as a store clerk in Lockhart. Although he expressed no prejudice, Ash advised striking him with a peremptory challenge, whispering to Will that a northerner would not likely believe a former confederate soldier's testimony.

The prosecution used a peremptory challenge on the next panelist, a man who said Gilbert Adams was "white trash," but who would not admit to bias in favor of the defense.

Ish Friedman was called up next. He was known to everyone as the owner of a general store and saloon in Lockhart and as a good friend of Ash Maitland and Will's father, Wes McCulloch.

"Wouldn't you find it hard to reach a verdict of guilty in this case, Ish?" Clark asked.

"I don't think so, if the evidence was clear."

"You mean you would find against your friends?"

"I believe I would follow the law, wherever that may lead."

"And the evidence?"

"Yes, sir. And the evidence."

"But you know the defendant and his lawyers. Wouldn't it be hard to find against them?"

"I don't know the defendant that well. I've seen him in my store."

"Recently?" Clark asked.

"Yes, I saw him in the saloon last week."

Ash nudged Will.

"Just last week, huh?" Clark beamed.

"Yes. He has been in frequently."

"So he is a regular customer of yours."

"Your Honor," Clark said. "This man is obviously prejudiced and we challenge him for cause."

"Overruled," the judge said.

"Then we strike him," Clark said.

Five jurors were seated by the noon recess. Clark had used four of his ten peremptory challenges. Will had exercised five of his twenty. At lunch, in a private room at the Davis Café, Ash immediately confronted Ev Hardeman.

"I thought I made it very clear that you were to steer clear of public places, particularly saloons," he said briskly.

"I don't have much to do at night," Ev responded.

"There's nothing wrong with that," Will said.

"Who have you been talking to at Friedman's?" Ash asked.

"Just some of the boys," Ev replied.

Ash shot Will a stern look.

"Listen," he said. "The word gets around pretty quick around here. If you're drinking in a saloon, you are not being responsible. It's dangerous and I won't have it."

"I haven't said anything about the case," Ev said.

"I find that hard to believe," Ash said. "I know damn well the subject would have come up."

"I haven't said anything."

"Just being there is bad enough." Ash had a disgusted look that exceeded anything Will had seen in him before.

After lunch, jury selection resumed. By the end of the day, eight jurors had been selected. Clark had exercised peremptory challenges on some men who had not appeared to be defense jurors, but Ash said afterwards that he was probably relying on his card catalog of past jury service in the county. Will had used up another three of the defense strikes. Thus far, no panelist had been successfully challenged for cause. The judge was not likely to strike any man for cause who did not admit to bias.

On Tuesday morning, three more jurors were seated without challenge, leaving only one more to go. Next to take the witness stand and be sworn in was a portly man wearing black-rimmed spectacles. He was not known to Ash or Will, but Clark seemed to have a confident look on his face when the man sat down.

"State your name, please," he said.

"Parker Bronson," the man replied.

"What is your profession, sir?"

"I am a salesman."

"Who do you sell for?"

"I work for the Remington Arms Company."

"And you are a resident of Caldwell County?"

"Yes, sir."

"This man is acceptable to us, Your Honor," Clark said.

Ash leaned over to say something to Will, but Will placed his hand on his wrist, effectively pushing him away.

"Mr. Bronson," he said. "This case involves a shooting, an alleged homicide, with a firearm. A person of your expertise might become an expert witness in the jury room, which would be improper. I therefore suggest that you would not be a fair juror to the defense in this case. Would you agree?"

"Not at all," Bronson replied. "I don't know anything about the case and would have to listen to the evidence."

"But there may be testimony about firearms that you might not agree with, based on your knowledge of firearms. Wouldn't that be a problem for you?"

"I think I can keep an open mind."

"Do you understand that if some of the testimony is contrary to what you believe to be true about the subject matter based on your special knowledge, you cannot then tell the other jurors what you know that is not in evidence?"

"Yes, I understand that, sir."

"Your Honor, we strike this panelist," Will said.

Not only did the man appear to be a danger because of his line of work, his answers seemed to be too pat, as if rehearsed. Ash made a note on his tablet. He looked over to the other counsel table and saw a smirk on the face of Singleton, the assistant prosecutor. Ash wondered what had been happening outside the courtroom.

A blacksmith was the next panelist. Although there may have been a danger of his special knowledge influencing him, Ash whispered to Will to let him on. A man who knew something about firearms and was a local might be a good juror for them, and he felt it was worth the risk to leave him on the jury. With that, all twelve chairs in the jury box were filled, and the judge asked the jurors to stand and be sworn. After they were sworn, the judge dismissed the remainder of the panel seated outside the railing and instructed the sheriff's deputy acting as bailiff to escort the jury to the jury room while the court took up other matters. When the jury was gone, the judge looked down at the lawyers standing before the bench.

"It is almost four o'clock, gentlemen, and I do not wish to begin the evidence this late in the day. We will start with the reading of the indictment and opening statements, followed by the state's case, at nine in the morning. Until then, the court will be in recess."

SIXTEEN

WONSLEY HAD BEEN WITH MCNELLY'S RANGERS FOR months. They had slept outdoors around campfires, which he was used to. The Nueces Strip, the land that lay between the Nueces River and the Rio Grande, had been disputed territory prior to the Mexican War, claimed by Mexico and the Republic of Texas. It was brush country, dry and barren for the most part. There were few fences and many roaming cattle. Rustlers from across the Rio Grande had taken advantage of the character of the land by taking herds of cattle and driving them across the river into Mexico, evading posses raised to catch them. Wonsley had been assigned as a tracker as soon as the sergeant confirmed his tracking skills. They had tracked rustlers over the Strip, all the way to the Rio Grande, then watched them cross over to the far side of the river beyond rifle range. There were many roving bands of men, claiming to be posses looking for rustlers, but McNelly did not trust anyone who was not part of his Ranger company. He had forced a posse to leave the area, telling their leaders that he did not need any more men and they had best get home if they did not want to be treated as outlaws.

They had taken prisoner a member of a rustler gang and, after he was persuaded to talk, learned that his cohorts were driving a stolen herd of cattle near the Laguna Madre on the Texas coast. The Rangers caught up with them after many hours in the saddle. The rustlers had erected a brush barricade on the other side of a shallow salt marsh. The Rangers charged and killed most of them with shots from their Sharps rifles. A few escaped across the river, but the herd was recovered.

On one occasion, McNelly led the company across the Rio Grande into Mexico to recover a stolen herd, against general orders from the governor. They fought a battle against the rustlers on Mexican soil and took hostages back across the river with them, to persuade the outlaws to drive the stolen herd back across. Although McNelly was a man of principle, his tactics were unorthodox, but effective. No longer did large gangs of rustlers cross over to the Texas side. The few smaller groups that came across were handled by the ranchers themselves, who had been instructed by McNelly about being diligent around their herds. Wonsley also noticed that the local stockmen and Tejanos seemed to revere Captain McNelly. Local newspapers contained glowing articles about his venture into Mexico and his fearless manner. Word of his actions had obviously spread on both sides of the river.

When McNelly finally sent a written report to Austin, it contained evidence of his displeasure with the routine of filing reports and answering to his superiors. He had received a wire from Ranger headquarters asking how he had handled the surrender of the cattle, what terms he had made with the outlaws. McNelly responded, "Do you think I'd make a dicker with outlaws? Why would a Texas peace officer ever have to beg peace terms from bandits?"

The Rangers were in a comfortable camp at Retama, on the Rio Grande. They received good food and drink from the locals. Captain McNelly had consumption. His wife had been sent for and he spent most of his time in a cotton wagon that Mrs. McNelly had fixed up for them to live in. She fed him goat's milk, supplied by the local ranchers, for his ailments. The men would routinely go out on patrol, but all was quiet. Wonsley began to be restless, and after a couple of weeks thinking about it, decided he had had enough of Ranger life. After receiving his pay at the end of the month, he told Sergeant Armstrong he was needed at home and headed for San Antonio.

In spite of his best efforts, he had been thinking of Martha daily since he had last seen her. Maybe he had been wrong in assuming that they would never marry. School teachers married farmers and ranchers all the time. It took him two days and nights to reach San Antonio, where he took a room at a boarding house he was familiar with. He had decided that he needed some new clothes before seeing Martha and that he should get a haircut, a shave, and a shine on his boots. She was not likely to be there in the middle of the day, so he waited until six in the evening to call at Mrs. Elliot's door on Soledad Street. Rosa came to the door and showed surprise when she saw him.

"Mr. Wonsley," she said. "Come on in out of that cold wind."

She held the door open for him and he stepped into the hallway.

"I'll tell Miss Martha that you're here," she said. "Would you like to wait in the parlor?"

A fire was blazing in the fireplace. He stood and warmed his hands. There was a framed photograph of Martha on the mantle. It was a studio portrait. She was standing next to a column wearing a flowery dress, her hair up under a small hat. The smile on her face was broad and happy. The picture seemed to be in such contrast to the life he had been leading with the Rangers that he began to feel uncomfortable standing there. Then he heard her steps in the hallway and turned in that direction. She came in the doorway quickly and reached for his hand as she came up to him.

"Oh, Wonsley," she said. "I can't believe it."

Her hand was warm in his. He could not speak.

"I hadn't heard from you," she said. "I didn't know if you were still alive. You have had adventures, I'm sure. You must tell me all about them. Please, let's sit here by the fire."

She gestured for him to sit in one of the fireside chairs, then took a seat in the opposite one.

"So, tell me what has happened."

"Aw, I've been with Captain McNelly's Ranger band," he said. "Chasin' outlaws."

"Where did you do that?"

"Down in the Nueces Strip," he said. "Down on the Rio Grande."

"How exciting. I'll bet that was dangerous."

"Somewhat. But most of the time we were tracking and trying to find 'em. How about you, Martha? How have you been?"

"I've been well," she replied. "I've been going to college. I love it."

She was leaning forward in her chair, smiling broadly. Although she was the Martha he had known, something about her had changed. She was even more beautiful than before, and there was something else about her. She had a look of confidence that he had not noticed before.

"So are you on leave or something?" she asked.

"Naw. I've quit the Rangers," he said. "I've had enough of that."

"Oh?"

"Yeah. I've come back to become a farmer again, I guess. I've always wanted to be on my own, to be my own man."

"Well, good for you," she said. "I'm so glad you're safe. I didn't hear from you and the last time I saw you, I felt you were . . . I didn't know what you were thinking."

Her hands were clasped together. She looked down at them.

"I felt like you were disappointed, somehow," she said. "I've thought about it since, and I thought you were not happy that I was going to go to college."

"Oh no," he said abruptly. "I'm glad you're going. I just decided I needed to see how the Rangers would be."

"Are you sure? I really felt funny about it. And then you didn't write. And you seemed sad."

"I guess I was just sad about going away and not seeing you."

She looked up at him.

"I'm sorry," she said.

"It's all right," he said.

"Well, you're back now and we'll see more of each other."

Wonsley felt out of place. He had been living with a hard group of men for months, out of touch with civilization. The young woman who sat across from him seemed like someone he had once known, but did not know anymore. He found it difficult to carry on a conversation with her. They talked for some time about nothing of substance, and he wondered what he had been thinking in holding out hope that they could be together as a couple. Listening to her, he realized that he had held the image in his mind of her under the shelter on the hill overlooking the San Saba valley, covered with a blanket, her red hair wet and disheveled. The young woman who sat across from him was not that frightened girl, but a sophisticated person that he hardly knew. They chatted for a few more minutes. Then he said he had better get going. Before he left, she extracted a promise from him that he would come and visit at least once a month, and as he walked out the doorway he felt a kind of relief, as if a burden had been lifted from him and he was now free to move on with his life.

SEVENTEEN

ON THE DAY THE EVIDENCE WAS TO BEGIN IN THE TRIAL OF *State vs. Hardeman*, the courtroom was full, which was unusual. There were seldom more than a few people sitting on the benches outside the rail, but on this morning all of them were full, and the observers sat closely packed in. There were even a number of people standing in the outside hallway, waiting to be admitted in the event some of those inside left. A notorious case in the county was about to begin.

Frank Clark rose from his chair beside the counsel table, walked up to the clerk's desk, and picked up the indictment, then read it to the jury. He stood straight and proud as he enunciated every syllable in a grave tone. When he finished, he returned the indictment to the desk, walked to the middle of the jury box railing, and placed his hands on top of it, looking up and down the two rows of jurors.

"The evidence in this case will show that this is a case of cold-blooded murder. This defendant was not satisfied with placing the stain of sinful adultery on his victim's wife. He took his life in a cold-blooded manner, without regard to the two Adams boys, who were there to witness the evil deed. He shot their daddy down in front of them. They will be here as eyewitnesses, to tell you what happened out there that day. We will bring witnesses that will prove that this man, this defendant, was intent on killing Gilbert Adams because he was sinfully involved in an adulterous relationship with Mrs. Adams. His actions were deliberate and premeditated.

He left the home of Mrs. Moore, Mrs. Adams's mother, and went after Mr. Adams with the intent of killing him. Although it was a killing that was motivated by passion, it was not done in the heat of passion. The evidence will show that a significant period of time elapsed after he set out on his deadly journey. He then encountered his victim, who was setting out to find his estranged wife, with his two boys in his wagon with him. Mr. Adams was unarmed and was surprised by the defendant on the lane near his home. He was shot without even being given the chance to defend himself. When all the evidence is in, you will find this defendant's guilt beyond a reasonable doubt. You will find that he is guilty of murder in the first degree."

Clark turned and strode confidently back to the prosecution's counsel table. Will stood and approached the jury box.

"The district attorney would have you believe that this is a case of premeditated murder. It is not. Gilbert Adams was not unarmed on the day in question. He was reaching for a shotgun that lay in the bed of his wagon. Ev Hardeman did not draw his pistol until Adams made his move. It was self-defense."

He paused for effect, looking to his right and left at the faces of the jurors.

"It is extremely important for you to withhold judgment on this case until all of the evidence is in. The state gets to go first. But to follow your oaths as jurors, you must keep an open mind until you have heard all of the evidence. All of you have experienced times when things were not what they first seemed. This is such a case. The judge will charge you regarding the law of self-defense when the evidence is all in. If the shot the defendant fired was fired in self-defense, then he should be found not guilty. That is the verdict I believe you will reach when you have considered all of the evidence.

"Remember also, that the state has the burden of proving the defendant guilty beyond a reasonable doubt. The defendant does not have to prove his innocence. He is presumed innocent until proven guilty. And that proof has to be beyond a reasonable doubt. If you have a reasonable doubt as to the defendant's guilt, then you must find him not guilty, under your oaths as jurors. I am confident that this will be your verdict after you have heard all of the evidence."

He turned and walked back to the counsel table. After sitting down, he placed his hands under the table in his lap, to hide the fact that they were shaking. The judge turned to Clark.

"The state will call its first witness," he said.

Clark stood.

"The state calls as its first witness, George Adams. He is in the hallway, Mr. Bailiff."

The bailiff, an elder deputy, escorted the witness through the back door of the courtroom to the railing. From there, George Adams, his hair cut short, cleanly shaven and wearing a new suit of clothes, stepped to the witness chair where, without being prompted, he turned and raised his right hand. He answered "I do," quietly after the reading of the oath, then sat down as if he had been through the motions before, as if he had been rehearsed.

"State your name for the jury, please," Clark said.

"George Adams." He was staring straight ahead and had not made eye contact with the jury.

"And your father was Gilbert Adams."

"Yes, sir."

"Were you present on the day your father was shot?"

"Yes, sir."

"Tell the jury what happened that day," Clark said.

"Well, when my brother Harry and me got up that morning, Ada was gone."

"And who is Ada?"

"She's my daddy's wife."

"Your stepmother."

"Yes, sir."

"What time did you and Harry get up?"

"Before dawn."

"Where was your daddy?"

"He was still asleep."

"Did you and Harry normally get up before your daddy?"

"Yes, sir. We done chores before daddy would get up. We had to feed the hogs and do our milking."

"How did you know your stepmother wasn't there?"

"'Cause she wasn't up yet. She was usually up before us."

"When did your daddy get up?"

"Oh, about his usual time. It was light outside."

"And after it was discovered that your stepmother was not there, did your daddy start out to look for her?"

"Yes, sir."

"Did he take you and your brother Harry with him?"

"Yes, sir."

"Tell the jury what happened then."

"Well, we was over the bridge on the lane in front of the house, when Ev Hardeman come riding up from the other direction and he shot my daddy in the chest."

"And were you riding in the family wagon?"

"Yes, sir."

George was still looking straight ahead and avoiding turning toward the jury box. Ash passed a slip of paper to Will, who nodded after reading it.

"Was your father armed on that day?" Clark asked.

"No, sir, he was not."

"So you and your brother were in the wagon and your father was driving?"

"Yes, sir."

"And this defendant just rode up on horseback and shot him."

"Yes, sir."

"Were any words exchanged?"

"No, sir."

"Did he use a pistol like this one?" Clark held up a Colt revolver that had been marked with a tag.

"Yes, sir."

"Please let the record reflect that this pistol is marked State's Exhibit One," Clark said. "We will not offer it into evidence at this time, Your Honor."

"Very well," the judge said.

"Pass the witness," Clark said.

Will was listening to Ash, who was whispering in his ear. The judge waited a moment, then asked, "Cross examination, Mr. McCulloch?" Will then stood up.

"Yes, Your Honor." He then returned to his seat and thumbed through his pages of notes. "George, your father owned a shotgun, didn't he?" he asked, without looking up.

"Yes, sir."

"And you and your brother had one just like your father's, didn't you?"

"We used to," George said. "But we lost it."

"You lost it?"

"Yes, sir."

"How did you lose a shotgun?"

"We was hunting hogs one day and got charged by a big boar and Harry dropped the gun and run away. We never found it."

"Harry dropped it, huh? Where did this happen?"

"We was on the Barton place."

"Did you go back and look for it?"

"Uh, no, sir. We wasn't supposed to be there, so we didn't go back."

"So you were trespassing?"

"I guess so." George shifted uncomfortably in the witness chair.

"When did this happen?"

"Oh, I don't know. A few months ago, I guess."

"Was it before or after your father was shot?"

"Oh, it was before. Quite some time before."

"I see. On the day you have testified about, the day your father was shot, what time of the day did that happen?"

George's brow furrowed.

"I guess it was early afternoon," he said.

"And you have testified that your father got out of bed about dawn and found that your stepmother was gone. Why did it take so long for him to go after her?"

"I don't know. I guess he thought she would be coming home like she had done before."

"Like she had done before." Will paused for effect. "Then this wasn't the first time she had run off?"

"Uh, no, sir. I guess not."

"You know it wasn't, don't you, George?"

"Yes, sir. I guess so."

"Do you know why she left on those occasions?"

"No, sir."

"Do you know why she left on the morning in question?"

"No, sir, I don't."

"Were your father and stepmother fighting or arguing during the night?"

"No, sir. They wasn't."

"How do you know that?"

"I think I would've heard 'em."

"Had you heard them before?"

"Sir?"

"Had you heard them arguing or fighting before?"

George hesitated, then looked down at his feet before replying.

"I don't remember," he finally said.

"Was your father a drinking man, George?"

"Naw, not so much."

"So he drank."

"Not so much."

"He drank whiskey, didn't he, George?"

"He had some."

"He always had a jug of corn whiskey around, didn't he?"

"Yes, sir."

"Ever see him drunk?"

"Naw. I never seen him drunk. No, sir."

"Would he still be drinking when you and your brother went to bed at night?"

"I don't know."

"You don't know." Will again paused and looked at his notes. "That shotgun you and your brother had. It was just like your father's, wasn't it? In fact, they were both purchased on the same day, weren't they?"

"Yes, sir."

"And your father kept his on a rack over the inside of the front doorway. Where did you boys keep yours?"

"In our room, mostly," George replied.

"Were you at home when the sheriff came on the day of the shooting?"

"Yes, sir."

"You didn't tell anyone about the shotgun you and your brother lost, when the sheriff and other people were there that day, did you?"

"Nobody asked me," he said.

Will reviewed his notes again and conferred in whispers with Ash, then stood.

"We pass this witness at this time, Your Honor, but we wish for him to be subject to recall."

"He will be, counselor," the judge said.

"And, Your Honor, may counsel approach the bench?" Will asked.

"Very well," the judge replied.

The four lawyers came to the side of the judge's bench away from the jury box and spoke in whispers.

"Judge, we don't want to invoke the rule, but this witness should be instructed not to discuss his testimony with any other witnesses," Will whispered.

"Your Honor, he can invoke the rule if he wants that instruction," Singleton said.

"The jury will retire to the jury room while the court takes up a matter of law," the judge said aloud. "Mr. Bailiff, see to it, please."

The bailiff showed the jurors through the jury room door and shut it behind them. The judge then turned to the lawyers, who had regained their places at the counsel tables.

"Now, Mr. McCulloch, you have requested an instruction to this witness, even though the witnesses have not been placed under the rule. Can you explain the basis of your request for the court?"

"Yes, Your Honor. We have no objection to the witnesses being placed under the rule as long as Mr. Maitland is allowed to remain in the courtroom during the testimony of the other witnesses, but we are not requesting that. We simply assert that once a witness has been sworn in and has testified, he should not be able to discuss his testimony with other witnesses even though the rule has not been invoked. It would not be proper for him to do so, Your Honor, and the court has the power to order him not to do it."

The judge turned to Clark and Singleton. "What says the prosecution?" he asked.

Singleton stepped forward and responded.

"If the rule is invoked, as the court well knows, all of the witnesses are sworn and then instructed that they are not to discuss their testimony with anyone other than the lawyers in the case, but if the rule has not been invoked, there is no precedent for one witness to be so instructed. If the other witnesses have not been sworn, it is impossible to tell who is a witness and who is not."

The judge smiled. "I am sure the prosecution has its reasons for not invoking the rule, and I understand that the defense does not wish to do so because of Mr. Maitland's somewhat unique position, but I think that the solution is this. I will order that the rule has been invoked by defense counsel's request, but that Mr. Maitland is excused from the rule insofar as he will be allowed to continue to participate in the trial of the case. He will not, however, be allowed to interview any witnesses outside the courtroom, just as he will not be allowed to interrogate any witness inside the courtroom."

"But, Your Honor . . . " Singleton began.

"You have heard the court's ruling, Counselor. Have I made myself clear?"

"Yes, Your Honor," Singleton replied.

The judge looked at Ash and Will. "Gentlemen?" he asked.

"Yes, Your Honor," Will responded.

"Very well, gentlemen. You will present all witnesses who are to testify in this case to be sworn in, and they will be instructed that they are not to be present in court during the testimony of any other witnesses and that they are to discuss their testimony with no one other than law enforcement personnel and lawyers in this case. The court will stand in recess to allow counsel time to summon their witnesses. And counsel are instructed that they are to inform any witnesses that are not in attendance today of the court's ruling and to instruct them to abide by it. The court stands in recess."

Ash, Will, and their client made their way to a small room in the rear of the county clerk's office, where Ash shut the glass-paned door behind them. When they returned to the courtroom after the recess, they noticed George sitting on a hallway bench with Harry. Then the judge directed counsel to have their witnesses sworn. Harry was brought in and sworn. Clark said none of his other witnesses were in attendance. Will said that none of the defense witnesses were in attendance, but that he would make sure they were instructed not to enter the courtroom during the testimony of other witnesses and to otherwise obey the rule.

After they had returned to their places in the courtroom and the jury had been brought in and seated, Clark called Harry Adams as the state's next witness. Harry was eighteen. He had sandy hair and a pockmarked face. He smiled sheepishly at the jury as he took his seat on the witness chair.

"Was Gilbert Adams your father?" Clark asked.

"Yes, sir."

"And were you present on the day he was shot?"

"Yes, sir. I was standin' in the back of the wagon."

"And so you saw the shooting?"

"Yes, sir."

"Tell the jury what you saw."

"We was ridin' up the lane and that man came up on horseback and shot Daddy."

He pointed to Ev Hardeman.

"Let the record reflect that he pointed to the defendant," Clark said. "Did your father have a firearm that day?"

"Naw. He didn't."

"Were any words exchanged before he was shot?"

"No, sir."

"Pass the witness," Clark said.

"Did your father own a shotgun?" Will asked.

"Yes, sir."

"Where was it that day?"

"Uh. I don't know." Harry looked over at Clark when he said it.

"Did you see it that day?"

Harry hesitated, still looking in Clark's direction.

"Did you understand the question?" Will asked.

"Yes, sir. I don't remember."

"You don't remember seeing the shotgun that day?"

"No, sir."

"Did you and your brother have a shotgun that was just like your father's?"

"Uh, yes, sir."

"Where was it on the day of the shooting?"

"Uh. I don't know."

Ash touched Will's coat sleeve. Will turned to look at him, then rose from his chair.

"We have no further questions of this witness at this time, Your Honor, but reserve the right of recall."

Harry turned and smiled uncomfortably at the jury, then stepped down from the witness chair. Clark stood.

"As its next witness, the state calls Sheriff Augustus Ellison," he said.

The sheriff, a tall man with a full moustache, was summoned from the hallway. There were smiles of recognition from several of the jurors as he took the witness stand and was sworn in.

"You are Sheriff Augustus Ellison?" asked Clark.

"I am Gus Ellison, yes," he responded.

"Did you get called out to the Adams place on Easter Sunday last year?"

"I did," the sheriff answered.

"Please tell the jury what you found when you got there and go through the course of your investigation."

"Well, I rode up with Ash Maitland and a couple of deputies. The Adams wagon was in front of the yard gate when we got there. We found Gilbert Adams inside the house, dead. His two boys, George and Harry, were there. Ash told us about the Adams shotgun in the bottom of the wagon, so we looked for it."

"And did you find it?"

"Yes, it was hanging over the doorway in the front room."

"Did you look over the wagon when you got there?"

"Yes, sir. There was blood all over the wagon seat and the bed down near the seat. And some on the wagon wheel, where the boys drug him out of the wagon."

"Was there any blood on the shotgun?"

"No, sir. The shotgun was clean. That is, there was no blood on it."

"Is that shotgun in your custody, sheriff?"

"Yes, sir. It is."

"Is it here at the courthouse?"

"Yes, sir," the sheriff replied.

"Would you have it brought in, please?"

The sheriff nodded to the bailiff, who stepped into the hallway and came back carrying a single-barreled shotgun, which he carried to the sheriff. When the sheriff had it in hand, Clark asked him, "Is this the shotgun you found over the doorway that evening?"

"Yes, sir," the sheriff replied.

Clark reached for the shotgun and the sheriff handed it to him. Clark tied a cardboard tag to the barrel with a piece of string, then held the shotgun up.

"I have marked this weapon as State's Exhibit Two," he said. "Now, Sheriff. Is this shotgun in the same condition you found it in at the Adams place last Easter Sunday?"

"Yes, sir. It is."

"Has it remained in your custody ever since you took it from the Adams home?"

"Yes, sir."

"Has it been cleaned up at all?"

"No, sir."

"Now, Sheriff. Is there any sign of blood on that shotgun?"

"No, sir."

"Have you examined it carefully?"

"Yes, sir."

"Are you familiar with firearms and, in particular, firearms that have had blood on them?"

"Yes, sir," the sheriff replied, looking at the jury. Several of the jurors smiled.

"Did you find any trace of blood on this weapon?"

"No, sir. Not a trace."

Clark stood to address the judge, holding the shotgun.

"Your Honor, we offer State's Exhibit Two into evidence."

The judge looked at Will, who stood and said, "No objection."

"State's Exhibit Two is received in evidence," the judge said.

Clark picked up the pistol from the clerk's table and handed it to the sheriff.

"Do you recognize this weapon, Sheriff?" he asked.

The sheriff looked closely at the pistol as he held it. "Yes, sir," he said.

"Where have you seen that before?"

"It's the Colt we took off Ev Hardeman when he was arrested."

"Let the record reflect that he has identified State's Exhibit One," Clark said. We offer it into evidence, Your Honor."

"Very well," the judge said. "Hearing no objection, it is admitted."

"We pass the witness, Your Honor," Clark said.

Will cleared his throat, then began.

"You said Ashley Maitland was out there at the Adams place that day?"

"Yes, sir."

"And he told you he was there at the time of the shooting?"

Singleton rose from his chair.

"Objection, Your Honor. That calls for hearsay," he said.

"I'll rephrase it, Your Honor," Will said. "Do not repeat what he said that day. Did he identify himself as a witness to the shooting?"

"Yes, sir, he did."

"And that is why you were looking for the shotgun?"

"Yes, sir."

"How long have you known Mr. Maitland, Sheriff?"

"Oh, about twenty-five years or so," the sheriff replied.

"Are you familiar with his reputation in the community as to truth and veracity?"

Singleton again stood. "That calls for hearsay, Your Honor. The state objects."

"It's an exception to the hearsay rule, Your Honor. The defense intends to call Mr. Maitland as a witness. His reputation in the community as to being truthful is therefore relevant," Will replied.

"Objection overruled," the judge said.

"You may answer, Sheriff," Will said.

"Mr. Maitland has a good reputation as a truth-teller," the sheriff said.

"This defendant, Everett Hardeman, did he surrender himself after the indictment came down?"

"Yes, sir, he did. Mr. Maitland brought him into my office and he made bail."

"So, you didn't arrest him on the day of the shooting?"

"No, sir. I wasn't sure he would be indicted."

"Did he try to hide his pistol from you?"

"No, Will. He turned it over to us. Said it was his."

Ash pulled on Will's sleeve. Will leaned down to listen to his whisper, then stood.

"That's all we have for this witness at this time, Your Honor, if he is subject to recall."

"I am sure the sheriff will be available," the judge said. "It is well into the noon hour. The court stands in recess until one thirty."

EIGHTEEN

HENRY JACOB WAS ROLLING HIS SALES CART DOWN NORTH Railroad Avenue in Luling during the noon hour. It was the best part of the day in which to catch potential customers, except for the afternoons when the passenger train stopped to unload its passengers. Henry's cart was a two-wheeler with two long handles for pulling and two legs that folded up when he was moving. He had been halfway across the continent pulling it, stopping to make sales of goods in small towns along the way, much like his cousin, Ish Friedman, had done more than twenty years before. Henry was given the opportunity to work for Ish in Lockhart, but decided that the new town presented more opportunity for an aspiring merchant. And he had spent enough time working for his uncle in New York, while saving up enough to stock his cart. He knew he wanted his own business.

The new town was bustling. At the end of the line for almost a year, it had grown rapidly. New buildings lined the avenues on each side of the railroad tracks. Two banks, several hotels and restaurants, and about a hundred businesses were open. There were also a number of saloons and two dance halls, with the usual collection of gamblers and bar girls. Shots rang out almost every night. Ladies required escorts during the day and were not to be seen on the streets after dark. Luling soon gained a reputation as one of the toughest towns in Texas. The criminal activity led a group of citizens to petition the legislature to grant a charter to the town, so that it could be incorporated and a mayor and aldermen elected, with the power to employ peace officers. After the election, some law and a bit more order had been implanted, but there were still a number of rowdy characters. And gambling, women, and whiskey formed a combination that regularly led to violence in the streets of the town.

Henry set up his cart near a saloon that served lunches, hoping to catch a lucky gambler or two as customers. He put down the legs and opened the double doors at the rear of the cart to reveal his wares, which were spread on the floor and hung on the inside of the doors and the interior walls of the contraption. As he finished and turned around, he was confronted by a tall young man whom he recognized. The man wore a white Stetson tilted back on his head and a pistol hung low in a holster.

"Mr. Hardin," Henry said. "Are you interested in something?"

The young man stepped near the cart and looked at the ironware on the bottom of the open box.

"Maybe," he replied.

"I'll be happy for you to take anything you like, Mr. Hardin," Henry said. He clasped his shaking hands behind him to hide them.

"You know me?"

"Oh, surely, Mr. Hardin," Henry replied.

"How is that?" Hardin asked. "How do you know me?"

"You were pointed out to me the other day, sir," Henry said.

Hardin glared at him before turning back to the cart.

"I was thinking about some cookware for my wife," he said.

"Take whatever you want."

Hardin turned toward him abruptly.

"I am not a thief, sir. I will pay for whatever I might take."

"Yes, sir," Henry said. "I didn't mean to imply . . . "

"You appear to be an educated man," Hardin said. "You should not take everything you hear about me as gospel."

"Yes, sir," Henry replied.

"How much is that Dutch oven?" Hardin asked.

"That one's normally three dollars, but I can let you have it for less," Henry said.

Hardin glared at him. His blue eyes were steady and cold.

"I'll pay full price. I am not a thief," he said, reaching into his vest pocket. He pulled out three silver dollars and handed them to Henry, then grabbed the iron pot, which had the lid tied to one of its handles with wire.

"Have good day, sir," Hardin said, then turned around and carried the pot and lid to his horse, where he tied it onto the saddlebag behind the cantle, mounted, and rode off.

Henry Jacob stood looking after him, holding the silver dollars in his hand. He would tell his grandchildren about the day he met the notorious John Wesley Hardin on the streets of Luling. It would become one of their favorite stories among the many told them by their grandfather.

NINETEEN

AFTER THE NOON RECESS, THE PROSECUTION CALLED A gunsmith named Adolph Gruning as a witness. Singleton questioned him and established that he was an experienced gunsmith from Austin who was familiar with guns and had had experience identifying weapons with dried blood on them. Singleton then handed him the shotgun.

"Mr. Gruning," he asked. "What type of gun is this?"

"This is a Stevens Model 30 twelve gauge single-barrel shotgun," he replied. "A fairly new breach loader."

"Have you examined this weapon previously at the request of the State of Texas?"

"I have," he replied.

"How can you tell it is the same gun you examined before?" Singleton asked.

"Because it has my mark on it right here," he said, holding the shotgun up toward the jury and pointing to a spot on the stock. "I always make my mark in pencil and it's still here."

"Is there any sign of blood on that weapon?"

"No, sir. Not a bit."

"Any trace of dried blood at all?"

"No, sir, not a trace."

"And did you examine it thoroughly, looking for any trace of dried blood?"

"Yes, I did. Didn't find a trace."

"Pass the witness, Your Honor," Singleton said, his back to the jury, smiling at Will.

"Is this a fairly common shotgun?" Will asked immediately.

"No, sir. Can't say that it is," the gunsmith replied.

"You say it is a fairly new one, is that right?"

"Yes, sir. Sure is."

"In fact, it's a new model, isn't it?"

"Yes, sir, the Model 30 has only been out a couple of years."

"I see," Will said. He then turned, reached to the floor behind his chair and pulled up a blanket wrapped around a long, narrow object. He held it up in front of the jury and unwrapped it, revealing another single-barreled shotgun. He walked to the witness stand and handed it to the witness.

"Would you look at this gun, please sir?" he asked.

Singleton immediately rose to his feet.

"Your Honor, the state objects," he said. "There is nothing in the evidence that shows that this weapon has any relevance to this case. Counsel is trying to play a trick here."

"It will be identified as having a great deal to do with this case, Your Honor," Will said. "I promise the court that I will tie it in when we present our evidence."

"Objection overruled," the judge said.

Gruning looked the gun over, turning it around and closely examining it.

"All right, sir," he said. "I have examined it."

"What kind of gun is that, sir?" Will asked.

"It is a Stevens Model 30 breech loader, sir. Just like the other one."

"It is in fact identical except for the serial number, isn't it, sir?"

"It looks to be, yes, sir."

"May I have it, please?" Will said, reaching for the gun. The witness handed it to him and Will carried it to the clerk's desk, wrote on a cardboard tag and then attached the tag to the barrel of the shotgun with a string.

"Please let the record reflect that I have marked this weapon as Defense Exhibit One," he said.

"The record will so reflect," the judge said.

Will walked to the witness stand and handed the gun back to the witness.

"Mr. Gruning," he said. "Please examine this shotgun and tell me if you see signs of dried blood on it."

"Yes, sir," Gruning said, without looking at the gun again. "There are signs of dried blood on the stock, on the case, and on the barrel."

"Is there quite a bit on there?"

"Yes, sir, quite a bit. Looks like it was lying in blood."

TWENTY

WILL AND ASH WERE IN THEIR OFFICE HAVING A WHISKEY after what they considered a good day in the courtroom. Ash was leaning back in his chair with his feet on the desk.

"That gunsmith was the best witness we could have had," Ash said. "It's refreshing to find an honest witness for a change."

Will nodded his agreement. He then turned toward the reception room, where he had heard footsteps. In a few seconds, a deputy sheriff, Marvin Hoskins, appeared in the doorway. Ash stood up.

"Good evening, Deputy Hoskins," he said. "Come on in."

The man, tall and thin, stepped into the room.

"Can I offer you a drink?" Ash asked.

"No, sir. Not when I'm on duty. I just wanted to let you know something. Sheriff Ellison wanted me to tell you that I have just served a subpoena on Mrs. Olivia Moore."

"On Mrs. Moore? The state subpoenaed her?"

"Yes sir. The sheriff wanted me to tell you about it."

Ash and Will exchanged looks.

"Well, I appreciate it, Marvin," Ash said. "Tell Gus I appreciate it. When is it returnable?"

"She's subpoenaed for tomorrow morning."

"Well. It's good to know about it now. Thanks again, deputy."

"You're welcome," the deputy replied. "I best be going."

After the deputy left, Will turned to Ash.

"We thought that would happen," he said. "Should we go talk to her?"

"I don't think so," Ash replied. "It's best that we leave her be. I know Clark and he's likely to ask her if we talked to her about the case. Nothing wrong with woodshedding a witness, but the jury won't know that. Besides, she's going to be nervous enough without us contributing."

"All right," Will replied. "What about Ada? I thought they might subpoena her, too."

"They might yet," Ash said. "We'll just have to wait and see."

The next morning, they were at the courthouse early, as was Ash's habit. Mrs. Moore was not in the hallway or the courtroom when they arrived. When Ev Hardeman arrived shortly before nine, Will looked in the hallway for her, but she was not there. Clark and Singleton came up the stairs as Will was looking through the courtroom doorway. They smiled at him and nodded as they walked past. A small, elderly woman came up the stairway after Clark and Singleton. She looked familiar to Will, but he did not know her. Instead of coming into the courtroom as a spectator would have, she took a seat on a bench just outside the doorway.

After the judge had entered and the jury was brought in and seated, Singleton stood and addressed the judge.

"Your Honor," he said. "The state calls as its next witness, Mrs. Esther Bagley."

The elderly lady who had been in the hallway entered the doorway, accompanied by the bailiff.

"Come forward and be sworn, ma'am," the judge said.

She approached the bench and was sworn in by the judge. When told she should take the witness stand, she had to be shown its location. When she was finally seated, Singleton began his examination.

"State your name, please, ma'am."

"Esther Bagley."

"Where do you reside, Mrs. Bagley?"

"I live out on the Prairie Lea road, out of Luling," she said.

"Are you a married woman?" Clark asked.

"I'm a widow," she replied.

"Are you a neighbor of the Gilbert Adams family?"

"Yes, sir. I live just up the road from them."

"Is your house in sight of the lane that turns into the Adams place?"

"Yes, sir, it is."

Singleton walked to the side of the counsel table where Everett Hardeman sat and pointed him out.

"Have you ever seen this man before?" he asked.

"Yes, sir. I've known Ev Hardeman since he was a boy."

"Have you ever seen Hardeman out by the Adams place?"

"I seen him out there a number of times."

"When do you recall seeing him out there?"

"I seen him turn into their lane a number of times over the last few years," she said.

"A number of times." Singleton paused for effect. "How many times would you say?"

"Oh, I don't know. Maybe a dozen."

"A dozen?"

"Yes, sir."

"What time of the day or night was he out there?" Singleton asked.

"During the day," she replied. "It was always during the day that I seen him. I'm inside at night."

"What time of the day?"

"Usually in the late morning," she said.

"What were you doing outside at those times?" he asked.

"Usually hanging out my wash or feedin' the chickens or the hogs. I'm usually outside durin' the day if the weather's good."

"Was this during the week or on Sunday?"

"During the week," she said. "I don't do no chores on Sunday. That's the Lord's day."

"You didn't happen to see him out there last Easter Sunday did you?"

"Yes, but it was after I heard a shot."

"You heard a shot?"

"Yes, sir. A pistol shot, I reckon. Heard it sittin' in my front room."

"So your house must be pretty close to the Adamses' lane."

"Right across from it."

"What time of the day did you hear the shot?"

"It was around three o'clock, I think."

"And you say you saw Hardeman that day?"

"Sure did. It was a few minutes after the shot. He come riding out of the lane in a big hurry."

"On the previous occasions that you saw Hardeman out there, did you ever find out what his business was at the Adams place?" Singleton asked, while looking at the jury.

"No, sir. I asked Ada once and she . . . "

"Your Honor," Will said, rising to his feet. "We object. That answer is hearsay."

"Sustained," the judge said. "You can't say what someone else has told you, Mrs. Bagley, unless I rule it's all right."

"She didn't say nothin', Judge. She wouldn't answer me."

Will sat back down. Singleton looked at the jury again, then stood.

"The state passes this witness, Your Honor," he said.

"How long had you been a neighbor to Gilbert Adams, Mrs. Bagley?" Will asked.

"A lot of years," she replied.

"Do you remember how many?"

"No, sir. I don't."

"Now, are you sure that you saw Mr. Hardeman out there a dozen times?"

"That's my best guess," she said.

"That's a guess?"

"Well, yes. I didn't keep no record."

"Could it have been less than a dozen?"

"Could have been."

"Less than a half dozen?"

"I don't know. I just give my best estimate."

"The road you live on is the road between Prairie Lea and Luling, isn't it?"

"It is."

"And there's quite a bit of traffic on that road, isn't there?"

"Yes, sir. Quite a bit."

"Is it possible that some of the times you saw Mr. Hardeman out there, he didn't turn into the Adams lane, but was coming and going on the main road?"

"I don't think so."

"In fact, your house is around a bend in the road from the entrance to the Adams lane, isn't it?"

"It's a little curve there. I wouldn't call it a bend."

"I see. You say you were standing in your yard when you saw him?"

"Out the side of the house," she said.

"But aren't your hog and chicken pens out back, Mrs. Bagley?"

"Yes, sir, they's out back, but . . . "

"You were outside feeding your chickens and hogs and maybe hanging up your wash, you said. Correct?"

"Yes, sir."

"Where's the clothesline you hang that wash on, Mrs. Bagley?"

"Now, see here, young man. I seen him out there several times. I don't remember exactly how many, but I sure seen him."

Will studied his notes, then turned to Ash, who shrugged.

"We have no further questions of this witness, Your Honor," Will said, half-standing.

"The state will call its next witness," the judge said.

"The state calls Deputy Constable Horace Walker," Clark said.

Ashley whispered to Will as the young man entered the courtroom, was sworn in, and took the witness stand.

"You are Horace Walker?" Clark asked.

"Yes, sir."

"And you are a deputy constable here in Caldwell County?"

"I am some of the time, yes, sir," Walker replied. "I help Constable Stagner out some."

"Were you helping him out some last Easter Sunday?"

"Yes, sir. I was."

"Tell the jury where that was and what happened."

"The constable had me stationed on Mrs. Moore's front porch. I was sittin' there when a man rode up."

"Do you see that man in the courtroom?"

"Yes, sir. He's sittin' right over there by Mr. Maitland."

"Let the record reflect that the witness has pointed out the defendant," Clark said.

"The record will so reflect," the judge said.

"What happened then?" Clark asked.

"He came on the porch and grabbed my rifle."

"Then what happened?"

"He went in the front door."

"How long did he stay inside?"

"Not very long."

"Could you hear him through the doorway?"

"I heard him say something." The young man looked down at his folded hands.

"What did you hear him say?"

"He used some bad language," Walker replied.

"That's all right," Clark said. "You can repeat what he said."

"He said, 'I'll kill the son of a bitch.'"

"Then what happened?"

"He come a barrelin' out of the house and rode off."

"Did he appear to be in a hurry?"

"Yes, sir. He was in a big hurry."

"Pass the witness," Clark said.

"Do you know why Constable Stagner posted you on Mrs. Moore's porch?" Will asked.

"Yes, sir, I do. It was to look out for Mr. Adams."

"Did you see Mr. Maitland that day?"

"Yes, sir. I did. Mr. Maitland rode out there to the Moore place with me and Constable Stagner."

"And that's when they left you there on the porch?"

"Yes, sir."

"Did you see Mr. Maitland again that day?"

"Yes, sir. He come ridin' up as that man was leavin' the Moore place. Then he rode after him."

"Did you also see him at the Adams place later that day?"

"Yes, sir. I was out there with the sheriff and his deputy and Mr. Maitland."

"Did you ride from the Moore house to the Adams house?"

"Well, yes, sir. I followed the sheriff and his deputy out there."

"Did it take you very long to get there from the Moore place?"

"Naw. It didn't take too long."

"Did you see the wagon out in front of the Adams house?"

"Yes, sir."

"Did you see any blood on it?"

"Yes, sir. There was blood all over the bed in front of the wagon seat and some on the seat itself. There was also blood on the side of the wagon and some on the ground."

"Don't tell me what he said, but did you hear Mr. Maitland tell the sheriff what he saw out there that day?" Will asked.

"Yes, sir. He told him."

"No further questions," Will said.

During the noon recess, Ash and Will ate at their usual table at the rear of the Davis Café, away from several of the jurors who were seated near the front of the room. They had still not seen any sign of Mrs. Moore at or around the courthouse.

"I checked the clerk's file," Ash said. "She's on the state's subpoena list. She may be disobeying it."

"Unless they have her hidden out," Will said.

"I doubt that," Ash replied.

"Seems like they would have applied for a capias before noon if they hadn't heard something from her."

After they had finished their lunch and were returning from the café, they noticed that the Moore wagon was tied up at the edge of a side street and the man who worked for Mrs. Moore was standing nearby. They walked over to him.

"Afternoon, Felix," Ash said. "What brings you to town?"

Felix, a Hispanic with a long mustache, had an uncomfortable look.

"Miz Olivia was ordered to come to court," he said. "I brought her up here."

"I thought she was supposed to be here this morning," Ash said.

"They told her to be here this mornin'," Felix replied. "But she don't find me in time. We just got here a while ago."

"Is Miz Ada still at home?" Will asked.

"Yes sir. She and Miz Olivia had some words about it. But she stayed home."

"Where is Mrs. Moore now, Felix?" Ash asked.

"She was told to go to the district attorney's office, I think," he replied. "That's where she said she would be."

It was only a quarter 'til one, and court was not to reconvene until one thirty. Clark had obviously sent her a message to arrive after nine, when court convened that morning, and report to his office. They would be spending the noon recess questioning her. It was always a concern of Ash's when the prosecution was able to use its power of the office to coax a reluctant witness into testifying to suit the state's case.

"Let's go pay Mr. Clark a visit," he said to Will.

As with most offices in the courthouse, the district attorney's office was small. A small anteroom opened onto the downstairs hallway, leading into a single office, which contained only enough room for four or five to sit at one time. When Will and Ash arrived outside the door to the anteroom, they found a deputy posted there, blocking the doorway.

"We are here to see Mr. Clark," Ash said.

"Sorry, sir. He said he was not to be disturbed."

"You know who I am, don't you, deputy?"

"Yes, sir, Mr. Maitland. I know you. But I have my orders."

"Mrs. Moore's in there, isn't she?" Ash asked.

The deputy hesitated before speaking.

"Yes, sir. She shore is."

"She is a client of mine, deputy. I have a right to be present when she is being interrogated."

The deputy looked from Ash to Will and back. His eyes showed confusion.

"Well, all right," he said. "I guess you can go in." He stepped aside and Ash and Will entered the anteroom, where they could hear crying through the transom over the doorway to the inner office. Ash quickly opened the door and pushed his way inside.

Clark was seated behind his desk. Mrs. Moore was seated in a chair to his right, sobbing into her handkerchief. Singleton sat in a chair next to her. He stood up abruptly when Ash entered, followed by Will.

"What the hell are you two doing here?" he asked.

"Just thought it might be fair for all of us to hear what Mrs. Moore has to say," Ash said. "Don't you think that would be fair?"

"We have a perfect right to interview a witness in private," Singleton said.

"And she has the perfect right to decline the interview," Ash replied. "Have you advised her of that?"

"She is here voluntarily," Clark said.

"How about that, Mrs. Moore? Were you advised that your presence here was voluntary?"

Her face was red. She held the handkerchief in both hands.

"I didn't know that," she said, looking at Clark. "I was told to be here at eleven. I got a subpoena."

"Well, you certainly have to obey the subpoena, but that only means you are required to come to court. Mr. Clark's office is not the same thing. You are free to talk to these gentlemen outside the courtroom, but you are not required to do so."

Clark and Singleton gave each other a troubled look.

"Do you wish to continue this interview, Mrs. Moore?" Will asked.

She looked from Will to Ash and then to Singleton and Clark.

"I want to do what I am supposed to," she said.

"You are supposed to come to the courtroom in answer to the subpoena, Olivia. That is all that is required. Who you talk to outside the courtroom is entirely up to you," Ash said.

"Then I don't want to," she said.

"This interrogation is at an end, gentlemen," Ash said, looking at Clark.

Mrs. Moore followed Ash and Will out into the hallway. They led her to a bench at the opposite end from Clark's office. Once she was seated, she began crying again.

"I don't want this to go on," she said. "Do I have to be here?"

"Yes, ma'am, I'm afraid you do," Will said.

"It won't be that bad, Olivia," Ash said. "Just remember when you're on the witness stand not to let them put words in your mouth. Just listen carefully to the question and take your time in answering. You'll do fine."

"They were asking me about what Everett said that day," she said, her voice breaking with emotion. "I didn't know what to say."

"Just tell the truth of it if they ask you, but don't volunteer any information. That's my best advice," Ash said. "And don't let them lead you into saying something you wouldn't say otherwise. You'll be okay."

She stopped crying after a while and they led her slowly up the stairway to the second floor and left her seated on a bench outside the door to the courtroom. It was not yet time for the court to reconvene. Ash and Will had the time for a whispered discussion at the counsel table before the prosecution and the other court officers returned.

"That was good," Will said.

"What? I was just letting her know her rights," Ash replied.

"No. I mean saying she was your client."

"She is my client," Ash said. "I drew up her will several years ago."

After the judge came in and the jury was seated, Mrs. Moore was called to the witness stand. Some redness lingered on her cheeks, but her eyes were clear and she appeared to have regained her composure. Clark began by asking her questions about her background, then about Everett Hardeman.

"How long have you known the defendant, Hardeman?" he asked.

"For a number of years," she replied.

"This defendant and your daughter, Ada, were in a relationship, weren't they?"

"They were friends."

"Weren't they engaged to be married?" Clark asked.

"Yes, they were. Many years ago." Mrs. Moore straightened up in the witness chair.

"And yet your daughter married Gilbert Adams, the decedent, the victim in this case, didn't she?"

"Yes, sir. She did."

"When did she inform this defendant that she was breaking their engagement and marrying Gilbert Adams?"

"We all thought Everett was killed in the war," she said. "Nobody knew anything else for years. Ada thought he was dead."

"But he turned up again years later, didn't he?"

"Yes, sir."

"And by that time, your daughter was married to Mr. Adams, wasn't she?"

"Yes, sir."

"Then your daughter began seeing Hardeman again after he came back."

"No, sir. That's not true. She was faithful to her husband."

"Isn't it true that Hardeman visited her at the Adams home numerous times?"

"Not that I know of," she replied.

"Not that you know of." Clark paused for effect. "Do you know that he was seen going onto the Adams place numerous times?"

"No. I do not know that."

"Now I want to ask you about last Easter Sunday," Clark said. "Was your daughter at your home on Easter Sunday?"

"Yes, she was."

"And did Everett Hardeman visit her there?"

"No. She was asleep when he came."

"But you had a conversation with him then, when he visited, didn't you?"

"Yes, sir."

"And he was angry, wasn't he?"

"He was upset. So was I. Mr. Adams had beaten Ada."

"How do you know that?"

"You could tell by looking at her."

"What did Hardeman say?"

"I don't remember," Mrs. Moore replied.

"Oh, I think you do, Mrs. Moore," Clark said. "Didn't he say, 'I'll kill the son of a bitch' when he was at your house?"

"I don't remember," she replied.

"You don't remember?"

"He was upset and so was I. He might have said something like that. It wasn't a long conversation."

"In fact, he hurried away from your house, on his way to murder Gilbert Adams, didn't he?"

Will arose quickly. "Objection, Your Honor," he said loudly. There was a pause.

"On what grounds, Counsel?" the judge asked.

"That's highly prejudicial, Your Honor. And it's argumentative."

"Objection sustained," the judge said. "The jury will disregard the question."

"He left in quite a hurry, didn't he, Mrs. Moore?" Clark asked.

"Yes, sir."

"And he appeared to be angry or upset, didn't he?"

"He was upset. So was I."

"No further questions of this witness," Clark said.

"Are you ready to proceed, Mrs. Moore?" Will asked. "Or do you need a break?"

"I'm all right," she said.

"Very well. Would you please describe for the jury when and in what condition your daughter Ada arrived at your house last Easter Sunday?"

"It must have been around two in the morning," she replied. "She had walked all the way barefoot in her nightgown."

"How do you know that, Mrs. Moore?"

"She had no horse with her and her feet were bloody and all messed up."

"Was there evidence that she had been abused?"

"Oh yes, sir. She was bruised all over. Her left eye was swollen shut and there were scratches and bruises all over her face. There were bruises on her back and the back of her legs where he had whipped her."

"Objection, Your Honor," Singleton said, standing up. "That's a conclusion by the witness, not an observation."

"Overruled," the judge said. "I'm going to let her tell it in her own way, counsel."

"Had you seen signs of abuse before on your daughter, Mrs. Moore?" Will asked.

"Yes, sir. Many times. I asked her to leave him, but she wouldn't do it."

"Over what period of time did you see those signs of abuse?"

"For years," she replied. "For a long time."

"Have you seen Everett Hardeman since that Sunday, before today?"

"No, sir."

"He hasn't been to your home since then, has he?"

"No, sir."

"Has your daughter Ada been with you every day and night since that Sunday?

"Yes, sir. She has."

"But you have not seen anything of Everett Hardeman since last Easter?"

"Not until today," she replied.

"No further questions," Will said.

TWENTY-ONE

WONSLEY BAKER WAS IN LOCKHART TO SHOP FOR SOME tack which he could not find in Luling. It was late in the day, and he decided to stop in to Friedman's Saloon for a beer before returning homeward. As he stood at the bar waiting for his beer to be poured, he thought he recognized a voice from the back of the room, coming from Friedman's "home" table, where Ish and some of the regulars usually sat. When he turned and looked, he saw it was Everett Hardeman. Ev was talking to two men at the table who were unknown to Wonsley. He walked over and could hear Ev more clearly as he approached.

"The son of a bitch had her on the stand for quite a while," Ev said, then looked up as Wonsley approached.

"Wonsley," he said. "I haven't seen you in years. Pull up a chair."

"Hi, Ev," Wonsley replied. "I'll sit for a spell."

"This here's Herman Frank and Arthur Carter," Ev said. The two men nodded at Wonsley. "I was just telling these two gentlemen about my day in court."

"I heard," Wonsley said.

The tone of Wonsley's voice made Ev pause. He looked from one to the other of the two men.

"Wonsley here is Billy McCulloch's uncle, from Guadalupe County. Only he doesn't like to be called Billy anymore, does he?"

Wonsley did not answer. He looked down at his beer glass. It was only about five thirty, but Ev appeared to be well on his way. He spoke with a slurred antagonism that puzzled Wonsley. Ev took another swig of whiskey and refilled his glass from the bottle that sat at his place. The bottle was three-fourths full. "So the bastard subpoenaed her," he said to the other two. "She's worried as hell about Ada, who is broken up good right now and he makes her come to court. And she doesn't know anything anyway." He turned to Wonsley, as if suddenly remembering he was sitting there. "So I thought you were still off with the Rangers. What brings you home?"

"Oh, I had enough of Ranger life," Wonsley replied. "Figured out farming ain't so bad after all. At least I get to sleep inside most nights."

"Well, hell yes. I get that." Ev took another shot of whiskey.

"I was thinking about supper over at Dot's," Wonsley said. "Would you like to join me?"

"No, you go ahead," Ev said. "I've got some more work to do on this bottle here."

Wonsley finished his beer and left. He decided to stop in at Ash's office on his way through Luling. He found Ash and Will in the inner office, going over their notes and talking about the trial.

"Uncle Wonsley," Will said. "Come in and sit down. Can I pour you a drink?"

"Sure," Wonsley replied.

He sat down in a side chair and Will placed a crystal glass on the desk and poured a shot for him.

"I've been to Lockhart," Wonsley said. "Had a beer at Friedman's. Your client was in there drinking and shooting his mouth off. Just thought you'd like to know."

The next morning when they met as usual in the courtroom hallway, Ash pulled Ev aside. "I've told you to steer clear of Friedman's or any other public place, Ev," he said. "You know that's just asking for trouble."

Ev looked a bit hungover.

"I just meant to have one drink," he said. "It won't happen again."

"When we have more time, during lunch, I want you to tell me who you talked to," Ash said.

After they had returned to the courtroom and the judge and jury had been seated, Clark stood and announced that the state rested its case.

Will and Ash were surprised. At the end of the day before, Clark had indicated he had another witness.

"You represented to the court yesterday that you had at least one more witness, Mr. Clark," the judge said.

"We decided to rest instead, Your Honor," Clark said.

The judge turned to Will.

"Are you ready to proceed with the case for the defense, counsel? Or do you need more time?"

"We are ready, judge," Will said. "The defense calls Ashley Maitland."

Ash stood and was sworn, then took the witness stand. Will asked him to state his name and profession.

"Ashley Maitland. I'm a lawyer," he said.

"And you are assisting in the defense in this case?"

"Yes."

"How long have you known the defendant, Everett Hardeman?"

"I've known him since he was a boy. I knew his parents."

"Why did you decide to represent him, knowing you are a witness in this case?"

"He asked me to," Ash replied. "I have always been his family's lawyer."

"Under what conditions are you representing him in court in this case?"

"I am allowed to assist counsel, that being you, in the courtroom, but I will not examine witnesses or address the jury in argument."

"Is that consistent with the rules, as you understand them?"

"Yes, and that is what Judge Daughtry has ruled in this case."

"Very well. Mr. Maitland, did you receive a message from Mrs. Olivia Moore last Easter Sunday?"

"I did. She had her maid deliver a message. She asked me to come to her home."

"What did you find when you arrived there?"

"Mrs. Moore was there with her daughter, Ada. Ada was in bed. She had been beaten."

"How could you tell she had been beaten?"

"There were bruises on her face and her eye was swollen shut. It was obvious."

"Was anyone else there with you?"

"Yes. Constable Quill Stagner and a young man he had deputized, Horace Walker."

"When you and the constable left, did you leave the deputy there at the Moore place?"

"Yes."

"Why was that done?"

"For Ada's protection."

"Against what or whom?"

"Her husband, Gilbert Adams."

"Then where did the constable and you go after you left the Moore house?"

"The constable went to send a message to Sheriff Ellison and I went to an Easter Sunday dinner at Lily Poe's."

Several members of the jury looked at each other when Lily Poe's name was mentioned.

"Did you see Everett Hardeman that day?"

"Yes, he was at Lily Poe's when I arrived."

"Did you tell him about what you had found at the Moore place?"

"I did."

"How did he react?"

Ash paused before answering.

"He was visibly upset. He left Miz Poe's immediately."

"Did you follow him?"

"Yes. When I got to the Moore place, he was already leaving. I met him on the front porch."

"Did you know where he was going?"

"It was obvious he was going to the Adams place."

"Did you follow him?"

"I did."

"What was his demeanor when you saw him on the Moore front porch?"

"He was still upset."

"What happened next?"

"I followed him on horseback, but his mount was faster than mine. I caught up with him after I had turned into the lane to the Adams place."

"What did you observe?"

"Gilbert Adams was stopped about fifty feet from Everett, in his wagon. The two Adams boys were in the wagon with him. They were coming from the opposite direction."

"Then what happened?"

"Adams reached down in front of him to the bed of the wagon and Everett pulled his pistol and shot him."

"Were any words exchanged between them?"

"No."

"How far behind Everett Hardeman were you when the shot was fired?"

"Maybe fifty yards. I could see everything clearly."

"Did you come closer after the shot was fired?"

"Yes. I rode up beside Ev's horse and dismounted. I went over to the Adams wagon. Adams was slumped over in his seat."

"Did you notice anything in the bed of the wagon?"

"Yes. There was a shotgun lying there."

"Did it appear to be in a place where Adams was reaching?"

"Yes. It was on the bed of the wagon, in front of the seat."

Will picked up the blood-stained shotgun and handed it to Ash.

"Does this appear to be the shotgun?"

"Yes, it does."

"Let the record reflect that the witness is referring to Defense Exhibit One," Will said.

"The record shall so reflect," the judge said.

"What happened next?"

"I advised Ev to leave and go home. Then I went to meet the sheriff and constable."

"Did you leave the wagon and Adams in place?"

"I did."

"Did you then return to the Adams place with the sheriff and a couple of deputies?"

"I did."

"What did you find then?"

"The wagon had been moved. It was sitting in front of the yard fence in front of the Adams house. Gilbert Adams's body was not in it. There was a trail of blood where it had been moved into the house. We found him in his bedroom, laid out on the bed."

"Where were the Adams boys?"

"We found them hiding behind the well house in back. We had to look for them for quite a while."

"Behind the well house?"

"Yes. Adams has a well house. I guess I should say he did have a well house. It was in the German style, built around the well."

"And the two boys were hiding behind it?"

"Yes. A deputy found them there."

"Was the shotgun still in the wagon?"

"No. It had been moved."

"Was there a shotgun in the house?"

"Yes. Over the door in the front room."

"Did it look like the one in the wagon?"

"Yes, except there was no blood on it."

"Was there blood on the one in the wagon?"

"Yes, there was. Gilbert Adams was bleeding on it when I looked in at it."

"Did you think the one in the house was the same as the one in the wagon?"

"At first I did. I thought it had been wiped off. But later it seemed that there was no trace of blood on it, so it couldn't have been the same one."

Will picked up the other shotgun and handed it to Ash.

"Does this State's Exhibit Two look like the shotgun that was over the doorway?"

"It does."

"Are the two shotguns alike?"

"Yes, they appear to be identical. Except this one has no bloodstains on it."

"Are you sure that Everett Hardeman did not go for his pistol until Gilbert Adams reached down to the bed of his wagon?"

"I am certain. It was clear that Adams was reaching for something."

"No further questions," Will said.

Singleton arose from his chair and picked up the rifle with no bloodstains. He held it in front of Ash as he spoke.

"You say this is the same shotgun that was hanging over the doorway in the Adams house when you and the sheriff got there?" he asked.

"It looks like the same one," Ash replied.

"And it looks like it because there was no trace of blood on it, correct?"

"That's one reason," Ash said.

Singleton returned to the clerk's desk, laid down the shotgun and picked the other one up. He held it up in front of Ash.

"This one, Defendant's Exhibit One. Do you know where this came from?"

"I do," Ash answered, suppressing a smile.

"Of your own personal knowledge?"

"I was not there when it was found, no," Ash replied.

Singleton laid the shotgun back on the clerk's desk and resumed his seat by the counsel table.

"You say the defendant was visibly upset when you told him about Mrs. Adams having been beaten?"

"Yes. He was."

"You did not see her being beaten, did you?"

"No."

"And you don't know that Gilbert Adams did it to her, do you? Of your own personal knowledge?"

"I didn't see him do it, no."

"Did you know that Ada Adams had a paramour?"

"She did not."

"How do you know?" Singleton asked pointedly. "You weren't around her all the time, were you?"

"Of course not."

"So you don't really know what caused the bruises you described, do you?"

"I didn't see him do it, if that's what you mean."

"And therefore, you don't know how they got there, do you?"

"I have a good idea."

"That's your conclusion," Singleton said.

"Yes, based on what I saw and what she said."

"Objection, Your Honor," Singleton said. "That's hearsay."

"It was invited, Your Honor," Will said from his seat.

"Overruled," the judge said.

"Very well," Singleton said. "But for all you know, it could have been her paramour, your client, who caused those injuries."

"Not hardly," Ash replied.

"You don't know where he was the previous evening, do you?"

"No, I don't." Ash appeared to be irritated.

"What did the defendant say when you told him that his lover had been beaten?"

"I didn't actually say that to him."

"Did you have a conversation with him at the widow Poe's house?"

"I told him she had been hurt, the best I can remember."

"And what did he say?" Singleton asked.

"He said he was not going to let him get away with it."

"Did he say anything else?"

"Not that I recall. He was heading for the front door right away. He didn't say much."

"Who else was present at that time?"

"Lily Poe and her daughter, Barbara Ann," Ash replied.

"Do you expect to call Lily Poe as a witness?"

Will stood.

"Objection, Your Honor," he said. "That inquires into counsel's legal strategy and it's not proper."

"They made the decision to call this defense counsel as a witness, Your Honor," Singleton said. "They have to live with the consequences."

The judge rubbed his chin while looking from Singleton to Will.

"Objection overruled," he finally said.

"You may answer, counsel," Singleton said.

"We have no plans to call Miz Poe as a witness," Ash replied.

"You tried to stop Hardeman from going to the Adams place, didn't you?" Singleton asked.

"I did."

"Why was that?"

"To avoid any trouble."

"You knew he was out to kill Gilbert Adams, didn't you?"

Ash hesitated. The jurors were leaning forward in their seats.

"I did not know that," he finally said. "I just thought there might be trouble."

"You knew that Everett Hardeman and Ada Moore had been engaged to be married, didn't you?"

"Yes."

"And you knew they were carrying on a love affair after she was married to Gilbert Adams, didn't you sir?"

"I did not."

"You didn't know that?"

"No."

"You were at the ball and dinner for Colonel Hays several years ago, weren't you, counsel?"

"I was," Ash said.

"It was at the Menger Hotel in San Antonio, wasn't it?"

"It was."

"And Ada Adams was there without her husband, wasn't she?"

"She attended with her mother," Ash replied.

"Gilbert Adams was not in attendance that night, was he?"

"He was not."

"And Mrs. Adams was seen to be dancing with this defendant, wasn't she? In the absence of her husband?"

"Yes, they danced together once that night."

"And they were seen to be alone together on the patio that evening, weren't they, sir?"

"I don't know about that."

"You don't know about that," Singleton said.

"No, I don't."

Singleton turned toward the jury.

"I have no further questions of this witness, Your Honor," he said in a confident tone.

TWENTY-TWO

DURING RECESS, WILL AND ASH MET IN THE SMALL CLERK'S office they had previously used. Ash was visibly upset.

"You did okay," Will said.

"I shouldn't have let that smartass get to me," Ash replied. "I think the jury sensed it."

"Don't be too sure they weren't on your side of it. At any rate, it's done. We need to get to our next witness."

After recess and after the judge and jury were seated, Will stood.

"As our next witness, we call Constable Quill Stagner," he said.

Stagner, a portly man with long gray sideburns, stood up from his seat in the first row, came through the gate in the rail, was sworn and seated in the witness chair.

"You are Constable Quill Stagner?" Will asked.

"I am," he replied.

"Were you called on by Ashley Maitland last Easter Sunday?"

"I was, yes. He came to my house."

"And did you follow him out to Mrs. Moore's place?"

"Yes, sir. I surely did."

"Why did Mr. Maitland call you out there?"

"He said Gilbert Adams had beaten up his wife and she needed some protection."

"Objection, Your Honor," Singleton said loudly, having risen to his feet. "That's hearsay."

"Sustained," the judge said. "Constable, you are not to say what someone has told you." Stagner nodded.

"Did you leave a deputy there, Constable?" Will asked.

"I did. I deputized Horace Walker and brought him out there with me."

"And was that for Ada Adams's protection?"

"Yes, sir, it was."

"Then last Thanksgiving week, did I contact you about going out to the Adams place with me?"

"Yes, sir, you did."

"And did we stop by Mrs. Moore's place on the way?"

"Yes, sir."

"Did you obtain the permission of Mrs. Ada Adams to search the Adams premises?"

"Yes, sir. She said I had her permission to go search."

"And did you accompany me to the Adams place?"

"I did."

"Was anybody home?"

"No, sir. Nobody was home."

"Did you search the premises?"

"Yes, sir, we both did."

Will went to the clerk's desk and picked up the bloodstained shotgun, then handed it to the constable.

"Do you recognize this shotgun that has been marked Defendant's Exhibit One?"

Stagner reached into his vest pocket, pulled out a pair of spectacles and put them on, then held the shotgun up and looked closely at the top of the barrel near the stock. He then looked back at Will.

"Yes, sir. I found this shotgun out at the Adams place. I memorized the serial number," he said proudly.

"Where did you find it?" Will asked.

"It was hidden behind a loose board in the inside wall of the well house," he said. "Somebody had gone to a lot of trouble to hide it. Took a while to find it."

"Did you keep it in your custody until the other day when you delivered it to me here at the courthouse?"

"Yes, sir, I did."

"Is it in the same condition today as it was when you found it out at the Adams place?"

"Yes, sir, it is."

"Do you notice any stains on it?"

"Yes, sir. There're bloodstains on the stock and the barrel."

"Have you had experience in identifying bloodstains on weapons, Constable?"

"Yes, sir. Many times," Stagner replied, turning and smiling at the jury. "Those are definitely bloodstains."

"Was it loaded?"

"Yes, sir. Sure was. Had a load of buckshot."

"Pass the witness," Will said.

"Did you obtain a warrant to search the Adams premises, Constable?" Singleton asked.

"No, sir. I did not," Stagner replied.

"Then that was an illegal search, wasn't it?"

"I don't know about that," he said. "Nobody was home."

Singleton picked up the bloodstained shotgun and stood to address the court.

"Your Honor, this exhibit has not yet been offered, but I move to strike all of the testimony concerning it. It was obtained illegally."

The judge looked at Will. "Do you have a response, counsel?"

"It was not obtained illegally, Your Honor," Will said. "Constable Stagner was given permission by Mrs. Adams to search the premises. A peaceable search of the premises was reasonable under the circumstances, and the constable was within the law in searching them. I meant to offer this shotgun, Defendant's Exhibit One, into evidence at the conclusion of the constable's testimony, but I offer it now."

"Very well," the judge said. "The objection is overruled and Defendant's Exhibit One is admitted." He turned to Singleton. "Do you have further questions, Mr. Singleton?"

"No, Your Honor," Singleton replied.

"Then this witness is excused," the judge said.

"It is close to the noon hour," the judge said. "The court stands in recess until one thirty."

Will and Ash told their client they would need to confer and that they would meet him back in the courtroom at one o'clock. They again met in the small clerk's office and continued a discussion that had been going on for months.

"We can't afford to put him on," Ash said.

"Only he can say that he did not intend to kill Adams before he reached for the gun," Will said. Ash stared at Will before speaking. He had a stern look about him.

"I had forgotten a couple of things Ev said when I gave my testimony," he said. "We can't afford for him to take the stand."

"What? You haven't said anything about that before. What did he say?"

"I don't remember," Ash replied, with the same stern look about him, which Will had trouble reading.

"He said he was going to stop him and arrest him if he had to, to protect Ada," Will said.

"And you believe that?"

Will hesitated. Ash continued his unwavering stare.

"You are not telling me everything," Will said. "I can't believe this."

"I have had experience placing my client on the stand in criminal cases before," Ash said. "You must do so only when there is no other hope for an acquittal and when you are sure he can stand up under cross examination. There is no way we can have that assurance in this case."

"Then you don't believe his story," Will said.

"That matters not at all," Ash replied. "The question is whether the jury will believe it. If they think he is lying to save his skin, they'll come down hard on him."

"All right. Then I guess we rest."

"Yes. It's time to do so."

TWENTY-THREE

AFTER THE JUDGE AND JURY WERE SEATED, Will announced that the defense rested. The judge then asked if the state had any rebuttal testimony. Singleton stood and addressed the court.

"We do, Your Honor," he said. "The state calls Arthur Carter. He is in the hallway, Mr. Bailiff."

The bailiff went into the hallway to get the witness. Ash and Will were conferring in whispers. Several members of the jury noticed Ash turning and whispering to Ev. After a minute or so, Carter was brought in by the bailiff and directed to stand before the bench, where the judge administered the oath. He then took the witness stand.

"You are Arthur Carter," Singleton said.

"Yes, sir," Carter replied.

"Where do you live, Mr. Carter?"

"Here in Lockhart."

"What do you do for a living?"

"I shoe horses," Carter replied.

"Do you know the defendant, seated there, Everett Hardeman?"

"Yes, sir. I do."

"Have you seen him recently?"

"Yes, sir."

"Where was that?"

"At Friedman's Saloon."

"When was that?"

"Last evenin'."

"He was at Friedman's last night?"

"Yes, sir. He was."

"Did you know at the time that this trial was going on?"

"I did."

"Did Hardeman say anything that would relate to this case?"

"Huh?" Carter appeared to be puzzled by the question.

"Did he say anything about Gilbert Adams?" Singleton asked.

"Well, yes he did. He said he needed killin'."

"Did he say anything else?"

"Well, we was in there for a while. He said y'all shouldn't oughta called Miz Moore to the stand."

"Anything else?"

"Oh, I don't remember everything he said. We was in there quite a while"

"Pass the witness," Singleton said, with a smile on his face.

Ash whispered in Will's ear.

"You supported Frank Clark in the last election, didn't you?" Will finally asked.

"Yes, sir. I shore did."

"You went around giving out flyers for him in his contested race, didn't you?"

"I gave out a few flyers, yes sir."

"Had you talked to Mr. Clark or Mr. Singleton about this case before last night?"

Carter hesitated and looked at Clark, who was looking down at the table before him.

"Well, yes, I guess I did."

"You guess you did. When was that?"

"I don't remember," Carter replied.

"Did Clark or Singleton put you up to spying on Everett Hardeman?" Will asked.

"I wasn't doin' no spyin'," Carter replied. "I was just listenin'."

"But you had talked to Clark or Singleton before you listened," Will said.

"Well, yes, sir."

Ev whispered in Ash's ear and Ash in turn whispered to Will. It took a while and the judge looked down at them from the bench.

"Do you have further questions, counselor?" he asked.

"Yes, Your Honor," Will replied. "Mr. Carter, did Everett Hardeman make the statement you have told us about, or was he just agreeing with something you said?"

Carter looked at Clark again.

"Mr. Clark can't help you with the answer, sir," Will said. "You are sworn to tell the truth."

Carter looked down at his folded hands.

"I guess he might have been agreein' with me," he finally said.

"You said 'Gil Adams needed killing' and he said 'probably so,' didn't he?"

"Well, yeah, I guess so."

"You guess so. And he didn't agree with you until you had repeated it several times, did he?"

Carter shifted uncomfortably in the witness chair.

"I guess I might have repeated it," he said.

"And everybody at the table was drinking whiskey, weren't they?"

"Well, yes, sir."

"Including Ev Hardeman," Will said.

"Yeah, he was drinkin'."

"In fact, you and the others were drinking out of his bottle, weren't you?"

"Well. Yes, sir. We was."

"And Mr. Clark put you up to it, didn't he? Put you up to tricking Ev Hardeman into saying something that could be used against him in court?"

"I didn't trick him," Carter said.

"You were there to try to get something out of him, weren't you?"

"I was just there to drink some whiskey," Carter said, his eyes again looking in Clark's direction.

"But Mr. Clark put you up to going there, didn't he?" Will's voice, steadily rising, was full of indignation.

"He asked me to go over there, yes, sir."

Will stood. "No further questions of this witness," he said.

"Mr. Clark and I didn't tell you what to testify to, did we?" Singleton asked.

"No, sir," Carter replied.

"No further questions," Singleton said.

"When did you tell Mr. Clark what you had heard?" Will asked.

"Last evenin'," Carter said.

"Did you go to his home to tell him?"

"Yes, sir. He told me to."

"He told you to."

"Yes, sir."

"No further questions," Will said.

The judge displayed a bemused expression as he addressed Clark and Singleton.

"Any other rebuttal witnesses, gentlemen?" he asked.

Clark stood. "No, Your Honor. The state closes."

The judge turned and looked at Will, who stood and said, "We also close, Your Honor."

"Very well," the judge said, then turned to the jury. "Gentlemen of the jury, the court will need to confer with counsel to prepare the court's charge and it being Friday afternoon, I am going to ask you to come back to court on Monday morning. As I have previously said, you are not to discuss this case with anyone, not even your family, and if anyone tries to discuss this case with you, tell the sheriff or one of his deputies about it right away. All right. This court is in recess until nine o'clock, Monday morning."

TWENTY-FOUR

WILL WAS AT THE OFFICE ON SATURDAY MORNING, AS HE often was, but this Saturday was different. He was reading and rereading his copy of the court's jury charge and making notes, in preparation for his jury argument. Ash had not yet arrived. He was probably sleeping late for a change. The ride to Lockhart took about two hours, and they had been making some early mornings during the trial. And it was probable that Ash had had a few the previous evening.

The lawyers for the prosecution and defense had met the previous afternoon with the judge, and each side had presented written charge requests, proposals as to what the judge would read to the jury as being the law that applied to the case. Each lawyer, as an officer of the court, was duty bound not to misrepresent the law to the court, although there were usually enough differences in precedent and interpretation of precedent to support argument on both sides of most issues. Written charges were seldom reported in published appellate court decisions, an indication that assignments of error in regard to the charge to the jury were rare. The judge had wide discretion in interpreting the law for the jury.

He heard footsteps on the stairs. He did not think it was Ash this early and stood and walked to the doorway to the outer office. Then the footsteps halted at the top of the stairs. Ada stood at the edge of the stairwell, pale and out of breath from the climb. He came to her and extended his hand.

"Ada," he said, "you've come to see me."

"Yes," she replied. "I need to talk to you."

Her voice was weaker than he had ever heard. He led her to a chair and sat beside her.

"What is it, Ada? Did you come all the way into town alone?"

"Billy, I am worried about Ev," she said.

"But things are going pretty well," he said. "You shouldn't be worried."

"He came to the house again last night," she said. "And he had been drinking. I'm afraid he's going to kill himself."

"Did he threaten to do that?"

"Oh, yes, he did. He was talking crazy. About the judge and the jury. Even about you and Ash. I'm afraid he's losing his mind. Oh, Billy, I'm afraid. I couldn't sleep all night."

"I've warned him about seeing you," he said. "It does nobody any good. I'll talk to him."

"I don't know what to do," she said, tears brimming. "He's acting crazy."

"Did you come into town alone?"

"Mattie drove me," she replied.

"I'll go and see him today. I'll settle him down."

She refused his offer of coffee, then sat quietly for a while. He could not help thinking of her as he used to when he would have dreams about her. Now, thin and pale, she seemed much older than her years.

"I'm proud of you," she finally said, looking down at her folded, gloved hands.

"Don't be too fast with praise. The jury isn't in yet."

"You didn't ask me to testify."

"You would hardly talk to me about it."

"I will now. I don't want him to die for me."

"The evidence is closed. We've rested. I would have to represent to the judge that we had discovered unanticipated evidence in order to be allowed to reopen and put you on the stand. Even if he would allow it, you'd have to testify on cross-examination. We can't pick and choose the questions you'd be asked."

"I don't care," she said. "I want to help him if I can."

"Then I have to let you know what you would be asked. And what they would want the jury to believe."

"That I am an adulteress," she said, looking at him coldly. "Is that it?"

"Yes."

"I will swear to almighty God that Everett and I have never had intimate relations. He would never do that to me. You may think of him as weak, but he is strong. Now he's acting crazy, thinking he's going to be hanged and acting like a drunk, but he still wouldn't do anything that would cause disrespect to me."

"He's been coming to you in secret, hasn't he?"

She began to cry.

"You wouldn't understand."

"I'm his lawyer. I have to understand."

He handed her his handkerchief. She dabbed her tears.

"He has never loved anyone else," she said. "I believe him when he tells me that. And it's so hard."

He stood and walked to the window, his back to her.

"Will you testify about how your husband treated you?"

She did not respond. He resisted the urge to turn and look at her. A minute passed.

"I will," she finally said. She was standing behind him when she said it and the tone of her voice reminded him of when they were children, cousins who were often engaged in verbal combat. Her voice had a confident sound that told him she was not bluffing. He turned to her.

"You'll have to be prepared to answer all questions," he said. "I'll have to go over everything with you today."

"All right," she said, in the same tone.

"Then we had better have some coffee. It's going to take a while."

"Aren't you going to see Everett?" she asked.

"Not now. It's more important to hear what you have to say."

"All right. Then I'll have some coffee."

Ash arrived at noon, eager to have Will join him for some lunch at a local café. He was surprised to see Ada there.

"You have decided to testify?" he asked.

"She has," Will said. "I have been going over it with her."

"Have you explained the danger to her?"

"He has," Ada said. "I understand the risk."

"Do you understand that the risk is not to you?" Ash said. "It's to

Everett Hardeman." He paused. "I think Will and I need to confer in private about this. Sorry, Ada, but I'll have to ask you to step out for a few minutes."

"If you wish," she said, rising from her chair. She stepped quickly through the doorway into the outer office. Ash pulled the door shut and looked up at the closed transom before walking back to where Will stood by the double desk. He spoke quietly.

"She could put the noose around his neck. I don't think it's worth the risk."

"I disagree," Will said. "The jury needs to hear the whole story."

"I was in favor of exploring her as a witness originally, but her emotional state is not good. Can you imagine what that Austin lawyer could do to her on cross?"

"She's got some grit to her, Ash. I think I know her better than you do. She can help with her testimony. She swears she has not committed adultery."

Ash walked over to the window and looked out. He was silent for a few moments.

"I'll sit in with you going over it with her," he finally said. "But let's reserve our final decision until we are through with our talk." He turned to Will. "I've woodshedded a lot of witnesses in my day. What they say on the stand, particularly under cross-examination, is often a lot different from what they tell you in private."

"Fair enough," Will said. "You know I respect your opinion."

They called her back into the office. At Ash's suggestion, Ada asked Mattie, who had been waiting in the Moore wagon, to take some money from Ash and bring them some lunch from the café. They then kept up questioning her for another three hours, until Ash finally said she should go home. She assured them that her mother knew she was there and that she would accompany her to court on Monday morning.

Ash left soon thereafter, obviously tired and in need of rest. They agreed to meet back at the office the next morning, on Sunday, to finish their preparations. After Ash had gone, Will locked up and left. He rode down the street two blocks to the Pincheon Hotel, where Ev Hardeman had a room. He entered the small lobby and then walked up the creaky stairs to the second floor and knocked on the door to the room. After a minute passed without a sound from within, he knocked again, louder.

He could hear a muffled sound from within and after another minute, the door was opened. Ev stood there, unshaven, his hair tousled, his clothes rumpled, rubbing his reddened eyes.

"Billy," he said, his voice a sad whisper. "Come in. Sorry about the mess. I had a rough night.

On the table near a rumpled bed lay an ashtray overflowing with cigarette butts and an empty whiskey bottle. One of the chairs was overturned. Ev picked it up and gestured for him to sit in the other one. After sitting for a few seconds, Will said, "Ada came to see me this morning."

Ev visibly stiffened. "Why?"

"She's worried about you. And the trial. But mainly about you. She thinks you want to kill yourself."

Ev ran his fingers through his hair.

"I went to see her last night," Ev said. "I know I shouldn't have, but I had to see her."

"And you were drunk," Will said quickly.

"I was," he replied, looking down at the empty bottle. "I'm sorry."

Will stood. "She has agreed to testify," he said. "She will be in court Monday morning."

"What? She wasn't going to. Did you talk her into it?"

"Not at all. She came to the office on her own. She wants to help you."

"I can't believe it," Ev said.

"It's true. You'd better get something to eat and get some rest. I'll see you in court on Monday."

TWENTY-FIVE

ON MONDAY MORNING, THE JUDGE ASKED IF THERE WAS anything to cover before he brought the jury in to hear the reading of the charge. Will stood and announced, "We move to reopen, Your Honor. New evidence has come to our attention."

Clark rose immediately. The judge looked his way.

"We oppose, Your Honor. The jury has already been told to expect final arguments today."

The judge had a bemused look. "I can hardly overrule the defense motion before I have heard the grounds. What say you, Mr. McCulloch?"

"The widow, Mrs. Adams, came forward this weekend with new evidence, Your Honor."

"What is the nature of her anticipated testimony, Counselor?" the judge asked.

"The prosecution has been attempting to smear her name with the insinuation that she and the defendant were having an extramarital affair, Your Honor. She is prepared to offer testimony to rebut that. She can also offer testimony that bears upon the personality of the decedent, Mr. Adams."

"And why would his personality be relevant?" the judge asked.

"As you know, Your Honor, we believe that the defendant acted in self-defense, but that is in dispute. Mr. Adams's tendency toward violent acts is therefore very relevant."

The judge rubbed his chin, then turned toward Clark. "You may respond now, sir."

"Your Honor, there is nothing in what counsel says that indicates that the widow's testimony could have not been put on when the defense presented their case."

"Mr. McCulloch, I believe counsel has a point," the judge said. "Why could this testimony not have been presented last week?"

"Because Mrs. Adams had not been forthcoming until this past weekend, Your Honor. My impression is that she was overcome emotionally because of the events surrounding the death of Mr. Adams and did not want to be involved. She came to our office last Saturday of her own accord and furnished information we had not had before."

"But Your Honor . . . " Clark began.

"I will allow the widow to testify," the judge said. "Is she present and ready to testify, Mr. McCulloch?"

"She is in the hallway, Your Honor."

"Very well. Is there anything else to bring before the court before we bring the jury in?"

"No, Your Honor," both lawyers said simultaneously. The judge gestured to the bailiff, who opened the door to the jury room. The twelve men walked through the door in single file to the jury box. When they had taken their seats, the judge addressed them.

"Good morning, gentlemen. We are to have some more testimony this morning, on motion of the defendant. Mr. McCulloch, you may call your next witness."

"The defense calls Mrs. Ada Adams, Your Honor," Will announced.

Several jurors exchanged glances as the bailiff walked slowly to the hall door and leaned through the doorway for a moment before letting Ada Adams in. He escorted her to the rail gate, opened it for her to pass through, then followed beside her as she approached the bench. The judge administered the oath. She was then escorted to the witness stand, the bailiff extending his hand to steady her as she stepped up. When she was seated, Will spoke from his seat at the counsel table.

"State your name, please."

"Ada Adams."

"Your husband was Gilbert Adams?"

She glanced at the jury before answering.

"Yes."

"When were you and Mr. Adams married?"

"March 4, 1867."

"So you had been married over eight years at the time of his death?"

"Yes."

"Mr. Adams had two sons by a previous marriage, is that correct?"

"Yes."

"And they have previously testified. Did you and your husband have any children of your own?"

"No. We didn't." She looked down at her clasped hands.

"Are you still of child-bearing age and condition?"

She was visibly surprised by the question.

"Yes," she said.

"Did you and your husband try to have children of your own?"

"No. We didn't."

"Was there any particular reason why you did not try?"

Singleton stood and addressed the judge.

"Objection, Your Honor. This could not possibly be relevant."

The judge looked at Will, who stood.

"It will become clearly relevant, Your Honor," he said. "It has a bearing on the personality of the decedent."

"The decedent is not on trial here, Your Honor," Singleton said.

"Overruled," the judge said. "You may proceed, Counselor."

"Why didn't you and Mr. Adams try to have children, Mrs. Adams?"

Ada hesitated, looked at the jury, then back at Will.

"He said that wasn't what I was for," she said.

"Were those his exact words?"

"No."

"What did he say?"

"He said that was not what I was hired on to do."

"'Hired on'? Did he use those words?"

"Yes, he did. He said I was hired on to take care of his boys and to wait on him and obey him and that was all."

"And was that the way the marriage went?"

"Yes."

"How were you treated, Mrs. Adams? How did your husband treat you?"

"Like a servant girl," she said, her eyes reddening.

"Did he beat you?"

"Yes," she said, beginning to sob.

"With his hand?"

"With his fists," she said. "And sometimes he used other things to whip me."

"What other things?"

"He would cane me. And sometimes he used a saddle quirt."

"Would there be anything you would do to bring on a beating?"

"He would say I wasn't doing as I was told, but I think he liked to do it."

Singleton stood.

"Objection. That's her conclusion."

"Sustained," the judge said.

"I ask that the jury be instructed to disregard that testimony, Your Honor," Singleton said.

"I will give one instruction on that subject," the judge said, smiling, and turned to the jury. "Gentlemen of the jury, when I sustain an objection to testimony, you will not consider that testimony as evidence. You will disregard it." He turned to Will. "You may proceed, Mr. McCulloch."

"Did he ever whip you in front of his sons, your stepsons?" Will asked.

"Yes," she replied, tears running down her cheeks. "He would call them into the room where he whipped me and tell them to watch. He said they needed to see what happened when he was not obeyed."

"Did you ever see him whip his boys?"

"No. He never did."

Will hesitated before asking the next question.

"Did he ever . . . make you expose yourself in front of his two sons?"

She put her face in her hands, sobbing. Her sobs were the only sounds that could be heard in the courtroom. After a few moments, she looked up, her lips quivering.

"He made me bend over and pull up my skirts when he whipped me," she said, spitting out the words.

The jury, the lawyers, and the onlookers in the courtroom were completely still and quiet. The judge sat back in his chair, looking down at her. Tears were rolling down her cheeks. Will stood, walked to the witness stand, and handed her a handkerchief. He turned and faced the jury before returning to his seat at the counsel table.

"Are you able to continue?" he asked.

"Yes," she said, dabbing the tears from her cheeks.

"How long have you known Everett Hardeman?"

"Since I was fifteen," she said.

"Were the two of you engaged to be married?"

"Yes. Before he went off to war."

"Did he come back when the war was over?"

"No. He did not. Everyone said he had died in a Yankee prison."

"So you believed your fiancé was dead?"

"Yes. Everyone did."

"But you waited before marrying, anyway?"

"I waited for years, but I finally gave up. I didn't believe Everett was alive."

"And when you had given up on him being alive, you married Gilbert Adams."

"Yes, I did. It was a bad time. He said he would take care of me and my mother. He said he would be good to me and I could help him raise his two boys."

"When did you find out Ev Hardeman was alive?"

"Not until he came back. That was in 1870."

"And you were already married to Adams then."

"Yes."

"Did you see the defendant while you were married to Gilbert Adams?"

"I saw him a few times," she replied.

"Did he ever visit you at your home?"

"He came to the house once. I was in the yard, hanging up clothes to dry."

"Was your husband home?"

"No. He was off somewhere. But he came home after Everett left."

"Did your husband ever accuse you of having an affair with Everett Hardeman?"

"He did," she replied. She was sitting upright now, no longer crying.

"Mrs. Adams, were you and the defendant ever intimate during your marriage to Gilbert Adams?"

"No. Absolutely not. Everett always showed me the greatest respect. He would have never done anything like that to me."

"Did you see him at the ball for Colonel Hays in San Antonio?"

"Yes."

"Were the two of you ever alone that evening?"

"No. My mother was with me all the time."

She looked at Ev for the first time.

"Have the two of you discussed marriage since he came back?"

"No." Hesitating . . ."We haven't discussed it."

Will looked at the jury, then back at Ada.

"I want to ask you about the day before Easter last year," he said. "Did your husband whip you that evening?"

She looked down at her hands again.

"He beat me with his fists and with a cane," she said.

"Did you go to your mother's house that night?"

"Yes."

"How did you get there?"

"I ran all the way," she said.

"How far is it that you ran?"

"I don't know exactly. About four miles."

"Did your husband know you were leaving?"

"No. I waited until he was asleep."

"Did you see Everett Hardeman that day?"

"No."

"How long had it been since you had seen him?"

"I hadn't seen him in months," she said.

"Why did your husband beat you that night?"

"He accused me of being with Everett."

"Had you been with him?"

"No."

Will paused again. Ada was sitting upright, looking straight ahead, her head held high. Will looked expectantly at Ash. Ash shook his head. Will stood.

"Pass the witness, Your Honor," he said.

Singleton stood in a crouch and slid his chair forward to the front edge of the counsel table, then retook his seat.

"Mrs. Adams," he asked. "Have you ever kissed Everett Hardeman?"

She hesitated. "Yes," she finally said, softly.

"What was that? I'm not sure the jury could hear your answer. Was that a yes?"

"Yes," she said, quite aloud, looking at the jury. "We were engaged to be married and we certainly kissed."

Several of the jurors smiled.

"Has he held you in his arms?"

"Yes," she replied.

"Has Everett Hardeman ever held you in his arms during your marriage to Gilbert Adams?"

She looked down again before answering.

"Yes."

"More than once?"

"No. Only once."

"When was that? Do you remember?"

"Yes. It was in 1870."

"Only once since you were married?"

"Yes."

She was still sitting upright, looking straight back at Singleton with every answer she gave, her pale face held high, as if she had nothing to hide.

"How many times has Everett Hardeman visited you at your home since you were married?"

"Only once," she replied.

"And when was that?"

"In 1870," she said.

"And your husband was not home that day."

"No. He wasn't."

"Did you kiss Everett Hardeman that day?"

"No. We did not kiss then."

"Did he take you in his arms?"

"No."

"Was that the first time you had seen him since he came back after the war?"

"Yes, it was."

"And you did not embrace?"

"No. We did not."

"Did you kiss him at some other time during your marriage?"

"One time."

"You did? When was that?"

"At the ball in San Antonio."

"The ball for Colonel Hays?"

"Yes."

"That was in 1870, wasn't it?"

"Yes."

"I thought you said your mother was with you at all times during the ball."

"She was."

"So you kissed this man, a man other than your husband, in the presence of your mother?"

"She was on the patio with us."

"On the patio."

"Yes."

"Were any others present on the patio with you?"

"No."

"And you allowed him to kiss you? You let him?"

"Yes. I . . . I wasn't expecting it."

"So you had a romantic attachment to this defendant during your marriage to your husband?"

"No. He was very respectful to me."

"Did the defendant express his feelings toward you? During your marriage?"

"He told me he still loved me."

"He told you he still loved you?"

"Yes."

"Did you respond?"

"What do you mean?"

"Did you say you loved him, too?"

"No."

"Are you sure you didn't?"

"Yes. I am sure."

"Why didn't you?"

"Because I was married. It wouldn't have been proper."

"Was it proper for you to kiss another man?"

"No."

"But though you might not have said words of love to the defendant, you felt them nevertheless, didn't you Mrs. Adams?"

She hesitated, as if holding her breath.

"You still love him, don't you, Mrs. Adams? In spite of your marriage. In spite of the fact that he killed your husband in cold blood."

"No," she said, her voice weaker. "It wasn't like that. I hadn't seen him in so long. I thought he was dead. I thought I'd never see him again."

"Because you and he had been and are lovers, aren't you, Mrs. Adams?"

"No. Just because I care about Everett doesn't mean we are lovers. He has always shown me respect."

"Like kissing you when you were married. He knew you were married when he took you in his arms and kissed you, didn't he?"

"Yes."

"Did he ask you to divorce your husband and marry him?"

She hesitated and looked at Ev again. Singleton was smiling.

"Did he?"

"Yes," she finally said.

"Did he ever threaten to kill your husband?"

She was staring at Ev, who was returning her stare.

"No," she said. "He never did."

Singleton paused for a few moments. The courtroom was silent. All eyes were on her. She again looked down at her clasped hands. Then Singleton slowly stood.

"Those are all the questions we have for this witness at this time, Your Honor," he said quietly.

The judge looked at Will.

"Do you have any further questions of this witness, Mr. McCulloch?"

Will stood.

"No, Your Honor. The defense rests."

TWENTY-SIX

AFTER THE LUNCH RECESS, THE JUDGE READ THE CHARGE of the court to the jury.

"Gentlemen of the jury, I charge you that the law that applies to this case is as follows. The evidence you will have received from the testimony in this case. The law you will receive from this charge and only from this charge.

"Murder in the first degree is the intentional taking of the life of another without just cause and with malice aforethought. Murder in the second degree is voluntary homicide, committed under the immediate influence of sudden passion without adequate cause. Manslaughter is voluntary homicide committed under the immediate influence of sudden passion, without malice, arising from an adequate cause, but neither justified nor excused by law. Homicide is justifiable when committed in the lawful defense of the person when there shall be reasonable grounds to apprehend a design to commit a felony or to do some great personal injury, and there shall be imminent danger of such crime being accomplished. No assault, however violent, will justify killing the assailant under a plea of self-defense, unless there be a plain manifestation of felonious intent. If the defendant had reasonable grounds to believe a felony upon his person to be intended, it matters not that such was really not the case. It will be necessary for the jury to examine the evidence to determine whether a reasonable belief of an intended felony can be deduced. Where the apprehension of a felony is found to be present and honest, but the grounds unreasonable, then the crime might only be manslaughter. If you believe from the evidence that a combat ensued between the parties, then the combat must not have been of the defendant's own seeking and he must not have put himself in the way of being assaulted, in order that when assaulted and pressed he might take the life of the decedent.

"In your deliberations, you will first determine whether the defendant is guilty of the crime of murder in the first degree. If you do not find him guilty of that crime, you will then consider whether the defendant is guilty of the crime of murder in the second degree. If you do not find him guilty of that crime, you will consider whether the defendant is guilty of the crime of manslaughter.

"In order to find the defendant guilty of any crime, you must find his guilt from the evidence beyond a reasonable doubt. Certainty is not required, but if there is a reasonable doubt in your minds as to the guilt of the defendant, after hearing all of the evidence, you must find him not guilty.

"Your verdict must be unanimous. When you first enter the jury room, you will elect one of your number foreman of the jury. Your foreman will communicate with the court, through the bailiff, in writing, if you have any questions or requests. You will be sequestered until you reach a verdict. When you have reached a verdict, you will let the bailiff know and you will be returned into court and announce your verdict."

The judge looked up at the jury.

"You will have this charge in the jury room with you. Now you will hear final arguments, first from the State of Texas." He turned to Clark. "Mr. Clark, you have indicated you will open for the State."

Clark stood and approached the jury box, placed both hands on the railing, and leaned forward. He looked each juror in the eye, one by one, then began in a soft voice.

"You have heard the evidence. It is clear from the evidence that Everett Hardeman was in an inappropriate relationship with Gilbert Adams's wife. On Easter, he became enraged at what he perceived to be cruelty on the part of Adams toward his wife, which was none of his business. None of his business. And he set out from Mrs. Moore's that day saying he would kill Adams and that is exactly what he did. In cold blood. Deputy Constable Horace Walker heard him say, 'I'll kill the son of a bitch.'

"Counsel for the defense would have you believe that Gilbert Adams was reaching for a weapon just before Hardeman shot him, but their so-called evidence doesn't hold up. At a time when no one was at home, they find a shotgun conveniently hidden where it could be easily found. A gun that had been lost months before, but that conveniently turned up after the shooting. Who knows how that gun got there? Anybody could have planted it there after the shooting had occurred. And it's not unusual, as all of you know, to get blood on a shotgun while out hunting.

"The only testimony that a shotgun was in the wagon that day came from the defendant's own lawyer. There is no independent, unbiased evidence that it was there. No. Everett Hardeman was intent on killing Gilbert Adams when he left the Moore place. He said he was going to kill him and he did. That is premeditation. That is malice aforethought. That is murder in the first degree.

"We don't know everything that went on between this defendant and his former fiancée, but we know that they kissed at least once while she was married to Gilbert Adams and he embraced her. They had an illicit relationship. Hardeman even asked the married woman to divorce her husband and marry him. She admitted that. Gilbert Adams was in their way. And remember, Gilbert Adams is not on trial here. If he was indeed harsh in punishing his wayward wife, who is to say that it was not his right as a husband who had been wronged? He certainly did not deserve to be killed for it.

"When you look at the believable evidence in this case, there is only one conclusion to make. Everett Hardeman killed Gilbert Adams in cold blood to eliminate him as an obstacle to his illicit designs on Mrs. Adams. He made up his mind to kill him before he had left the Moore place that day. That's murder in the first degree."

Clark walked slowly to his seat by the counsel table and sat down. After a pause, Will stood up and approached the jury box. He held his hands clasped behind him to keep them out of sight, to keep the jury from seeing that they were shaking. He cleared his throat before speaking.

"Gentlemen, you have heard the evidence. Everett Hardeman did not reach for his pistol until he saw Gilbert Adams reaching for his shotgun. He had the right to defend himself. Adams was known to be violent. He beat his wife. Not only did he beat her, he made her expose herself to his two sons. Yes, Everett Hardeman was upset when he found out what Adams had done to Ada Adams. Yes, he started for the Adams place while he was riled up, and who wouldn't have been? But you heard the testimony of Ada Adams. She had never been unfaithful to her husband, and Everett Hardeman had always shown her respect and would never have compromised her virtue."

Will turned and pointed toward Ev, who was sitting at the counsel table.

"This is not a cold-blooded murderer. This is a man who returned from the war maimed, only to find that he was given up as dead and that his fiancée had married another. Should he be condemned for still being in love with his fiancée? Certainly not. He respected her status as a married woman, but was understandably disturbed by how she was being treated. Should love be condemned? Not in any civilized society.

"You will recall what George Adams testified to. He said his brother lost the matching shotgun, the one that was just like the one his father had, while on a hunting trip on an adjacent place, and they didn't go back and get it because they would be trespassing. But they were trespassing when the shotgun was lost, if that's what happened. Why trespass once, but not afterwards? And you will recall that when the sheriff and the others arrived at the Adams place after the shooting, the two boys were found hiding behind the well house, the very place where the bloodstained shotgun was later found, hidden behind a loose board in the inside wall. Mr. Clark would have you believe that *someone* planted it there, I guess meaning the defendant or us two lawyers, officers of the court. Shame on you, Mr. Clark. It is clear from the circumstances how the shotgun got there. You will recall that Harry Adams, nervous as a cat on the witness stand, said he didn't know what had happened to his and his brother's gun. He said nothing about losing it while being charged by a wild boar. Well, it is obvious what happened to it. One of the boys, probably the older one, George, placed it over the doorway to the front room and hid the other one, the one used by their father, the bloodstained one, in the well house wall, so it would not be found.

"Now I want to talk about the testimony of Ashley Maitland. The state gets the last word here today and I'll bet that Mr. Singleton tells you not to believe Ashley Maitland's testimony because he is one of the lawyers for Everett Hardeman. You heard his testimony. He represented the family and felt duty bound to represent Everett Hardeman when asked to do so. And you also heard that the judge ruled that it was proper for him to do so as well as testify as a witness, so long as he did not actively participate in the trial by questioning witnesses or addressing the jury. In other words, it was entirely within the rules for him to testify. And you heard Sheriff Ellison say that Ashley Maitland has a good reputation for telling the truth. He is a credible, believable witness.

"He saw what happened out there. He saw Adams reach down toward the bed of the wagon and he saw that Everett Hardeman did not reach for his pistol until Adams made his move. He also saw the shotgun in the bed of the wagon after Adams had been shot. And you heard Sheriff Ellison testify that there was blood in the bed of the wagon where Ash Maitland saw the shotgun, but no blood on the shotgun that was found over the doorway. And the sheriff acknowledged that there was dried blood on the shotgun that was found in the well house. Adolph Gruning, the gunsmith, testified that it looked like that shotgun had been lying in a pool of blood.

"It is clear what happened. After the shooting, the boys, probably with George, the eldest, in the lead, took their father's bloodstained shotgun from the bed of the wagon and hid it in the wall of the well house, then took their shotgun and placed it over the doorway, so that there would be no evidence that their father had been reaching for his shotgun when Everett Hardeman shot him. So that there would be no evidence that he was shot in self-defense. In order to make their father look good and in order to get Everett Hardeman for shooting him.

"And you heard Constable Quill Stagner testify that he found the bloodstained shotgun in the well house wall and it took a long time to find it. The prosecution did not look for it, of course, because they were hell-bent on getting Ev Hardeman convicted. But you will recall that Sheriff Ellison did not arrest Everett Hardeman that Easter Sunday, because, as he said, he wasn't sure he would be indicted. That's because he had heard Ashley Maitland, who is a believable, trustworthy witness, say that Adams was reaching for his shotgun before Ev Hardeman reached for his pistol.

"When you consider all of the evidence, it is clear that Everett Hardeman shot in self-defense and that he is not guilty. But the judge has told you in his charge that if you have a reasonable doubt as to the defendant's guilt, you must find him not guilty. So you don't have to be certain that it was self-defense. This is not a perfect world, as we all know.

And it is not up to the defendant to prove he is not guilty. It is up to the State of Texas to prove his guilt beyond a reasonable doubt. That is a rule of law and of our constitution that protects us all from tyranny, and it is not to be taken lightly.

"Finally, let me say to you that I apologize for my youth. I hope that I have not offended any of you for speaking bluntly about the evidence in this case. It is my duty to do so, and I do not mean to be presumptuous about my age and relative lack of experience. I trust that you will do the right thing by Everett Hardeman and our society by finding a verdict of not guilty in this case, based on the evidence. Thank you."

Will returned to the counsel table and took his seat. Singleton slowly rose from his chair and approached the jury box. He stood quite erect, holding the lapels of his coat in both hands.

"The defense in this case would have you convict Gilbert Adams of wife-beating. But he is not on trial here today. He can never be here again, because this man," pointing to Ev Hardeman, "took his life away from him last Easter Sunday. He is the absent voice here. He is not here to defend himself. I think if he was here, he would tell you that any discipline he administered to his unfaithful wife was necessary and reasonable, because he had caught her being unfaithful to him and to their marriage, a marriage which the church and society regards as holy wedlock. And how did she and this defendant honor that holy pact? By sneaking around and engaging in adultery, a sin before God.

"But Gilbert Adams is not on trial here today. This man," again pointing at Hardeman, "is on trial, and the evidence is clear that he threatened to kill Gilbert Adams and did so in cold blood. He left Mrs. Moore's house, some four miles away from the Adams place, after vowing to kill Adams and that is exactly what he did, without any warning. No words passed between them. He merely pulled his pistol and shot an unarmed man.

"But the defendant would have you believe that he shot in self-defense because Gilbert Adams was reaching for a shotgun, in spite of the fact that no shotgun was found in the Adams wagon afterwards, when the sheriff arrived. But think about it, gentlemen. Everett Hardeman could not see into the bed of the Adams wagon and it is undisputed that Gilbert Adams did not have a weapon in his hands when he was shot. The defense would have you believe that a small gesture, a slight movement, is all it takes for a shooter to be shooting in self-defense. Well, it certainly takes more than that to establish self-defense. When you read the judge's charge you will see that he tells you that the law requires a plain manifestation of felonious intent to be reasonably perceived by the defendant. That means that Hardeman had to see a plain movement with a weapon. That's all that can mean. But there was no weapon. Ashley Maitland, the defendant's lawyer, is the only witness to this *movement* they are relying on. The *defendant's lawyer.* From a distance away from the wagon. What kind of movement was it? Ashley Maitland may be a credible witness in a case where he is not involved on behalf of one of the parties, but he can hardly be considered credible in this case. Besides, if Gilbert Adams was making any movement at all, he may have been merely laying down his reins or reaching for the brake pole on the wagon. There was no clear sign that he was reaching for a weapon, even if there was a shotgun in the bed of the wagon and, remember, one of the defendant's lawyers was on the Adams place when the other shotgun was found. How convenient that was! There was no plain manifestation of felonious intent on the part of Gilbert Adams, no evidence that he had a weapon and was threatening to use it against this defendant. This was an intentional killing. It was murder with malice. It was a killing that was intended to eliminate Gilbert Adams as an obstacle to this man's illicit desires towards Mrs. Adams. He was seen at the Adams place numerous times when Mr. Adams was not at home. There is no doubt what he was doing there. And Ada Adams admitted that Hardeman asked her to divorce her husband, so she could marry him. Why didn't she divorce her husband? I submit to you that she did not divorce Gilbert Adams because she had no grounds for divorce. Her husband is the one who had grounds for divorce. Adultery is grounds for divorce in Texas. He had grounds, but she did not. That is why Gilbert Adams was killed.

"Remember what Ev Hardeman said during this trial, at Friedman's Saloon just last week. Gilbert Adams needed killing. He needed killing, gentleman, because Gilbert Adams was in the way. He stood between this defendant and the object of his adulterous desires, his lust for Adams's wife. Everett Hardeman murdered Gilbert Adams in cold blood, in front of his two sons, in broad daylight. He is guilty of murder in the first degree, and I ask that you return that as your verdict in order that justice be done. Thank you for your attention."

As Singleton returned to his seat at the counsel table, the jury's eyes were on the defendant, who sat beside his lawyers, looking down.

TWENTY-SEVEN

WILL, ASH, AND EV HARDEMAN WERE WAITING FOR THE verdict at Friedman's Saloon. Ash had informed the bailiff where they would be, so that he could notify them when the jury announced that they had reached a verdict. Judge Daughtry often joined the lawyers at Friedman's while waiting for a verdict, but this time he did not issue an invitation from the bench, instead telling them that they should let the bailiff know where they would be waiting. Clark said he and Singleton would be waiting in Clark's office. Ash merely nodded at the gray-haired bailiff, who was used to notifying him of verdicts at Friedman's. No words were needed.

They sat down at the round "home" table in the back, where Friedman's friends and regulars gathered. It was early afternoon. and no one else was there. Friedman was not in the saloon. He was usually in the general store up front until after business hours. The bartender poured whiskeys for them and they downed their shots without speaking. Ash gestured to the bartender to bring another round. The quiet of the afternoon in the saloon was unusual, and each man seemed to be unwilling to break the silence.

Will was going over in his mind the details of his final argument, when Ev finally spoke.

"I should have testified," he said.

Will and Ash exchanged a look.

"How long have I known you, Everett?" Ash asked.

"I guess all my life."

"That's right. And I knew your father well before you came into this world. Lawyer McCulloch and I have given you our best advice about that, and this is no time to be second-guessing."

The bartender came with the bottle and poured another round. Ev downed his shot immediately.

"How long do you think they'll be out?" he asked.

"No telling," Ash replied. "But I expect them to be out for a while."

They sat and drank for another hour, then returned to the courtroom, where the bailiff sat with his ear to the door of the jury room. He straightened up quickly when he saw them enter the courtroom. Ash walked over to him.

"How's it going in there, Mr. Bailiff?" he asked.

"It's been pretty loud most of the time," the bailiff replied. "But it's gotten real quiet recently."

They took their seats at the counsel table and sat quietly for a long time. For the first time, Will could hear the clock at the back of the courtroom ticking. The sound seemed to emphasize the slow pace of time passing. He had sat with Ash waiting for juries before, but this time the wait was painful. After what seemed like an hour, there was a loud bang on the jury door, which startled all three of them. Ev jumped to his feet. The bailiff opened the door and leaned inside, then shut it and turned the key in the lock.

"They've reached a verdict," he said. "I'll notify the judge and the district attorney."

He walked through the door to the hallway. Ev was looking down at his boots, his shoulders slumped. Ash looked at the clock.

"It took 'em three and a half hours," he said.

Judge Daughtry entered through the hallway door and made his way to the bench. Clark and Singleton soon followed and took their seats at the prosecution counsel table. The judge looked down at the lawyers and Ev, a solemn expression on his face.

"Gentlemen, I understand that we have a verdict. Do counsel have anything to bring up before the court before we bring the jury in?"

Clark and Will both said, "No, Your Honor."

"Very well. Bring them in, Mr. Bailiff."

The bailiff opened the door to the jury room and leaned in. The jury filed in and took their seats in the jury box. The former Gonzales County deputy was seated last, in the near chair on the front row, and carried the court's charge with him.

"Mr. Slade, it appears that you are the foreman," the judge said.

The man stood.

"That's right, Your Honor," he said.

"Have you reached a verdict?" the judge asked.

"We have, Your Honor," Slade replied.

"Please state your verdict," the judge said.

"We find the defendant guilty of manslaughter," Slade replied.

The courtroom was completely silent. Ev was staring down at his left hand, which he held in a tight fist on the counsel table.

"Is that the verdict of all of you? You may signify by saying 'aye' or 'nay.'"

The jurors said "aye" in unison.

"Very well, gentlemen. The jury is hereby discharged with the thanks of the court. You will each be getting a small check in the mail for your service. You are now free to leave."

They left the jury box, returned to the jury room for their coats and hats, and soon filed out of the courtroom. The judge then turned to counsel.

"The defendant has elected to have the court pass sentence," he said. "You may request time for argument or I can pass sentence now, gentlemen. How do you wish to proceed?"

Singleton began to rise from his seat, but Clark stopped him by grabbing his arm. He then stood.

"The state is ready for sentencing by the court," Clark said.

"What say you, Mr. McCulloch?"

"The defendant is ready, Your Honor," Will replied.

"Very well. The defendant will stand and be sentenced."

Will, Ash, and Ev stood.

"Everett Hardeman," the judge said. "You have been found guilty by a jury of your peers of manslaughter, for which the punishment is confinement in the state penitentiary for a term of not less than two nor more than five years. Do you have anything to say to the court before sentence is passed against you?"

"No, Your Honor," Ev replied.

"Very well. The court hereby sentences you to confinement in the state penitentiary at Huntsville for a term of four years. The bailiff will summon the sheriff and you will remain in the courtroom until the sheriff has taken you into custody to be transported to the state penitentiary. Are there any questions, counsel?'

"No, Your Honor," Clark and Will responded simultaneously.

"Court is adjourned," the judge said.

TWENTY-EIGHT

IT WAS AFTER TEN WHEN WILL RETURNED HOME, BUT HIS mother was waiting up for him. She had kept supper warm for him in the warming bin of the kitchen woodstove. He had not eaten anything all day and attacked the plate with abandon. Laura sat quietly and watched him eat. She knew her son well. He would tell her what he wanted her to know in his own good time. After he had finished, he told her about the verdict and sentence and Ev's quiet reaction to it. She had not seen Everett Hardeman since the ball at the Menger, five and a half years earlier, and she asked how he looked.

"How does he look? Tired, I guess. We're all pretty worn out."

"I can see that you are. I'll let you sleep in the morning."

"I have to get up early. I have something to do tomorrow."

She knew what he meant.

He arrived at the Moore place around eight the next morning. It was a cold morning, and smoke was pouring from the kitchen chimney when he rode up. Mattie admitted him into the living room.

"They's in the kitchen, Mr. McCulloch. Miz Moore said for you to go on in."

Mrs. Moore and Ada were seated around the kitchen table.

"Good morning, Billy," Mrs. Moore said. "We heard about the verdict. Mattie told us. The news made it to Luling last night. Won't you sit and have some coffee? Have you had breakfast?"

“I’ve had breakfast, but I could stand a cup of coffee.”

“When can I see him?” Ada asked.

“Anytime. The sheriff has not limited visits to him.”

“Then I’ll get dressed and go right away,” she said. “Is he well?”

“Well as can be expected. He’s been drinking quite a bit, Ada.”

“I know,” she said. “Will he have to serve the whole four years?”

“He will have to.”

The morning light was shining through the east window onto her face, revealing lines he had not noticed before.

“It won’t be as long as you think,” he said.

“You know how long I waited before,” she said.

“It won’t be that long.”

He took a seat at the table as Ada left the room. Mrs. Moore sat and looked at him while Mattie poured him a cup of coffee.

“What was the verdict, exactly?” she asked.

“Manslaughter.”

“What does manslaughter mean?”

“The legal definition?”

“Of course not. You know what I want to know. Is it a kind of murder?”

“It means a killing without malice, which really means in the heat of passion.”

“In the heat of passion,” she repeated.

“Yes. Without thinking clearly.”

“Meaning accidental?”

“Not exactly.”

She had known him all his life. He felt uncomfortable with her, as if she thought he was trying to hide the truth from her, the same as when he was a boy.

“He won’t be a convicted murderer,” he said.

“I think Ada will marry him,” she said. “Then they’ll move away, up north. I’ll never see her again.”

“I don’t know about that. Maybe they’ll stay around here. He’s lost his job with the railroad, but he can find work.”

“From what I know about Everett Hardeman, he won’t want to come back here,” she said. “He didn’t come back after the war. For years.”

He had finished his coffee when Ada returned, dressed in a light blue dress that matched her eyes.

"Are you going to Lockhart?" she asked.

"I am," he said, standing.

"I would like for you to accompany me," she said.

Felix already had the mules hitched to the wagon. Will tied Julie on behind and drove the team, sitting next to Ada on the wagon seat. The road was rough, and she was quiet for the first few miles. She grasped his arm a couple of times as they went over low spots. She was thin and fragile. She had the same good looks as before, but she lacked vitality. When they were growing up, Ada had always been full of energy and optimism.

"I'm sorry you had to go through all this," he said.

She kept staring at the road ahead.

"I'll be all right," she said.

"Your mother thinks you'll marry Ev after he gets out and you'll move up north."

"If he'll have me. And I'll go where he goes."

When the wagon pulled up in front of the jail, he stepped down and reached up to give her a hand, but she was staring at the crude stone building and did not see his gesture at first. When she finally took his hand and he helped her down, she wavered and almost fell. He held the door to the jail office open for her. They entered a large room with filing cabinets, desks and chairs, and a locked gun rack on the wall by the door. He asked the jailer if they might use the sheriff's office, a small room just off the main office. Indicating the sheriff had authorized it, the jailer led them to the room, which contained a desk and four chairs and was dimly lit by a small, barred window. Ada's hands shook as they waited for the jailer to bring Ev in from his cell. It was unusual for a prisoner to be allowed outside the barred cell block in the rear of the jail, but the jailer brought him into the sheriff's office, unshackled. As soon as he stepped inside the room, Ada stood and embraced him. They held each other as Will looked on.

"I'll come out with you, Seth," he said to the jailer, following him through the doorway.

Ev held onto Ada for a long time after the door was shut. Ada, her arms around his neck, was crying, her face against his shoulder.

“I should have divorced him,” she said. “You were right. I should have divorced him.”

“I got off light,” he said. “I didn’t sleep last night and I been thinking. I can do four years standing on my head. Don’t worry.”

“I didn’t sleep either,” she said. “I can’t bear to think of you in prison.”

“Will you wait for me?”

“Of course. I’ll wait for you, this time. And I’ll come to see you, if they’ll let me.”

“The jailer says they have visiting days, but I’ll be in Huntsville. That’s a long way from here.”

“I’ll come every time they’ll let me,” she said.

“No, you won’t,” he said. “But I’ll see a lot of you. I know that.”

“I should have divorced him. Billy said I had grounds. I should have talked to him or Ash about it.”

“It’s all right,” he said. “It’s all right. I’ll be out before you know it. And I think they got it right. The jury. They got it right.”

They spent an hour together. When Ada opened the door, Will and the jailer were sitting at one of the desks with Sheriff Ellison. All three men rose from their seats when she entered the room. Although it was obvious she had been crying, she was smiling and her eyes had brightened. She walked over to the sheriff.

“I want to thank you, Mr. Ellison, for your kindness to Everett.”

“Don’t mention it, ma’am,” the sheriff said.

“I’m ready to go home now,” she said to Will, then turned to Ev. “I’ll be here tomorrow,” she said.

On the way back to Mrs. Moore’s house, Will explained that Ev’s sentence would not commence until he was signed in at Huntsville, and that every day he stayed in jail would delay his release from prison. She agreed that Will could tell the sheriff after her visit the following day that he could transport his prisoner to Huntsville as soon as he was ready. Three days later, a deputy accompanied him to Luling to board the train to Huntsville, by way of Houston. She was there to say goodbye at the station.

TWENTY-NINE

THREE WEEKS AFTER THE VERDICT, WILL RECEIVED A TELEGRAM.

Will be in S. Antonio on the 29th inst.
Dinner at the Menger on the 2nd at 8 p.m.
Independence Day. You and Baker boys join me.
Hays.

He had heard nothing from Colonel Hays since Hays had returned to California in the summer of 1870. He decided to ride to Wonsley's place to tell him. He crossed the river at Sam's Ford and took the Gander Slough road the remaining two miles to the wooden gate at the edge of Wonsley's pasture, then down the lane through the pasture, where mixed breed cattle grazed around him as he rode to the high place above the river where Wonsley had built his small cabin. The front door to the cabin was open. Will dismounted, tied his horse to a porch post, stepped up to the doorway, and leaned inside.

The single room of the cabin was dimly lit with late afternoon light from the open doorway. A pot-bellied iron stove stood in the middle of the room, trash around it on the floor. A small table beside two straight wooden chairs was cluttered with empty, dirty plates and an assortment of dirty cups, knives, and forks. A wooden single bed against the wall was covered with dirty sheets and blankets. A sad, bare pillow lay askew at the edge of the bed.

Will turned and walked around the corner of the cabin toward the river. The path led downward into a lower bottom which was overgrown with blood weeds and Johnson grass. He found Wonsley at the river's bank sitting on a cypress root, leaning against the trunk of the tree, a cane pole held loosely in his hand with its butt end lodged in the fork of two tree roots. He had been asleep, but he had heard Will approach and was grinning at him as he walked up.

"So the lawyer visits the country bumpkin," he said, his even teeth showing in his smile.

"I have some good news," Will said. "Got a telegram here. Guess who from."

Wonsley's smile vanished.

"I don't know," he said. "But wires don't usually bring good news."

"This one does. It's from Colonel Hays."

Wonsley quickly stood up.

"You're kidding me," he said. "And it's good news, not bad?"

"He wants us to join him in San Antone for dinner at the Menger."

"Damn." Wonsley's face was alive. He took his cap off. "Colonel Hays. He's still kickin'."

"He's asking me, you, and Uncle John."

"Damn."

Later, Wonsley followed him back downriver to John Baker's place, where they found John and Susan Baker sitting on the front porch. John seemed happy about receiving the news. Susan was quiet. After discussing the details, they agreed to meet at Luling on the second, where they would take the train to the end of the line at Marion and a coach the rest of the way into San Antonio. The railroad was still under construction west of Marion, which lay twenty-five miles east of San Antonio. They did not discuss who else might be invited to the dinner.

Wonsley was uncharacteristically quiet during the train ride to Marion and in the coach into San Antonio, staring out the window at the rolling countryside, his feet propped up on the empty seat opposite him. Watching the scrub brush pass by outside, Will thought of Gruder and a cold feeling ran through him. He remembered Hays seating Gruder at the head table at the dinner and ball in '70 and he could not imagine that he would not have invited him to dinner along with the others. The coach followed the winding dirt street to the front of the Menger. He looked around for Gruder, but did not see him. Will would have expected that if he had been invited, he would have ridden horseback to San Antonio and would be meeting them at the front door of the hotel. Instead, a black porter, a thin old man with gray hair, took their bags off the top of the coach before they had stepped down and stood holding them and slightly bowing until they had entered the doorway, then carried the luggage in. They tipped him when he set their bags down at the front desk. The old man said, "Thank you, suh" to each of them, standing stooped over and peering over his gold spectacles.

John Baker had a separate room. Will and Wonsley shared one. When they were checking in, John asked the desk clerk if Colonel Hays was registered. He replied that he was indeed, but was out at the moment. They agreed to meet in the bar after they had settled in their rooms. Will asked the desk clerk to let Colonel Hays know they were in the bar if he came in. Hays walked into the bar when they were ordering their second round.

He looked older. The gray streaks in his beard had broadened. He wore a black suit with a vest and string tie, much like the one he had worn at the ball years before. He greeted them all warmly and ordered a whiskey, then sat down to join them at a round table near the outside door. They exchanged news and a few personal stories. John Baker told Hays that Will was now a practicing attorney who had dropped his boyhood name. Wonsley, at John's urging, shared some stories about his time with McNelly's Rangers in the Nueces strip. None of them asked Hays what he was doing in San Antonio. Will figured he would tell them what he wanted them to know in his own good time, as always, although he seemed to show more interest in what they were telling him than he did during the chase after Morgan and the girl. He even smiled at some of Wonsley's anecdotes about McNelly, saying that he had never met him, but had heard of him. After a pause in the conversation, he looked down at his glass before speaking.

"I have come back here to see my niece," he said. "And I've just been to see her. She's doing well."

"Glad to hear it," John Baker said, glancing at Wonsley, who briefly met his glance.

"Doing quite well in school. A college student. She'll be joining us for dinner tonight."

"It's good that she's doing well," John said. "I understand Wonsley has seen her a few times in the last couple of years."

"She mentioned that," Hays said. "She said Mr. Baker here was quite a gentleman and had been very kind to her."

Wonsley stared at his glass.

"It will be good to see her again," Will said. "I haven't seen her since the night of the ball here at the Menger."

"I've reserved a private room for our dinner so we won't be disturbed," Hays said.

They agreed to meet him at the room on the second floor at eight. He said he had arranged for Martha to be brought to the hotel in a carriage and that she should be arriving around that time. They split up after leaving the bar. John Baker said he was going to take a nap during the two-hour wait. Wonsley and Will decided to go for a walk.

It was a breezy day. They walked down Commerce Street across the bridge past rows of Lone Star flags posted on the fronts of buildings. At the edge of the gravel street the ditches were covered with alternating patches of wildflowers—bluebonnets and Indian blankets and wild onions. The wooden sidewalks had stalks of grass growing through the cracks along the edges where foot traffic was light. There were more stone buildings than Will remembered. They passed St. Mary's Street without speaking. At Main Plaza a wooden stage had been built, a crowd of people gathered around it. Will and Wonsley walked up to the rear of the crowd. After a few minutes, a man appeared at the front edge of the stage and raised his arms for quiet. The people in the crowd gradually stopped their chatter.

"Our Most Honorable Judge Lewis is our next speaker. We all know him and he needs no introduction, so welcome . . . Judge Henry Lewis."

There was a smattering of applause and a portly man with long gray sideburns emerged from the rear of the stage and took a wide stance front and center, his hands grasping the lapels of his gray coat. He looked over the crowd before speaking.

He spoke in a low voice about heroism and sacrifice, the past as a book to open and learn from, of destiny and faith, gesturing dramatically, like an actor in a travelling show. The heroes of Texas should be revered and emulated, he said, referring to them in intimate terms, as if he had known them.

"How shall we make this day acceptable to them and serviceable to ourselves? Shall I tell you? By consecrating ourselves to their firm purposes and their high resolves; by avowing this day that the ends we aim at shall be our country's, our God's, and truth's. Let us strike hands with them and pledge ourselves to love the truth and seek it, to learn the right and do it, and, however wealth may tempt or popular applause allure, to be the sole rulers of her own free speech, masters of our own untrammeled thoughts, captains of our own unfettered souls. In this spirit, to those ends, may we worthily celebrate this day."

Another smattering of applause. Wonsley gave Will a look. Will shrugged his shoulders. The man caught his breath before continuing. Will and Wonsley turned and walked away.

"I think we've heard enough," Will said.

"Yep," Wonsley replied. They had both heard Texas Independence Day speeches before.

On the south side of the plaza, at the corner of Soledad and Commerce, they passed the two-story building that had been the Cosmopolitan Bar. A large sign on the front of the building proclaimed it as Jack Harris's Saloon and Vaudeville Theatre. They stopped for a moment and looked in the front doorway, then continued east on Commerce until they came to the intersection with St. Mary's Street. Gas street lighting had been installed since that June night in 1870, and they could see down the street to the lighted bridge. Without saying anything, they turned and walked to the edge of the bridge, stopped, and stood there looking across it.

"It's been over five years," Will said. "A lot of water under this bridge since then."

He was standing at the spot where Ephraim McLane had fallen. He half-expected to see blood in the gravel in the light from the street lamp. Memories came flooding back to him. The walk from the Menger with the three women and Wonsley. The man at the other end of the bridge in the moonlight, standing defiantly in the middle of the street, hands at his sides. The quick shot he had made. The sound of the gunfire. He felt for his Remington in its holster at his side reflexively, as if his unconscious mind wanted reassurance because of the place and the atmosphere. It was a cooler night than that June night many years ago, and there was no moon, as there had been then, but the light from the street lamps recreated the scene in his mind.

"You did good with that shot," Wonsley said.

For some reason, Will thought of Eli Baker, his grandfather, now in his seventies and becoming less mobile every day, and the day his grandfather had shown him the Plum Creek battlefield. It puzzled him that he would think of that here, in this place. He thought of McLane following them from the Menger that night; he learned afterwards that he had done it on his own and that Hays had not put him up to it.

They walked across the bridge to the other side. The cattails that had grown up beside the bridge had been cut, and buildings had been built along the street on the north side, where there had been a pecan orchard. It did not look the same.

"Kind of makes you feel funny, doesn't it?" Wonsley said. "It's the place, but it's different."

"Yeah. It's the place, all right."

They got back to the Menger just in time to wash up at the washstand in their room before going down the hall to meet Hays and Martha for dinner.

"How does she look?" Will asked.

"She looked real good the last time I saw her," Wonsley replied, awaiting his turn at the wash basin.

"You saw her in January? When you came back from South Texas?"

"Yep. She looked good."

When they reached the room where the dinner would be, John Baker and Hays were alone, sitting at a round table in the center of the room. The room was elaborately decorated, with paintings of Texas landscapes on the wall. Six ladder-back chairs with cane seats were placed around the table. A bar had been set up in the corner, tended by a black bartender wearing a white jacket. Gas lanterns lit the room well. A large candelabrum was centered on the table.

Hays and John Baker stood to shake hands with them. Hays asked what they were drinking and invited them to step up to the bar. They chose glasses of local lager, which the bartender poured for them from a pitcher.

"John here's been telling me about your trial," Hays said after they were seated. "He's very proud of you."

"I told what I knew. But you didn't tell me the whole story on the train," John Baker said.

"It could have turned out worse," Will said. "The main thing is Everett Hardeman will be a free man in a few years."

"You still practice with your pistol?" Hays asked.

"I haven't been, no. Not much."

"Better keep that practice up," Hays said. "I don't think we've achieved civilization yet. It's coming, but it's not here yet."

They turned toward a sound from the doorway. Martha entered, wearing a green dress that accented her red hair. She was followed by Gruder, who was dressed in his Sunday best. The four men at the table stood when she entered. She was captivatingly beautiful, entering the room with an air of confidence.

"Gentlemen, you may remember my niece, Martha," Hays said, approaching her and extending his hand.

"Amazing," said John Baker. "I can't believe how grown up you are."

"Thank you, sir," she said, smiling broadly. "Hello, Wonsley," she said, turning to him and extending her gloved hand. He took her hand lightly in his.

"And this is Billy," she said. "The lawyer."

"Yes," Will said.

"Only now he goes by Will," Wonsley said.

Gruder had remained by the doorway, a black hat in his hand. Will walked over to him as the others made a place for Martha at the table.

"I'm glad you're here," he said. "I forgot to tell you about this."

"Captain Hays sent me a wire," he said. "First one I ever got. He arranged a room for me at a colored establishment just around the corner."

"Shall we visit the bar?" Will asked. He had not seen Gruder drink whiskey since they had been on the trail together. Gruder smiled a knowing smile.

"Don't mind if I do," he said, following Will to the bar. The bartender nodded a greeting to him. They ordered shots of bourbon, which the bartender poured. They then joined the others at the table. Martha was telling the others about her school experiences. She turned to Will as he sat down.

"I want to hear about the famous murder trial," she said. "I've heard you were quite something in the courtroom."

"I did all right," he said.

"Better than all right," Wonsley said. "I wasn't there in the courtroom, but I heard about it."

"You must be the youngest lawyer to ever be in a murder trial," Martha said. "I'm proud of you."

"We all are," John Baker said.

He gave them a brief version of how the trial went. How he and the constable found the other shotgun. The help Ash gave him. How he felt the verdict was a close thing that represented a compromise.

"From what I heard, the man needed killin'," Wonsley said.

Dinner was served, and they continued discussing what each had been doing since that night at the Menger and the aftermath, except for Hays, who said he had nothing to report. Martha said that was surprising to her.

"I read that you were sheriff of San Francisco County out in California," she said.

"That was long ago," he said. "I'm just a banker and stockman now."

"And that you surveyed the plan for the city of Oakland."

"That's true. It was a long time ago. Oakland's quite a city now."

After dinner and cordials, Martha said she had to be going. She had classes the next day. Gruder was to take her home, and before she got up to go, she took Will's hand in hers.

"I'm so happy to have seen you again," she said. "I hope it's not so long 'til next time."

After she left, the men stayed and drank for another hour. Hays talked more than he ever had before in their presence. He talked about how California was growing too fast for the water supply, how the railroad had made Oakland a commercial center, with warehouse after warehouse near the terminus at the edge of the bay; and the clustering of people in the cities, like the cities of the east. He said he had heard reports that the plains were littered with buffalo bones and that the great herds of the past had been obliterated, with only a few left in preserves in Canada and on Charles Goodnight's ranch. And that the last great Comanche war chief, Quanah Parker, had surrendered in Oklahoma over a year ago, unable to feed his people.

"Civilization is not here yet, gentlemen," he said. "But it's coming. They tell me the railroad will be here in San Antonio before long, and it's only a matter of time until it hooks up with California. There's already the central route. And with civilization, old ways will die out. Some good. Some bad. It's the way of things."

"The railroad has been good for farming and ranching," John Baker said.

"Moving goods to market is a good thing all right," Hays said. "And having nice store-bought clothes is certainly a good thing."

"But there's sure a lot of people gettin' off that train," Wonsley said. "There won't be no more wilderness in a few years."

"The Indians saw it coming," Hays said. "The Comanche lived off the land. They didn't spoil it for anyone else."

"Barbed wire. I've heard it's coming, too," Will said. "There will be fences everywhere. I heard about a demonstration here in San Antone by a fellow named Gates, from Illinois. You buy it in rolls and staple it to cedar posts. It'll close off the range."

"I can't see it," Wonsley said. "I kind of like things the way they've been."

"Well, get ready," Hays said. "Things are going to keep changing. I'm leaving for Galveston tomorrow, and I go from there to New Orleans on business. There's a railroad across Panama now, and I'll take a ship from New Orleans to Panama, then a train across to the Pacific and a ship to San Francisco. Won't even have to get my boots dusty. The next time I visit, I expect to be able to travel by train across the desert."

After they retired to their rooms, Will had trouble getting to sleep. He kept thinking about Martha.

THIRTY

EVERETT HARDEMAN HAD BEEN IN THE HARRIS COUNTY JAIL for three weeks, waiting for transportation to Huntsville. Ned Allen, the deputy who had accompanied him from Luling to Houston on the train, had told him it might be awhile before the Harris County sheriff would transport him to the state penitentiary. He was told he had to wait until there were enough prisoners from Harris County to justify the trip.

"We ain't goin' to send a man up there just for you," one of the jailers finally told him after a week had passed. "There's plenty comin' out of the courts here, though. You shouldn't have to wait long."

Two more weeks had passed and now he was part of a group of five that was loaded onto a train from a siding adjacent to the jail, four of the five men chained together in pairs. He was the solo, due to his one arm. The pairs were chained, hands and feet, to the seats in the rear of the last passenger car, which was otherwise empty. He was chained by his left wrist in a seat in front of the others. Two black prisoners were one of the pairs chained together in the rear. The one deputy accompanying the prisoners sat in the last row across the aisle from them, a shotgun across his lap. It was not possible for the prisoners to reach him due to their constraints. They were told they were not to talk among themselves and were only to talk to the deputy if they needed water, which he would provide from a canteen he carried. He did not carry a canteen for the blacks.

The trip took two hours. When it reached the station yard at Phelps, the car was disconnected on a siding, then connected to an engine that would haul it on the Huntsville Branch Railway, also known as Tilley's Tap, eight miles farther to the station between downtown Huntsville and Austin College, and the penitentiary. There, a prison van pulled by two mules was waiting for the train, along with the mule driver and three prison guards dressed in dark-blue uniforms. The deputy who had accompanied them was relieved of duty and was free to spend the night in Huntsville until the morning train back to Houston.

"I'm going to see the town tonight, boys," he said, leaning into the rear door of the van after they had been loaded in. "Hate to say it, but I'm going to have a better time than you will."

One of the guards rode up front with the driver. The other two stood on the tailgate, outside the barred door at the rear of the van. They jostled down a slight incline over a dirt road. Seated on benches built into the side walls of the van, the prisoners could see through the back door, but not to the side or ahead. Ev looked at the faces of the other men. But for the chains, they could have been out on a hunt together. Each of them was looking out the back door at the receding roadway without showing any concern for their destination. One, an older black man with graying temples, wore a slight smile, as if he had been along that road before.

After what seemed like a half hour, the van came to a jostling halt and was still for a few moments, then started up again as they passed through the gate in the wall of the prison. The brick walls in the "Walls Unit," as it was known, ranged in height from fifteen to twenty-two feet, with an average thickness of three feet. They could see the iron gate in the wall closing behind them as the van came to a stop in the prison yard. The two guards in back jumped down and opened the door, then gestured for the prisoners to get out. They jumped out two at a time, as if used to doing it, then Ev followed clumsily. He was not used to fetters, as the others seemed to be. The chains connected at his ankles were just long enough for a short step, but too short to allow running. The guards lined them up by twos and marched them across the empty prison yard, with Ev bringing up the rear. They were then herded into a room where the manacles and fetters were removed and they were made to stand at attention in line, where a prison official wearing sergeant's stripes and carrying a walking cane strode in front of them, staring into their faces with a scowl.

"I recognize most of you," he said in a gruff voice. "Those of you who are here for the first time ought to know what the others already know. To get along here and avoid trouble, you gotta work and obey the guards. Escape attempts will be punished, and you won't like the punishment. If you shirk or don't mind, you will be put in a dark hole and you won't like it. Do something worse and you'll be whipped and you won't like it. And there's no talking among yourselves. You will speak only when you're spoken to."

He paused at the end of the line of men and pointed at Ev's pinned right sleeve.

"What in the hell are you gonna be able to do with that?" he asked.

"I can read and write and do figures," Ev replied.

"Oh? Well, there ain't much of a call for that kind of work here. I don't guess you can do any paper hanging, can you? Not much of a call for a one-armed paper hanger is there, boys?" He turned to the guards, laughing. They laughed in response. "We'll find something for you to do. Now all of you get along by that window and we'll get your information."

Each of them came up to a Dutch door with the top half open, where a prisoner trusty wrote down the information about each of them given him by one of the guards, who held a clipboard with sheets attached. Each was asked to confirm the information given, which included name, date of birth, the crime of which each was convicted, and the sentence, as well as the county of conviction. Ev was the last one to pass by the window. The trusty looked at him after receiving the information and writing it down on a sheet of paper.

"First time, huh?" he asked.

Ev nodded, then moved on behind the others in line. They were taken to a barbershop, where a prison barber gave each of them a burr haircut. Then they were herded to a shower room, where they were made to undress and take cold showers. Bars of lye soap were furnished. A trusty then handed each of them striped pants and shirts, giving some thought to proper fit. They were then made to wait while another trusty sewed numbered patches on their shirts. The guard with the clipboard checked the shirts after they had been handed back to the new prisoners. Prison-made shoes were given them. After they were dressed, they were marched down several corridors to the mess hall, where they were given a meal of beans and cornbread. Twenty minutes was the standard time for meals. When time was up, they were marched to four-by-eight cells. Ev was placed in a cell with an older man, who did not speak and looked his way only briefly as he entered. It was furnished with two metal bunk beds, two buckets, and a metal wash basin. The mattress and pillow were stuffed with corn husks. As night fell, he lay awake in the upper bunk, contemplating his new surroundings. He had been in a Yankee prison during the war, but had been assigned by his doctor-mentor to help as an aide in the prison hospital as soon as he had the strength to walk. He had never been confined in a small cell before.

After dark, he could hear a faint rumbling sound coming from the cells around him. Each of the cells was separated from those adjoining it by concrete walls, but the other two walls in each were made up of bars. Each cellblock had three floors of cells in a row, like a rabbit warren. After a while, he realized that the rumbling was the sound from the voices of the prisoners, talking to each other. Although there was a guard on each floor of each cellblock, they were not enforcing the total silence rule. He could hear his cellmate moving below him and leaned over the edge of his bunk to look down. The old man's bare feet were visible beneath him, his legs hanging over the edge of his bunk. Then he spoke in a low voice.

"Hey," he said.

"Hey," Ev said in reply, looking down at the bare feet below.

"What's your name?" the man asked.

"Hardeman," he replied.

"Hard man, huh? That's a good one."

"What's yours?"

"Ike. They call me Ike. What's you in for?"

"I shot a man," Ev replied.

"Kill him?"

"Yes. I killed him."

"That's good. I ain't never killed nobody, but I robbed a few. That's what got me in here. Two times."

"Is it pretty tough in here?" Ev asked.

"Stick around, you'll find out," the man said with a low chuckle.

THIRTY-ONE

IT HAD BEEN A FULL DAY AT THE LAW OFFICE OF MAITLAND and McCulloch. Will had seen a number of clients in the anteroom while Ashley Maitland saw even more in the inner office. Ash had called him in to meet a roughly dressed older couple, the man wearing cotton jeans and a khaki shirt and the woman wearing a flour-sack dress. He introduced Will and then made it known that he was excused. Normally, when called into the inner office to meet clients, Will was expected to take them over, their cases being below a level of importance that Ash deemed worth his time, so it was puzzling that he had merely been called in to meet the old couple. Late in the day, after all were gone from the waiting room, he leaned into the inner office door. Ash gestured for him to enter, rose from his desk, and reached for the whiskey bottle on the bookshelf. After pouring two shot glasses, he returned and they both sat and sipped.

"You're probably wondering about Mr. and Mrs. Strong," he said.

"As a matter of fact," Will replied.

"Bee Strong is one of the biggest landowners in the county. He has an old ramshackle store out in the sand hills. Sells on credit and has taken deeds of trust on land as security. I'm sure he has his first earned dollar in a safe hiding place. Didn't convert to Confederate money during the war. Always thought gold coin was the only real money. So looks can be deceiving."

"I wondered," Will said.

"He's been very fair with his customers," Ash said. "He got deeds from those who couldn't pay. Only once did I have to foreclose on a deed of trust for him. And that was on a man who was a scoundrel. He's still carrying some war vets. There's no telling how much he's worth."

They talked about a few other clients until Will got around to what he wanted to say.

"I'm thinking about visiting the Alamo city," he said.

This drew a knowing smile from Ash. Will had mentioned Martha several times since the San Antonio visit in March.

"Someone you want to visit there?" he asked.

"Yes, there is. But there may be a problem."

"Oh?"

"I think Wonsley is sweet on her," Will said. "And I want to respect his feelings."

Ash leaned forward in his chair.

"Is he doing anything about it?"

"What do you mean?"

"Well, is he going over there and seeing the girl, or is he just sitting around out at his place?"

"As far as I can tell, he's not doing anything about it, but I haven't talked to him about it, either."

"Maybe you should," Ash said, staring at his shot glass.

It was dusk when Will rode onto Wonsley's place. As expected, Wonsley was sitting on the front porch of his cabin. He watched as Will rode up, then stood as he dismounted.

"Welcome, Lawyer McCulloch," he said with a smile. "What brings you way out here?"

Will stepped onto the porch before answering.

"I need to talk to you about something," he finally said.

"Then have a seat, cousin." Wonsley had always called him "cousin" rather than "nephew," which Will always took to be a compliment that spoke to the slight difference in their years. Will sat on the split log bench and Wonsley resumed his place in his rocker.

"I'll bet I know what you want to talk about," he said, upon taking his seat.

"You do?"

"It's about that red-headed girl, ain't it?"

"Well, yes."

"I'll tell you, Will. I was in love with that girl, but I've decided she's not the one for me. So you've got a clear field."

"You sure about that?"

"I'm sure. You see, I had this dream that she would want to come out here and live on this little place I got and be a farmer's wife, but that would never work. It just took me a while to figure that out, that's all. She's more likely to be a schoolteacher. Gettin' educated. I think she'd make a good lawyer's wife, if anybody's."

"Well, I find myself thinking about her a lot," Will said.

"I could see that in San Antone," Wonsley said. He reached for an earthen jug beside his chair, then handed it to Will. "Here. Let's drink on it."

Will took it, pulled the corn cob stopper out, couched the jug in the crook of his arm, and took a swig. It was moonshine and had quite a kick. He handed the jug back to Wonsley, who did the same. They sat for a while, looking at the darkening sky to the west.

"I didn't want to step on you," Will finally said.

"I know," Wonsley said. "I appreciate it."

THIRTY-TWO

ADA WAS SHOWN INTO THE VISITORS' ROOM BY A PORTLY guard, along with five other women. She was the youngest and best-dressed of the group. They were told to sit on one side of a long table that had a vertical plank down the middle and were warned that there was to be no touching between prisoner and visitor. They were made to wait fifteen minutes before she could hear the tramp of footsteps coming down an adjacent hallway. The steps were marching in unison, as if made by soldiers on parade. A moment flashed by from her memory of the first time she had seen Everett Hardeman, marching with his company at Camp Clark during the war. Then the men came in through the doorway, one by one, the five others first and finally Ev, who looked pale and worn, his hair shorn short and his shoulders bony under the cloth of his striped prison shirt. His beard, a stubble, showed a tinge of gray on the chin. His eyes had dark bags under them. She instinctively placed both hands on the sides of her face as he sat down without smiling, unable to hide her surprise at his appearance. He looked at her briefly as he took his seat, then looked down at his lap without speaking.

"Oh, Ev," she said. "What have they done to you?"

"Do I look that bad?" he asked, meeting her stare.

"Oh, I'm so sorry," she said. "I didn't mean to . . . "

"It's okay," he said, managing a tired smile. "It really hasn't been that bad. I guess my grooming habits here haven't been so good, but I'm all right."

It had taken her weeks to learn when he had been transferred to prison. She had written him before the transfer, but he had not received the letters. She finally wrote the warden and received a reply from a lesser official, who informed her that there would be no visits allowed during the first two months of confinement. It had therefore been three months since she had seen him board the train for Houston.

"You've lost weight," she said.

"Yeah, I was probably getting a little fat anyway," he replied. "How have you been?"

"Just fine," she said. She realized that tears were welling up in her eyes and she reached in her sleeve for her handkerchief.

"How is your mother?"

"She's well," she said, dabbing at her eyes.

"Ada, I can do this easy. I'm all right. If you go along with them it's not so bad here. They've given me the job of keeping track of production in the furniture factory here, so it's kind of like a job on the outside. Except you can't leave."

She noticed that his right sleeve was tied up with a piece of twine, rather than pinned as before. He noticed her looking at it.

"I've had a few jokes about one-armed paper hangers to put up with," he said. "But I can put up with that all right."

"They tell me I can visit once a month," she said. "I'll be here every time."

He looked down again before speaking.

"It might be better for you not to come so often," he said. "The trip must be hard on you and expensive. It must take a couple of days and nights."

"I've had some help," she said. "The expense is not a problem."

"Help? What kind of help?"

"Lily Poe has been helping me. She wants to come see you, too."

He smiled.

"Ah, Lily. She has been a good friend." He paused. "But I haven't seen her since before the trial. I wasn't sure she was still with me."

"I think Mr. Maitland had something to do with that," she said.

He nodded.

"That makes sense. He was trying to keep me away from bad influences."

"Is she a bad influence?" She smiled.

"She's been a good influence since I was a teenager," he replied, smiling again. "Look. These four years will pass quickly, and I'll be out in no time. You should take care of yourself."

"I'm going to wait for you," she said. "And I'm going to visit every chance I get."

"You don't have to do that. But it's great to see you."

The guard at the doorway said that time was up and the visitors were to remain seated until all the prisoners had left the room and they were told they could leave. They were reminded that there was to be no touching. Ev and Ada said a quick goodbye before the prisoners were commanded to stand and march out of the room, leaving the six women seated at their side of the table.

He had not told her of the stifling lack of ventilation in his cell, or the putrid beef in the stew served up for meals. Or that talk among prisoners was prohibited, but for the whispers in the cells at night and the occasional grumbling at work. There were other things he would never tell her. He had seen men in stocks in the prison yard. They were on display as a deterrent against further disobedience to the rules and the orders of the guards. The stocks were adjustable wooden contrivances in which a prisoner's head and hands were fixed in place at a point where the prisoner is made to stand on tiptoes, causing the pain from the position to increase over time. And there was the "horse" for more grievous offenses. It consisted of a wooden peg one inch in diameter driven at a right angle into a wooden post. The offending prisoner was placed astraddle the peg with his hands tied behind to the post and his ankles tied below, so that he could not touch the ground with his feet. This caused excruciating pain, which increased as time passed and often resulted in injuries to the testicles of the prisoner and sometimes in the loss of urinary function for a period of time. Everyone feared having to take a ride on the horse.

Whippings were also administered by the guards for even minor offenses, although most of these were done outside in the fields, where men were expected to work through fatigue and illness without stoppage or complaint. Work inside the walls was greatly preferred to field work. The worst of all was work on the railroads, where prisoners were "leased out" to railroad companies to work on construction. Almost all of the field hands and railroad workers were blacks, whom the prison authorities thought to be "conditioned" to the harsh work that these jobs entailed. He had noticed that the prison graveyard had several freshly covered graves in it. Most of these were said to be field hands and railroad workers.

He had not been fully forthcoming about his work, either. Being a one-armed man in prison made him unable to do much manual labor, so he had been assigned to assist a trusty in the furniture factory. He was able to hand tools and parts to workers as they required them, but he was also tasked with informing the trusty when men were lagging behind in their work. The trusty had the run of the factory wing and would leave him alone with the workers for long periods of time, during which he was expected to keep an eye on them. It took him some time to learn that he was in a position that drew hatred from the workers if he performed his job too well.

At least those working in the furniture factory were able to talk to each other when no guards were present. Enforced silence was something he had not thought of as being a burden, but after several weeks he realized that it caused him to be left with his thoughts too much, without the distraction of conversations, the whispered words exchanged with his cellmate notwithstanding. Several of the furniture workers had been put in solitary confinement in a small, dark cell, where the days and nights were indistinguishable and the only contact with the outside was twice a day when a wooden bowl of gruel and a cup of water was passed through a small opening in the door to the cell. Once placed in solitary, a man would obey without complaint to avoid going back there.

Marching down the hall from the visiting room, he felt as if he had already been there for years, rather than months. He had doubts as to whether he could survive until the end of his sentence.

THIRTY-THREE

WILL WALKED UP SOLEDAD STREET TO MRS. ELLIOT'S. He could scarcely believe it had been six years since he had last been there, after the services for Sister Rosella. He had written Martha about a visit, falsely indicating he had business in San Antonio anyway, and was excited when he received her reply that she would be pleased to see him on the Saturday evening he had suggested. Mrs. Elliot's maid, Rosa, met him at the front doorway and showed him into the front parlor. It was a hot June day. The late afternoon sun shone through lace curtains moving in the breeze over windows opening onto the street to the west. He declined the chair offered and stood looking at the sketches and photographs on the mantel until Martha came into the room wearing a light green summer dress. He had mentally rehearsed what he would say, but was speechless when he saw her.

"Well, Mr. McCulloch," she said, extending her hand. "It's a pleasure to see you again."

"The pleasure is all mine," he replied.

"Won't you sit down?" she asked, taking a chair by the windows. "It's more pleasant here in the breeze."

He took the chair opposite hers but was still unable to utter his rehearsed speech.

"How are things in your part of the world?" she asked after a somewhat embarrassing pause.

"It's pretty quiet right now," he replied. He realized that his palms were sweating. He had not been so nervous since his first court appearance.

"No recent shootings?" she asked.

"Oh, you hear shots from time to time," he said. "But no one has been killed lately."

"I have read that your town is known as the toughest town in Texas," she said. "It must be quite exciting."

"It's actually pretty peaceful most of the time during the week. Picks up quite a bit on the weekends and when a cattle drive is in town. They bring cattle from South Texas now and the cowboys can get a little rowdy with money in their pockets."

"So you haven't had any more murder cases?"

"No. Not yet." He paused. "How is school?"

"Oh, I'm not in school in the summertime, but I've been enjoying it so far."

"So, do you plan on teaching?"

"I think so," she said. "I think I would make a good teacher. I'm good at grammar and literature. Not so good at math and science, but I suppose I could teach them anyway."

"I'm also fond of good literature," he said. "I used to think I wanted to teach."

"But you seem to be well placed as a lawyer."

"I suppose I am, but it's a little uncomfortable for me at times."

"Maybe that's the way of things," she said.

She did not seem at all the same girl that he first encountered at Adam Bradford's cabin in the San Saba valley. She still had the air of confidence he first noticed when she told him she wanted to teach, although beneath it he could sense something else. She had a way of looking him in the eye that had a directness to it, but then she would look away and the smile would briefly leave her face.

They talked about San Antonio and his law practice, friends she had met at school, and his time at college in Mississippi. After a while, Ellen Elliot came into the room. She remarked on how grown up he seemed and after exchanging pleasantries, she invited him to stay for supper, insisting that they had planned on having him for supper ever since she and Martha had discussed his visit. He became more relaxed during supper.

"I enjoyed the visit from Colonel Hays last spring," Mrs. Elliot said. "I did not get to see you then, but I understand from Martha that you had a nice dinner party."

"Yes," he replied. "I should have come to see you, but we were only here overnight. I had to get back to work the next day."

"Well, I am pleased to see you here this evening. And I hope we will see more of you." She glanced at Martha as she spoke.

"I hope so," he said.

"I hope so, too," Martha said.

They chatted about current events in San Antonio, and the weather and cattle prices, with Mrs. Elliot taking the lead in the discussion. After the supper dishes were cleared, Mrs. Elliot excused herself, and he and Martha were again alone in the parlor.

"Perhaps you could recommend some books for me," she said.

"I'm not sure what you would like. My mother is a reader. She liked *Little Women.*"

"I've read it and it was all right, but I think I liked Hawthorne better. *The House of the Seven Gables* held my interest."

"Have you read *The Innocents Abroad* by Mark Twain? It was very funny," he said. "And a good travelogue."

"No, but I read a story by him in a periodical about a jumping frog, which was quite nice."

"My mother taught me to read when I was quite small," he said.

Her smile disappeared. She looked down at her hands, which were tightly clasped together in her lap. When she looked up again, she was the girl on horseback on the way to San Antonio from the San Saba valley, her face a still mask of resignation, without life or emotion. Then she suddenly smiled again, but this time it was forced.

"My mother read to me," she said. Her eyes were moist.

"I'm sorry," he said.

"Why? It's a good memory. I have some good memories."

When he had seen her at the dinner with Hays and the others at the Menger, he had been impressed with her appearance. She was no longer a girl. She had become a young woman. He had not been able to get her out of his mind since that evening. Now he had an even better impression of her as a young person who could be a friend and companion, who shared an interest in literature with him, and when she smiled the forced smile and held back her tears, he had a feeling for her that was unlike anything he had felt before. It was as if all space between them had evaporated.

They continued to discuss literature. She loved Poe's poetry and was frightened by his dark stories. He talked about Melville and Fenimore Cooper, acknowledging that they were probably not popular with the ladies. She loved Dickens, but preferred George Eliot. He recommended that she read *The Atlantic* for its essays, poetry, and fictional pieces. When the parlor clock struck ten and he decided it was time for him to go, she showed him to the door and stood there as if she did not want to see him leave. He agreed that he would visit again soon, and as he walked back to his hotel, his step was lighter than he could remember.

THIRTY-FOUR

THE RAILROAD RIGHT-OF-WAY WAS THREE HUNDRED FEET wide and lay between North Railroad Avenue and South Railroad Avenue in Luling. A passenger depot and a freight depot were located on the south side of the tracks, but most of the rest of the area was used as a park for the people of the town. For special events, local citizens were allowed to use the grassy, cleared area on each side of the tracks for erecting temporary stalls for the sale of goods, including the stock of goods at Runge's outdoor bar.

The drinking started early on July 4, as it always did. Will and Wonsley met at the outdoor bar on North Railroad Avenue at ten thirty in the morning, a half hour before the scheduled start of the parade. It was a sunny day. A crowd of drinking men had already gathered in front of the planks set on sawhorses that served as the bar. The only date that rivalled the Independence Day celebration for alcohol consumption was Election Day, and that was still months away. A fresh keg of beer had been opened and was being poured for free. From the second keg on it would be a nickel a mug. It was considered early for hard liquor. Will and Wonsley took their mugs and stood apart from the others, watching the crowd gather. Domino tables had been set up adjacent to the bar area. Old men were already in the heat of battle around the tables, their beer mugs at hand. Will was acquainted with only a few of the old-timers and a few of the younger members of the crowd. The railroad was regularly bringing in new blood. It was a town of strangers.

They recognized one of the domino players immediately. A dark-haired man with a receding hairline and a long mustache, Rowdy Joe Lowe was a well-known gambler and saloon owner who had been in town for months. He was sitting with two of the local barflies and a young cowboy. The cowboy seemed to have found some of the hard stuff. He looked to be well on his way. As they watched the game, it became clear that he was not paying good attention to the dominoes. The game was usually for a penny a point, which were high stakes. The cowboy had been in town for a week. Having come back from a trail drive, he had been in touch with gamblers and ladies of the night, saying every day that he was going on back to South Texas the next day, then staying another night after another day of drinking and gambling. Rowdy Joe had already taken him on the faro table and in poker games. It was hard to figure out how the cowboy could have any money left, in spite of the fact that a drover's pay for an entire drive could amount to hundreds of dollars.

Will and Wonsley sipped their beers and watched the crowd gather along the street. Many wore "1776-1876" sewn on men's shirts, ladies' aprons and sunbonnets, and children's clothing. Others wore horseshoes, fleurs-de-lis, clover leaves, horses' heads, and jockey caps embroidered on their shirts and blouses. The storefronts on the opposite side of the street were dressed with red, white, and blue bunting. People began to gather on the wooden sidewalk in front of the stores on the north side of the street and along the edge of the street on the south side. It was the middle of a dry spell, so there was no mud to deal with. Dust rose from horse and mule hooves as well as the boots and shoes of the men and women walking across and along the street.

Will and Wonsley wandered to the east, passing booths that had been erected by churches and civic organizations. The St. John's Catholic Church booth was selling tamales, carne guisada, and bowls of menudo. Several of the men sitting at folding tables eating menudo had been in saloons the night before. They were dipping tortillas into their menudo bowls, looking hung over. The Presbyterians had barbecued a hog in a pit dug the day before. Laid over coals and covered with sticks and dry earth, then dug up at midmorning, the meat was falling off the bone when cut and brought to the serving booth, where it was served with onions, tomatoes, and loaves of bread. The ladies' aid society had pies and cakes for sale. Wonsley was particularly fond of Mrs. Bronson's Dutch apple pie.

He sidled up to the booth to look at the tags for her name, although he had no intention of buying one. He had no money to spare. And he had no place to keep a pie on horseback for the ride home.

He had not noticed the other people looking at the pies and cakes. When he finally looked up he was surprised to see Ashley Maitland, Lily Poe, and Lily's daughter, Barbara Ann, standing nearby. Will was right behind Wonsley. He stepped up and offered his hand to Ash.

"Happy fourth," Ash said.

"Same to you," Will replied.

Lily stepped forward and extended her hand, palm down.

"It's good to see you, Counselor," she said, smiling. "You will remember my daughter, Barbara Ann."

Barbara Ann was even prettier than the last time he had seen her, over two years ago. Her hair was done up under a lacy bonnet. She smiled broadly.

"Of course," Will said. "And you know my uncle, Wonsley Baker?"

"Yes, indeed. But it has been a long time since I have seen you, Wonsley," Lily said. "Where have you been keeping yourself? I didn't see you at the gin all last season."

"Didn't make much of a crop last year," Wonsley said. "I was only there a couple of days and you was out of town or somethin'."

"I hope this is a better year for all of us," she said.

Wonsley noticed Barbara Ann looking him over and was glad he had worn his Sunday clothes. He wished he had gotten a haircut and beard trim. As it was, his long, sun-bleached hair fell over the back of his collar.

"I see you boys found the beer keg," Ash said. "I could use one myself. How about you, Lily?"

"You know I'm not much on beer, Ash," she replied. "I'll wait until the whiskey is served. But Barbara Ann and I will go along with you."

They walked down the street to the bar, where Ash ordered a beer. The free keg was already gone. It cost him a nickel. He paid for beers for Will and Wonsley. Lily and Barbara Ann stood near the street in front of the bar. Several men and women passed by, the women all looking quickly away after giving them the once-over. They did not exchange greetings with the notorious Lily Poe and her daughter. Some of the men gave signs of recognition when they looked their way, but turned their heads back quickly. Ash came up to Lily, followed by Will and Wonsley.

"I see the good people are still acting upright," he said.

"I'm used to it," Lily replied, glancing at Barbara Ann, who nodded.

After a while, they heard a loud voice from the direction of the domino tables. The cowboy was standing unsteadily by the table where he and the others had been sitting, his right hand on the butt of his pistol.

"I saw you palm that rock," he said to Rowdy Joe.

"Not so," Rowdy Joe replied. "If you knew anything about dominoes, you'd know better."

"You're a liar," the cowboy said, slurring his words.

Rowdy Joe's stare was unwavering. A black cigar was clenched between his lips. His hands were below the edge of the table.

"I'm gonna forget you said that, son," he said coldly. "This one time."

Wonsley quickly walked over to the table and stepped between them, facing the cowboy.

"You don't want to be doin' this, Rafe," he said. "You need to sober up and calm down." His voice was steady and calm. The cowboy rocked back on his heels, staring glassy-eyed at Wonsley.

"This ain't none of your business, Wonsley," he said.

"You need to stop and think. Don't let the whiskey do your talking for you," Wonsley said.

The cowboy looked down, then up again, and seemed to relax, almost keeling over. Wonsley slowly put his hand on his right arm and moved the cowboy's hand away from the pistol.

"I think you need a nap," Wonsley said, then, turning to Rowdy Joe, "You collected enough for today, Joe. I'm takin' this man where he can get some rest."

"Suits me," Rowdy Joe said in the same cold voice.

Wonsley turned to Will, who had walked up.

"I'm takin' him to Reese's," he said, now holding the cowboy up by his shoulder. "That's where he's stayin'."

He walked the cowboy across the street just ahead of the parade.

Barbara Ann leaned toward her mother.

"That was something," she said into her ear.

By the time Will and Ash had finished their beers and Ash had paid for two more, a bugle from the east sounded the beginning of the parade. The crowd on both sides of the street gathered closer to the street edge, the children standing in front for a better view. The first men on horseback came into view, led by the mayor and the sheriff, who were flanked by two young men carrying the US and Texas flags, followed by members of the board of aldermen and a carriage with the mayor's and aldermen's wives. The carriage was pulled by a team of four mules decorated with red, white, and blue garlands. Next came a series of wagons covered with decorations, carrying local club members, children, and church members, each pulled by decorated horses and mules, followed by the town band, marching in step to the music. The last part of the parade consisted of local citizens on horseback, many of them young men and boys, some of whom wore decorations on their mounts.

After the last horses passed, Wonsley made his way back across the street to where the others stood.

"Did you put the young gambler to bed?" Lily asked.

"I managed to get him up the stairs to his room," he replied. "He fell into bed without any argument."

"It's a good thing you stepped in," Ash said. "Rowdy Joe was ready to shoot him."

They stood and talked for a while, then walked to the picnic grounds in the next block. Tables and benches had been set up. Barbecue pits had been dug and filled with beef and pork over oak wood fires since before dawn. Black men wearing white aprons were serving from a long table. Beef brisket and pork ribs were the main fare, but there were also bowls of pinto beans, macaroni and cheese, and coleslaw. Ash suggested that the ladies find seats at one of the tables and the men would go through the serving line and bring plates to them.

When the men returned, Ash had a plate for Lily and Wonsley carried one for Barbara Ann. He sat beside her as they ate the meal, but said little, although Lily would at times try to draw him into the conversation. The tables had been arrayed in an arc in front of a small wooden dais with a podium. After most of the picnickers had finished the meal, the mayor stood to deliver his Fourth of July speech. He read from a sheaf of paper that fluttered in the wind so much he had trouble keeping it straight in his hands and paused for long shuffling intervals. The founding fathers, Old Glory, and the centennial's significance were the obligatory topics, which he haltingly delivered in a high-pitched voice. In mid-speech, Lily drew a small flask from her purse and offered it to Ash, who took a quick swig and passed it to Will and Wonsley. When it returned to her, Lily drained it, tipping it up and holding it high in full view of the good citizens who surrounded them. After the speech ended, the crowd stood and gradually dispersed. As they walked away from the tables, Ash, Lily, and Will walked together and Wonsley and Barbara Ann followed close behind.

THIRTY-FIVE

ON A TUESDAY MORNING, WILL RECEIVED A NOTE FROM his mother that Gruder was gravely ill and he should come quickly. He rode immediately to Gruder's cabin. Several horses and a couple of carriages were outside when he arrived, one belonging to his mother, the other a buggy that belonged to Dr. Young. Several black people he knew were gathered on the front porch. Inside, Laura sat beside the cot where Gruder lay, with the doctor standing nearby. The old man was lying on his back, taking shallow breaths, his eyes closed. Laura saw Will as he entered and motioned for him to follow her out to the porch. She turned as they passed through the doorway.

"The doctor has only been here a little while," she said. "He says it's pneumonia. Lettie found him this morning and told me. I sent for the doctor."

"Is he awake?"

"Yes, but he's real weak. It's okay for you to talk to him."

Will turned and reentered the cabin. When he approached the cot, Gruder's eyes slowly opened and he gave a sign of recognition.

"Billy," he said in a weak voice.

"Gruder," he replied.

Dr. Young placed his stethoscope into his black bag and turned toward the door.

"You'll want to spend some time with him," he said, with a solemn look.

"I took sick," Gruder whispered. "But I'll be all right."

"Sure," Will replied. He sat down on the stool beside the cot. "It's a good thing Lettie came by to check on you."

"She's gonna bring me some chicken soup. That'll fix me up."

He appeared to be having trouble keeping his eyes open. He would close them while speaking.

"You doin' all right, Billy?"

"Yes, I'm doing all right. But I haven't been to see you in a long time."

"That's all right." He was taking shallow breaths between episodes of talking. "You been busy bein' a lawyer. I know that."

"I've been keeping busy, all right."

"Fightin' for justice in the courtroom."

"Some of that, I guess."

"You see that wood box on the mantel?" Gruder asked, looking toward the fireplace.

"I see it."

"Fetch it for me, please."

Will walked to the mantel and picked up the small wooden box. It had a curved lid with intricate patterns carved on it. He brought it to the cot.

"Open it, Billy."

Inside, something was wrapped in a woman's handkerchief. Gruder's eyes were closed.

"What do you see?" he rasped.

"Something in a handkerchief," Will replied.

"Go ahead. Take it out."

Will pulled the object out and unwrapped it. It was a gold pocket watch.

"Got it out? Go ahead and open it."

He flipped open the case, revealing the face of the watch and a miniature portrait of a young black woman on the inside of the lid.

"You see her?"

"Yes, I see her. Was that your wife?"

"It is. My Lois. Your daddy gave me that watch as a wedding present. I want you to have it."

"Me?"

"You're the only family I have. You and Miz Laura. There's somethin' else in there."

Will pulled a folded yellowed paper from the bottom of the box. Gruder looked at it.

"Go ahead and read it," he said.

He unfolded it. It was written in Gruder's precise hand.

> My Last Will and Testament, written in my own hand this 13th day of November 1870.
>
> I, Gruder McCulloch, being of sound mind, do make this my Last Will. I leave all my worldly goods to William Wesley McCulloch and ask that he dispose of them as he sees fit and he handle all things pertaining to my estate. I wish to be buried beside my wife and child on my place.
>
> Gruder McCulloch

Will looked up. Gruder was staring at him. He had seen that look before, many times. It was a look that he gave him when he expected his attention, indicating he was going to tell him something important.

"I owe lots to your family. I'm proud of you. Your daddy would be proud of you, too. Take care of your mother."

He closed his eyes again, as if he had used his last bit of strength to say what he had to say and was relieved that he was able to do it, then opened them and looked at Will. A smile came on his face.

"We had us some times, didn't we?"

"Yes, we did."

"We got that girl from that outlaw," he said. "Or the Cap'n did anyway."

"Yes."

"And you got him. That half-breed."

He closed his eyes again. Will sat looking at him. His breathing was labored, but otherwise he looked as if he was sleeping soundly, as Will had seen him so many times before. Memories came to him. Following Gruder through the woods when he was a boy, hunting squirrels and jack rabbits. Learning how to whittle sticks into artistic objects, although he could never do it as well as Gruder. Learning from him how to listen in the woods, for birds and animals. Hearing about how it had been before the war, when almost all the other blacks were enslaved and had to have a written pass to go past the boundaries of the land they were tied to and how Gruder, after Wes McCulloch had freed him, had had to carry a document with him that certified that he was a free man and did not need a pass. Gruder taking him to a Juneteenth picnic after the war, where he was the only white person present, and announcing that it was also his birthday. And accompanying Gruder and his father to register Gruder to vote, his father having to accompany him because of a frivolous prior refusal by the voting clerk to register him. He remembered the proud look on Gruder's face as he watched Wes McCulloch dress down the voting clerk, telling him that he was sworn to uphold the law and should be ashamed of himself.

He remembered the trek in pursuit of Morgan, the renegade, and the respect shown Gruder by Colonel Hays and Will's uncles as they rode. Gruder's treatment of Julie the mare's mountain lion wounds, and how he had talked Will into leaving her. The gunshot wound in Gruder's side and the fever it caused.

He did not know how long his mother had been sitting beside him, but he turned and she was there on a log stool. After a long time, Lettie, the McCulloch house servant, who had stayed with them after emancipation, came with a pot of chicken soup. They tried to rouse Gruder to get him to eat some, but they could not awaken him. Laura felt his forehead and said he was burning up. Lettie and Laura applied damp cloths to his face. Laura said the doctor indicated there was nothing else he could do and that it would just be a matter of time, so they waited together, looking at him, until, after hours, his breathing stopped and he lay still, having gone quietly to his rest.

The funeral was held at the Sweet Canaan Baptist Church on the Prairie Lea to Kingsbury road. Will and his mother were the only white people in attendance. When they arrived in front of the church, the churchyard was filled with people. Will and Laura recognized a number of the attendees, but the two of them were recognized by many more, which was apparent, particularly when the crowd parted and encouraged them to enter the church, which was already full. Will realized for the first time that one effect of slavery and its aftermath was a massive anonymity, which he thought was welcomed by those who were part of it. It made sense. It was best not to be identified as an individual among whites. Such identity could often lead to bad consequences.

The church itself had been founded in 1867 by a group of men and women who had previously been members of the otherwise white congregation of the Shiloh Baptist Church in Prairie Lea. They had come to Caldwell County along with their masters and their families from San Augustine in East Texas and had been baptized into the church family while still slaves. Nelson, property of Asa Wright, the white preacher, was authorized to "preach to his colored brethren within the bounds of the church," but only in the presence of a white male member of the congregation, until the news that they had been emancipated reached Galveston on June 19, 1865, and quickly spread by telegraph and word of mouth to all corners of the state.

The first meetings after the founding of the church as a separate congregation were held on the banks of a creek on the Guadalupe County side of the river, and the church was first called Brushy Creek, but was known colloquially as "Brusha." The present sanctuary had been erected a few years later. Once inside, Will and Laura were politely ushered to the front pew, where places had been reserved for them. The walls on the inside were whitewashed. The windows were not arched and contained no stained glass, but they were in good repair and open to the mild September morning. The pulpit was of stained oak, as were the pews, which had been roughly hewn by hand. The congregation had built the church themselves, and it was a clean and orderly place, without frills. The congregants were dressed in black suits and dresses. The casket lay closed beside the pulpit, surrounded by flowers. The preacher sat nearby. Once Will and Laura had been seated, he rose and stepped behind the pulpit, slowly and deliberately opening his Bible before speaking. He read the Twenty-third Psalm and led the congregation in a prayer that set the theme for the service, thanking God for the good life that they had witnessed and expressing gratitude that his worldly cares were over and that he had finally reached the streets of gold. The hymns sung were about the joys of salvation and deliverance from evil and worldly cares and the sermon celebrated the good life of the man, stressing his unselfish assistance to others and his role in teaching his fellow human beings the value of honesty and dignity. Will felt tears running down his cheeks and was embarrassed until he self-consciously turned and saw that most of the congregation was also crying openly, many of the women dabbing their eyes with lace handkerchiefs.

After the benediction, a deacon announced that the services would continue at the graveyard, and that afterwards there would be a dinner on the ground. The casket was lowered into the grave by the six pallbearers, hemp ropes supporting it as it was carefully laid down, the congregation standing without any movement until each pallbearer had placed a shovel full of earth on top of it. Laura's jaw was set as she watched. She remembered Gruder coming to her when Hays and her brothers were about to embark on their pursuit of the renegade, Leo Morgan, how he had sidled into the room where she sat knitting, waiting until she looked up before speaking, as he always had. And how he had slowly and skillfully persuaded her that it was time for her son to take his father's place in the family and go along with them, indicating that Billy would be holding the horses and mules and that he would watch out for him and keep him safe. He had always been a reliable, calming influence on her husband, and he had always been trustworthy. So she had let Billy go, and when he came back with his shoulder injured, it was Gruder, more seriously wounded, who had told her how it had happened.

"He was holding onto old Gray," he said. "Doin' his job."

After the graveyard service, a place had been prepared for them at the head of one of the tables set up under the oak trees beside the church. Most of the benches had been moved outside and set beside the planks placed on sawhorses that served as tables. Pork loin, turnip greens, and potatoes were the main portions of the meal. They were seated across from the preacher, Nelson Wright, and his wife. A light-skinned young man sat nearby. Will thought he looked familiar, and when he looked his way the young man stood and slightly bowed.

"Mr. McCulloch, I'm Lucius Jackson and this here's my wife, Sally," he said, pointing toward a young black woman seated beside him. "I help Miz Poe run the mill and also do some work for Miz Moore. I've known your man, Gruder, since I was a boy. He taught me to read and write and do sums. He was a guiding light to us all."

"Thank you," Will replied. "And this is my mother, Mrs. McCulloch."

The young man bowed again.

"Please to meet you, ma'am. If there's anything me or Sally can do to help, just let me know. We live on Miz Moore's place."

Laura nodded. "Thank you," she said. "I may need some more help. I'll let you know."

When they left, several people accompanied them to their carriage and Lucius Jackson untied the hitching rope and stood holding it until they had both boarded. He then put it in its place on a hook inside the dashboard, smiling as he did so, then turned the lead horse away from the hitching post. Those who had followed them to their carriage stood at the edge of the road watching as they drove away.

THIRTY-SIX

AFTER TWO YEARS IN THE WALLS, EVERETT HARDEMAN WAS made a trusty and assigned to the wheelwright shop. He had casually mentioned to a guard that his uncle had been a wheelwright before the war and that he had apprenticed with him until he joined the army. When he was told he had been made a trusty and was to report to the wheelwright shop, he was given no explanation as to why this had happened, nor did he seek one. To be designated a trusty was a privilege afforded to a small number of prisoners who had been deemed a low security risk and who usually had a particular skill or ability. Trusties had day passes that let them have the run of most of the prison and were housed and fed separately from the general prison population. Although some bore grudges against trusties and it could be a dangerous position, it was generally sought after for the greater freedom it afforded.

His job at the wheelwright shop included oversight of the work of building and repairing wheels for wagons and carts used throughout the prison system. Most of the workers in the shop were knowledgeable and needed little supervision. Ev was also tasked with visits to the blacksmith shop to deliver measurements for braces, bands, bolts, and wheel rims to be used in wheel repair and construction. He had been at his new job for six months when word spread about a new arrival at the Walls Unit. Another trusty, known as Shad, stopped him on his way between shops one afternoon.

"You heard about who's just got in?" Shad asked. "The baddest man in Texas just got here."

John Wesley Hardin had been found guilty by a jury in Comanche, Texas, of murder in the second degree and sentenced to twenty-five years in prison. The evidence showed that he goaded a deputy sheriff into a gunfight on the streets of Comanche. Although the deputy apparently drew first and Hardin claimed self-defense, the appeals court ruled that he could not coerce the man into a gunfight and then make that claim. Hardin's reputation as a cold-blooded killer may have influenced the verdict. He was known to have killed more than twenty men in gunfights and was said to have once shot a man who was snoring in an adjoining hotel room by shooting through an interior wall. Whiskey and gambling were often involved in his fights, and his temper was easily aroused. He was said to have killed a number of black state policemen, but had not been convicted of any crime until the Comanche verdict. He was twenty-six years of age when he arrived at the Walls in early October, 1878. He was assigned to the wheelwright shop.

When Ev first met him, Hardin had been brought to the shop midmorning by a guard, who told Ev to "find some work for this man to do." The sounds of activity in the shop stopped and everything was quiet until Ev asked, "Know anything about wheelwrighting?"

"Not much," Hardin answered, looking Ev steadily in the eye. He stood very straight. His blue eyes glanced around the shop interior.

"Any idea why they brought you here?"

"Not a clue. Except I heard one of them say I couldn't be worked outside the walls because I was a first-class prisoner."

"That's not a compliment," an older man standing nearby said.

"I didn't think so," Hardin said, smiling at him.

"Can you use a helper, Pete?" Ev asked the man.

Pete looked Hardin up and down.

"I guess so," he said. Then to Hardin, "Can you use a plane?"

"I have," he replied.

"Know how to saw?"

"I've done some sawing."

Pete smiled. "Are you good with your hands?"

Hardin had a twinkle in his eye.

"You know who I am, don't you?"

Pete looked down at his own hands, which he held palm up before him.

"I used to use these for other things. Now I work wood with them." He looked up at Hardin. "You can do the same, I reckon."

"Pete's in charge of making spokes," Ev said. "How long you been in, Pete?"

"Eight years, seven months, and eighteen days," he replied.

"I don't plan on staying that long," Hardin said.

Ev and Pete exchanged a glance.

"You can work with Pete here, for the time being," Ev said. "If he'll have you."

"It's all right with me," Pete said. "But you can keep that kind of talk to yourself," he said to Hardin.

Pete showed him the spoke work area and the tools used to split and cut the oak used for making spokes—the adzes, saws, planes and shavers, and the measuring sticks and tapes. By lunch break, Hardin was measuring and marking pieces of oak and sawing them into spoke roughs for a wagon that needed a replacement wheel. Pete was pleased with his new helper as far as the work went, but the young man's air of confidence worried him. It was as if Hardin believed that he was capable of anything; and he was far too cheery for someone who was sentenced to twenty-five to do.

As the days passed, Ev noticed that Hardin was talking in whispers with others in the shop. Pete finally came to Ev during a break and motioned him aside, then spoke in a low voice.

"Hardin's planning a breakout," he said. "Thought you might want to know."

"I don't want to know anything," Ev said. "I've got about eighteen months to do and I don't want to do anything that would mess that up."

Pete shook his head. "I don't want to know either, but there it is. We're all gonna be in it whether we want to or not."

"Not me," Ev replied. "We didn't have this conversation."

A couple of weeks later, Ev returned from the blacksmith shop to find Hardin surrounded by several others in the corner of the workroom. He walked up to the group, where Hardin was speaking in a low voice. When Ev's presence was noticed, Hardin stopped talking and the group quickly dispersed, leaving Hardin standing alone, looking at Ev with unwavering eyes.

"You seem to be getting along pretty well," Ev said. "Got people crowding around you."

"I usually get along with those who are fair," Hardin said.

Ev looked around the shop. The others had returned to their workstations.

"I don't want any trouble in here," he said. "You know what I mean?"

"I'm not a trouble causer," Hardin replied, smiling. "You got nothing to worry about from me."

Later, near the end of the workday, Hardin came over to where Ev stood, near the door to the shop.

"I think you might have the wrong idea about me," he said in a low voice. "I'm really not the bad man folks have made me out to be."

Ev looked at him but did not speak.

"I've had some education. My daddy is a minister and a lawyer. I got railroaded into here and I don't plan to do any twenty-five years."

"Look, Hardin. I don't care. I don't want to know anything about it. I've got about eighteen months left in here and I don't want anything messing me up."

"Don't worry. I won't do anything to mess you up." Hardin had the same knowing smile as he turned away.

THIRTY-SEVEN

ONE MORNING IN DECEMBER, WHEN WILL GOT TO THE office, a black man was waiting for him. Will thought he looked familiar, but he could not place him. He was dressed in a work shirt and cotton pants. He stood when Will reached the top of the stairs, holding his hat in his hand and bowing slightly.

"I don't know if you remember me, Mr. McCulloch. I'm Nelson Wright, Preacher Wright. I presided at Gruder's funeral."

"Oh, yes," Will replied. "What can I do for you?"

"A young man is in serious trouble, Mr. McCulloch. He needs your help."

"Oh? Who is he?"

"He's Lucius Jackson, Mr. McCulloch. You met him and his wife, Sally, at the funeral."

"Yes, I remember him. What kind of trouble?"

The preacher looked down at his scuffed boots before speaking.

"He's been accused of raping a white girl, Mr. McCulloch. But I know he didn't do it."

"Who is the girl?"

"It's Miz Lily Poe's daughter, Barbara Ann, sir. But I know he didn't do it."

Will felt a chill.

"Lily Poe's daughter?"

"Yes, sir. That's what she says. But I know it ain't true."

"How do you know that?"

"Because Lucius Jackson is a good man," the preacher said. "He's got a wife and two babies he loves. He would never do nothin' like that."

"I don't see how I can represent him," Will said.

"He's in serious danger, Mr. McCulloch. Word is gettin' around that there's a mob that's going to lynch him without even giving him a trial."

"Where is he?"

"They got him in the county jail in Lockhart," he said. "If they haven't already taken him. I saw him an hour ago."

"I don't see how I can help him, Nelson," Will said. "You'll have to find someone else."

"But Mr. McCulloch, you're the only one who would help a poor Negro man," he said. "I know that because of Gruder. He always spoke well of you and how you weren't like most white men."

"I can't do it," Will said. "The court will appoint a lawyer for him. And Sheriff Ellison and his men will protect him through the trial. He'll get a fair trial."

The preacher stared at him for a long moment, his eyes showing a kind of recognition. They both knew the young man was doomed. The court would appoint someone all right, probably Matt Barton, who would barely interview his client, perform no investigation, call no witnesses, and put up a token defense. If he survived the mob, he was not likely to survive the trial. Then the memory of the night after his father died came rushing back to him—Lily Poe, his father's mistress, and her daughter, a young girl then, clinging to her mother's skirts, at the family home, wet from the rain, come to view the body; and his mother's stoic acceptance of the fact of her husband's infidelity and the finality of his death as if it was the only thing to do. He thought he had moved on from his feelings about Lily, but they had come back to him in the form of a cold, dark thing that pulled on him.

"I'll have to think about it," he finally said.

"Mr. McCulloch, he may not be there tomorrow. They may take him today."

"He'll be all right in the jail," Will said, but there was no air of confidence in his tone of voice. Nelson Wright's eyes were moist.

"All right, then, Mr. McCulloch. I hope you can at least go see him."

After the preacher left, Will stepped inside the inner office and went to stand at the large arched window behind the desk, looking at the street and railroad below in the early morning light. He recalled Lucius Jackson and his wife at the funeral. He had looked Will straight in the eye and stood erect when they talked, showing respect for Will and his mother without attempting to ingratiate himself to them. Will had been impressed by his directness and the expression of his regard for Gruder. He could not imagine him being a rapist, but it would be almost impossible to find a jury that would acquit him if Barbara Ann testified to facts amounting to rape, even if the evidence was otherwise weak. And if he agreed to represent him, it would likely destroy his law practice. Few white people would continue to be clients.

He was still standing at the window a half hour later when Ashley Maitland entered the office. Will turned toward him. Ash stood at the office doorway staring in his direction.

"I guess you heard the news," Ash said.

"About the rape? Yes, I heard."

"Well, Lily is beside herself. Understandably."

"How is Barbara Ann?"

"She's refusing to go to the doctor," Ash said. "She says she's too embarrassed."

Ash took a seat in a side chair.

"There's something about it that doesn't add up," he said. "She didn't tell her mother until yesterday and she says it happened last week."

Will had turned and was looking out the window again.

"You think she's lying?" he asked.

"I don't think so, but she may be hiding something."

"Like what?"

"I don't know. But there's something about her story that doesn't add up."

"What about physical evidence?" Will asked. "Was there blood?"

"She says she washed it all off. Too embarrassed to tell her mother at first. Then she told her and the maid washed the dress she says she was wearing and the sheriff's men didn't find any bloodstains on it."

"I've been asked to represent him," Will said.

"What? Who asked?"

"Nelson Wright, the Negro preacher from the Sweet Canaan Church.

He was here when I got here this morning."

Ash stood up.

"You're not considering it, are you?" he asked.

There was a silence.

"Are you?" Ash asked again.

"I think I'll go see him. The preacher says there are rumors of a lynch mob. I would hate to stand by and let that happen, whether or not he's guilty."

"And you think you could stop the mob?"

"I don't know, but I would hate not to try. What if he's not guilty?" he asked.

Ash hesitated before answering. He had known Lily Poe for a long time and had always had a strong affection for her. He could not fathom representing a black man who was accused of raping her daughter. On the other hand, he had always had an uncomfortable feeling about Barbara Ann. She was willful and headstrong, a spoiled child who had been doted on by her mother, and he was troubled by the circumstances of the alleged rape. But Will representing her would be tantamount to his own representation and he could not allow that to happen. Lily would never forgive him.

"You can't do it," he finally said.

Will's face hardened.

"I can't?"

"There's Lily," Ash said. "She would be hurt."

"Because of you or because of my father?"

"Because of you," Ash said, his voice rising. "She has a lot of respect for you. It would be crushing to her."

"I'll go see him and then make up my mind about it," Will said.

"I strongly object," Ash said. "Just know that I strongly object to you having anything to do with the case."

An hour later, Will was riding up to the jail, which was a block from the courthouse square. He had expected to find a crowd outside the jail, but no one was there. He hitched his horse and walked through the door into the front office without encountering anyone until he came to the front desk, where a guard stood by next to a seated jail employee.

"You have a Lucius Jackson?" he asked the jailer.

"Yes, sir," the jailer answered. "You want to see him?"

"Where's Sheriff Ellison?" Will asked.

"In his office."

"I'd like to see him first," Will said.

"You can go on in, Mr. McCulloch."'

He found the sheriff seated at his desk alone. He rose to meet him.

"You come to see my new prisoner?" he asked.

"I'd like to talk to him," Will replied. "But I thought you would have more of a guard up. I heard there was a lynch mob."

"Naw. I haven't heard of one, anyway."

The sheriff's face was immobile. He had a look of studied unconcern.

"You haven't?"

"Not a word," the sheriff replied. "Course, I guess I might be the last one to hear."

Will remembered how solicitous the sheriff had been toward Everett Hardeman. He seemed like a different man.

"Well, I've heard that there has been some talk. At any rate, I would like to see him."

"Sure, Will. I'll show you back there myself."

He followed the sheriff past the front desk, where he retrieved a set of keys, through the door into the cellblock, past empty cells to a cell in the rear, where Lucius Jackson sat alone on a cot, holding his head in his hands. He looked up when they approached, and Will noticed that he had bruises and swollen areas on his face. He wore a shirt with a torn sleeve. He stood as the sheriff unlocked the cell door and stepped aside for Will to enter. The sheriff shut the cell door behind him but did not lock it.

"You got this whole jail to yourselves," he said. "I'll wait for you outside. Come on out when you're ready." He had a slight smile on his face as he turned to leave.

"Mr. McCulloch," Jackson said. "Thank you for coming to see me."

Will pulled up a stool and sat. Lucius sat down on the edge of the cot.

"You sent for me?" Will asked.

"Yessir. I didn't know anyone else. I know I'm in big trouble." His eyes were wide with fright.

"I don't know that I can represent you," Will said. "But I'll keep whatever you say to me confidential if you tell me what happened."

Lucius Jackson stared at him, a pained look on his face.

"It'll have to be the truth," Will said. "I can't help you if you lie to me."

"I didn't rape that girl," Lucius said. "I didn't do nothin' to her. She was teasin' me all the time, but I didn't do nothin' to her."

Will hesitated.

"Teasing you?"

"Yessir. Teasing me all the time, but only when no one else was around. Down at the gin. I work there for Miz Lily, you know. And she would be down there some of the time. And some of the time when I was working alone, she'd . . . " He stopped speaking for a moment and looked over Will's head toward the door to the jail office. "I know nobody's goin' to believe me. I can't say what really happened, Mr. McCulloch. Nobody's goin' to believe it."

"You've got to tell me," Will said. "Or I can't help you."

"She come on to me, Mr. McCulloch."

"She did what?"

"I know you won't believe it. Nobody's goin' to believe me."

"You mean she flirted with you?" Will asked.

"You know I can't say that about a white girl," Lucius said. "I know I can't say that. They'll hang me for sure if I say that."

"Just tell me what happened."

"She come around and said things like 'you're such a big black man, aren't you?'—things like that. And I'd say she shouldn't be talking to me at all and she'd just laugh and say more things, like 'you're real strong, ain't you?'—only she wouldn't say 'ain't.' And she started touching me on my arm, on my arm muscle and sayin' things like that."

"What did you do?"

"I didn't do nothin' to her. But . . . "

"But what?"

"She come up and rubbed against me one day. And I took her by the arm to push her away. And she said 'you grabbed me' and 'don't you know you're not supposed to be touching a white girl'—and she backed off and smiled at me and said 'you could be in big trouble for doing that, you know'—and I was real scared then. Then she said I would have to do as she said or she would tell on me."

"How did she rub on you?"

"I can't tell this," Lucius said. "Nobody's goin' to believe me. They'll hang me for sure."

"What did she do?"

"She come up to me and . . . I didn't expect it, you see . . . she come up and rubbed herself against the front of me. And I was in my work clothes, which wasn't too clean, and I didn't expect her to do that, and that's when I grabbed her."

"You grabbed her?"

"Yessir. Just to push her away. Just to get her off me."

Will hesitated, looking at him. One of his eyes was almost swollen shut.

"How did you get those bruises?" he asked.

"They roughed me up a bit when they brought me in."

"Getting back to the girl, Barbara Ann," Will said. "How did you grab her?"

"I grabbed her by the arms. That's all. Just to get her off me."

"By both arms? I thought you said you took her by only one arm."

"I grabbed her, Mr. McCulloch, but it was only to push her away."

"By both arms."

"Yessir, it was by both of her arms. But I didn't hold onto her. I just pushed her away."

"What did she do then?"

"She said I should'na touched her, like I said."

"Then?"

"Then she walked away. She backed off and smiled at me, then she just walked away."

"Where did this happen?"

"It was in the counting office, by the scales."

"Did anyone see this happen?"

"No, sir, we was alone."

"Did you see her again after that?"

"Yessir, a number of times, but not when we was alone. She only did that stuff when we was alone."

"When did this happen?"

"When she come up against me? It was in September, after the cotton harvest."

"So it was several months ago?"

"Yessir. It was about that time. It was after the cotton harvest. I was catching up on the books in the counting office."

"And that's the only time you touched her?"

"Yessir, that's the only time, I swear it."

"Do you know why she said you raped her?"

"No, sir. I sure don't. I never touched her but that one time."

Will stood and looked down at Lucius Jackson, who sat there looking up at him. Everything the young man had told him had the ring of truth to it, but he was right. A white jury wouldn't believe a black man who accused a young white woman of making advances to him. In fact, Will thought, that is why his story was logically true. If he was going to make up a story, it would not have been the one he told. And the young man was very direct in the way he said it. Though obviously agitated and afraid, he spoke convincingly, without hesitation.

"I don't know if I can help you," he said. "I'll have to think about it. In the meantime, I'll see if I can convince the sheriff to increase the guard here at the jail."

Lucius quickly stood.

"Why's that?" he asked.

"There's a rumor about that some men are planning to take you out of here," Will replied.

"Take me out of here? You mean to hang me?"

"I'm afraid so. But I'll see what I can do to prevent that."

"Thank you so much, Mr. McCulloch. I appreciate it."

When he left the cell, Lucius sat back down on the cot. Will found the sheriff in the jail office. After he instructed the jailer to go back in and lock the cell, he invited Will into his private office. Once inside, he turned and shut the door behind them.

"Are you going to be his lawyer?" he asked.

"I haven't decided that yet, but I think you are going to need more of a guard here, from what I hear."

"Who told you this?"

"Nelson Wright."

"Preacher Wright? He's likely to know the word that's getting around."

The sheriff seemed to be more serious than he was before.

"You know that young lady, don't you?" he asked.

"Yes, I know her."

"And her mother."

"Yes, I know her, too."

"And you're considering representing this Negro?"

"I'm considering it," Will said.

"And you believe there's a lynch mob out there?"

"Lily Poe has a lot of friends, Sheriff. You know that. I think it's a real possibility."

"Very well. I suggest you go over to Friedman's and see who you can get to come here and help. I'll round up some of my reserves."

It was now midmorning, and as he walked the block to Friedman's Store and Saloon he thought about the situation. Lucius Jackson was obviously frightened, and a black man in his position was not likely to admit he had raped a young white woman, but it did not make sense that he would have molested the daughter of his employer at his place of work. Ash was a close friend of Lily Poe and had always felt a fondness for her, perhaps more than fondness. Yet he had said there was something that was not right about Barbara Ann's story. Her father had been killed in the war when she was six years old, and she had always been pampered by her mother, who obviously took pleasure in pampering her—buying the nicest dresses for her and generally catering to her every whim. Although Will was four years older, he had noticed her because she was dressed more richly than the other children her age and had a noticeable air of superiority about her.

He had heard other boys speak of Lily Poe as being a tarnished woman, who had run a gambling house and was a "shady lady," according to some. He was fourteen when he heard them talking about how Mr. McCulloch was a "special friend" of the notorious Miz Poe. He asked his father about it, who said that Mrs. Poe was indeed a friend of his, that they had done some business together and that she was a good woman, cautioning him not to believe every rumor he heard. Wes McCulloch had always been honest with him, trusted him, and believed in him. When he told him Lily Poe was a good woman, he had said it with emphasis. He had defended her, but he had not said that she was his mistress. Will learned that on that rainy night when she and Barbara Ann showed up to view his father's body. His mother, admitting her into the parlor where his father's body lay, showed respect for Lily Poe without saying a word. She had never said anything to him that indicated that she had bad feelings about her. It was left to Gruder to tell him about it, later that night, after he had asked what she and her daughter were doing there, and Gruder told him as he thought his father would have, indicating that sometimes a man's heart would go in more than one direction and there were things in life that he would understand better when he was older. Lily had always exhibited a fondness for Will, and he had always had a good feeling about her. When he saw her that rainy night, it was obvious that she was shaken by Wes McCulloch's death and felt it as fully as any member of the family would have.

When he approached Friedman's Saloon, which opened onto the side street he was on, he noticed an unusual number of horses hitched up outside the doorway. He stepped inside the swinging doors and found a crowd of men drinking and speaking in loud voices. Will recognized most of them. Some of them had been friends of his father. A young dark-haired man, Scotty Bowen, was raising his whiskey glass toward the crowd as Will entered.

"Here's to Texas justice," he said.

A chorus of agreement followed, with several men raising their beer and whiskey glasses in a toast.

"We need to make sure white women and girls are safe in this country," Bowen said. "We can't have raping niggers running around doin' their evil deeds."

Several men in the crowd noticed Will as he walked through the doorway. Bowen saw them looking and turned to face him.

"Well, what have we here?" he said. He appeared to have been drinking for a while, in spite of the early hour. The rest of the crowd was silent. Will walked up to him.

"Looks like you gentlemen must be celebrating something to be partying this early," he said. He looked around at their faces, one by one. "I saw the horses outside and figured there must be a wedding or something."

"It's not that kind of party," said Harvey Otto, who had done some cattle trading with his father. Several of the others murmured their agreement.

Will noticed Henry Davies in the crowd, a blacksmith who had served on the jury in the Hardeman trial. A large swarthy man standing next to him spoke up.

"It's a necktie party, son," he said. "You heard of those, ain't you?"

"Yes, I have," Will replied. "I was thinking that might be going on here." He paused, looking them over once again. "I've known most of you for as long as I remember. That's not the kind of justice you men have stood for."

"You gonna represent that nigger?" one of them asked.

"I'm considering it," he said. "He deserves a fair trial."

"Fair trial?" the swarthy man asked. "He didn't give that Poe girl much of a fair trial, did he?"

"I guess that's based on what you've heard," Will said.

"You damn right it is. And I heard enough. Ain't that right, gentlemen?"

Several murmured their agreement, but the majority were silent, which Will took as a good sign, a sign that a number of them had not made up their minds about lynching Lucius but had come there to talk and listen.

"I haven't been practicing law for long," Will said. "But I know that every man is entitled to a fair trial, even if his skin is black. Each of you know good Negroes, good people who have worked for you. Many of you had ones who stood by you after the war was over, when money was scarce. They didn't run off. They stayed and helped. And you would have been hard-pressed to do without them."

"They can't be allowed to rape our women," one man said.

"You can't assume this man is guilty and condemn him without a trial," Will said.

"He's as guilty as sin," the swarthy man said. "We all know it. We ain't goin' to let him get off with some smart lawyer talk."

Several of the men said, "Yeah, that's right." Will sensed that a crucial point in the meeting had arrived. Then Henry Davies, the blacksmith, spoke out.

"I think we should listen to Lawyer McCulloch," he said. "I was on the jury in that case he tried some years ago. I think he did a good, honest job for that man, that Hardeman. I think we should pay him some heed."

"We'll save the county the expense of a trial," one man said. Several uttered their approval, but the majority were silent.

"If it was a white man who was accused, would this meeting be happening?" Will asked.

"If he had done what this nigger done, it sure would," Scotty Bowen said, his words slurred.

"Sounds like you're trying to get your courage up, Scotty," Will said.

"Why, you son of a bitch," Bowen replied. His right hand moved toward his holstered pistol, but Carl Nethery grabbed his hand. Nethery had been a friend of Will's father.

"You're not going to start that here," Nethery said.

Bowen stood still, his hand held in Nethery's firm grip, his eyes glaring glassily at Nethery. Then Henry Otto stepped forward from the back of the crowd.

"He's right, Scotty," he said. "Let it go. You don't want whiskey talking for you."

Bowen slumped a bit. "All right," he said. "I'll let it go this time. But don't try me again, Billy McCulloch."

"I think it's time we all went home," Otto said. "We got better things to do."

"That's right," Henry Davies said. Several others agreed. The tense mood had lifted.

"You ain't speaking for me," the swarthy man said. "I say let's go get him."

No one responded to him and several quiet seconds passed. The crucial moment had passed. Several of the men came up to Will and shook his hand.

"I knew your father," Harvey Otto said. "He was a good, fair man and you carry a lot of weight with me on his account. I got to know him when we were both members of Hardeman Lodge."

Within a few minutes, they had all filed out of the door, leaving Will short of breath as he realized that he had been tensed up the entire time he had been in the saloon. Jack, the bartender, slid a whiskey bottle down the bar in his direction. Will put his palm up and turned to go.

"You gonna represent him, aren't you?" Jack asked.

Will did not answer. He pushed his way through the bar doors and stepped into the street, where Henry Davies stood. Davies extended his hand.

"You done good," he said. Will shook his hand and then turned and walked away. After Will had walked a few feet in the direction of the jail, he noticed gray smudges on his hand that the blacksmith's handshake had left there. It was only a matter of skin color. It was only a matter of something so inconsequential as the color of one part of a man's body, the part that was most visible, but only one part. And it dawned on him that he was on his way back to the jail to see his client.

THIRTY-EIGHT

A BARREL WAS KEPT IN THE BACK OF THE WHEELWRIGHT shop for scraps and other trash. It was periodically loaded onto a dolly and carried to the far side of the prison yard, where its contents were dumped on a burn pile. It was a large barrel, and it was usually necessary to empty it only every other day or so. One day Ev noticed that Owens, the man who normally took the barrel out, was taking it out more often, or at least he thought he remembered seeing him taking it out the previous afternoon. The next day, he was on the lookout for him and stopped him as he was about to roll the dolly through the doorway of the shop. Owens gave him a nervous look. Ev stepped closer and looked in the barrel. It was full to the brim with scraps of wood and wood shavings, which looked normal, but Ev noticed a piece of cloth sticking out through the shavings that did not look right. He reached down and pulled on the cloth, which was firmly lodged in the shavings somehow, although they were too light to exert the pressure he felt. He pulled harder and more of the cloth came into view. It was a pillow case. He pulled aside a flap of cloth and looked inside. It was full of dirt.

"You don't want to know about this, do you?"

It was Hardin, who had walked up behind him. Ev turned to him.

"I don't see how I can keep from it," Ev said.

"Just don't look," Hardin replied. "You won't see anything if you don't look."

Ev hesitated, then nodded for Owens to move along with the dolly. When Owens had made it outside the doorway, Ev turned back to Hardin.

"How can I avoid this? You are going to get us all in trouble."

"Then join us," Hardin said. "Two more weeks and we'll be out of here."

"Not likely," Ev replied. "They'll catch you for sure."

"You want to know my plan?" Hardin asked.

"I don't think so. I think the less I know the better."

"Then keep quiet and you'll be all right. But you better not tell. He who tells gets it good." Then Hardin smiled, turned, and walked to the back of the shop.

The burn pile was on the far side of the yard and was protected from the view of the guard towers by a toolshed. It would be a simple matter for Owens to empty the dirt from the pillowcases and spread it around the edge of the pile without being seen. It had been a month since Hardin had been assigned to the wheelwright shop. If they had been digging a tunnel for three weeks or more, a considerable amount of dirt would have been deposited and would have been seen if any alert guard had ventured behind the toolshed, but the guards did not go there often, leaving it to the prisoners who carted scraps from the various shops to burn the pile regularly. A trusty was in charge of supervising the burning and was normally in charge of the matches used to light the fires. Years of burning had left a large heap of accumulated ash that formed a small hill, making the deposit of dirt from a tunnel less conspicuous.

Hardin had recruited eleven men from the wheelwright shop to participate in the digging of the tunnel. The entrance was in the very back of the shop behind a lathe that hid it from view. A large wooden box used for scraps was placed over it, except when a man was entering or leaving it. Whether or not the escape attempt was successful, Ev was surely to be accused of being in on the conspiracy. He was the trusty in charge of the wheelwright shop. It would be hard to convince the prison administration that he was not involved if he did not come forward and report it. On the other hand, he did not like the idea of telling the authorities. And Hardin's threat had an air of seriousness about it. John Wesley Hardin was known throughout Texas as a cold-blooded killer, and a threat from him was not to be taken lightly. There were stabbings that took place within the walls with some regularity, some of them unsolved murders of prisoners by other prisoners. If he took up Hardin's offer and joined them, it was highly unlikely that the escape attempt would be successful. His eighteen months could be enhanced by his participation. It would probably be best to do nothing. At least there was a chance of convincing the administration that he had not known about it.

THIRTY-NINE

LILY POE CLEARED OFF THE DINNER TABLE. Normally, Barbara Ann would have done so, but Lily had sent her to spend the night with her aunt. Ash figured that she wanted to talk about some things that she did not want Barbara Ann to hear. It had been one of Lily's seemingly offhand dinner invitations, delivered by her that afternoon in a casual manner that was familiar to him. During drinks, before dinner, and as they dined, they had engaged in small talk, and Lily spoke sparingly, which was not like her. She was not normally willing to settle for small talk. She also seemed to have a less confident manner than usual. Knowing her as well as he did, he knew she would get around to what she had to say in her own good time. When he followed her into the kitchen and offered to dry the dishes as she washed, as he always did, she was silent for a good while, handing him the dishes and silverware as usual. Finally, she asked, without looking at him, "Is Billy going to represent that Negro?"

Although he had expected it, it sprang out of her uncharacteristic silence and he was not ready for it. He paused before answering.

"He is," he said.

"Why?" She turned abruptly and looked him in the eye as she asked it.

"He's entitled to a lawyer," Ash replied.

"Does he think he's innocent?"

He knew it was coming and here it was. The ultimate question. He could avoid it, but she would know he was lying.

"Reasonable doubt, in his mind," he said. "He thinks there's reasonable doubt."

"Reasonable doubt? What reasonable doubt? Does he think Barbara Ann is lying?"

He wanted to say that she should ask him herself, but he knew better.

"That's hard to say," he said.

"Hard to say?" Her voice had risen.

"I think he thinks that there's reasonable doubt about her version of what happened."

Having finished with the dishes, she was holding the damp dish rag tightly. Her eyes bored through him, unwavering.

"Well, I want to talk to him about that," she said. "I want to know why he thinks that."

"You are a witness, Lily. He'll talk to you, but he can only do so as a lawyer. I don't think you'll like that."

She continued to stare, twisting the dish rag in both hands.

"I thought we were okay. I thought Billy and I were okay."

"I don't think it has anything to do with that," he said.

"You don't? Well, I don't understand it."

"I don't think it has anything to do with you. He has a strong sense of duty."

"Duty! To do what?"

"Duty as a lawyer. He takes it seriously."

She turned then and leaned against the sink, still holding the dish rag.

"What would Wes think?" she asked, staring at the wall. "What would he think?"

He hesitated before speaking.

"Wes would support him if he thought his motives were fair," he finally said. "At least, that's what I think."

Tears were welling up in her eyes. She stared at the wall for a long moment.

"Of course he would," she said, her voice firm. "Of course he would. But he hasn't even talked to me or Barbara Ann. Why wouldn't he do that first? I don't understand why he didn't talk to me first."

There was no satisfactory explanation that he could give her. He had known it would come to this.

"I know it doesn't make sense to you," he said.

"You're right about that. It makes no sense to me at all. At all."

She turned and hung the dish rag on the hook over the drain board and walked out of the kitchen, taking short, hurried steps, as if she was holding herself against falling. He followed her into the parlor and for a moment thought of taking her in his arms, but he had never taken the initiative with her that way and decided instantly that it would not be a good idea. For the first time since he had met her, he felt uncomfortable in her presence. She walked to the side board and poured two shots of bourbon, then handed him one of the glasses.

"Here's to justice, Lawyer Maitland," she said. "May she prevail."

The next morning, Ash was at the office early, before Will arrived, which was unusual. He had acquired the habit of sleeping later than usual, a change from past years when he had resisted the pull on him that age exacted, sensing somehow that slowing down would accelerate the downward spiral that the passage of time rendered inevitable. And he had come to rely on Will's presence to give him more time to spend a leisurely morning at home, which was still in the small cabin on the other side of Plum Creek, where he had once had his office as well as his dwelling place, in the near ghost town of Atlanta. Only a handful of families remained there, most having moved on to the new town of Luling a few miles to the west.

He sat in his chair in the inner office, beside the window overlooking the street, resisting the urge to puff on a bit of cannabis that lay in his pipe, as an antidote to the hangover that pulsed in his head from drinks the night before. He wanted to be sober when Will arrived. He had postponed talking to him about the case for a couple of weeks, which had caused some uncomfortable silences between them. Now he felt that the time had come. Knowing Lily as he did, it was obvious that she would come to talk to Will, and it would be a crucial confrontation. Will should be warned. And it was not too late for him to change his mind and let Judge Daughtry appoint counsel for Lucius Jackson.

Will walked in at seven thirty, his normal arrival time when he was not attending court. Ash turned the chair around to face him.

"Good morning," he said.

"Good morning," Will replied. "Here a bit early, huh?"

"I wanted to talk to you before the public started coming in." Ash had always referred to those coming to the office as "the public," as if their clientele included the entire community. Will nodded and sat down in his chair, on the other side of the railroad desk.

"All right," he said.

"I know you have your mind made up about the Negro's case, but I want to have a talk with you about it."

"Okay."

"I had put this off, but I was at Lily's for dinner last night," Ash said.

"And she brought it up," Will said.

"Yes."

"And she wanted to know why I had agreed to represent that Negro."

"Yes."

"What did you tell her?"

"It was hard, Will, hard to explain. I did the best I could. I told her it was a matter of principle for you, that you believed every man was entitled to a competent defense."

"And did that satisfy her?"

Ash stood and turned toward the window.

"Of course not," he said, his back to Will. "She is going to come see you. She didn't say she was, but I'd bet on it. She's going to ask you why you don't believe Barbara Ann's story even though you haven't talked to either of them."

"I thought she would," Will said. "I thought she would have already come and asked about that. I'm surprised she hasn't."

"She thinks very highly of you, Will. It's not an easy thing for her to understand."

"I guess this is a warning. Thanks for that."

"Yes, but I would like for you to reconsider. I could talk to the judge. He could appoint competent counsel for him."

"You and I both know that won't happen," Will said. "He'll wind up with Matt Barton. Might as well have left him for the lynch mob."

"There is a young lawyer, new to Lockhart," Ash said. "You may have met him. Fly is his name."

"I have met him. We had coffee together not long ago."

"He is a former assistant DA from Dallas County," Ash said. "And he has a wife and a young child. He can't afford to take the case."

"But you can?"

"As I've said before, Ash, I'll go out on my own, if you wish. I know it's likely to hurt your practice for me to do this."

Ash turned to face him.

"I'm not worried about me," he said, with an air of indignation. "I've had my run at things, and I've got clients that will stick with me until I hang 'em up, no matter what. I'm concerned about you, about what it will do to you. You've got a bright future that's likely to be spoiled."

"I knew that going in," Will replied, looking him in the eye.

"Well, all right then. But keep it in mind that I can talk to the judge. He might even appoint someone from out of county, someone who'd come from Seguin or Gonzales."

"For what, appointed counsel fees? That's not likely."

"There may be unknown resources that could be brought to bear," Ash said.

Will stood.

"That's obscene," he said. "Just to save my reputation from the exercise of my convictions? I don't think so."

"Let me ask you this," Ash said. "Do you think you're the only lawyer that can do right by this man?"

"No. But I may be the only one who will."

FORTY

HARDIN'S PLAN WAS TO TUNNEL ABOUT SEVENTY-FIVE yards from the wheelwright shop to the armory, where weapons were stored, then to wait until the guards had put up their guns and gone to supper. They would then cut through the pine floor of the armory, take the guns, and force their way out of the prison, taking with them every man who wanted to go, except for convicted rapists. Hardin didn't think that "rape fiends" should be liberated, although he did not seem to hold the same concern about murderers and thieves. In addition to the twelve men from the wheelwright shop, who actually shared in the tunneling, he had let dozens more in on the plot. They were to assist in the escape by taking keys from guards and trusties and opening cell and cellblock doors. Hardin had even chosen men to become snipers, who were to target the guards in the guard towers at the corners of the walls.

On the day before the planned break, Owens confided in Ev that he and one other, Bill Terril, were going to go to the superintendent and tell him of the plan. He invited Ev to join them.

"You know you'll be a suspect if you don't go with us," he said.

"I don't want to know anything about it," Ev replied.

"Suit yourself. We're going after supper tonight."

After the superintendent was informed, he ordered Hardin and nine others who were in on the plot arrested. Owens and Terril obtained pardons for their disclosure. The other nine eventually confessed to having been involved, but Hardin denied all knowledge of it.

He was put in a dark solitary cell on bread and water, with a ball and chain attached to his ankle, for a fifteen-day period, as punishment. The other five who worked in the shop, who were not reported as part of the plot, were interviewed by the superintendent and the captain of the guard. Everett Hardeman was interviewed last. A stenographer was present, taking notes.

"You were the trusty in charge of the wheelwright shop," the captain stated. "Did you know of this plot?"

"I did not," Ev replied.

"A great amount of dirt was smuggled out of the shop and into the yard. How was it that you did not notice this?"

"It was brought out with the scraps and it was covered up. I found out about it afterward."

"Hmm. And how was it that a tunnel was dug from the shop without you knowing it? You were the trusty in charge."

"It was done in the back and covered up every day by the time I did my inspection."

"You took an oath when you became a trusty," the superintendent said. "Do you remember that?"

"Yes, sir."

"And part of that oath was that you would report any suspicious activity. Do you remember that part of your oath?"

"Yes, sir."

"It is not believable that all this was going on in your shop and you were not aware of it," the superintendent said. "Two of the men in the shop, two who worked there, reported it to us. They knew of it and reported it. You did not."

Ev was silent.

"They told us that you did not know this was going on, but I find that hard to believe," the superintendent said. "You are relieved of your trusty duties as of now. You will be back to the prison population and will be removed from the trusty cellblock. Do you have anything else to tell us?"

"No, sir," Ev replied.

He was placed in a cell with a lifer named Collins at the rear of a cellblock. It was five days before he was assigned to the furniture factory again. Ten days later, Hardin was brought to the furniture factory by two guards, who told the trusty in charge that he was a plotter who would probably try to escape in some way and that he should keep an eye on him and on anyone he talked to or hung around with. The trusty escorted Hardin past Ev to his place of work. Hardin gave him a hard look as he passed.

FORTY-ONE

IT HAD BEEN THREE WEEKS SINCE THE ARREST OF LUCIUS Jackson. The Grand Jury was in session and was due to return indictments, and perhaps no-bills, on Friday. Will McCulloch had made an appointment to see Dr. Phillip Watkins on Thursday. He had learned from the sheriff that the doctor had examined Barbara Ann Poe. He was not sure the doctor would talk to him about his examination. He was likely to cite the physician/patient privilege, although it was probable that the doctor had performed the examination on behalf of the state, according to Sheriff Ellison, and not as Barbara Ann's treating physician. The doctor's office was upstairs above the Gem Pharmacy, on the corner of the courthouse square. When he reached the top of the stairs from street level, he was surprised to see Frank Clark, the district attorney, seated in the reception area along with several patients. Clark stood when he saw Will and walked over to him.

"Good morning, Will," he said, extending his hand.

"Good morning," Will replied.

"I'd like a word with you," Clark said, gesturing toward a side door marked "Private." Will followed him into an anteroom containing a small table and three chairs. Once inside, Clark shut the door and turned around to face him.

"I assume that you were not aware that you should notify opposing counsel before interviewing an expert witness," he said. "So I take no offense, personally, but it would have at least been common courtesy to let me know about it."

"I was not," Will said hesitantly.

"Well, that's what I thought. If you had asked, I would have consented to an interview and have no objection now, as long as I am present."

"Of course. I'm sorry about that. It just didn't occur to me."

"I'll let the nurse know we are both here," Clark said. "Wait here, please."

Clark left the room and returned shortly. "The doctor will see us now," he said.

They entered the doctor's office, which contained a roll-top desk covered with stacks of papers, an examination table, two chairs and a stool, as well as a faux human skeleton hanging from a hook atop a metal pole. A table against another wall held an assortment of jars and boxes, full of medical supplies. Dr. Watkins, a tall, sandy-haired man in his mid-fifties whom Will had met before, greeted them as they entered.

"Welcome, gentlemen," he said. "Won't you have a seat?" He gestured toward the two chairs and, once they were seated, sat on the edge of the exam table.

"As you know, Doctor, Mr. McCulloch here represents the young Negro accused of raping the Poe girl," Clark said. "I have agreed that he can ask you questions about your examination and findings, and you are free to answer him if you wish, but you are not required to do so."

"I am willing," the doctor said.

Will pulled a pad and pencil from his briefcase. "Doctor," he asked, "when did you examine this young lady?"

"It was a week ago yesterday," the doctor replied. "Wednesday of last week."

"Did you take a medical history from her?"

"A brief one," he said. "I asked her when the rape occurred."

"And what did she say?"

"Weeks ago. She said it happened weeks ago."

"Did she recall a specific date?"

"I don't remember asking her for a specific date," the doctor said.

"Did she tell you what happened?"

"I did not ask her that."

"Why not, Doctor? Wouldn't that be relevant to your exam?"

"No, not at all. I was told to examine this young lady for evidence of the outrage that was committed upon her. I did not need the details from her. A physical examination was all that was called for."

"I see. What were your findings?"

"I found the absence of a hymen, indicating penetration by a male organ."

"Anything else, Doctor? Did you have any other findings?"

"No. Nothing else was required."

"Did you find any evidence that violence had been committed upon her?" Will asked.

"I found no marks upon her other than a birthmark," the doctor replied.

"A birthmark?"

"Yes."

"What did it look like?"

"Just a round spot, about a centimeter in diameter," the doctor said. "Brown. On her inner thigh. I think the right thigh, if I recall correctly."

"And you found no other marks indicating violence?"

"No. None."

"Thank you, Doctor. That's all I have."

As Will and Frank Clark walked down the stairway together, Will asked, "Are you going to indict this man?"

"I won't. The Grand Jury will," Clark replied.

"This is a weak case, Mr. Clark," Will said, stopping on the stairway. "I think you know that."

"We'll see about that," Clark said, and moved on down the stairs ahead of him.

The Grand Jury returned an indictment for rape against Lucius Jackson the next day. Judge Daughtry set the case on the jury docket for the next session of court, one month away. Lucius was led out of the courtroom in chains, with manacles around his wrists and ankles. On the ride back to Luling, Will considered the situation. He could hardly expect the jury to believe Jackson's version of what had happened between him and Barbara Ann, and putting him on the stand might ensure his conviction, but he probably had no other choice. That, and a careful attention paid to the prosecution's case, was all he had to work with. He would have to listen carefully and be skillful in his cross-examination of the state's witnesses. Under the penal code, the punishment for rape was a penitentiary term of not less than five nor more than fifteen years. So fifteen years was the outside risk, if a lynching could be avoided.

When he reached the sidewalk outside his office, he noticed Wonsley Baker's gray mare hitched to the post by the stairway door. He found him waiting for him in the reception room. Wonsley stood as he approached.

"You've come to see me, Uncle?" Will asked.

"I need to talk with you," Wonsley replied, not responding to the usual joking manner Will had used in referring to their kinship.

He showed him into the inner office, which was vacant. Ash was apparently away. Wonsley took the seat Will offered him and after Will was seated, leaned forward to speak in a low voice.

"You gonna represent that nigger boy?" he asked.

"I am already doing so," Will replied.

"You can't do that, Billy. You can't."

"Why not?"

"Because it's Barbara Ann. You know it ain't right."

"I think it's the right thing to do," Will said.

"I'm sure you do, but it ain't right. Have you talked to her?"

"No. I haven't."

"She's real upset about this whole thing," Wonsley said.

"So you've talked to her about this?"

Wonsley looked down before speaking.

"I been seeing her some," he said.

"You mean socially?" Will asked.

"Not exactly. Her mama don't approve of me."

"So you've been seeing her in secret?"

"Yeah. Some."

Will stood and walked to the window, then turned to face Wonsley again.

"What do you know about this?" he asked.

"I know she was raped."

"How do you know that?"

"She told me, that's how."

"What did she tell you?"

Wonsley rose to his feet.

"She said that boy raped her in the seed house," he said, raising his voice.

"What was she doing in the seed house?"

Wonsley hesitated.

"I don't know," he said. "It's her mama's gin. She's got the right to be there."

"But she doesn't work there, does she?"

"She don't work at all," Wonsley replied.

"Lucius Jackson says he didn't do it," Will said.

"Sure he does. That's what he'd say."

"Look. If she says it happened in the seed house, then why was she in there? What was she doing in there in the first place? That's not a place for a young lady. It's a dirty place. I don't see why she would be in there."

Wonsley's brow furrowed. "I don't know," he finally said.

Will returned to his seat behind the desk. He waited for Wonsley to speak. Finally, Wonsley took his seat in the side chair.

"I don't know," he repeated. "I never thought of that."

"Did you have relations with her?" Will asked.

"Relations?" Wonsley looked down at his hands, clasped together in his lap.

"Yes. Did you lie with her?"

He kept staring down.

"I don't think she is telling the truth about what happened with Lucius Jackson," Will said. "That's the main reason I agreed to represent him. He says he didn't do it and I believe him."

"I asked her to marry me," Wonsley said. "But her mama wouldn't approve."

"I understand," Will said. "What do you want me to do?"

"I don't know," Wonsley replied. "Just don't represent him, I guess."

He stood, his hat in his hand.

"I must," Will said. "Her story doesn't add up. I believe there's reasonable doubt."

Wonsley left without shaking hands.

FORTY-TWO

THE JURY PANEL FOR THE JACKSON CASE WAS SWORN IN. They were all white males. Because it was not a case involving possible capital punishment, questioning of the panelists was done while all of them were seated outside the rail in the courtroom. Frank Clark went first. He merely asked if every man could follow the evidence from the witness stand and the law as the judge instructed them, after describing this as a case of rape in which the accused, a young Negro man, was the defendant and the victim was a young white woman. None of the panelists looked surprised on hearing what the case was about. They had all obviously heard about it beforehand. They all agreed that they could find the defendant guilty if they believed the evidence showed his guilt. Clark spoke with confidence, failing to ask any individual questions. He probably had information on all the members of the jury panel and did not need to learn any more. It was unlikely that any of them would be leaning toward the defendant in this case.

Will stood up and introduced himself, then asked Lucius Jackson to stand and introduced him as the defendant. Several of the panelists exchanged solemn glances. When Will asked if anyone knew the defendant, nobody raised their hand. Then he asked if anyone knew the complainant, Barbara Ann Poe. No one raised their hand. When he asked if anyone knew her mother, Lily Poe, a dozen raised their hands. He marked their names on his list.

"Would any of you who know Mrs. Poe require less proof of the prosecution just because of that?" he asked.

"What do you mean?" asked a gray-haired man in the second row.

"The state must prove its case by believable evidence beyond a reasonable doubt," Will replied. "That's the burden of proof. If you have a reasonable doubt as to the defendant's guilt, then you must find him not guilty."

The man and several others nodded.

"The defendant is a Negro," Will said. "He is entitled to a fair trial, as fair a trial as a white man. He has the same rights in this courtroom as any of your friends and neighbors would have. Just because he is a black man, you should not assume that he is guilty of a crime. I am representing him because I do not believe he is guilty. And he is entitled to a presumption of innocence."

Will noticed skeptical looks on several faces.

"Lucius Jackson is a law-abiding citizen who has never been in trouble with the law. He has a good reputation in the community and is a married man with a young child. This is the only time he has been accused of any wrongdoing. I ask you to wait until you have heard all of the evidence in the case before arriving at an opinion as to guilt. I ask you to presume he is innocent of this crime until you have heard believable evidence that convinces you beyond a reasonable doubt as to his guilt, just as you would do if you were sitting in judgment of your neighbor. Do you all think you can do that?"

Only a few nodded their agreement. There were only a few men on the list that Will did not know or know of. He asked questions of them about how they made their living and where they resided. There were three farmers, one rancher, one wagon maker, a carpenter, and a blacksmith. Each of them said he could return a verdict of not guilty if he was not convinced by the evidence beyond a reasonable doubt that the defendant was guilty. One of the farmers, named Collins, had to have the question rephrased several times before he understood it.

Will had ten peremptory challenges, or strikes, to five for the prosecution. He struck ten off of his jury list based on his knowledge of their probable deep prejudice against black men and the knowledge that some of them were either friends or debtors of Lily Poe. None of the men who had been at Friedman's Saloon that day were on the panel, but one was a neighbor of one of those men and another was a relative of one. Will struck both of them. In spite of what they said in answer to questions, he knew that practically all of the men on the panel were likely to have already formed an opinion that the defendant was guilty, solely by reason of his race and the fact that a young white woman was his accuser. He had struck the ones on the panel that he knew to be former slaveholders. Clark turned in his list first. Later, when Will looked at it, it was obvious that Clark had struck poor working men, including three who were relatively young. The jury that was seated included three merchants, one saloon keeper, a banker, two ranchers, a preacher, and the one blacksmith. They stood and the judge swore them in, then declared a recess until after the noon hour.

Will visited with Lucius Jackson in a holding cell on the first floor of the courthouse. He had considered that the judge might be convinced to assess the minimum sentence of five years in return for a plea of guilty, but a black man convicted of raping a white woman was not likely to survive five years in prison. Will felt that he was under a duty, however, to discuss the possibility of a guilty plea with his client one more time before the trial began. Jackson's response was the same. "I won't say I'm guilty," he said. "I didn't do it."

As Will ascended the stairs on his way back to the courtroom, he was thinking about his cross-examination of Barbara Ann Poe. He would have to be very careful. An approach to questioning her that appeared to consist of gratuitous insults would likely be held against his client. On the other hand, his only chance to obtain an acquittal involved contradicting her story of what had happened. As he passed the door to the district attorney's office, he could hear a loud female voice coming from within. It was a voice he recognized as Lily Poe's. He could not make out what she was saying, but it was clear that she was agitated. He paused by the doorway, listening. He could also hear Frank Clark's voice, at a lower volume. The two of them appeared to be in strong disagreement about something. After a moment's silence, Will passed on and entered the courtroom, where he spent the rest of the noon hour going over his notes and thinking about the probable testimony to come.

Clark and his clerk entered the courtroom shortly before one o'clock, followed by the sheriff and a deputy, who led Lucius Jackson in and seated him at the counsel table with Will. The judge entered shortly thereafter, those in the room rising as he entered, then retaking their seats when instructed, after the judge was seated at the bench. Judge Daughtry cleared his throat before speaking.

"Are you gentlemen ready to proceed?" he asked, looking at the lawyers.

Clark stood to speak. "Your Honor, I request an adjournment until the morning, due to the illness of the prosecuting witness."

The judge looked surprised. "Did you just learn of this illness, counsel?" he asked.

"Yes, Your Honor," Clark responded. "Apparently it came on suddenly." There was something in the way he said it, as if he was not convinced of the truth of what he was saying.

"Hmmm," the judge intoned. "What says counsel for the defense?"

"We have no objection, Your Honor," Will said.

"Very well," the judge said. "I will have the jury brought in and instruct them that we are in recess until nine in the morning. Do counsel for the state and for the defense agree that the jury may be allowed to separate during court recesses and adjournments?" Both Clark and Will agreed. The judge then asked, "Is there anything else we can take up outside the presence of the jury today?"

Will rose to address the court. "We invoke the rule, Your Honor."

"Very well, Counsel. We can take that up first thing in the morning. Is there anything else?"

Both lawyers shook their heads.

"All right. Bring in the jury, Sheriff Ellison. As soon as the jury has been discharged, I want to see counsel in my chambers."

The jury was brought in and instructed not to discuss the case with anyone, to report to the bailiff if anyone attempted to discuss it with them, and to be in the jury room by nine in the morning. The judge gestured for the two lawyers to follow him to his office. Once inside, he offered them seats, took off his robe, and hung it on a hook on the wall before taking his seat.

"What is going on, Frank?" he asked Clark.

"I just learned that the girl is ill," Clark said, in an unsteady voice. "I just found out over the noon hour. I expected her to be here ready to testify, but her mother came alone and said she was ill."

"What is the nature of the illness?" the judge asked.

"It's that time of the month," Clark responded. "She's having cramps."

"I see," the judge said. "Does Mrs. Poe expect her to be able to testify tomorrow?"

"I believe she will be available, Your Honor."

"All right, Frank. I want the two of you here by eight thirty. Have your witnesses ready to be sworn under the rule. And, Frank. I will not hold this jury over another day. I'll declare a mistrial if the girl does not show up ready to testify in the morning."

"Yes, sir," Clark said.

"I'll see you both in the morning," the judge said, giving Will a look.

As they left the judge's office, Will noticed that Clark no longer had the air of confidence he had displayed earlier. Outside the courthouse on the lawn, Will was approached by an elderly black man he did not recognize. The man took off his hat and made a slight bow before speaking.

"The lady over there wants to have a word with you," he said, nodding toward a buggy standing across the way. He could not see who was seated inside until he approached it. He was not surprised to see Lily Poe seated there. She stared at him with a grim look for a moment before speaking.

"Billy, I don't understand why you are doing this," she said. "You are causing my daughter to suffer and I won't forgive you for it."

He knew that nothing he could say would be well received, so he did not speak.

"Don't you have anything to say for yourself?" she asked. Her eyes were moistening.

"I'm just doing what I believe to be right, Mrs. Poe."

"Mrs. Poe. Aren't you the formal lawyer now? Calling me Mrs. Poe."

"The man is entitled to a defense," he said.

"He's lucky to be alive after what he did," she said, tears running down her cheeks. "Prison's too good for him."

He stood there, taking it.

"Don't you have anything else to say?" she asked.

"No, ma'am."

"The hell with you," she said, then grabbed the reins and flapped them hard against the back of the horse, which caused the buggy to lurch forward, past where he was standing. He stood and watched her drive away down the street.

FORTY-THREE

WILL WAS IN THE COURTROOM, SEATED AT THE DEFENSE counsel table with his client by his side when the judge entered and took the bench. The courtroom was packed with observers. Neither Frank Clark nor his clerk were present. The judge took his pocket watch out from beneath his robe and looked at it before setting it down before him.

"It's eight thirty-five by my watch, Sheriff. What time do you have?"

Sheriff Ellison arose from his seat by the railing gate. "That's what I have, Your Honor."

Judge Daughtry pursed his lips. "Is the jury present and accounted for?"

"Yes, Your Honor," the sheriff replied.

The judge signaled for the sheriff and Will to approach the bench, then leaned down to speak to them in a soft voice.

"Sheriff, go see if you can find Mr. Clark. I don't want our audience to get any impressions from his absence if I can help it, so keep it quiet. Do you understand, Counsel?"

"Yes, Your Honor."

Will took his seat at the counsel table as the sheriff left the courtroom. The crowd had been silent since the judge had entered, but was now filled with a cacophony of conversations. The judge leaned back in his high-backed chair and closed his eyes. After a few minutes, Clark and his clerk entered the doorway from the hall and came inside the railing. Clark stopped in front of the counsel table.

"Sorry for the delay, Your Honor," he said, almost out of breath.

"That's quite all right, Mr. Clark. Is the state ready to proceed?"

"Yes, Your Honor," Clark replied.

"And is the defense ready?"

"Yes, Your Honor," Will said, standing.

"Very well. The rule has been invoked. All witnesses that are present will be brought forward to be sworn, except for the defendant, of course."

"We have two in the hallway," Clark said.

"We have none present at this time," Will said.

The judge gestured toward the sheriff, who was standing by the doorway. He opened the door to the hallway and leaned through it, gesturing. After a few moments, Lily and Barbara Ann Poe entered. They walked slowly toward the railing, waited for the sheriff to open the gate for them, then stepped inside, Lily first and Barbara Ann following. They stood before the bench. Lily wore a dark blue dress that stood out among the dull colors of the crowd, which consisted mostly of men in weekday clothing. She stood straight, staring at thc judge. Barbara Ann was looking down, her head slightly bowed. She wore a dull brown dress and though dressed neatly, she slumped, giving her the appearance of being somewhat disheveled. Though her face appeared to have been made up, her eyes were red and she had a flushed look.

"Ladies, you will each state your name, please," the judge said.

Barbara Ann looked at her mother, who spoke first. "Lily Henchard Poe," she said. She then looked to Barbara Ann and nodded. Barbara Ann hesitated before speaking softly.

"Barbara Ann Poe," she said.

"Please raise your right hands to be sworn," the judge said. Lily did so promptly. Barbara Ann followed. "You do solemnly swear in your testimony to be given before this court to tell the truth, the whole truth, and nothing but the truth, so help you God? You may signify by saying, 'I do.'"

Lily said, "I do," firmly. Barbara Ann's response could barely be heard.

"Ladies, the rule has been invoked. That means that you will not be present in the courtroom when other witnesses are testifying. Furthermore, you will not discuss your testimony with anyone other than the lawyers in the case, Mr. Clark and Mr. McCulloch. That means, of course, that you will not discuss your testimony with each other or with any other witness. If anyone tries to talk to you about your testimony, you are to report it to me immediately. Any violation of the rule may result in disqualifying a witness from testifying and may even cause a mistrial in this case. Do you understand?"

They both nodded.

"I will need a verbal response for the record, please," the judge said.

They both quietly said, "Yes."

"Very well. You will wait outside the courtroom until you are called to testify. Sheriff?"

Sheriff Ellison escorted them through the railing gate and through the doorway to the hall. All eyes of the audience were on them as they left and a murmur arose. The judge slammed his gavel down.

"I want to say to those present that there will be no demonstrations in my courtroom during this trial. This is as full as I have seen this courtroom in years and I do not want any interference with the testimony. You will therefore refrain from comments or conversation during the testimony and during any other proceedings in open court. If you violate my instructions, I may clear the courtroom. Does everybody understand?"

Several murmurs of "Yes, sir" could be heard.

"All right. Is there anything else to take up before we bring the jury in, gentlemen?"

Both lawyers said, "No, Your Honor."

"Bring them in, Sheriff."

The sheriff walked over to the door to the jury room, opened it and leaned inside, speaking inaudibly, then the jury filed in through a side gate in the railing and took their twelve seats in the jury box. The judge turned their way.

"Gentlemen of the jury, the court appreciates your patience. You were here early this morning and had to wait awhile in the jury room while the court took up other matters, which were important. We are now ready to proceed with testimony." He turned to Clark, who stood by the counsel table. "The state will call its first witness," the judge said.

"The state calls Lily Poe."

She was again escorted through the hallway door by the sheriff. When she was inside the railing, the sheriff showed her to the witness stand, where she took a seat.

"You are Lily Poe?" Clark asked.

"Yes."

"Do you reside in Caldwell County with your daughter, Barbara Ann?"

"Yes."

"And you are a widow?"

"I am."

"When did your husband pass?"

"During the war. He was killed at Shiloh."

"Fighting for the Confederacy?"

"Yes."

"Is Barbara Ann your only child?"

She hesitated before answering, "Yes."

"How old was she when her father died?"

"She was five."

"And how old is she today?"

"She is twenty-one."

"Does she live at home with you?"

"Yes."'

"Last year, did Barbara Ann report something to you?"

"Yes." She looked down at her hands, folded in her lap.

"What was that, Mrs. Poe?"

"She said Lucius Jackson had raped her."

"When did the rape happen, according to what she told you?"

"It had been about a week."

"Do you believe that she was chaste before this happened to her?"

Her eyes widened. "Certainly," she said.

"Pass the witness," Clark said.

Will hesitated before speaking. Lily Poe was not looking at him. She was staring straight ahead toward the rear wall of the courtroom.

"Mrs. Poe," he finally said, "did your daughter appear to be upset when she told you this?"

"Yes, of course she was upset," she replied, still looking straight ahead.

"What time of the day did she tell you this?"

She hesitated. "I don't recall the exact time," she said.

"Do you recall if it was in the morning, afternoon, evening?"

"It was in the morning."

"Before or after breakfast?"

"It was after."

"Was anyone else present when she told you?"

She looked at him for the first time since she had entered the courtroom.

"No. No one else was there."

"Where were you when she told you this?"

"In my dining room. We had finished breakfast."

"Don't you have a maid, Mrs. Poe?"

"Yes, I have a maid."

"Was she at work that morning?"

"I don't recall. It could have been a Sunday morning. I give her Sunday mornings off after she cooks, so she can go to church."

"What is your maid's name?"

"Effie."

"Is she a Negro woman?"

"She is."

"And you're not sure whether she was there that morning?"

"I don't think she was."

"Do you and your daughter attend church?"

She hesitated, glancing at the jury. "No, we do not."

"Do you recall what you did the rest of the day?"

"No, I don't recall. I was upset."

"When did you report it to the authorities?"

"The next day."

"The sheriff's records indicate you reported it on a Wednesday. Does that sound right?"

"I don't remember."

"If you reported it the next day, she would have told you on a Tuesday morning. Is that possible?"

"I told you, I don't remember the exact date."

"Where does Effie work when she is at work? Does she cook and serve you breakfast?"

"She does the usual household chores. She cooks and cleans and does the wash," she said, her voice at a staccato clip.

"Is she normally at work on a Tuesday morning?"

"What are you getting at?" she asked angrily. "I have told you I didn't think the maid was there and you keep asking about her. If she was at work, she wasn't in the room."

"All right, Mrs. Poe." Will waited, staring at her as she again looked at the back wall. A few moments passed before he asked her the next question.

"Did you and your daughter have an argument that morning?" he asked.

She turned and looked sternly at him.

"No. We do not argue."

"You and your daughter never argue?"

"No. We sometimes have disagreements, but I wouldn't call them arguments."

Will stood to address the judge.

"Your Honor, subject to recall, I have no further questions of this witness at this time."

"We have nothing further at this time, Your Honor," Clark said.

"She will be available. Make sure the sheriff knows your whereabouts, Mrs. Poe. You are excused for now," the judge said.

She stood promptly, stepped down from the witness stand, and the sheriff escorted her toward the railing gate. She gave Will a stern look as she passed by the counsel table. After she was through the hallway door, the judge said, "The state will call its next witness."

Clark rose and said, "The state calls Barbara Ann Poe."

The sheriff again leaned through the doorway to the hall, then, after a few moments, stepped through it and shut the door behind him. The courtroom was silent as a minute passed, then the sheriff opened the door and reappeared, holding the door open. Barbara Ann entered. Her face was flushed and she appeared to have been crying. She held her head down as the sheriff escorted her to the witness stand, where she hesitated before unsteadily mounting the two steps and taking a seat in the chair.

"You are under oath, miss," Judge Daughtry said. "The state will proceed."

Clark cleared his throat before speaking.

"State your name, please."

"Barbara Ann Poe." Her voice was barely audible.

"Are you a resident of Caldwell County?"

"Yes."

"And you live with your mother, who just testified before this jury?"

"Yes, sir." She glanced at the jury.

"And are you a single woman?"

"Yes."

"How old are you?"

"Twenty-one."

"Miss Poe, I am going to ask you some delicate questions about what happened to you last fall. Do you understand?"

"Yes, sir."

"You and I have talked about this, haven't we?"

"Yes, sir."

"Something bad happened to you at your mother's place of business, her mill and gin, last fall, didn't it?"

"Yes, sir."

"Tell the jury what happened."

"I was raped." She started crying.

"Can you tell who did it to you?"

"It was that nigger," she said, pointing at Lucius Jackson.

"Let the record reflect that she is pointing out the defendant," Clark said.

"It will be so," said the judge.

"Do you know this defendant?" Clark asked.

"Yes, sir. He worked at the gin."

"Where did this happen?"

"It was in the seed house."

"Was anyone else present when it happened?"

"No, sir."

"Tell the jury in your own words what happened."

"He came at me and threw me down and had his way with me."

"Were you a virgin?"

"Yes, sir."

"I have to ask this question. Did his organ penetrate you?"

She looked down, then looked directly at the jury.

"Yes. It did." She was no longer crying, although her face was still flushed.

"And did you report this to your mother?"

"Yes, sir. I did."

"When did you do that?"

"It was a few days later."

"Why didn't you report it before then?"

She hesitated. "I was embarrassed, I guess."

"And did this happen on or about the twenty-fifth of November 1878?"

"Yes, sir."

"Pass the witness," Clark said.

Will remained seated at the counsel table. Barbara Ann looked directly at him, tears welling in her eyes.

"Do you need some time to compose yourself before I question you?" he asked, his voice soft and polite.

"No. Go ahead," she answered.

"Do you remember what day of the week that this happened?"

"No."

"You were asked if this happened last fall. Can you tell us which month?"

"It was in November, I think."

"Was it early November or late November?"

She paused before answering. "I think it was late November."

"But you do not recall the date it happened?"

"No."

"Do you recall why you were at the gin that day?"

"I think," she said, hesitantly, "I was there to see my mother."

"You do not normally work there, do you?"

"No, but I go there sometimes, to see my mother."

"Did you see her that day?"

"Yes, I did."

"At the gin?"

"Yes."

"Was she there at the gin when this happened to you?"

"Yes, she was."

"But you did not report it to her?"

"No. I was too embarrassed."

Will waited a few moments before asking his next question.

"Why were you in the seed house?"

"I don't remember."

"Was Lucius Jackson there when you got there?"

"Yes, he was there." She dabbed her eyes with her handkerchief.

"Was anyone else there when you got there?"

"No."

"Had you been in the seed house before, on other days?"

"Sure I had. It was my mother's place of business. I had been all over."

"You didn't work at the gin, did you?"

"Sometimes I ran errands for my mother," she said.

"Were you on an errand that day?"

"I don't remember."

"What was done in the seed house? By that I mean, what was it used for?"

"To store seed," she said curtly.

"What kind of seed?"

"Cottonseed," she answered.

"Was it stored in sacks?"

"Yes, sir."

"Did you know Lucius Jackson before that day?"

"Of course. He worked for my mother at the gin."

"Had you had any previous encounters with him?"

"What do you mean?"

"Had he made any advances toward you before that day?"

"Advances?"

"Yes. Had he done anything to you that was in any way disrespectful?"

"He called me by my first name once."

"You mean he referred to you as Barbara Ann?"

"Yes."

"Might he have said, 'Miss Barbara Ann'?"

She paused before answering. "He might have."

"Had he ever touched you before this time?"

"No."

"And no words were exchanged between you on this occasion?"

"He didn't say anything. He just grabbed me when I walked in and threw me down."

"Did you yell or scream?"

She hesitated again. "I don't remember," she finally said.

"If you had screamed for help, might someone nearby have heard you?"

"I don't know."

"Was any part of your clothing damaged in this attack?"

"I don't know," she answered.

"You waited almost a week to tell your mother about this, didn't you?"

"I guess it was about a week."

"Why didn't you tell her sooner?"

She hesitated again. "I was too embarrassed," she finally said.

"Why did you tell her when you finally did?"

She did not answer.

"Were you and your mother having an argument?"

"I don't remember," she said, softly.

"Had you been seeing a young man that your mother didn't approve of?"

"What do you mean?"

"Did you and your mother have an argument that morning about your seeing someone socially, or perhaps in private, that she didn't approve of?"

"I don't remember," she said.

"Had you and your mother had disagreements about a person you were seeing before this day?"

"I don't think so," she said.

"Did you tell anyone else about this alleged assault before you told your mother about it?"

"No."

"Had you been seeing someone before this happened?"

"I see a lot of people," she replied.

"I mean, had you seen a male friend or acquaintance, socially or in private, before this happened?"

"I had not."

"You did not have any boyfriends?"

Clark rose to his feet. "May counsel approach the bench, Your Honor?" he asked.

"You may," the judge responded.

Clark and Will came to the side of the bench away from the jury, where Clark leaned in and spoke in a low voice.

"He is about to pursue a line of questions about her chastity, Your Honor, which is improper. I have an objection to make outside the presence of the jury."

"Very well," the judge said. He then turned to the jury. "Gentlemen of the jury, there are times when the court will need to discuss matters of law outside of your presence. This is one of those times. You will retire to the jury room at this time for the court to consider such a matter. You will not consider this as affecting the facts in this case. The sheriff will escort you to the jury room."

The jury stood and followed the sheriff to the jury room. When the sheriff had closed the door, the judge said, "You may make your objection, Mr. Clark."

"Your Honor, counsel's question asking if Miss Poe had a boyfriend opens a line of inquiry that would not be proper. It is obviously intended to raise questions about her chastity, which is only permissible in a rape case when it relates to the question of the woman's consent to the act and even then the questions must be limited to her reputation for chastity in the community, not to any alleged specific acts of misconduct."

The judge turned to Will. "Any response, Counsel?" he asked.

"The question did not relate to her chastity, Your Honor, but only to her seeing other men socially or in private. It did not relate to acts of sexual intercourse."

"In that case, it has no relevance," Clark said.

"It is relevant if her mother did not approve and they argued about it," Will replied.

Judge Daughtry rubbed his chin and stared at Will. "I think I see where you're going with this, Mr. McCulloch," he said. "I will allow the question, but I warn counsel for the defense to keep in mind that specific acts of misconduct shall not be inquired about. You may proceed."

"But Your Honor . . . " Clark said.

"I have made my ruling, Mr. Clark," the judge said. "The sheriff will return the jury to the jury box."

After the jury was seated, the judge looked at Will and said, "You may proceed, Mr. McCulloch."

"Did you and your mother ever have an argument about a man you were seeing?" he asked the witness.

"We might have had a disagreement. We didn't have an argument."

"Did you have such a disagreement on the day you told her about what happened with Lucius Jackson?"

"No. I don't think so."

"But you may have had a disagreement with her about a man you were seeing, at some other time?"

"I don't remember," she said, looking down at her lap.

"Who was the man your mother didn't approve of?" Will asked.

"I don't see that that's any of your business," she said.

The judge held his hand out toward Will. "Young lady, you will answer the question, if you can," he said. "It is not your place to make objections. That is for the lawyers, not the witnesses."

"I don't remember," she said.

"You don't remember? Were you seeing more than one man socially?"

"No. I don't see anyone."

Will paused, looking toward the jury. "Who were you seeing at the time?"

"I don't remember," she replied, looking down at her clasped hands in her lap.

"Did you bleed after this attack?" Will asked.

She kept looking down. "Yes," she said.

"Was there any blood on your clothing?"

"There was some."

"Where is the clothing that had blood on it?" Will asked. He noticed a man on the jury leaning forward in his chair. He was the blacksmith.

"It's at home," she said.

"Can you describe the garment?"

"Bloomers," she said. "They were my bloomers."

"Were they white?"

"Yes, of course they were white."

"Do you know what Lucius Jackson was doing in the seed house that day, before you got there?"

"No."

"Do you know why he was there?"

"No, I don't."

"And you can't tell the jury what you were doing in the seed house that day?"

"I may have been sent there by my mother," she said. "I don't remember."

"Why would your mother have sent you to the seed house?" Will asked.

She paused, still looking down. "I don't remember," she finally said.

"I have no further questions," Will said.

"Nothing further," Clark said.

"Very well," the judge said. "It is time for the noon recess. This court will be in recess until one thirty this afternoon."

FORTY-FOUR

DURING THE NOON RECESS, WILL HAD A BRIEF CONVERSATION with the sheriff, then with his client. He spent most of the lunch break going over his trial notes and notes he had taken from interviews with witnesses. At one thirty, Judge Daughtry entered the courtroom, where both Frank Clark and Will were seated at the counsel tables. After the judge had determined that both sides were ready to proceed, he directed the sheriff to bring the jury in.

"You may call your next witness, Mr. Clark," the judge said.

"The state calls Dr. Phillip Watkins," Clark said.

Dr. Watkins entered and took the oath.

"Are you Dr. Phillip Watkins?" Clark asked.

"I am," Dr. Watkins replied.

"Are you a doctor of medicine duly licensed to practice medicine in the state of Texas?"

"I am."

"Where is your practice located, doctor?"

"Here in Lockhart."

"At my request, have you examined Barbara Ann Poe?"

"I have," the doctor replied.

"When was this examination performed?"

"Last December."

"What kind of examination, doctor?"

"It is called a pelvic examination," the doctor said. "It involves examining the female organ."

"Why did you perform this type of examination, doctor?"

"To determine whether the young lady's female organ had been penetrated by a male organ."

"And how can you tell that, sir?"

"By determining the presence or absence of a hymen."

"And what is a hymen?"

"It is a membrane that is found in the female organ. It exists at birth. The presence of a hymen would indicate that the female organ had not been penetrated by a male organ."

"What did your examination reveal, doctor?"

"No hymen was present."

"Did this indicate that the young lady was not a virgin?" Clark asked.

"Yes. Or at least, that no hymen was present," the doctor said, glancing in Will's direction.

"Pass the witness," Clark said.

"Dr. Watkins," Will asked, "Does the absence of a hymen indicate that the female organ was penetrated by a male organ, or could there be some other cause of its absence?"

"The hymen could be ruptured by objects other than the male organ," the doctor replied.

"How long have you been practicing medicine here in Lockhart?" Will asked.

"For over twenty-five years."

"During that time, how many pelvic examinations have you performed?"

"Too many to count."

"Have you found the absence of a hymen in other examinations, where the woman denied that she had been with a man?"

"Yes. A few."

"And it is possible, is it not, that there were other causes on those occasions than that the female had had intercourse with a male?"

"Yes, that's possible."

"Might one possible cause of an absent hymen be that the lady had been riding horseback?"

"That's possible," the doctor replied.

"Or that some object other than a male organ had penetrated the female organ?"

"Yes."

"Did you ask Barbara Ann what happened on the day she said the alleged rape occurred?"

"No, I did not."

"Why not?"

"I was only asked to determine if the young lady was a virgin."

"And the absence of a hymen does not necessarily mean that she was not a virgin, does it?"

"I believe that it is evidence of that fact, sir, although certainly not conclusive."

"Did you examine Miss Poe to determine if there were signs that violence had been committed upon her?"

"I did, somewhat."

"What do you mean by 'somewhat'?"

"In cases of rape, there are often bruises or scratches on the legs of the victim. So I looked to see if any were present."

"And what did you find?"

"There were none."

"Did you find any other marks on her?"

"Yes. She has what appears to be a birthmark on her inner thigh. I believe it was her right thigh."

"Please describe it, Doctor."

"A round, brown spot, like a mole, about a centimeter in diameter."

"And what would that be in inches?"

"Approximately a half inch across."

"Did she say when this alleged rape occurred?"

"Yes. She said it had happened a few weeks before my examination."

"And that would put it around the last week in November of last year, wouldn't it, doctor?"

"Yes, that's correct."

"Doctor, would a rape that caused the rupture of the hymen result in bleeding?"

"Yes, certainly."

"Would there be enough bleeding for it to be noticed on the clothing of the victim?"

"If she was clothed at the time, yes, it would."

"I have no further questions," Will said.

The judge looked at Frank Clark. "Redirect, Mr. Clark?"

"Yes, Your Honor," he replied. "Doctor, can bruises and scratches on the skin disappear in a period of several weeks?"

"Certainly, particularly on a young person," the doctor replied.

"In your experience, what is the most common cause of the absence of the membrane in the female organ?"

"Sexual intercourse with a male."

"No further questions," Clark said.

"I have nothing further," Will said.

"Very well," Judge Daughtry said. "You may call your next witness, Mr. Clark."

"Your Honor, the state rests," Clark said, glancing at the jury.

"All right," the judge said. "Are you ready to proceed, Mr. McCulloch?"

"I have a motion for the court outside the presence of the jury, Your Honor," Will said.

The judge turned to the jury. "Very well. Gentlemen of the jury, the court will take up matters of law outside your presence and due to the hour, the court will recess until nine in the morning. Do not discuss the case with anyone, including each other, and be back in the jury room by nine in the morning. The court will be in recess for fifteen minutes."

During the recess, Will let Clark know that he intended to call Lily Poe the next morning, so that Clark would have her present. After the recess, the judge overruled Will's motion to dismiss. Will then went to the office of the district clerk to have subpoenas issued.

FORTY-FIVE

WILL RETURNED TO THE OFFICE IN LULING IN LATE AFTERNOON. The mid-February sun was already low on the horizon. Ash was in the inner office, alone, seated in a side chair by the bookcase, reading. A glass of whiskey was on the side table beside him. He looked up as Will entered.

"So how's it going?" he asked.

"I don't know, really," Will said. "I'm surprised you asked."

"Why is that?"

He gave Ash a look. Ash had been carefully avoiding any conversation about the Jackson case since Will had decided to represent Lucius Jackson against Ash's advice and warnings.

"I didn't think you wanted to know about it," Will said.

"You're going to call Lily back to the stand, aren't you?"

"Yes, I am."

Ash took a sip from his glass.

"She came to see me this afternoon," he said.

"Oh?"

"She's very troubled by this," Ash said, staring at his glass.

"I know she is," Will said.

"It's more than that," Ash said. "She's troubled by what she has testified to."

"What do you mean?"

"Let's just say she has not been as forthright as she could have been.

When you recall her, you may want to go over some of that plowed ground again."

"Why was she telling you that?"

"She wants this to be over with," Ash said. "That's all I can say about it. If you ask the right questions, it will help your case." He stood and drained his glass. "I respect you for what you are doing. Good luck."

He extended his hand and they shook.

"I'll leave you to it," Ash said, then turned and walked out of the office.

The next morning, after the judge and jury had been seated, the judge asked Will if he was ready to proceed.

"Yes, Your Honor," he said. "The defense recalls Lily Poe as an adverse witness."

The sheriff showed her to the witness stand.

"You are still under oath, Mrs. Poe," the judge said. "You may proceed, Mr. McCulloch."

"Mrs. Poe, when your daughter told you she had been raped, what did you do?"

"I reported it to the sheriff the next day, as I said."

"Did you examine her clothing, the clothing she wore that day?"

"No. It had already been washed."

"Who washed it?"

"The maid."

"Effie?"

"Yes."

"Is her name Effie Washington?"

"Yes."

"In your experience, would a washing take out bloodstains?"

"Sometimes it would," she replied.

"Do you recall the sheriff asking about them?"

"Yes. He asked and I told him they had been washed."

"Did he ask to see them anyway?"

"Yes."

"And did he look at them?"

"Yes, he looked at some bloomers."

"Were there any bloodstains on them?"

"No."

"At the time of the alleged rape, was your daughter on an errand for you?"

"An errand?" she asked.

"Yes. At the gin that day, was she visiting you or on an errand?"

"No. I don't recall sending her on an errand around that time."

"What would Barbara Ann have been doing in the seed house that day?"

"I don't know, but she was used to wandering around the gin and the mill. She had been going there since she was a child, as long as I have owned it."

"Would Lucius Jackson have had any work to do in the seed house that day?"

"Not that I know of," she replied.

"I asked you previously whether you and your daughter had an argument about a man she might have been seeing. As I recall, you said that the two of you did not have arguments, but might have had disagreements. Is that correct?"

"Yes, we have had disagreements. Or I suppose you could call them arguments."

"Did you have a disagreement that morning?"

"Yes."

"What was it about?"

"She had been seeing a man behind my back. A man I didn't approve of."

"Who was that?"

Clark quickly rose to his feet. "Your Honor, I object. That is irrelevant. Dragging some man's name into this serves no purpose and has no relevance in this case."

"Overruled," the judge said. "You may answer the question, Mrs. Poe."

"His name is Scott Bowen," she said.

This came as a surprise to Will. Scotty Bowen was the young man who had been leading the lynch mob the day Will encountered the men in Friedman's Saloon. He had a reputation as a drinker and gambler, who had trouble holding down a job.

"And she had been seeing him in private?"

"Yes. She admitted that she had."

"Why did you object to her seeing Bowen?" Will asked.

"He had a bad reputation regarding women. And he was a drinker and a gambler. I did not approve of him."

"And you were arguing about this when she told you that Lucius Jackson had raped her?"

"We had been. She became upset and was crying. Then she told me about the rape."

Lily Poe's jaw was set, her lips pursed. She sat straight in the witness chair, tense and rigid. Will hesitated. He recognized the strain she was under and was not sure how far he could safely go with his questions. He also saw something in her he had not noticed before, something his father must have seen in her, a firmness of purpose, and courage.

"Were there others?" he finally asked.

"Others?" Her eyes were moist. "You mean other men?"

Clark again rose to object. "Your Honor, this gets into acts of alleged misconduct that are clearly not admissible and are irrelevant. The state objects."

"Overruled," the judge said, then turned to the witness, but did not speak. She looked up at him, then back toward Will.

"She had admitted to others," she said. "She had been seeing your uncle, Wonsley Baker, for one."

"Did you object to her seeing Wonsley Baker?" Will asked.

"I do not have anything against Wonsley Baker. He is an honest man, but I did not think the two of them would make a good couple. She said he wanted to marry her and I did not think she would do as a farmer's wife."

"I see. Mrs. Poe, do you actually recall seeing Barbara Ann at the gin the day she said she had been raped?"

She hesitated before answering. "I saw her there many times, but I do not recall which day that may have been."

"Has Lucius Jackson been a good employee?"

"Yes, he has."

"Had you ever had any trouble with him before?"

"No. I had not."

"Were you surprised when your daughter told you he had raped her?"

"Yes. I was. I was stunned." She seemed relieved to say it.

"Thank you, Mrs. Poe. I have no further questions."

"Any questions, Mr. Clark?" the judge asked.

"No, Your Honor," Clark replied.

"May this witness be excused?" the judge asked. Both lawyers said, "Yes." Lily glanced at Will as she left the courtroom.

"You may call your next witness, Counselor," the judge said to Will.

"I call Effie Washington," Will said.

There were murmurs in the courtroom as the sheriff went to the hall door, opened it, and escorted a thin, middle-aged black woman in through the rail. She wore what must have been her Sunday dress, which, although probably a hand-me-down, was presentable. She stood still and straight before the bench as she took the oath and pronounced "I do" in a calm, strong voice. When she passed by the jury box on her way to the witness stand, she looked over the jury with no display of shyness. After taking her seat, she looked directly at Frank Clark, then at Will, her head held high.

"You are Effie Washington?" Will asked.

"Yes, sir," she replied.

"Where do you live, Effie?"

"I live in the south part of the county, near old Atlanta."

"Did you come here in response to a subpoena?"

"Yes, sir. I did."

"Do you work in the household of Mrs. Lily Poe?"

"Yes, I do."

"Do you recall a morning last fall when the sheriff came to the Poe house and asked you about laundry?"

"Yes, sir. I recall."

"And did the sheriff ask you about a specific item of clothing?"

"Yes, sir. He asked about a pair of Miss Barbara Ann's underwear."

"Did you show him the underwear?"

"Yes, sir. I had washed it the week before and he wanted to see it."

"What kind of underwear was it?"

"They're called bloomers, Mr. McCulloch. They were white bloomers."

"Can you describe them?"

"Yes, sir. They're white cotton underpants with legs that go down almost to the knee. And they have ribbons to tie off over the young lady's stockings."

"And you had washed them the week before?"

"Yes, sir."

"Were there any bloodstains on them?"

"No, sir. There wasn't any."

"Were there any bloodstains on them before you washed them?"

"No, sir. There wasn't."

"Were these underpants worn by Miss Barbara Ann the week before the sheriff asked about them?"

"Yes, sir."

"How do you know that?"

"I do the laundry once a week and she changes every week in cold weather."

"How long have you worked for Mrs. Poe, Effie?"

"Ever since before Mr. Poe went off to the war," she said, still sitting upright.

"Since Miss Barbara Ann was a young girl?" he asked.

"Oh, she was a baby when I went to work there, sir."

"Was part of your job to care for Barbara Ann when she was growing up?"

"Yes, sir. I looked after her when Miz Poe was off at work."

"Did you bathe her and dress her?"

"Yes, sir. I did."

"And have you done the laundry all these years?"

"Yes, sir. I have."

"Have you ever seen blood on Miss Barbara Ann's underwear?"

"Well, yes, sir, I have. During her monthlies, since she reached womanhood."

"Effie, did Miss Barbara Ann use anything during her periods?"

"Yes, sir. She used rags."

"Rags?"

"Yes, sir. Like a diaper."

"Was she using one of these the week before the sheriff came?"

"No. She had not got her period for some time before that."

"For how long before that?"

"Oh, for a couple of months, sir. She had not got her period for a couple of months."

Will paused, looking toward the jury.

"Do you know Lucius Jackson?"

"Yes, sir. I've knowed him since he was a child."

"Do you know his reputation in the community as to whether he is a law-abiding citizen?"

"Yes, sir. He has a good reputation for that."

"Pass the witness," Will said.

"You are a friend of the family of Lucius Jackson, aren't you, Effie?"

"Yes, sir. I know his family."

"And you've known Lucius Jackson since he was a little boy, haven't you?"

"Yes, sir."

"And you'd want to help him out if he's in trouble, wouldn't you?"

"I wouldn't tell no lie for him, sir."

"But you'd want to help him out, wouldn't you?"

"If I could do it honestly," she said, still sitting erect and looking directly at Clark.

"You colored folks stick together, don't you, Effie?"

She did not answer at first, continuing her unwavering stare at Clark, then said, "We've had to, Mr. Clark."

"And you talked to Mr. McCulloch here about your testimony, didn't you?"

"Yes, sir. Mr. McCulloch came to see me and asked me questions."

"What about?"

"The same things he asked me about here today," she said.

"Did you tell your employer that Mr. McCulloch talked to you?"

"No, sir, I didn't."

"Didn't you think that she would have wanted to know that you had talked to him about her daughter?"

"I didn't think I should tell her," she replied, looking down.

"Why not?"

"I didn't think it was the thing to do."

"Don't you think she would want to know that you were going to be testifying about her household laundry and her daughter in a court of law?"

"I didn't know I was going to be here today, sir."

"You didn't? Didn't Mr. McCulloch tell you he expected to call you as a witness?"

"No, sir. Not until I got the paper telling me I had to be here today."

"And when was that?"

"Last night, sir. Then I told Miz Poe this mornin'."

"I see." Clark showed a surprised look. He hesitated. "No further questions," he finally said.

Effie Washington left as she had entered, her head held high.

"The defense may call its next witness," Judge Daughtry said.

"We call William Barger," Will said.

The sheriff escorted a tall, slim man with a black moustache into the courtroom. After taking the oath, he was seated in the witness chair.

"State your name, please," Will said.

"William Barger," he answered in a deep voice.

"Are you employed at Lily Poe's gin and mill?"

"I am."

"What is your job there?"

"I'm a practical engineer. I make sure the machinery is kept in running order."

"Are you on the premises most working days?"

"Yes, I am."

"Were you working at the gin last fall, in the latter part of November?"

"I was."

"Do you know Lucius Jackson?"

"Yes."

"What are his duties at the gin?"

"He's the straw boss. He's in charge of the colored men who work there. Or at least, he was."

"Are you also familiar with the seed house and what it is used for?"

"I am. The seed house is where the cottonseed is stored after the cotton harvest."

"In the latter part of November last year, was there any seed in there?"

"Hardly any."

"Why is that?"

"Because of the drought last year. Cattlemen were buying up all the seed early. We had sold all the seed by the middle of November or so. There might have been some spilled seed scattered on the floor, but there were no more sacks of seed in there then."

"Would there have been any reason for Lucius Jackson to be in there during that time?"

"No. There was no seed to load out and there wouldn't be any men working in there."

"Would there particularly have been any reason for Lucius Jackson to be in there alone?"

"No. There wouldn't ever be any reason for him to be in there alone, unless he was counting seed sacks. He was the foreman. He would be in there with his men."

"And there were no seed sacks there in the latter part of November?"

"None. I was in there the third week of November or so working on a hoist and there weren't any sacks in there then."

"Were you subpoenaed to come here and testify today?" Will asked.

"Yes, I was," Barger replied.

"No further questions," Will said.

"Might Jackson have been in there sweeping up?" Clark asked.

"I don't think so," Barger replied. "He's not likely to do that himself. He would order one of his men to do it."

"But the latter part of November is past the harvest season isn't it?"

"Yes."

"And Mrs. Poe wouldn't have a full crew working at that time, would she?"

"Not a full crew, but there would be at least one helper there and the straw boss wouldn't do work like that himself if there was anyone else there to do it."

"But he could have been in there for some other reason," Clark said.

"He could have been, yes," Barger replied.

"No further questions," Clark said.

"I have nothing further from this witness," Will said.

"Very well," the judge said. "It is close to the noon hour, so the court will be in recess until one thirty."

Will walked over to Clark. "I'll want to recall the doctor this afternoon, Frank," he said.

"Well, I don't know if he's available," Clark said.

"Okay," Will said. "I'll contact him and see, but I wanted to let you know."

At one thirty, when the court reconvened, Dr. Watkins was seated in the first row outside the rail. Will called him as a witness, and he took the stand.

"You are still under oath, Doctor," the judge said. "You may proceed, Counsel."

"Dr. Watkins, I have recalled you to ask you some questions about a woman's monthly periods." There was a murmur in the courtroom. "What are they referred to in the medical profession?"

"Menstrual periods," the doctor replied.

"What are they, exactly?"

"When a woman is of child-bearing age, she has monthly periods when her uterus is emptied of what you might call unused baby material."

"What happens when a woman becomes pregnant?"

"She no longer has menstrual periods until her body has recovered from childbirth."

"So if she stops having her monthly periods, is that an indication she is with child?"

"Usually that is the cause of the interruption of the menstrual cycle, yes."

"No further questions," Will said.

"But that is not the only cause?" Clark asked.

"No. Sometimes the periods are interrupted when there is no pregnancy, due to unknown illness, but those are rare," the doctor replied.

"Nothing further," Clark said.

"Doctor, what is a miscarriage?" Will asked.

"That is when the mother loses the fetus, the unborn child, before the pregnancy comes to full term," the doctor replied. "Sometimes trauma to the mother, sometimes due to illness. Many times the cause is unknown."

"Can the pregnancy be aborted?"

"Yes, although that is illegal."

"After a miscarriage or an abortion, does the woman eventually start her periods again?" Will asked.

"Usually that is the case, yes," the doctor replied.

"No further questions," Will said.

"Nothing further," Clark replied.

"Thank you, Doctor. You may step down," the judge said. "You may call your next witness, Mr. McCulloch."

"The defense calls Wonsley Baker, Your Honor," Will said. "He should be in the hallway, Sheriff."

The sheriff rose from his seat, opened the door, and stuck his head through the doorway. He could be heard calling out, "Wonsley Baker." After a few moments, he stepped into the hallway, then after a minute, returned to the courtroom and approached the bench.

"No answer, Your Honor," he said.

"Mr. McCulloch," the judge said. "Is this witness under subpoena?"

"Yes, Your Honor," Will replied.

"Very well," the judge said. Then, turning to the jury, "Gentlemen of the jury, the court will stand in recess at this time. You are to return to the jury room until called."

After the jury had filed out, the judge again addressed Will.

"Has the subpoena been served?" he asked.

Will looked at the sheriff.

"It was served last evening," the sheriff said. "I am not sure the return has made it to the clerk's office, but it has been served."

"And when was the witness compelled to be here?" asked the judge.

"By one thirty this afternoon, Your Honor," Will replied.

"Do you want to request the issuance of a capias, Mr. McCulloch?" the judge asked.

"I would rather not," Will replied. "This is my last witness. I would request that I have until tomorrow to bring him into court."

"I object to that, Your Honor. The subpoena was not issued until yesterday afternoon. The defense has not shown due diligence in getting this witness here. And, after all, this witness is Mr. McCulloch's uncle."

"The witness would not agree to appear voluntarily, Your Honor, in spite of family ties," Will said. "I would like to have the chance to convince him to obey the subpoena."

"The court will stand in recess until in the morning at nine," the judge said. "But if the witness has not appeared then, you will be required to proceed without him, Mr. McCulloch. Do you understand?"

"Yes, sir," Will replied.

"Sheriff, please have the jury return at 9 a.m. tomorrow," the judge said. "We will have a fifteen-minute recess, gentlemen, then we will spend some time working on the court's charge."

FORTY-SIX

WONSLEY BAKER WAS SEATED IN THE FIRST ROW OUTSIDE the railing when court convened the next morning. He was promptly sworn in and took the witness stand.

"State your name, please," Will said.

"Wonsley Allen Baker," he replied.

"Where do you live, Mr. Baker?"

"I live in Guadalupe County, across the river."

"Did you come here today in response to a subpoena?"

"Uh huh," he replied.

"You are my uncle, my mother's younger brother, aren't you?"

"Uh huh."

"But you would not come in to testify voluntarily, would you?"

"No."

"Do you know Barbara Ann Poe?" Will asked.

"Yeah, I know her," Wonsley said.

"Why would you not come in to testify without being subpoenaed?"

"Because I thought you wanted me to testify against her."

"Against Miss Poe?"

"Yeah."

"You had been seeing her against her mother's wishes, hadn't you?"

Clark rose to his feet. "Objection, Your Honor. Counsel is leading his witness."

"He is not here voluntarily and is a hostile witness, Your Honor," Will replied. "I should be able to ask leading questions."

"The court will allow it, Counsel," the judge said.

"You had been seeing her in spite of her mother's objections, hadn't you?"

"I don't think Lily wanted me to see her," Wonsley replied.

"But you continued to do so?"

"Yes, but I had honorable intentions."

"You had asked her to marry you?"

"Yes."

"When was that?"

"Several months ago," Wonsley replied.

"Would it have been in September?"

"Maybe. Or October."

"I will remind you that you are under oath," Will said. "Why did you ask her to marry?"

"Because I wanted her to be my wife," Wonsley replied.

"Was there another reason?"

"I loved her."

"Wasn't it after she told you she was pregnant?"

Wonsley was red in the face, looking down. He did not answer.

"Your Honor, I ask that the witness be instructed to answer the question," Will said.

The judge leaned forward toward Wonsley and said, "You will answer the question, Mr. Baker."

Wonsley looked at the judge before answering. "Yes. But we had talked about it before then."

"About getting married?"

"Yeah. And she told me her mother did not approve of it."

"So you had had conjugal relations with her?"

"Yes."

"And it was before she told you she was with child in September or October?"

"Yes," Wonsley replied.

"Pass the witness," Will said.

"Mr. Baker," Clark began. "Why didn't you and the lady in question marry?"

"She said her mother didn't approve."

"But that was before you lay with her?"

"She told me her mother didn't approve of me then," Wonsley replied.

"But you seduced her anyway?"

"Well, I didn't seduce her. It just happened."

"Where did this happen?"

"At her mother's gin," Wonsley said.

"Where at the gin?"

"In the seed house."

"Wasn't it busy in there?"

"No. It was on a Sunday afternoon."

"You talked to your nephew, Will McCulloch, about this before you came in to testify, didn't you?""

"Yeah."

"So you got your story about all of this straight with him before you were called as a witness."

"He asked me about it. He didn't tell me what to say."

"How did he know to ask you about it?"

"Huh?"

"Why would he ask you about Miss Poe's condition?"

"Her condition?"

"Didn't he ask you if she told you she was pregnant?"

"No. He didn't."

"How did you come to talk to him about your story?"

"He came by last evenin' to tell me I had to come to court because of the subpoena. He said the sheriff would come arrest me if I didn't."

"And he hadn't talked to you about any of this before last night?"

"I talked to him some a couple of months ago."

"I see. And that's when you told him about your seduction of that young lady."

"I went to see him to tell him not to represent that Jackson boy."

"Oh? Why did you do that?"

"Because it was going against Barbara Ann."

"I see. And that's when you and he came up with the idea that you'd testify against her?"

"No. I didn't have no idea of testifying," Wonsley said.

"Yet here you are. How do you explain that?"

"Billy told me that I would be arrested if I didn't come into court, because I had gotten that paper from the sheriff's deputy."

"And Billy is Mr. McCulloch here, the defendant's lawyer."

"Yes."

"Your nephew."

"Yeah. I'm only a few years older than he is, but I'm his uncle."

"And blood's thicker than water, isn't it, Mr. Baker?"

Wonsley did not answer. He stared at Clark. There was a moment of silence.

Clark looked toward the jury. "I have no further questions of this witness," he said.

"When you had intercourse with Miss Poe, was it in the daytime?" Will asked.

"Yeah, it was on a Sunday afternoon," Wonsley replied. He was still staring at Clark, who had taken his seat at the prosecution's counsel table.

"Did you notice any identifying characteristics on Miss Poe?" Will asked.

"Any what?" He turned and looked at Will.

"Did you notice anything on her leg?" Wonsley hesitated before answering.

"Yeah, I did," he finally said, looking back at Clark.

"What did you see?"

"She had a spot on her leg, kind of a mole," he replied.

"What did it look like?"

"Like a brown mole, about the size of a dime."

Clark could be heard sputtering in disgust.

"Do you remember where on her leg?"

"It was on the inside of her leg, up high," Wonsley said.

"Do you remember which leg?"

"No, I don't."

"No further questions," Will said.

"When did Lawyer McCulloch tell you about the spot on her leg?" Clark asked.

"He didn't," Wonsley replied.

"Uh huh. So when did you tell him you saw it? Was it a couple of months ago when you first talked to him or last evening?"

"I didn't tell him and he didn't ask me."

"You expect this jury to believe that the first time he asked you about a spot on the girl's leg was here today on this witness stand?"

"Objection, Your Honor," Will said, rising to his feet. "That's argumentative."

"Sustain the objection," the judge said.

"When did you first tell Lawyer McCulloch that you had had sexual intercourse with the young lady?" Clark asked.

"Here today," Wonsley replied.

"But you had talked to him a number of times since you claim this happened with you and the girl, hadn't you?"

"I talked to him a couple of times, yeah."

"Was that two or more than two?"

"I guess I seen him more than two times since then."

"And didn't he ask you if you had had sexual intercourse with Miss Poe on those occasions?"

"He may have," Wonsley said.

"But you didn't tell him?"

"No, I didn't."

"Did you deny it?"

"No. I didn't say or deny it."

"So he asked you and you just didn't say anything?"

"Yeah, I guess so."

"You guess so? Don't you know?"

"I didn't tell him she and I done it," Wonsley said angrily. "I didn't want to admit it."

"Uh huh. So your nephew calls you up here and puts you on the stand and asks his question about that without knowing what you would say? Is that what you are telling this jury?"

"That's the truth," Wonsley replied.

"We'll let the jury be the judge of that," Clark said. Will started to rise to his feet to object, but sat back down without saying anything. Clark looked his way, smiling. "I have no further questions of this witness," he said.

"No further questions," Will said.

"You may step down, Mr. Baker," the judge said. "The court will stand in recess for fifteen minutes." Judge Daughtry gave Will a look as he rose and left the bench.

During the recess, Will conferred with Lucius Jackson in the clerk's office. The sheriff had posted a deputy outside the door. Jackson sat across the clerk's desk from Will, his brow furrowed.

"I've told you in the past that it had to be your decision as to whether you testify or not and that's still true," Will said, "but I have the duty to advise you about it. Do you understand?"

"Yessir," Jackson answered, his eyes steadily meeting Will's.

"You can tell that Mr. Clark will be tough on cross-examination if you testify," Will said, returning his client's steady gaze. "If you testify, you will be at great risk. You must tell the truth, but you have to remember to only answer the question asked and not to volunteer anything. If you testify, it could be bad for you. On the other hand, I want the jury to know why Miss Poe would have accused you of rape. The way the testimony stands now, there wouldn't seem to be a reason she would accuse you of that if something hadn't happened. Do you understand?"

"Yessir, I think so."

"It may be all right to leave it as it is now, but I have a feeling that I may not have done enough to raise reasonable doubt. It's a long shot. The jury will have a hard time believing a black man over a white woman. You understand that, don't you?"

"I understand," Jackson replied.

"I wish I could advise you to do one thing or the other, but I can't," Will said. "To me, it's a close call. If you testify, the jury may not believe you, but if you don't, they may think you have something to hide. The judge would instruct the jury that they should not take into account your failure to testify as an indication of guilt and that you are not required to take the stand, but it would be hard for them to do that. It's hard to disregard something that's already in your mind."

"What do you think?" Jackson asked.

Will hesitated. His client had asked him the question he had been dreading.

"I think if you want the truth out there for the jury to see and you feel confident in telling it, you should take the stand. But if you try to say anything but the truth, the jury will see through it and it will hurt your case."

"I don't know what to do," Jackson said.

The time had come. It was going to be Will's decision. His client would do whatever he advised, and it was a close call. The odds were against Lucius Jackson. If he testified, it was likely the jury would not believe him. If he didn't, they were likely to feel that it was evidence of his guilt.

"I think you are telling me the truth," he finally said. "I've felt that since I first met with you. There are twelve men on that jury. I have to believe that there will be at least some of them that will believe what you say. If you feel confident enough to testify, I think you should do it."

"All right, Mr. McCulloch," Jackson replied. "I'll do it."

FORTY-SEVEN

THE COURTROOM WAS CROWDED AND SILENT WHEN THE sheriff brought the defendant in after the recess. The judge took the bench and looked toward Will without saying anything at first. His face showed concern, although it was impossible to tell what he was concerned about. Then the judge said, "The defense will call its next witness," with an emphasis that made it sound more like a command than an offer.

"I call the defendant, Lucius Jackson," Will said.

Every eye in the courtroom was on Jackson as he walked over to the witness stand and stepped up, then settled into the witness chair after taking the oath. No sound could be heard other than his boots on the wood floor as he approached, and the words of the oath seemed to echo, as if the room was empty.

"State your name, please," Will said.

"I'm Lucius Jackson, sir," he replied.

"Where do you live, Lucius?"

"On Miz Moore's place, outside of Luling."

"Are you married?"

"Yes, sir. My wife's name is Sally."

"Do you have children?"

"Yes, sir. We have two little ones. A boy and a girl."

"Do you and your wife attend church?"

"Yes, sir, we do. We're members of Sweet Canaan Baptist Church."

"And have you worked for Mrs. Poe at the gin and mill?"

"Yes, sir." Lucius was answering in a straightforward manner, keeping his eyes trained on Will.

"How long have you worked there?"

"Goin' on nine years," he replied.

"What are your duties there?" Will asked.

"I'm straw boss. I'm in charge of the workers."

"So you are in a supervisory capacity?"

"Yes, sir. But I work, too."

"Are you able to read and write?"

"Yes, sir."

"And do sums?"

"Yes, sir."

"Have you used those skills at work?"

"Well, yes, sir."

"How have you done so?"

"When there's cotton bein' ginned and corn bein' mashed, I run the scales and make up the billing."

"What is the seed house used for?"

"For storing seed. Mostly cotton seed, though there is some seed corn stored in there."

"Are you ever in there on the job?"

"Yes, sir. When there's loading or unloading seed. My men do that work with me."

"Do you know Miss Barbara Ann Poe?"

"Yes, sir."

"How long have you known her?"

"I've known Miss Barbara Ann since I been working there. Goin' on nine years."

"So if she is twenty-one now, she would have been twelve years old nine years ago. Does that sound right to you?"

"Yes, sir."

"How often have you seen her over the years?"

"She come to the gin every week or so."

"And that's where you would see her?"

"Yes, sir."

"Did you ever see her in the seed house?"

"No, sir."

"Were you in the seed house any in late November of last year?"

"No, sir."

"Why not?"

"All the cottonseed was gone by then. And we wouldn't be loading seed corn until the spring. So there wasn't no work to do in there."

There was a long pause before Will asked his next question. "I want to ask you directly. Did you rape that young woman?" he finally asked.

"No, sir, I didn't," Lucius responded emphatically.

"Well, did you ever give Miss Barbara Ann cause to dislike you?"

"No, sir. Not that I know of."

"Well, did you ever have an unusual encounter with her?"

Lucius hesitated, glancing toward the jury. "Yes, sir," he finally said.

"Please tell the jury what happened," Will said, his voice firm.

"Well, sir. One day I was in the scale house, in the counting office, toward the end of the workday. I was countin' up the sums for the day. And Miss Barbara Ann come in there."

"When was this?"

"Last September, at the end of harvest time," Lucius said.

"And what was unusual about it?" Will asked.

"She come up to me and started teasing me," Lucius responded. He hesitated, glancing at the jury again. "And I didn't do nothin' but push her away from me."

"What caused you to push her away?"

"Well, she come up to me and . . . "

"And what?"

"She come up real close to me. And I grabbed her by the arms and pushed her away. That's the only time I ever touched that girl."

"When you say real close to you, what do you mean? How close did she come to you?"

"Real close. So we was touching a little."

"What do you mean when you say she was teasing you?"

"Just sayin' stuff," Lucius replied.

"What was she saying?"

"She was saying stuff like, 'Oh, you're such a big, strong black man.' Things like that."

"And you grabbed her and pushed her away?"

"Yes, sir."

"What was her reaction?"

"She said I shouldn't oughta have done that. She said I could get into trouble for touching a white woman and that she might tell on me."

"Did she say anything else?"

"Well, she said if I didn't do as she said, she would tell on me."

"Had Miss Barbara Ann ever teased you before this time?"

"Well, yes, sir. Several times she done it."

"How did she tease you?"

"It was always her sayin' I was such a big, strong black man and stuff like that," Lucius replied.

"Did she ever touch you on those occasions?"

"One time she felt of my arm muscle."

"When was that?"

"I guess about a year ago."

"Did you see her after the time in the counting office last September?"

"Yes, sir, I saw her one other time."

"When was that?"

"It was a couple of weeks later, maybe early October."

"Did you have words with her then?"

"Yes, sir."

"What was said?"

"It was in the yard at the gin. I was a ways from the other men there and she come over to where I was and said I should remember what she told me, that I had better do as she says or she would tell on me."

"Did she say anything else?"

"She said everybody would believe her and nobody would believe me."

"What did you say to her?"

"I was respectful, but I told her, 'Miss Barbara Ann, you gotta stop coming over and talkin' to me and doin' that stuff.' That's all I said."

"And what did she say then?"

"She said how dare I talk to her like that and that I had no business tellin' her what to do. And that she could get me into some real trouble if she wanted to."

"What happened then?"

"She walked off," Lucius said.

"Have you seen her since?"

"No, sir. Not until I saw her here in court."

"Were you ever in the seed house alone with Miss Barbara Ann?"

"No, sir."

"Did you ever touch her other than the one time you have testified here about?"

"No, sir. I never did."

"No further questions," Will said.

Clark stood up and walked to a spot in front of the witness stand. He stood and stared at Lucius with his arms folded before speaking.

"Was anyone else with you and Miss Poe in that seed house?" he asked.

"I wasn't in the seed house with her," Lucius responded.

"Oh, so it was the counting house where you assaulted her, then?"

"No, sir. I didn't assault her."

"You pushed her away, you said. Didn't you?"

"Yes, sir. I pushed her a little bit."

"Just a little bit, huh? But she didn't invite you to push her, did she?"

"No, sir, but I had to get her away from me."

"A little girl like that. You had to push her?"

"I needed to get her away from me somehow."

"So you pushed her down?"

"No, sir. I didn't push her down. I just pushed her away from me."

"The truth is you pushed her down and had your way with her, didn't you?"

"No, sir."

"So you're telling this jury that the girl made advances toward you? That she came up to you, a Negro man, and was flirting with you?"

"She was teasing me some."

"Teasing you some. You mean she was flirting with you."

"I guess you could call it that," Lucius replied.

"And you say that wasn't the first time, that she had flirted with you before?"

"She had teased me."

"How many times?"

"A number of times, sir."

"Can you tell this jury how many times this young white girl flirted with you?"

"Several times," Lucius said, his hands gripping the sides of the witness chair.

"Was anyone else present any of those times that this young woman flirted with you?"

"No, sir."

"Including the time that you assaulted her?"

"I didn't assault her," Lucius said, raising his voice.

"You pushed her, didn't you?"

"Yes, I pushed her, to get her away from me."

"And it was in the counting house."

"Yes, sir."

"And there were no witnesses who saw it."

"No, sir. We was the only ones in there."

"Uh huh. Did you tell anyone that this young white girl was flirting with you?"

"I told my wife," Lucius said.

"Didn't you tell Mrs. Lily Poe?"

"No, sir. I didn't."

"Why not?"

"I didn't want to cause no trouble."

"You mean, you didn't want to get into trouble yourself, don't you?"

"No, sir. I didn't want to cause no trouble for nobody."

"Did you tell anyone else?"

"No, sir."

"I thought you said you told your wife."

"Yes, sir. I told my wife."

"What did you tell her?"

"Just that Miss Barbara Ann had been teasing me," Lucius replied.

"You didn't tell her that you touched her?" Clark asked.

"No, sir."

"Why not?"

"I don't know," Lucius said. "I just didn't."

"You didn't think that was important? That you touched a white girl?"

"I don't know. I just told her she had been teasing me."

"So you didn't tell her the whole story."

Lucius did not answer. He sat staring at Clark, who stood in front of the witness chair, staring down at him. After a few moments, Clark finally said, "I have no further questions, Your Honor."

"No further questions," Will said.

"Very well. You may step down," the judge said, then looked at Will.

"The defense rests," Will said.

"Does the state have any rebuttal?" the judge asked.

"No, Your Honor. The state closes," Clark said.

"The defense closes also," Will said.

The judge turned to the jury. "Gentlemen of the jury," he said. "That concludes the evidence in this case. The court has matters to take up outside of your presence for the rest of the day, matters of law. You are therefore recessed until nine in the morning. Please be in the jury room by then, and remember not to discuss the case among yourselves or with anyone else in the meantime. Both sides will present final argument in the morning."

After a recess, the lawyers and the judge finalized the court's charge to be read to the jury. The judge had already approved of the majority of it as requested by the state the day before. Will submitted charges for the defense and the judge approved most of them. Judge Daughtry was more solemn than usual. He would usually be joking about the conduct of the lawyers during charge preparation, but he was lacking in humor this time. When the charge had finally been completed, he merely said, "Okay, gentlemen. I'll see you in the morning."

FORTY-EIGHT

WILL HAD A RESTLESS NIGHT, TOSSING AND TURNING after finally taking to bed after midnight, having spent the evening going over his trial notes and preparing his final argument. During the ride into Lockhart that morning, he found himself being jarred awake in the saddle several times as the mare would move under him. He was in the courtroom before the man came to build the fire in the large wood stove behind the jury box. He went over his notes again and was seized with panic, doubting whether he could remember the points he intended to raise in argument. It was as if his energy had been expended during the weeklong trial to the point that his brain was not functioning. The district clerk showed up shortly before eight and put a pot of coffee on the stove in his office, the janitor having lit the fire in the clerk's stove earlier. Will entered and waited for the coffee. The clerk, an elderly man, had shown Will considerable deference. Now he stood behind the counter, waiting on the coffee pot also, greeting Will as he walked in, but otherwise not speaking. Normally, he would have engaged in small talk, courthouse gossip, but this morning he was silent.

When the coffee was ready, he poured a cup for Will, who thanked him and took the tin cup back into the courtroom. The coffee was strong and gave him a good boost. After a while, he settled down and, without looking at his notes again, decided he had done enough preparation. He sat and let his mind wander. The crowd starting shuffling in around eight thirty, taking their seats and talking, and it occurred to Will that this was the biggest show in town, as well attended as a barbecue or minstrel show. By the time the sheriff and his deputy brought Lucius Jackson in, the courtroom was packed with spectators. After Lucius was seated, Will shook hands with him. Lucius appeared to be calm and composed. During the trial up to now he had had an anxious look about him, glancing from time to time at the audience on the other side of the rail. Now he seemed confident, shaking Will's hand firmly and looking him in the eye.

Clark came in shortly before Judge Daughtry took the bench. The judge rapped his gavel and the courtroom noise subsided. He asked if the lawyers were ready to proceed, and when they affirmed their readiness, he had the jury brought in. Will noticed several of the jurors looking his way as they walked by the counsel tables on their way to the jury box, but he could not tell from their expressions if they were favorable or unfavorable looks. They just appeared to be solemn. The judge greeted the jury and began to read his charge. Will realized that his hands were damp with perspiration.

After the general part of the charge dealing with the burden of proof and consideration of only the evidence admitted by the court, the crux of the charge was given.

"Rape is the carnal knowledge of a woman without her consent, obtained by force, threats, or fraud. The force shall have been such as was necessary to overcome the resistance of the victim. Proof of penetration of the private parts of the female by the male member must be proven to your satisfaction, beyond a reasonable doubt, for the defendant to be found guilty, but such may be proven by circumstantial evidence, which is any evidence of one or more circumstances that tends to make the proposition more likely than not."

The judge also read the portion of the charge that Will requested.

"Evidence of circumstances that make it unlikely that the offense was committed by the defendant may also be considered."

As in all charges to juries, the judge concluded with these words: "You are the sole judges of the credibility of the witnesses and the weight to be given to their testimony, but the law you shall receive only as given to you in this charge by the court."

The judge then nodded to Clark, who stood and approached the jury box.

"Gentlemen of the jury," he began, "you have heard the evidence and, as Judge Daughtry said, you are the sole judges of the witnesses and the weight to be given to their testimony. That means that it is up to you, and solely up to you, to decide who is telling the truth and who is lying in this case. In that regard, I suggest that you consider who has the most to gain from lying. The young girl, who was obviously terrified and embarrassed to have to tell about the outrage that was committed upon her? Or this Negro defendant here, who is trying to escape punishment for his evil deed? You can determine his guilt by the nature of his perjury. Imagine a black man telling you that a young, attractive white girl was flirting with him. That she made advances toward him, which he rejected. That she threatened him when he asked her to stop. Shame on him.

"And his young lawyer, trying to cast aspersions on her character by having you believe that she became impregnated by a white man, and not just any white man, but the uncle of the lawyer, who told you that his nephew the lawyer had not even asked him about that until he was before you in this courtroom. If she was with child, what happened to the child? It was obvious that she is not pregnant now and there is no evidence that she had a premature child or that she miscarried. No, because that evidence would have to come from somewhere other than the fertile mind of the defendant's lawyer.

"And the colored maid, from the defendant's clan, who came in here and told you a tale about things which a lady would not have mentioned in public, about a young girl's underwear. Why? Because it was all part of this lawyer's plan to paint the young lady as a person of bad character, so you wouldn't believe what she had the courage to come forward and tell you under oath. And I can assure you that the lawyer will call your attention to some things she couldn't remember, like dates and time periods. I submit that these things merely show that her testimony is true and not rehearsed. She could not be expected to remember all of those details after the outrage she was subjected to.

"Keep these things in mind when you listen to his argument. You are the sole judges of the witnesses and the weight to be given to their testimony. The believable evidence points to a verdict of guilty as charged. I am sure you will do your duty."

Clark strode back to the counsel table. The judge looked at Will and nodded. As he rose from his chair and approached the jury box, Will was aware that his hands were still wet with perspiration. He paused and forced himself to look into the eyes of each of the twelve jurors. Each of them met his gaze with an unwavering stare. He cleared his throat before speaking.

"Gentlemen, you took an oath when you were sworn in. Just as serious an oath as that of any witness in this case. An oath that you would a true verdict render in accordance with the law and the evidence in this case. The law as given you by the court. The most important part of that law is that in order to find the defendant guilty, you must find from the evidence that he is guilty beyond a reasonable doubt. That means that the state has the burden of proving its case beyond a reasonable doubt and that the defendant is presumed innocent until proven guilty, based on the evidence, not the color of his skin. I am representing Lucius Jackson here today because I do not believe he raped Barbara Ann Poe. I believe he is innocent. The evidence introduced here does not prove his guilt beyond a reasonable doubt.

"The young girl who testified here before you certainly had a reason for telling you this young black man raped her. She had to back up what she told her mother when she lost her temper in an argument one morning about some men the girl had been seeing against her mother's wishes. So she made up the story that this young man had raped her. Why did she do this? Maybe it was because she thought she was pregnant and was fearful of what her mother would think of her when she found out. We don't know if she was pregnant, but she told Wonsley Baker that she was, and her menstrual periods had been interrupted, so she probably thought she was. And if she thought she was pregnant, she had to make up a story that would convince her mother that she had not disobeyed her and had sexual intercourse with one of the men her mother had forbidden her to see.

"It was not a very convincing story, if you look at its details. She says she was raped on a weekday at her mother's gin, in the seed house, but she doesn't remember what she was doing in the seed house that day. Her mother did not send her there on an errand, and the seed house was empty. She says Lucius Jackson was there alone when she got there and, without saying a word, grabbed her and threw her down and raped her, although he would not have been there for his work, because there was no work for him to do there that day. Her mother was at the gin that day, but she did not report the rape to her because she was too embarrassed. She doesn't remember if she yelled or screamed during this attack on her. She says Lucius Jackson had never touched her before, although he might have shown disrespect to her by calling her by her first name, but he might have just called her 'Miss Barbara Ann.' And she waited a week before she told her mother about the rape. She said at first that she didn't know why she told her when she did, and at first said she didn't remember if she and her mother were having an argument about a man she had been seeing against her mother's wishes. But then she said that she and her mother might have had a *disagreement* that morning about a man she had been seeing. When I asked his name, she said it was none of my business, and when the judge ordered her to answer the question, she said she didn't remember his name. Well, her mother remembered his name and it was not Wonsley Baker. It was Scott Bowen who she had been seeing, and her mother disapproved of him. Do you really believe the young lady did not remember his name?

"Now why would this young colored man, who had a good reputation in the community, who had been a good worker for her mother, who was a church-going husband and father, suddenly commit the horrible crime of rape upon the daughter of his employer at her business, on a workday when the lady boss was present on the premises? Why would he have been alone in the seed house when there was no work for him there? He would had to have been a monster, and a stupid one at that. Lucius Jackson is not stupid, and he is certainly not a monster.

"Consider what evidence there is tending to prove that Barbara Ann was raped, other than her inconsistent, incredible testimony. There is really none. The doctor found evidence that she was probably not a virgin, but he found no evidence that violence had been committed upon her. Nothing in his testimony supports her version of what happened to her. She says the defendant threw her down and violently raped her, but there is no evidence that violence was committed upon her.

"Now Mr. Clark would have you believe that I told Wonsley Baker about the birthmark on the young girl's leg. Well, I did no such thing. Wonsley Baker would not voluntarily appear here. He had to be subpoenaed. And it was obvious that he was a reluctant witness. He didn't want to testify. Barbara Ann told him she was pregnant. We don't know if she was or if Wonsley Baker was the father, but it is clear that she thought she was. Why would she have told Wonsley that if she didn't believe it to be true? She knew her mother would not approve of her marriage to Wonsley Baker, so it was not to lure him into making an offer of marriage.

"You might think, and Mr. Clark may argue, that if she thought she was pregnant, she would not have accused a colored man of raping her, because the baby would not have colored features. But she wasn't thinking clearly during that argument. It's likely that she didn't think that through. Just as she didn't think through why Lucius Jackson would have been alone in the seed house or why she would have been there that day. But the seed house is a key to understanding the motives for her testimony. That's where she lay with Wonsley Baker, on a Sunday afternoon when nobody was at work at the gin. I can see the young girl's mind, excited during an argument about seeing men her mother did not approve of, thinking of a place where she could say she was raped and picking, in a panic, the place where she had voluntarily lay with a man she was not married to.

"There is no credible evidence that this young lady was raped. Mr. Clark says you should not believe Lucius Jackson because he is a black man accused of raping a white girl. In so many words, that is his argument. If that is true, then you would have to believe that any man who is accused whose skin is not white should be found guilty, just because of the color of his skin. It is an appeal to base instincts. Surely we are better than that. Maybe Lucius Jackson is not our equal in many respects, but he is our equal in the eyes of the law. The statue of justice is blindfolded. She does not see skin color. She weighs the scales of justice without regard to the circumstances of the accused. Justice is for the poor as well as the rich, for the disadvantaged as well as those who are fortunate to be wealthier or healthier than their brethren, for black as well as white, for the low as well as for the high. That is the fundamental premise that this nation was founded upon, that liberty and justice is for all, not just the rich and privileged, not just for those with white skin. As a jury, you should hold the state to the same burden of proof when a black man is accused as a white man. No man should be convicted upon anything other than believable evidence, beyond a reasonable doubt. It's not here in this case, at all. You should find Lucius Jackson not guilty."

Will returned to the counsel table. The courtroom was completely quiet as Frank Clark stood and walked to the jury box.

"As I predicted, slander is this young lawyer's strategy in this case.

He would have you believe the slander that Barbara Ann Poe is not only a sinful tramp, but a perjurer to boot. He would have you believe that she would put herself and her mother through the ordeal of appearing in public in this courtroom to falsely accuse a Negro man of committing a felonious assault on her. Why would she do this? Lawyer McCulloch would have you believe that it is so that her mother would not know that she had become pregnant by Mr. McCulloch's uncle, Wonsley Baker. And he would have you believe that he and his uncle had not discussed his testimony before it was delivered in this courtroom, that he asked him those questions for the first time on the witness stand. Well, gentlemen, common sense tells you that cannot be true. A clever lawyer would never do that, and Lawyer McCulloch is certainly clever.

"And his lawyer would have you believe that the defendant would not have been in the seed house that day because he had no work to perform there, because the cottonseed had already been sold out. Well, he was probably not there to do work, but to escape work, as his kind is wont to do whenever they have the chance. I can see him lying there, avoiding work, when all of a sudden this young lady, his boss's daughter, comes into the seed house. What was she doing there? She said she didn't remember. It makes sense that she wouldn't remember why she was there after the outrage that had been committed upon her. And besides, she had a perfect right to be there. As her mother said, she had the run of the place. Maybe she just liked to wander around and went to the seed house that day as part of her wandering. And why would she say it had happened in the seed house if it didn't? The defendant's lawyer would have you believe that it was because that is where she had relations with Wonsley Baker and that somehow it just came into her mind to tell her mother it had happened in the seed house. Well, I tell you, it is more likely that the lawyer's uncle made that part of his story because he was told that this girl had said that is where the rape occurred.

"You don't have to abandon your common sense in that jury box or in the jury room when you go in there to deliberate. You know that people who are telling the truth don't have their testimony all stitched up perfectly, particularly when they have been through an experience that was a shock to them. Picture the young girl after this outrage occurred. Imagine what she must have been going through in the week afterward, during which time she had been unable to tell her mother about what had happened to her, because it was embarrassing for her to talk of such things. And it is understandable that on a morning when she and her mother had been talking about her seeing young men her mother did not approve of, she would have realized that she had to tell her mother what had happened, that her mother needed to know about it. And think about it. If she was going to concoct a story about being raped, if she was the liar the defendant's lawyer would have you believe her to be, wouldn't she have filled in some of those blanks in her account of what had happened? I guess he would have you believe that she made up the story during the week or weeks after she had surrendered her virtue to Wonsley Baker and told her mother her made-up story in some emotional outburst during an argument with her. But if she had all that time to make up a story, she would have filled in some of those blanks. She would have made up a better place than the seed house for the outrage to have been committed and maybe have said her mother was not there at work that day, to explain why she didn't report it to her. No, gentlemen, she was telling the truth, which is not always neat and done up. The truth is like life itself. It often contains seeming contradictions.

"When you examine all of the credible, believable testimony and evidence in this case, there will be no reasonable doubt in your minds about the defendant's guilt. And I know you will do your duty to protect the people of Caldwell County from criminal acts such as this Negro has committed. You, gentlemen of the jury, stand between the women and children of this county and the criminals who would perpetrate their crimes upon the community. You are the guardians of justice and civil order. You must do your duty and find this defendant guilty as charged."

As Clark turned and walked back to the counsel table, several jurors were looking solemnly at Lucius Jackson, who sat beside Will, his head down. After they retired to the jury room to deliberate, he looked up at Will, a look of fear across his face for the first time.

A deputy was left at the door to the jury room by the sheriff, who escorted Lucius Jackson to the jail for the noon hour. Will ate lunch at the Davis Café, after letting the deputy know he would be there. It was his first time waiting for a verdict alone. He could not help but think of things he might have done that affected the case and things he might have failed to do that had an effect, in spite of remembering Ash's advice not to worry about things that you could do nothing about. It seemed that Lucius had done well in his testimony, but it was impossible to tell what effect it had on the jury, and he could not help but wonder if his decision for Lucius to take the stand had been the right one. He ate his plate lunch alone at a corner table, having to force the food down. He thought he caught a few of the other customers staring at him, then turning suddenly away when he looked up from his plate. He recognized a few faces in the room, but no one said anything to him or gave a sign of recognition.

After lunch, he returned to the courtroom. Stewards from the sheriff's office had served lunch to the jury in the jury room and were leaving through the courtroom with empty plates. The courtroom was otherwise empty. The crowd had gone. The show was over. The sheriff appeared with Lucius a bit later on. Will sat with his client in the empty courtroom, waiting for the verdict. He read the local newspaper thoroughly. He walked around the room and looked at pictures of former judges and county commissioners that hung on the walls. He went to the office of the district clerk and made small talk with him, who was polite, but not cheerful. Hours passed.

Without realizing he had dozed off sitting in his chair, he dreamed he was on the trail again with Gruder, and his father was also there, riding alongside him. His father had the calm expression he often wore, his Stetson tilted at an angle over his forehead. He was riding beside his father with Gruder up ahead and he was Billy again, his father's quiet presence giving him a peaceful feeling he had not felt in a long time. They came to the edge of a stream, which at first looked like the San Marcos, but when they entered the ford and began to wade the horses across, he realized it was the San Saba. It was dawn, and the first rays of sunlight were coming over the hills to the east. He could feel the water lapping against his boots as they rode deeper into the stream. He could hear the sounds of the early morning birds in the trees along the bank. Then he heard a rather loud sound that sounded like knocking, and he came awake and realized where he was and that the sound he heard was the knock on the door to the jury room they had been waiting for.

The deputy at the door opened it and leaned in, then stood back, closed it, and said, "They say they have a verdict. I'll get the judge and Mr. Clark." He disappeared through the door to the hallway. Will had a cold spot in the pit of his stomach. After what seemed like an eternity,

Judge Daughtry entered the courtroom, followed by Frank Clark and the district clerk. After the judge had taken the bench, he said, "Gentlemen, they say they have reached a verdict. You may bring them in, Mr. Bailiff."

The deputy again opened the door to the jury room, leaned in and said something to those inside, then opened the door wide. The jury slowly filed out, walked through the side gate of the railing, and took their seats in the jury box. Not a single juror looked at the lawyers or Lucius as they passed. The last in line was a tall rancher named John Wallsmith, wearing a dark frock coat and string tie. He was carrying the court's charge. After the jury was seated, the judge asked, "Mr. Foreman, has the jury reached a verdict?"

Wallsmith stood and said, "We have, Your Honor."

"The defendant will stand and face the jury," the judge said.

Lucius stood slowly and was unsteady on his feet, weaving back and forth. Will stood with him.

"Mr. Foreman, does the jury find the defendant guilty or not guilty?" the judge asked.

"Not guilty, Judge," Wallsmith replied.

Will felt faint. He could feel the walls of the courtroom reeling about him. Lucius turned to him and grabbed his hand, shaking it vigorously.

"Very well," the judge said.

Frank Clark was seated at his counsel table, his head down.

The judge said, "The court thanks the jury for your service. You have rendered a verdict in this case, and you are discharged from your oath as jurors and from further service in this case. You are free to discuss your verdict and deliberations with counsel if you wish, but you are not required to do so. That is entirely up to you. If you will go through the district clerk's office, Mr. McDowell will have your checks for you. The pay is low, but the court's appreciation for your service is great. You are discharged."

The jurors filed out, not looking at the lawyers or the defendant. When the last one had passed through the door to the hallway, the judge said, "The defendant is discharged from custody. Is there anything else, gentlemen?"

Clark stood. "No, Your Honor. The jury has spoken."

"It has, indeed, Mr. Clark. I want to compliment counsel in this case for an orderly trial," the judge said, looking first at Clark and then at

Will, his attention seeming to linger a bit longer when he looked Will's way. "Court is adjourned."

After the judge had left the courtroom, Clark turned and walked through the door to the hallway without saying anything to Will. Lucius, standing beside him, grasped Will's hand again.

"I'll try to repay you for this, Mr. McCulloch," he said. "I don't have much and now I don't even have a job, but I'll repay you, sir. It might take a while, but I will. I can't thank you enough."

"It's all right," Will said. "I didn't take your case for the money. Go home to your wife and kids. I'm going to ask the sheriff if he can give you an escort."

"I can't do that, Mr. McCulloch," the sheriff, who was standing behind Will, said. "I'm afraid he's on his own now, but he has some friends waiting outside the courthouse."

Will and Lucius walked to the window behind the jury box and looked down at the courthouse lawn below. A dozen or so black men were standing on the lawn. They were armed with pistols and rifles. The preacher Nelson Wright was among them. Will recognized several more as being members of the Sweet Canaan congregation.

"I'll accompany him to the courthouse door," the sheriff said. "He should be all right from there. I would advise you to leave this county with your folk soon, however, Jackson. It will be safer for you somewhere else."

"Thank you, Mr. Ellison," Lucius said.

"I need to do something in the clerk's office," Will said to Lucius. "I'll let you go with the sheriff now."

Lucius shook his hand again and thanked him once more, then turned and left with the sheriff. Will walked to the district clerk's office, where the last few jurors were waiting in line for their checks. John Wallsmith was the last in line. Will pretended to be looking at the clerk's file in the case, until Wallsmith had received his check and was walking out the door, then he followed him into the hallway. He asked him if he minded talking to him.

"Not at all," Wallsmith replied.

"I would like to learn something about what the jury thought about the case and how you reached your verdict," Will said.

"Most of us didn't buy Mr. Clark's argument about your putting your uncle up to lying," he said. "There were a few in there that believed that, but we finally convinced them that you wouldn't do that."

"That's very good," Will said. "But I was not aware that you knew me."

"You don't remember me, Will, but I knew your father quite well. We were lodge brothers together. I first saw you when you were a little boy. Most of the other men on the jury also knew your daddy. Some of them are members of Hardeman Lodge. We also know your grandfather, Eli Baker, who is also a lodge member. We knew the son of Wes McCulloch wouldn't be putting on perjury. It took a little convincing of a few, but we finally got it done. And personally, I didn't believe that girl. Any girl who would see Scotty Bowen on the sly couldn't be worth much. Does that tell you what you need to know?"

"Yes, sir," Will replied. "Thank you very much."

"You're gonna lose some business for representing that Negro in this case," Wallsmith said. "But you got mine in the future and I think there will be considerable others that you'll get. A lawyer needs to stand up for what is right, no matter what. You did that. I'm sure your daddy would have been proud of you."

The lanky rancher walked to the stairwell and turned and nodded to Will as he stepped down. Will stood there. There was a strange quiet about the place, as if time had stopped.

FORTY-NINE

WILL STAYED AWAY FROM THE OFFICE OVER THE WEEKEND. When he arrived early on Monday morning, Ashley Maitland was already seated at the railroad desk, reading. He looked up as Will entered.

"Good morning, Counselor," Ash said. "Congratulations."

"Thanks," Will replied.

"I heard from the sheriff about your handling of the case."

"Oh?"

"Yes. I ran into him at Friedman's Saturday evening. Gus Ellison had nothing but good things to say about you. And he was telling all who would listen."

Will found that hard to believe. The sheriff had given the impression that he was on the side of the prosecution, although he was intent on doing his duty to protect Lucius Jackson, his prisoner, during the trial; and though it was not part of that duty to tell Will and Lucius about the preacher and the other black men waiting for Lucius on the courthouse lawn, he acted without any indication that he approved or disapproved of Will's conduct as defense counsel in the case or that he believed for a minute that Lucius was innocent.

Ash went on. "It took a lot of guts to represent that Negro. And from what Gus said, you did a good job."

Will walked to the window and looked at the street below. Ash swiveled in his chair to face him.

"Maybe I should move to Gonzales," Will said.

Although Will spoke as if calling for a response, Ash said nothing.

"I've been thinking about it," Will said. "I may not be welcome here anymore."

"Oh, I don't know about that. You may have done all right. The men at Friedman's certainly thought so."

"That's not what you thought. You said it would ruin me."

Ash smiled. "I may have been wrong about that. Maybe I wasn't giving the local folks enough credit for fair-mindedness."

"John Wallsmith was foreman of the jury," Will said. "Do you know him?"

"I do. He's a good man."

"He said he knew my father."

"He did indeed. They were lodge brothers."

"I may take a few days off."

"That's a good idea. There's a young lady in San Antone that would probably like to see you."

"Maybe later today," Will said. "There's something I have to do first."

Will rode through Wonsley's gate at midmorning. He found him at the corral behind his cabin, branding a young heifer. John Baker was with him, holding the heifer by her head in the corral chute as Wonsley wielded the branding iron. Intent on their business, they did not hear Will ride up and did not notice him until he had dismounted. They let the heifer back inside the corral as he walked up. John saw him first.

"Hello, Billy," he said. Wonsley turned toward Will and saw him for the first time, the hot branding iron in his gloved right hand. He did not speak.

"I wanted to talk to Wonsley," Will said. "I didn't have the chance to last Friday."

"I can let you two visit alone," John said.

"That's not necessary. I just wanted you to know, Wonsley, that I felt I had to subpoena you to represent my client."

"That's what you told me that evenin'," Wonsley said. "When you told me I'd be arrested if I didn't show up." He laid the branding iron down in the fire beside him.

"I just want you to know that I'm sorry I had to do it," Will said.

"Wonsley and I have talked about it," John Baker said. "We know you pretty well. We know you thought you had to do it."

"Well, I don't want there to be any hard feelings," Will said.

"I loved that girl," Wonsley said. "I didn't want to hurt her."

"I'm sorry," Will said.

"I'll get over it," Wonsley said. "But I don't know about Barbara Ann."

"The jury found the Negro not guilty, didn't they?" John asked.

"Yes, they did," Will replied.

"And you told the truth, didn't you, Wonsley?" John asked, giving Wonsley a stern look.

"Yeah. I told the truth," Wonsley replied.

"Well, then. You both did your duty."

Will and Wonsley stood and looked solemnly at each other. John Baker seemed to have put an end to it for both of them.

He was on the afternoon train, after having sent Martha a telegram that he would be visiting the city and would like to see her. He took a hack from the San Antonio station to the Menger that evening and walked to Mrs. Elliot's house the next morning after breakfast. Rosa greeted him at the front doorway and showed him into the front parlor as she had done before. In a few minutes, Martha was there and came up to him quickly, extending her hand.

"I'm so glad to see you, Will," she said, almost out of breath. "I haven't heard from you for the longest time. I was hoping you were well."

"I am," he replied. "I'm glad to see you, too."

It was a cold day. Martha invited him to sit across from her before the fireplace.

"Do you have business here?" she asked.

"No. I decided to take a break from work. And I wanted to see you."

She blushed and looked down at her hands, clasped in her lap.

"I'm happy to hear that," she said. "I was hoping you would come by this morning."

They discussed her college work and she inquired about his mother's health, then asked him how his law practice had been going. He told her about the Jackson case in detail. She listened intently and would occasionally ask a question or make a slight comment, each of which seemed to be on point and fitting. After almost an hour, he realized that he had not only told her about how the case went, but had also been pouring out all of his feelings about the trial and its aftermath, and that doing so had been easy and natural. He felt a great sense of relief in telling her about it and felt the urge to ask her opinion.

"I've been thinking about moving to Gonzales," he said. "I think it might be for the best."

"Because of this case you just tried?" she asked.

"Yes. I'm not sure I'm welcome in Luling."

She sat before him, a puzzled look on her face.

"What do you think?" he asked.

"I think you might want to wait awhile before making that decision," she said.

They talked for a while longer, and he then excused himself after making plans to take her out to dinner that evening. On the walk back to the hotel, he felt much better than he had in days and thought that he had a connection to this young woman that was hard to explain. It was as if she understood him better than anyone ever had, as if she knew what he was going to say before he said it. He could hardly wait until dinnertime to see her again.

FIFTY

ASHLEY MAITLAND HAD NOT SEEN OR HEARD FROM LILY POE since the day during the Jackson trial when she had come to see him at his office, ten days before. He had sent a note to her by the usual method, employing a young man who had acted as courier between them many times. When he had not received a reply by the next day, he decided to go to her place to see her. He did not think she would be at the gin. It was early March, and there would be no activity there. He rode up to her yard gate in late afternoon. The gate was ajar. He walked up onto the porch and pulled back the screen door and knocked. No one came to the door. He had heard about Effie Washington's testimony and assumed that Lily discharged her as soon as she found out about it, but she had a young girl that helped with the laundry and housework from time to time, and he did not expect Lily to be without help for long. It was a dark, cold day and he had noticed that there was no smoke coming from either of the chimneys as he came up the walk. He knocked again, harder, causing the door to shake against the doorframe, a noise that should have been audible throughout the house. Then he noticed the note he had sent lying halfway under the door.

He called out "Lily" in a loud voice. A minute passed and he called out again: "Lily, it's Ash." Then he thought he heard a sound from inside, which may have been a footstep, then another, less faint. Finally, after a couple of minutes, the door handle slowly turned and the door was cracked open slightly, revealing Lily's pale face. There were dark circles under her bloodshot eyes and her hair was disheveled. He was stunned at her appearance. She looked as if she had aged twenty years.

"Ash," she said in a raspy voice, staring at him, and he realized that she was quite drunk.

"May I come in?" he asked.

"Oh, Ash," she said. "I'm in no condition . . . "

"It's okay," he said.

She moved away from the opening and he pushed his way inside, grabbing hold of her just in time to keep her from falling. She was limp in his arms as he carried her to a chair by the dark fireplace, where he set her down carefully, leaning her back in the overstuffed chair. Her head rolled from side to side.

"I don't want you to see me like this," she rasped.

"It's okay, Lily. It'll be all right."

He bent down on one knee beside her chair. She was wearing a drab housecoat over a nightgown and some old worn slippers. The beautiful, self-assured woman he had known so well had been transformed. He tried to think of what to do.

"I need to light a fire," he finally said. "It's cold as hell in here."

"Whatever," she said, slurring the word.

Newspaper, kindling, and oak logs were on the hearth, and he soon had a crackling fire going. She was sitting back in the chair, her eyes closed, now still, as if she had fallen asleep. He went to the kitchen to get her some water and found dirty dishes stacked on the counter and kitchen table. He got a clean glass from the cabinet and pumped some water into it. He returned to the parlor and tried to get her to drink some of the water, holding the glass to her lips, trying to rouse her.

"Here, Lily," he said. "You need some water. Try to drink some."

At first she moved her head away, lolling back and forth to avoid the glass, but finally stopped long enough for him to get her to take a few sips.

"More," he said. "Try to drink some more."

She barely nodded, then took a swig from the glass, swallowed deliberately, then took another. She opened her eyes and stared at him.

"Oh, Ash," she said. "I'm so sorry."

"It's all right," he said. "I think you need to get some food down you.

I'll bet it's been a long time since you've eaten anything."

She leaned forward, indicating she wanted more to drink and he held the glass for her, tipping it so she could drink slowly. She then leaned back in the chair and closed her eyes again. After a few minutes, her breathing indicated she was sound asleep. He sat down in the chair opposite her and watched her sleep. When the fire died down, he put more logs on and kept it going, watching her in the firelight as it penetrated the growing darkness around them.

After what seemed like hours, he lit a lantern on the table in the center of the room and a candle, which he took with him into the kitchen. He found some eggs that were still fresh in the larder and built a fire in the kitchen woodstove. By the time he had scrambled the eggs and put them in an iron skillet with a dab of lard, he could hear her groans from the parlor. He put the skillet aside and stepped inside the parlor door. She was blinking, still sitting back in the chair, but appeared to be less addled.

"Do you think you can eat something?" he asked. "I'm fixing some eggs."

She nodded.

"You sit still. I'll take care of it."

"You'll take care of me?" she asked, her voice a whisper.

"I will," he said.

When he had finished cooking the eggs, he brought a plate of them to her in the chair and spooned them for her, a small bite at a time, interspersed with more swallows of water, until she could not eat any more. He then started a fire in her bedroom fireplace and lit her bedside lantern and helped her into bed. She fell asleep right away. He sat in the chair by the fireplace all night, keeping the fire going and drifting in and out of sleep.

He was asleep in the chair when she awakened at dawn and saw him there by the fire, which had died down to embers. He had placed a glass of water on her bedside table by the lantern. She drank the water and turned the lantern off, then quietly got out of bed, put her housecoat on, and went outside to the privy. When she returned to the house, he was standing by the back door, a concerned look on his face. She came up to him and took his face in both of her cold hands, which were shaking as she held his face. Tears rolled down her cheeks.

"Thank, you, Ash. Thank you," she whispered.

"I love you," he said.

"I know you do," she said, her voice rising, sobbing. "I know you do, my dear Ash."

Later, when she had washed herself in a tub with water he had heated on the kitchen stove for her and dressed herself in a brown dress, they sat in front of the parlor fire. She told him that Barbara Ann had gone off with Scott Bowen, having left her a note saying hateful things, that Lily did not love her and was always mean to her and that she would never see her again. She told him things about her daughter that he had suspected, but not known, about her erratic behavior, her indiscretions with men that Lily seemed powerless to prevent. She felt that she herself was at fault, because of the life she had led after her husband had not returned from the war, because of the gambling and the women she had engaged to work for her in her establishment and her foolishness in thinking that she could insulate her daughter from the bad effects of her lifestyle. And her longtime affair with Wes McCulloch.

He asked about her servants. She said she had not fired Effie Washington, but Effie had not returned to work after her testimony. She admitted that she needed some help and agreed that he could get in touch with the young woman she had sometimes employed to do some cleaning and washing for her. He also said he would send a young man with some groceries for her. She promised she would straighten up and not drink for a few days, at least until she had regained her strength. When he left shortly before noon, she kissed him warmly on the cheek.

"I value your friendship, Ash," she said. "Thank you for being here for me."

As he rode away, he felt cold in the pit of his stomach. She had always been so self-assured. The day before, she had seemed like another woman, someone he did not know.

FIFTY-ONE

THE WESTBOUND TRAIN PULLED INTO THE LULING STATION late in the afternoon in the latter part of February 1880. Everett Hardeman was standing by the doorway of his car before the train came to a halt. When the train had slowed sufficiently, he stepped onto the landing, holding the duffel bag containing his worldly possessions in one hand. Lily Poe had sent him some money for the train fare and meals, and he had several dollars left over. Although he had not sent word of his coming on this day, he was a bit disappointed that he did not recognize any of the people waiting for the train at the station.

It was a cold day and the worn coat he was wearing was a bit thin for the weather. He pulled up the collar and stood by the side of the station, waiting for the train to depart. He had lost weight, and his clothes hung on his shoulders. His belt was cinched tight against his trousers, bundling them at the waist. The old slouch hat he wore hung low against his ears, the prison burr haircut he had received at his discharge not providing the usual padding. When the train pulled out, revealing North Railroad Avenue across the tracks, he was stunned by the number of new buildings that lined the street in both directions. Considerable construction had occurred in the four years since he had last seen the town, and many new businesses were visible.

He crossed the tracks, walked through the park area on the other side and across the avenue to the door of the law office of Maitland and

McCulloch. He walked slowly up the steps to the reception room and found it empty. The door to the office was open. He stepped inside, into the anteroom, and peeked inside the doorway to the inner office. Will McCulloch was seated at the double desk, reading a book opened before him. Ev cleared his throat, and Will looked up and saw him. At first Will didn't recognize him and sat there with a puzzled look. The shabbily dressed and rough-looking character that was leaning in the doorway was unfamiliar to him.

"I guess you don't recognize me, huh?" Ev said, and Will recognized his voice.

"Ev," he said. "I didn't. I thought you'd be out soon, but I didn't expect you yet. Come in and have a seat."

He wanted to hear about Ev's life in prison, but that was not a subject Ev cared to talk about. Ev wanted to hear about what had been happening in Caldwell County, and Will told him about the Jackson case and Lily's involvement. Will had not been keeping up with Ada and her mother, so he had no news of them. Ev said he had been corresponding with Ada and that they planned to get married as soon as he could find employment. He thought he might look in San Antonio or Austin.

"I think Colonel Pierce is in San Antonio," Will said. "His personal car came through a couple of days ago. The GH&SA is building the line west of San Antone, and he's supposed to be making a deal to connect up with the Southern Pacific somewhere out in West Texas and maybe build a line to Eagle Pass. He's probably going to need some railroad right-of-way men with experience."

"I doubt that he would want an ex-convict," Ev said.

"I thought he knew you well," Will said. "Isn't he a good friend of the doctor who helped you?"

"Yes, but . . . "

Ev had not been in contact with the doctor who had saved his life in a Yankee prison and then befriended and employed him in Massachusetts, although he had been like a second father to him. He was too embarrassed about his conviction and imprisonment to write him from Huntsville. Dr. Wentworth was the uncle of Thomas Wentworth Pierce, the founder of the Galveston, Harrisburg, and San Antonio Railroad. He had introduced Everett Hardeman to Colonel Pierce at a gathering at the Pierce home in Topsfield, Massachusetts, the summer after the war ended. Pierce took a liking to the young, one-armed Texan and engaged in many conversations with him about Texas over the course of that summer. Pierce had investments in Texas. The Pierce and Bacon firm dealt in sugar, cotton, and hides, and before the war ran a line of packet ships that transported products to the East Coast and Europe from Texas. Before the war Pierce was also involved in the operation of the early railroad, the Buffalo Bayou, Brazos, and Colorado. The BBB&C had been built westward from Harrisburg, but the war had the effect of halting construction at Alleyton, near Columbus in Central Texas, and the line had gone bankrupt. When Pierce and a group of other investors bought the bankrupt company and its westward line in 1870, Pierce hired Ev as a general right-of-way man and troubleshooter for the new company, the GH&SA.

"I'll bet the colonel would understand," Will said. "Particularly if I explained it all to him. You went to prison for saving a woman's honor. That's not a bad thing."

"You don't know him," Ev replied. "I don't think he'd go for that."

"Maybe you should go see him, if he's still there. I'd be glad to write a letter for you to carry to him."

"Maybe. I want to see Ada. And Lily. How is Lily?"

"She's not spoken to me since the Jackson trial," Will said. "But Ash says she's been pretty down ever since. Barbara Ann has run off with Scott Bowen, and I don't think she's heard from her in about a year."

"She wrote and sent me some money and said she had a place for me to stay until I got on my feet. I guess she'll be at home."

"Ash says she doesn't go out much anymore."

"She doesn't," Ashley Maitland said from the doorway.

Ash stood there for a moment and looked at Ev, who returned his stare. They had both changed in the four years since they had last seen each other. Ash had visibly aged, and he was struck by Ev's gaunt, ashen appearance.

"Well, you're finally back," Ash said.

"I am," Ev replied, rising from his seat.

Ash walked over to Ev and grasped him by the shoulders.

"Welcome back, Mr. Hardeman," he said. "You're a sight for sore eyes."

"Thank you, Ash. It's good to be back."

The three of them sat around the railroad desk and talked for an hour. Ash wanted to know what had gone on in prison, and Ev reluctantly told them about his experience at the Walls Unit, about Hardin's escape attempts, the punitive tactics of the prison administration, and that during the last two years he had worked in the prison library, where Hardin, of all people, had been a frequent visitor, having apparently become interested in reading law books. Ev said he thought that initially the former outlaw was interested in trying to find some way to lessen his sentence, but as time went on, he realized that Hardin was already quite literate. Hardin told him he had been a school teacher as a teenager. Being the son of a preacher, he had read extensively as a boy and, according to him, had a gift for teaching.

Ash gave Ev a fuller picture of how the Jackson trial had affected the community and of Will's role in it, how he had fought for what he believed was right in the face of contrary public opinion, and how his work had had a positive influence. Will was surprised by Ash's words. Although speaking to Ev, Ash would from time to time look Will's way as he spoke, a proud look on his face. Ev asked Ash about Ada, and Ash replied that she looked good the last time he saw her; she was still living with her mother, and they had good help on the Moore farm, so he thought they were doing as well as could be expected.

"Are you going to surprise her?" Ash asked.

"I plan to ride out there as soon as I can rent a horse," Ev replied.

It was almost dark when he rode up to the yard gate at the Moore place. Lantern light shone through the parlor window. Ada opened the door before he knocked and fell into his one-armed embrace. She hugged him quietly for a good minute, then leaned back.

"I knew it was you when I heard your step on the porch," she said, teary-eyed. "I knew it was you."

He pulled her to him and they kissed. She was not used to his full beard, and she realized that they had not touched since he had taken the train to prison. She had visited him once a year at the Walls, but touching had been strictly prohibited.

"Oh, Ev, you are so thin," she said, feeling his bony shoulders.

"I wouldn't recommend the prison food," he replied.

"Well, come on in. We'll have a nice supper."

She led him into the parlor. He set his bag down near the fireplace, and she embraced him again, holding him tightly around the neck, sobbing.

"Oh, what you must have been through!" she gasped.

"It wasn't so bad," he said. "You get used to it after a while."

She backed away and looked him over.

"You could use some new clothes," she said. "We still have some of my daddy's that will probably fit you now, you're so thin."

"You look great," he said.

She was neatly dressed, and her black hair was tied back firmly in a bun. Her face had more color than he remembered from seeing her in the prison visiting room, and her eyes shone in the lantern light, glistening from her tears and as blue as the first time he saw her at the picnic area adjacent to the parade ground at Camp Clark, so many years ago. Her face was fuller with age and experience, but her smile was the smile of the fifteen-year-old girl he had fallen in love with before he went off to war.

Mrs. Moore hobbled into the room, leaning on a cane. She had also changed since he had last seen her. Her hair was completely gray, and she stooped over as she walked.

"Why, Everett!" she said. "It's so good to see you home at last."

The three of them sat by the fireplace and talked. He had not been eager to tell of his experience in prison, but he found himself pouring out a more detailed account of his experiences than he thought he remembered, with particular emphasis on the loneliness of the nights in his cell. Mrs. Moore had kept up with the local gossip and filled him in on events that had occurred during his absence that she considered important. Ada gleamed in the firelight as she sat by his side. They had a nice supper of roast beef, sweet potatoes, and stewed cabbage, with pecan pie for dessert. Ada had cooked the entire meal and had prepared much of it in advance, Mrs. Moore saying that she had been doing this every evening for a week, in anticipation of his arrival.

After dinner, Ada prepared a bath for him in the bathroom, heating water on the woodstove for it, laid a towel and some of her father's clothes out for him on a chair beside the metal tub, and smiled as she kissed him on the forehead and stepped out of the room. The candlelight showed his face in the mirror on the wall, and it was the face of a stranger. After the hot bath, he put on the nightshirt that lay on the chair and walked into the hallway carrying the rest of the clothes, where Ada was sitting beside a table with a candle burning, patiently waiting for him.

"I'll show you to your room," she said, smiling. The spare room was made up for him, with a picture of her on the bedside table. They embraced and kissed, standing beside the bed.

"I've waited so long for this," he said.

She could feel him weaving back and forth and knew that the day's journey was taking its toll.

"You're exhausted," she said.

He let her tuck him in under the quilts and blankets. She kissed him goodnight, then blew the candle out, and he fell asleep. She could see his bearded face in the moonlight shining through the window and stood there listening to his breathing for a while, then quietly left and went to her room.

He emerged the next morning in her father's clothes, looking much better, and they sat down for a breakfast of ham and eggs and biscuits. Mrs. Moore asked about his plans, and he told her he wanted to see Lily Poe and that she had promised him a place to stay until he got settled.

"You can stay with us," Mrs. Moore said. "That room is yours as long as you want it."

He hesitated before speaking.

"I'm not sure it would look right," he said. "The neighbors might talk."

"Let them," Mrs. Moore replied. "I know you and Ada plan to marry and I highly approve. This place will be hers after I'm gone, and only the good Lord knows when that will be."

He agreed that he would stay there after he returned from San Antonio, where he hoped to meet with Colonel Pierce about employment with the railroad. Once that was settled and he knew more about where they would live, they could get married. Ada trimmed his beard before he left and helped him pack some of her father's clothes into an old leather bag that had also belonged to her father.

He rode up to Lily Poe's house in midmorning. She opened her front door after his knock and stood there looking at him for a moment, no sign of recognition on her face, then stepped forward and grabbed his shoulders.

"Ev?"

Her frown displayed her surprise at his appearance. It had been three years since she had visited him in prison.

"Yes, Lily. It's me."

She embraced him, and he wrapped his arm around her. They stood there for a long minute, and when she pulled away and looked at him again there were tears welling up in her eyes.

"Oh, Ev," she said. "I didn't recognize you at first."

"I'm getting used to that reaction," he replied.

"Come in," she said and ushered him in the doorway. She had aged since he had last seen her. There were wrinkles around her eyes and her auburn hair was streaked with gray. He followed her into the dining room, where she had him sit at table while she asked her maid to make them some tea. "It'll warm you up," she said. "I want to hear all about what happened since I saw you last."

They sat and talked for over an hour. He told her that he had learned about the Jackson case from Ashley Maitland, and she bowed her head when he said it.

"I'm trying to forget about it," she said. "But it's hard."

He told about his experiences in prison. She talked about Barbara Ann going off with Scott Bowen and that she had not heard from her since. She told him how Ash had been providing moral support for her. She had been in touch with Ada and Mrs. Moore and felt that they had been doing well under the circumstances. He shared his and Ada's plans for marriage and told of his impending trip to San Antonio to try to find work. She gave him some money for his trip, and he promised to pay her back soon. He left for town shortly before noon, receiving her warm kiss on his cheek at the door.

He took the afternoon train to San Antonio. When he arrived at the depot he inquired of the stationmaster if Colonel Pierce's car was still in the city, and was told it was on a siding nearby. It was after dark, and he decided to wait until morning to visit the colonel. He took a room at a boarding house nearby. The next morning at nine he approached the colonel's car. An attendant was standing on the rear landing, and he told him he was there to see Colonel Pierce, telling him his name. After stepping inside the rear door, the man appeared and said the colonel would see him.

The room inside the rear door was an elaborately furnished parlor, with leather chairs, walnut tables, and standing ashtrays. The smell of good cigars filled the room. Colonel Pierce was sitting beside a table with a cigar and coffee cup in his hands, wearing blue trousers, a starched white shirt, and a smoking jacket. He wore the same long, bushy sideburns that Ev remembered. He rose to greet him.

"Mr. Hardeman," he said cheerfully. "It's good to see you're back."

"Thank you, Colonel," Ev replied. "I wasn't sure you would want to see me."

"Of course I would. Sit down and let's visit."

Ev took a seat opposite. He waited for the colonel to speak, and there was an awkward silence. The colonel took a long pull on the cigar, then cleared his throat before speaking.

"I know all about your difficulty with the law," he said. "I stopped in Luling one day and Ashley Maitland filled me in. I want you to know that I consider that you acted honorably, based on what Mr. Maitland told me. I hopc you've come to see me about employment."

"Yes. I thought it was worth a try."

"Of course. We're in need of good men right now. We are building the line west, and we are acquiring right-of-way. You have valuable experience and you have always been a good man for us. Welcome back." The colonel smiled broadly.

"Thank you, Colonel," Ev said. "I won't disappoint you."

FIFTY-TWO

AS THEY DID EVERY EASTER SUNDAY, WILL AND HIS MOTHER were to spend Easter at the Primitive Baptist Church service, followed by Easter Sunday dinner with his grandparents. Will still lived upstairs at the McCulloch place, but spent many nights during the week on a cot in the office downtown. Laura had hired a male servant after Gruder's death, a middle-aged black man by the name of Infantry Davis. He said his mother had named him that because his daddy had been a servant to one of the officers in Sam Houston's army during the Texas Revolution. Infantry was short and wiry and moved about his chores quickly. He drove Will and Laura across the river at Sam's ford up the lane to the church and the cemetery where Will's father was buried, where he had first encountered Jack Hays years before, after his father's funeral.

As usual, the little church was packed for the Easter service. Eli Baker, now approaching eighty, stood at the front of the room talking with several of the men of the congregation. Will's grandmother, Leonie, sat at the end of the front pew to the left, not far from the wood stove. Although it was a pleasant spring morning, the inside of the church still retained a bit of a chill. Eli Baker greeted Will and Laura as they approached the group of men, taking Laura's hand in his, then shaking Will's firmly, as strong in his grip as ever.

"Welcome, Daughter," he said to Laura, then to Will, "It's been a long time, Grandson."

"Yes, it has," Will said.

"I hear you've been busy as a lawyer," Eli Baker said, the trace of a smile on his face. Will understood the meaning of his sarcasm. He had not been attending church the past few years, except on Easter Sundays. "Happy Easter," his grandfather said, still gripping his hand.

Will and Laura walked over to his grandmother, who remained seated while Laura leaned down to hug her.

"We haven't seen much of you lately, Billy," Leonie said. "You should come visit more often."

"I know, Grandmother," Will said. "I'll do better. I promise."

"See that you do," she replied. "We would love to have your company."

Laura sat down next to her mother. Will walked over and greeted the men standing around his grandfather. John and Wonsley Baker were there. He and Wonsley had gone hunting several times since the Jackson trial and were on good terms again. After Wonsley heard about Barbara Ann Poe running off with Scott Bowen, he seemed to develop a philosophical attitude about his involvement with her. "You live and learn," he had said on their first hunting trip. John Baker's wife, Susan, was sitting near Will's grandmother, Leonie, and some other women, chatting. His aunt Jane and aunt Elizabeth were part of the conversation. There were Baker and McCulloch cousins and other kinfolk scattered throughout the congregation.

After a while, Eli Baker took his pocket watch from his vest pocket, looked at it, and said it was time to begin, then stepped behind the pulpit. The men took their places with their wives and families. Will sat next to Laura, beside his cousin Sally, who had married and was with child. She had said her husband was away on business, but Laura had told him the rumor was that he had abandoned her. His grandfather cleared his throat and said, "Let us pray."

All heads were bowed as he began the prayer. "Almighty God, on this day of the resurrection of our Lord and Savior, Jesus Christ, may we remember your everlasting grace and love for us and also those who have gone ahead to be with you and your son in paradise. May we walk in the light of your love and goodness. Help us to love our neighbors and forgive our enemies, as you have forgiven our sins through the sacrifice of your only son. We ask that you keep watch over those who are afflicted and guide those who have strayed from the path of righteousness. In the name of our Lord and Savior, Jesus Christ, we pray. Amen."

All voices followed in the "Amen." The prayer was followed by a hymn, without the accompaniment of any musical instrument, the notes in the hymnals being shaped in squares, circles, and triangles, then the reading of scripture and Elder Baker's sermon, which was a proper Easter sermon about the significance of the resurrection and the life everlasting.

After the service, the family met at the Baker house across the road for Easter dinner, with the adults seated around the large table in the dining room. Will sat next to his mother. After saying grace, Eli Baker carved the ham, and plates were passed from hand to hand around the table, then the bowls of sweet potatoes and spring vegetables were passed. The conversation was lively and warm.

After dinner, the men retired to the parlor with cigars and coffee, and the women cleaned off the dishes from the dining table and helped in the kitchen. Will sat next to his grandfather Baker, who had lit his pipe. John and Wonsley sat opposite them. They talked about hunting and fishing and how the spring planting had gone, the new calves, how many heifers and bullocks they had received, and that, all in all, it had been a good spring thus far. After a pause in the conversation, Eli Baker spoke in a serious tone.

"You know, General Sam Houston wore a ring his mother had given him when he was a young man. A gold band. He wore it his whole life. Nobody gave it much thought, but after Houston died, they took the ring off and inside the band one word was inscribed. 'Honor.' Nobody alive knew what was on the inside of that ring but him, for all those years, not even his wives. But he knew. It was a reminder for him. It was a good thing to have. He faced a lot of decisions in his lifetime, and that ring was always there to help him make the right ones."

Will, John, and Wonsley exchanged glances. Eli Baker seldom waxed philosophical.

"It's important to remember your heritage," he continued. "We come from a long line of honorable men and honest women. And I mean the McCullochs as well as the Bakers, Billy. Your ancestors didn't always make the right choices, but they lived honorable lives. We sometimes make mistakes, but that's part of life. I want you to know that I'm proud of you. You've lived right so far, and I have every reason to think you will continue to do so.

"Billy, some time ago, you made a decision to represent a Negro, when you knew it was a great risk to your reputation and might be the end of your law practice in these parts. I must admit that when I first heard about it, I thought you had made a big mistake. Then, as time went by, I heard from lodge brothers and other friends, men who had known your father, and I learned that you did the right thing. Instead of thinking of yourself, you chose the hard path of doing what was right. That's living up to your heritage.

"And Wonsley, son, you did right in showing up and telling the truth when it was a hard thing to do."

He paused, puffing on his pipe.

"I know you boys might think I'm laying it on a bit thick." He smiled as he said it. "I just think it's time to tell you these things. I'm getting to the end of my life. I'm already past my allotted time on earth. I've outlived most of my old friends. It seems like every day, another one passes."

"Aw, you'll live to be a hundred," Wonsley said.

"I don't think so," Eli replied. "I've got a feeling about it. I had a dream the other night. I was walking down a dark road toward a light that was in the distance, and I could hear voices all around. They were the voices of the departed. I couldn't make out what they were saying, but the sound of them was good and comforting. It was as if they were telling me it was going to be all right, that I was headed in the right direction."

Will remembered when Eli had taken him to the Plum Creek battleground and what he had said to him that day. Talking about slavery of captives by the Comanche and the enslavement of the Negros by the whites, his grandfather had said, "Don't compare whites to Indians. There's no comparison."

Will had thought then that the old-timers like his grandfather had a certain lack of understanding about Negros, Mexicans, and Indians, because of their encounters with them and because they clung to the old ways. But he had changed his mind about that. He now believed that knowing more about history and heritage gave the old-timers a background that his generation and generations to come would forget. The pioneer Texans had believed that they were bringing civilization to the wilderness, although many of them were bringing their slaves with them. They looked upon the Mexicans and Indians as inferior, not just because they were different, but because the early settlers saw them as enemies and obstacles to the destiny of advancing civilization, as primitives who would steal, kill, and maim, unwilling to learn the ways of the civilized. They saw them as obstacles to progress, which in the end meant that as latecomers who sought to impose their own ethics and religion in the land, they were blind to the inherent worth of cultures different from their own, just as they viewed the African cultures from which the blacks came as inherently inferior and primitive. And when they had conquered them and were no longer threatened by what in their view had been primitive cultures, they had resisted the assimilation into society of the minorities that lived among them because they still regarded them as primitive and inferior and incapable of being civilized.

It was ironic for Eli Baker to speak of honor in this context, but he did so without hesitation. And the people were proud of their heroes who fought against the other cultures and for a way of life that had been part of their heritage. They were proud of their history, though it had been slaked with violence and intolerance. They failed to realize that civilization brought with it a certain amount of necessary tolerance of cultures and beliefs that were different and required an understanding that things must change, that change is a good thing, and that the past should not be a pattern for the future, but merely a background, not to be forgotten, but not to be blindly followed.

Yet Eli Baker had acknowledged that slavery was a curse upon the South, as he had told Will at the Plum Creek battleground. And the jurors in the Jackson case followed the evidence and acquitted Lucius Jackson, a black man they all probably thought of as an inferior. Their code of honor encompassed fairness and compassion for those whom they considered inferior, because they were human beings, entitled to just treatment. Of course, there were those who were avidly racist and bigoted, those who would say, "The only good Indian is a dead Indian," and who would treat their horses better than their slaves, but they were in the minority, he believed, and would not lead Texas into darkness. He was still young and had illusions.

He also thought about the men of his father's generation he had encountered who seemed to know each other well through their association as members of Hardeman Lodge. They did not say much about their relationships, but Will had the impression that they had a certain faith in each other, in their common humanity, that somehow extended to their families, as if they knew that sons were likely to follow in the footsteps of their fathers. On the day he encountered the lynch mob at Friedman's Saloon, Henry Otto had told him he had faith in him because of his father, because he had known Wes McCulloch when they were both members of Hardeman Lodge. After the Jackson trial, John Wallsmith, foreman of the jury, said that several jurors were members of the lodge and therefore knew his father and did not believe that Will would have suborned perjury. His father had left him a greater legacy than he had thought of before, a legacy of honorable associations among fellow human beings. It was not always easy to live up to that code of honor, which required that a man should act unselfishly in furtherance of the rights of other people, regardless of personal consequences, but his father had lived his life as an example to him that led him along that path. He had learned things that he had not been aware of, and Wes McCulloch, in spite of his shortcomings, had left him much more than material wealth. Sitting with his grandfather and uncles on that Easter Sunday, he understood more about his heritage than ever before.

FIFTY-THREE

WILL WAS WAITING IN THE ELLIOT PARLOR FOR MARTHA TO appear. He had the ring in his vest pocket and kept feeling it through the cloth to make sure it was still there, as if it might have gone somewhere or as if he had dreamed of it having been there. Everett Hardeman and Ada Moore had been married for over a year, and the last time he had seen them at their home in East San Antonio, Ada had asked him when he was going to pop the question. "You've been courting that girl for a long time now," she said. "She won't wait forever." It was a pleasant evening in early May and he had telegraphed ahead, as he usually did, asking her to dinner.

When she finally entered the room, he stood too suddenly and her reaction indicated he must have had a stern look on his face. He stammered out a greeting and she extended her hand as she always had. She was a schoolteacher now and wore a white blouse and pleated skirt that he assumed was her teaching costume.

"I'm so glad to see you again, Will," she said. "I was glad to get your wire."

She took a seat by the front window and indicated that he sit opposite her.

"I'm glad to see you, too," he said.

She continued to smile, her eyebrows raised.

"I'll bet you've been busy," she said.

"Yes, pretty busy. How has the teaching gone?"

"I am enjoying my students," she replied. "It's close to the end of my first year."

She talked of her students and fellow teachers. He told of things that were happening in Caldwell County, his law practice and his family. There were pauses in the conversation that seemed awkward.

"I have something to ask you," he finally said.

"Yes?"

"Well, we've been seeing a lot of each other, and . . . "

She continued to smile and he had the impression that she was enjoying his discomfort.

"And I've grown to have feelings toward you . . . "

"Yes?" She was sitting upright on the edge of her chair.

"Will you marry me?" he finally blurted out, his voice cracking as he said it.

"Why, Mr. McCulloch, I would be proud to be your wife. Yes, I will." She said it as if she had rehearsed it and he was positive that she knew what he had come there to ask her.

"You will?"

"Yes, I will."

They were married at Ursuline Chapel, with his mother, her fellow teachers, some of her students, and some of the sisters of the cloth in attendance, as well as Ellen Elliot and her sewing circle. Her aunt, Katherine Johnston, was also in attendance. After the wedding dinner, they were driven in a carriage adorned with flowers to the Menger, where he had reserved a suite. He left her alone in the bedroom to dress down to her nightgown and when he came in, she was seated in the window seat on the far side of the four-poster bed, waiting for him. He came to her and she looked up.

"I have something to tell you," she said.

"It's not necessary," he replied, looking down at her.

"Yes, it is," she said. "Please listen."

"Of course."

"When I was taken by the outlaw," she said.

"I know. I know what he did to you."

"No, you don't. Not really. I have been frightened ever since."

"Certainly."

"You may have to wait."

"That's all right," he said. "I'll be patient."

"I want you to understand that I love you and I want you, but I'm afraid," she said.

"I understand."

"You do?"

"Yes. I do."

They lay in bed side by side and talked through most of the night. About Wonsley carrying her in the rainstorm. About Gruder getting shot in the side. About the first time he saw her, at the Bradford cabin. She finally fell asleep, cradled in his arms.

He lay there, thinking about the future. They would live with his mother in the McCulloch house, and he knew children would come, as well as some hardship, but he was ready for it. His law practice was doing well, and he knew if he kept at it, it would support his family quite well. Of course he could not foresee everything that would happen, and he knew that, but he was full of the optimism of youth and thought he had a certain destiny to fulfill, that he had been spared thus far to do something meaningful with his life, to fight for justice, to do what was right. To raise children to carry on the McCulloch legacy. To leave a mark on the world. To gain whatever portion of immortality human endeavors were given to bequeath.

EPILOGUE

Late in the year 1894, Everett Hardeman stepped off the westbound train in Luling, having come from Houston on railroad business. He had decided to stop off and spend the night and give himself the time to visit with some old friends, including Will McCulloch, before returning to his wife and children in San Antonio. As he stepped off onto the platform, he passed close by a man who was getting on the train to go further down the line. He did not recognize John Wesley Hardin, and Hardin did not recognize him.

Hardin was leaving Gonzales to move further west to Junction City, where he hoped to find work as a practicing lawyer. He had been released from prison only months earlier, had received a pardon from Governor James Hogg, and had been admitted to the bar in Gonzales by a crew of lawyers who examined him and found him well-versed in Texas law. He had spent his last ten years in the Walls Unit at Huntsville as a model prisoner and spent a great deal of time studying law in the prison library. His wife, Jane, had passed away, and he had been a supporter of the losing candidate for sheriff of Gonzales County. He had vowed to leave the county if the other man won and was being true to his word.

He would go on to marry a fifteen-year-old girl in London, Texas, but the marriage only lasted a week. He eventually wound up in El Paso, where he was shot in the back of the head in a saloon one night by a constable who claimed Hardin had threatened to kill him. His body lay on the floor of the saloon for a couple of hours, while people passed by to get a look at him. He was forty-two years old. He died seventeen months after he had been granted a pardon.

ABOUT THE AUTHOR

Photo by Steve Wood

W. W. MCNEAL is a retired trial lawyer and a sixth-generation Texan. He lives on the family ranch in Central Texas with his partner, Cathy, along with two cats and a dog. The land has been in his family for generations, and the original 1850 deed to the property is in his possession. McNeal is also a songwriter who has been a student of Texas and local history for many years. He published his first novel, *Plum Creek*, with TCU Press in 2016. *Hardeman Lodge* is his second novel.